The Druid's temple was covered with carvings, runes, and drawings. Two squared-off pillars rose up to the low cavern ceiling. The pillars contained six niches apiece; each niche contained a severed human head.

As the tallow candle took life and illuminated the entire cavern, the heads opened their eyes and, yawning, looked at Cathbad. With some reluctance, Cathbad asked, "What do you have for me?"

"Riddles," answered a head by the door.

"A big future," said another, high up on the right.

Groaning as he squatted down, he said, "All right, unravel your riddles. Tell me whose immense future we inspect tonight—and let's not waste our time with sniggering comments, please. I'm *very* tired. So, who are your conundrums about?"

The heads exchanged gleeful glances. In unison they proclaimed, "You!"

Cathbad coughed. "Me?"

"Mmm."

"A future coming."

"A virgin dethroned."

"A king dethroned, too, yes."

"And a charmed child on his seat." Then the heads fell silent, waiting, watchful.

Cathbad drew himself back up on his feet. "Is this some preposterous joke?"

Ace Fantasy books by Gregory Frost

LYREC
TAIN

GREGORY FROST

ACE FANTASY BOOKS
NEW YORK

This book is an Ace Fantasy original
edition, and has never been
previously published.

TAIN

An Ace Fantasy Book/published by arrangement with
the author

PRINTING HISTORY
Ace Fantasy edition/February 1986

ISBN: 0-441-79534-X

Ace Fantasy Books are published by The Berkley Publishing
Group, 200 Madison Avenue, New York, New York 10016.
PRINTED IN THE UNITED STATES OF AMERICA

To my triumvirate Moerae:
to Val for her indefatigable patience;
to Terri for her inestimable advice and navigation;
and to Mara, with love,
for riding out the storm.

PREFACE

The *Tain Bo Cuailnge* (tahn bō kōō'al-nyuh; translation: The Cattle Raid of Cooley) is the single surviving example of Irish Celtic epic. Although there are other stories such as the Book of Invasions that we still have, these are often apocryphal histories and do not reveal the life of the Celtic peoples as does the *Tain Bo Cuailnge*, which in many respects is the equivalent of The Iliad to the Greek culture.

How old is the story? No one knows for certain because no intact version of it survives. The pieces we do have are not the work of any individual, either, but of a body of scribes who were most likely writing down the oral tales told by the recitative artists of the day, who were called *filid*. By the seventh century the Celtic way of life had been absorbed into the Christian world that had arrived as much as two hundred years earlier. The monasteries that these missionaries built introduced the art of writing to the people, and the monks soon found themselves with a wealth of secular stories to put down on their wax tablets. No doubt there were many stories besides the *Tain*, but no record remains of these, due chiefly to a tendency on the part of invading Vikings to eradicate every monastery they came across, which included the burning of all manuscripts found within.

The earliest extant version of the *Tain Bo Cuailnge* exists in the *Leabhar na hUidhre*, The Book of the Dun Cow, which was produced in the early twelfth century. However, it and other manuscripts make reference to material dating from at least the seventh century, and the story is surely much older than that. Estimates place the actions contained within as occurring between 500–100 B.C.

The story has been translated numerous times, but this is not a translation. The best of those, for someone wishing further study, is by Thomas Kinsella and is available in an Oxford University Press edition. This book, like Lady Gregory's *Cuchulain of Muirthemne* (1902), is a retelling in a modern story form, which, it is hoped, does nevertheless maintain a close association with the numerous translations. Rather than copy verses, I have created modern parallels that utilize the elements which the *filid* found essential: irony, alliteration, and sarcasm. The quality of these verses is my own. Some of the tales have been rearranged for continuity; others have been set aside for a sequel volume, *Remscela*, forming a second story about Cú Chulainn; still other story fragments, consisting of lesser tales or deeds of the hero, make no appearance at all. Cú Chulainn is a hero in the true sense of the word. Half-human and half-divine, his godliness both aids and taints him.

The cattle raid itself was a common occurrence in prehistoric Ireland. By all indications it was not a theft as we would think of it so much as a method of antagonizing one's neighbor, of provoking a fight when you wanted one.

Two terms included in the text should be mentioned here. The first is *geis* (*geisa*, plural). This was an adjuration upon one's honor. A *geis* could go either way: it could compel someone to perform a certain act or, more commonly, it might prohibit the individual from doing something. The weight it carried is nearly inestimable, and the *geis*, occurring many times in the Celtic tales, always represents a turning point in the story. This adjuration was placed upon a person by a Druid, which gave it awesome religious significance, enough so that one's own belief in the power of it could, if the *geis* were violated, cause one to die from the belief, much as has been suggested about voodoo rituals. The strength of the *geis* could cause a person to alter his entire life, to pack up and leave, to stop speaking, to wither away to nothing.

The second term needing explanation is the word *Sidhe*. This represents an ancient and magical race that has gone underground and now lives in mounds strewn across the isle. I have distinguished the mounds from the people in them by spelling

the word for the mounds *sid* (*side*, plural) but the two words,
Sidhe and sid, are pronounced identically as 'shee' or 'sheedh',
the 'dh' being nearly a 'th' in sound. The variant spellings for
these people are numerous, as are the tales about them, most
of which have them performing nasty or cruel tricks upon
unsuspecting mortals.

Regarding pronunciation, I have included glossaries at the
end of the book. Old Irish is not a language where words are
often pronounced as they are spelled, and debate goes on about
proper pronunciations of many words. In researching this book,
I ran across many contradictory glossaries; etymologies are still
uncertain and some of the words spoken by the *filid* had already
lost any sense of meaning by the time they were written down.

So, let me close the introduction as a bard of that ancient
time might have begun his tale: "Once upon a time when there
was no time . . ."

G.F
1985

PROLOGUE

1. In the Feast Hall

The boy stood halfway up the green hillside, glaring down on all he saw. His stiff body was as thin as a hazel sapling and his hair, combed straight back and fanning across his shoulders, was so bright it could have been dyed with saffron. His large contemptuous eyes echoed the sky's blue, but were wet with tears of resentment. His cheeks burned bright red where his foster-father had slapped and then backhanded him. A rusty taste of blood tainted his saliva. He looked for all the world like an enraged young god: like Lugh of the Long Arm, the Sun, crisping the Fomoiri with his anger.

Rough stone steps under his worn sandals led up to a round feast hall whose thatched roof was visible just beyond the crest of the hill. Below, the stones divided the hillside, their discontinuous line extending past a dozen rickety round huts down to the valley where the objects of his hatred—his foster-father and brother—waded waist-deep in sheep.

At sixteen, Senchan was just a year shy of acknowledged manhood—of release from the bond of fosterage—and he had no idea who he was or what he was meant to be. His training had been left to chance, his growth to undernourishment, his brain to rot. His whole life it seemed had been robbed from him.

When he was a year old, his blood-father had fobbed Senchan off on Selden Ranoura, the ill-tempered man whose hand-

1

prints had tattooed Senchan's face on so many occasions that the sting never quite stopped. His blood father was a minor king in a world where minor kings were as plentiful as pimples, as distinguished as acorns. Life had changed on the island since the time when kingship mattered; the past lay buried beneath the steady and importunate tread of Christian soles; they who came to Ireland last of all invaders, ages after all neighboring island cultures had been assimilated. Gods and kingships alike were eradicated; goddesses were forged into saints, given new faces, new attributes. Still, some few aspects of the old society hung on tenaciously and forced the new order to adapt.

One such ancient custom was fosterage. It took two forms: that of affection and that of payment. In Senchan's case love never for a moment entered the bargain. In return for accepting the burden of his tutelage, Selden received four head of runny-eyed cattle given to explosive, toxic farting. Not much in the way of payment for fifteen years of tutelage. Selden had long ago ceased to exercise his responsibilities. He found instead that he preferred to train Senchan as a whipping boy.

With just one more long year to go, Senchan was determined to grit his teeth and withstand his torments silently, proudly. Few alternatives presented themselves. The old saying went that there were three ways to terminate a fosterage prematurely: Death, Crime, and Marriage. Senchan had no intention of dying. A criminal act he held beneath his dignity as the son of a king, however thin the royal blood running in his veins. And thus far he had yet to find anyone to wed. Selden's daughters had more bristles on their numerous chins than all the boars in Meath. Till Senchan earned the rights of a man he must abide; then he would repay Selden for all the ignominies shoveled upon him, for the bruises and the welts. Until then, his silence must continue. But the anger, the rage rising like a sun inside him, needed a safe means of release. And so, periodically, he sneaked off to vent his anger in the empty feast hall—where, in fact, he was forbidden to go until the ceremonies of maturity took place . . . which added a certain sweetness to the act.

In the center of the feast hall stood an octagonal arrangement of copper and brass screens that reached nearly to the ceiling. Their hammered surfaces revealed triskeles the width of a hand, spirals and trumpets, and faces—some hideous, others impassive. Old gods, stripped of their worth. Of them all, Senchan knew the identity of just one—an antlered character squatting cross-legged on the panel facing the doorway. This was Ruad Rofessa, also called the Dagda, which meant "the good god," although the Dagda had come to symbolize all forces satanic to the builders of monasteries. These screens were remnants of a pagan past, their value stamped out. Now they simply surrounded the central hearth to act as a chimney for peat smoke. Today, as Senchan stole inside, they had forsworn even this duty. The interior of the feast hall was clouded with smoke as thick as stirabout. Shields hung on the walls glimmered dimly, like the eyes of nocturnal monsters.

Senchan always found this place eerie, but never more so than today. Often he had thought someone sat beside him in the dimness listening to his muttered curses, his promises of evisceration and castration for both fathers, all brothers. He long ago rescinded all ties to this family. His few friends understood his intolerable situation, but they could only pity him. A mother might have soothed his blistered soul, but Selden's wife had died long before Senchan arrived, and the old bastard's squalid whore sided with Selden in everything.

"I hate you all," he hissed defiantly. The sound echoed around the empty hall as if the walls had sighed. "My spit should burn you. I could dig out your eyes with my *fingers.*" He went down on his knees and gouged the ground. "He has no worth. He measures his value in words tied to his tongue, so he can use them and reel them in again. Nothing but deceits and boasts. Why does he hate me? What choice did I have in where I went? He blames me! Oh, *God,* I hate him. His daughters I'll make shave their hairy chins in the foamy blood bubbling on his lips, while I watch him die and *laugh!* For all the times, I'll . . . I'll . . ." Senchan's fists pounded the dirt. He pounded and pounded until his rage was spent, then lay there, a swollen-eyed rag totem in a linen tunic. Ultimately he knew he would do none of these things. Not that he was a coward, but he was likewise no fool, regardless of what Selden called him. To slay Selden would bring the entire settlement out after his blood. Unfortunately, among all the other skills neglected in his teaching was the handling of weapons, and how long could he last when he cannot even fend off a blow? One hour? Two? He cried to the earth. He was trapped within traps within traps.

There came a soft scraping sound.

Forgetting his misery, acting by instinct, Senchan rolled across the floor and dove beneath a congeries of furs. He wriggled in amongst itchy leather that smelled of vintage sweat. His head emerged just enough to peer out. He sniffed, dabbed dirty fingers under his eyes, inadvertent makeup. If they saw or heard what he said, he was doomed in any case—a violator as surely as if he'd raped his own estranged mother. Selden would beat him to a cripple for being in here. But the feast hall looked empty. Possibly brighter than when he entered— could the smoke have thickened? He started to suggest to himself that it was just imagination that had made the sound, when the room grew brighter still.

Like a birch tree stuffed through the chimney hole, a shaft of pure white light shot down into the area enclosed by the screens. Heart pounding, his mouth tasting like bloody brine, Senchan tried to account for it, but knew that no errant beam of light could do that. The scraping sound began again. The ground beneath him shuddered.

The screens were parting.

Where they divided, brilliant light burst forth in a knife-edged line across the floor and up the pile of furs. Senchan's blue eyes sparkled with divine radiance. What was happening? He could not guess: it was like some tale of fairies and will-o'-the-wisps unfolding before him. He burrowed back further into the furs. Just one eye remained exposed, a single sapphire in a fuzzy niche.

What that one eye beheld left him in no doubt that the last beating he'd suffered had rattled his brains.

Inside the parted screens, on top of the smoldering bricks of peat, squatted an enormous black cauldron. Rings as big around as his wrists hung from its lip, and triskeles and figures much like those on the screens decorated its bulbous sides. It was the immensity of this vat that had pushed apart the screens. The thing seemed to have grown up out of the fire, to have swelled into being all at once. Were that all, he could almost have accepted it. But perched on the rim, as if someone lay inside the vat luxuriating in a hot bath, were two bare feet, soles wet and as pink as baby flesh. And the toes wriggled.

The feet slid down, out of sight, splashed. A lifetime of moments passed. Then a head began to rise up where the feet had been, the light grown so bright that the color was bleached from hair and skin—it was a face of chiseled chalk, a face of rigid bone, of death. Its wide eyes did not scan the room, oh no. They stared straight into the heap of furs, right at him. The nose was bent, maybe scarred across the bridge. The beard-ringed mouth when it appeared was grinning. A finger popped up beside it, crooked, and invited him to come on out, no good hiding from *this* apparition. The specter also had a voice, one full of life, lust, and humor. The voice said, "Senchan, Senchan, I spy Senchan," a man sing-songing a child's decree.

The furs trembled and shook.

2. The Ancestor

Down in the dark of the hot moist furs, Senchan rocked with laughter. A faint exhortatory voice cried out in his mind that he should not be acting this way—just a second ago he was frightened, wasn't he? But he couldn't contain the urge to laugh. He lifted his head and, with it, a huge piled cap of furs, and peeked out again.

The man in the cauldron disappeared below the rim with a splash, but the top of his head bobbed into view every few moments. Senchan heard gargling, followed by a spume of sparkling water. With the greatest of care, the boy burrowed like a timid mole out of the furs and began to crawl on elbows and knees across the smoky room. Discovery! The cauldron wasn't black at all, but copper gone glaucous, thick with verdigris as if dredged up out of a lake this morning. That old devil, the Dagda, sat in cross-legged bas-relief inviting the boy to pause and chat beside the fire.

A particularly loud splash sent a huge wave breaking over the rim above. Senchan had a moment to see it, but no time to crab away before it drenched his head and neck.

He got up on his feet, all fear and humor forgotten. The water should have turned to steam, he was so mad, stinking of those furs, dripping like a sheepdog. The man in the cauldron just floated, complacently naked. A bit of mockery was suggested by the look he tossed up to Senchan. What lustrous eyes! They were probably blue, but seen in this light the irises were barely distinguishable from the whites. As if acknowledging this problem, the light dimmed immediately, enough to let some color bleed in. The bather was revealed as flesh and blood rather than ghostly vapor. His hair was blond streaked with red, pulled back and drawn to the side of his head, behind his ear. A small filigreed device like a thimble-cup held it there, by what property Senchan couldn't imagine. At the man's throat, a thick silver necklace duplicated the fine work of the thimble-cup.

The overall impression the bather gave was of emaciation, dissipation: puckers of skin rode the recesses below his eyes; his cheeks were drawn, with fine lines in the hollows and around his bearded mouth. His body was pale, almost fish-belly blue; freckles stood out like pebbles on a beach. Below his navel was a round dark scar, looking slick and fresh. The bather, however, appeared not the least bothered by it.

"Who are you?" asked Senchan, no longer angered or scared. The bather had leached away his emotions with those moon-eyes and that smile full of irony and the promise of great japery.

"My name," the bather said, "is Laeg mac Riangabra." His tone suggested that Senchan ought to be impressed. The pale eyes searched him for some reaction and he grew uncomfortably embarrassed, enough that he had to look away—up.

"I shouldn't do that were I you," Laeg gently warned. "Often they prefer to keep a distance and would rather you didn't pry. They could, for instance, make you blind." He paddled up near Senchan. "Me, they keep blind drunk, which is not quite the same but does alter one's perception as unconditionally."

"Who are *they?*"

"What do you think of this gravid pot?" He slapped the rim. "The Druids used to bring dead warriors back to life in this very cauldron, back before the magic faded. . . ." He inhaled deeply through his nose, which *did* have a wicked scar across the bridge. "Good for the mind, a humid air is, especially a mind besotted for centuries. Are you aware that you have battle-dye under your eyes?"

Confused by this question, Senchan reached up and dabbed the hollows of his eyes, then saw the dirt on his fingertips. He made fists and rubbed hard at his stinging cheeks. Defiantly, he said, "Don't you answer people's questions?"

Laeg abruptly ended his deep breathing exercise. "Lugh's nuts, lad, don't you recognize a visitation when you see one? Or do you perhaps stumble upon my likes all the time? Seen a lot of pots like this?" He rapped the side and the cauldron bonged like a monastery bell.

"Of course not."

"Fine." He stretched out in the water once more. "Ask your critical questions then. I'm prepared to answer all inquiries."

Senchan repeated what he had already asked.

"They," replied Laeg, "are the Sidhe, the people of the mounds. The mounds also are called *sid*. The Sidhe live in *sid*. Naturally. I trust that clarifies everything?"

Senchan looked blank. Laeg might as well have quoted Tacitus at him. The joy went out of the man's eyes; the light surrounding him dimmed. In the cauldron, steam had ceased to wreathe off the water. Softly, almost fearfully, he asked the boy, "What is this at my throat?" His hand closed around the thick silver necklace. Senchan could only shake his head. Tension replaced the steam. "This is a *torc*. It is the symbol of the Dagda, lord of all animals, of forests everywhere. It girds the soul and binds us to nature, to the world, to the gods... nothing, I see it in your eyes," he said, pondered for a moment, then, "What about Druidry? Macha? Tell me at least that you know of Cu Chulainn?"

"I think, it means someone's dog?" hazarded Senchan, hysterically hopeful.

Laeg stared at the hole in the roof. "You were right, he *doesn't* know," he said. Then his eyes rolled up and he slid down into the water, turning to float there like a corpse, longer than was possible. Senchan fidgeted until he couldn't stand it anymore. He reached in, grabbed the body by the hair. It listed, then rolled over. In those few seconds the face had already begun to decay, the skin become yellowish, puffy. Senchan gasped and dropped the head. It sank out of sight. "No!" the boy cried out. He thrust his hand into the milky water, grabbed the hair again and pulled, but looked away before everything below the eyes was revealed. Those eyes stared straight up but did not see him or anything else this side of the grave. "Please," begged Senchan. "Stay up, wait." He towed the body to the edge of the cauldron and hung it from the rim by its dripping chin. "I'll be back," he promised. "I'll get Selden and the others to help." With a clot in his throat, he turned away.

"*Stop!*"

Senchan halted. His head hunched down—he didn't want to look back at that ghastly face, but finally he did. Laeg was whole again. Senchan's mouth dropped open.

"Surely not Selden?" Laeg continued. "That overbearing, solipsistic, base and vile example of the slug in human form? Think, Senchan, what he would do to you if you dragged him

in here for *any* reason. Skin you, I don't doubt. Take your head
and crush it in his fat hands like a grouse egg. And you," Laeg
said as he rose up like a sea god, "you'd like to do the same
to him, wouldn't you? Like to grab him by the balls and make
him obey your every whim; like to beat his stubbly face to a
purple dough. Wouldn't you?" He gripped the edge of the pot
to lean forward at Senchan, who was too stunned to move.
"Well, you *ought* to feel that way! He's a domineering swine.
His like have caused all our deeds to be forgotten. He's *chosen*
to be dim-witted, actually *chosen* it, you understand. It couldn't
be worse if the fornicating bastards all inbred! History's twisted
up like this neckring." He grabbed fiercely at the torc surrounding his throat, and in so doing lost his balance and fell
with a great splash back into the tub. With orange hair dripping
gray water, he eyed Senchan balefully. "And what's most ig-
nominious of all is that your foster father is descended from
my line." He reached out then toward the hesitating boy and
Senchan returned to him as if tied by an invisible thread. Laeg
gripped Senchan's shoulder. "It's you I'm for. You're young,
you can be shaped. A destiny awaits you, but you'll have to
go backwards to get it. Future answers lie in past deeds, Senchan.
I've come to give you what that wormy descendant of mine
can't—purpose and direction. A reason to be."

The shaft of light flared up. Senchan came out of his trance
into blindness as if a white sheet had shrouded him. Behind
him the copper screens swung shut; he heard them clank together, turned and ran, sightless, at the sound—two steps and
clang! he found them with his nose and chin.

He sat down.

From behind, Laeg's voice whispered into his ears. "There's
no escaping destiny, lad. You were yoked to yours the day
Selden accepted those flatulent cows."

Hands cupped over his bruised nose, Senchan noticed water
dripping onto his shoulder. He asked, "What's happening?"
and was surprised at how calm he sounded.

"We're traveling."

"I feel sick."

"Myself, as well. A good ale would have helped settle our
stomachs. I've asked a dozen times before, but they never think
of your needs any more than they consider your pride. Why,
I once saw a fellow—he had stumbled upon a *sid* at night by
accident, obviously didn't know where he was—suddenly pop
into the middle of a Sidhe feast, both feet in the meat platter.

And his pants down, tunic up, displaying both cheeks most rudely."

"What happened?" asked Senchan, his queasiness and bruised chin forgotten.

Laeg cast him that mocking glance. "Well, we all stood up and clapped."

Senchan eyed him askance. *We,* he had said. Didn't that mean that this man was one of those Sidhe? If not, then what else could he be? The screens shook, then rattled as thunder filled the air and Senchan cast speculation aside. "We're stopping," said Laeg.

3. The Circle of Stones

The light vanished so fast that Senchan and Laeg both gasped and looked up, snow-blind to the normal light. Above them now was sky—a great cloudy swatch the color of an oyster. Senchan pushed one foot against the cold copper screen in front of him. The screen dragged in the long grass, but opened. Through the slit he could see a sliver of gentle slope, a field not far below, in which stood a huge dark rock. Laeg hissed like a firestone dropped in water. Senchan looked up at him looming above and could see his coloration clearly now—the face, the orange freckles, the hair, and the clothing. When had he put on clothes? Maybe they'd just appeared on him. After everything else that had happened, Senchan wouldn't have been at all surprised. The clothes were similar to his own clothing, but different in design. Laeg's sleeveless tunic, for instance, was muslin white, but with a pattern of green chain links woven in. The edges actually seemed worked in gold. His knee-high boots—Senchan had to twist around to see them—were nothing more than wide strips of cracked leather wound around his feet and calves and tied down with thongs. They looked as if he had worn them since the Creation. Tight quilted leather breeches were tucked into the boots. Four bracelets encircled his left wrist, all similar in design to the thing he called a torc. His stringy arms were criss-crossed with scars.

All the while Senchan studied him, Laeg had not taken his eyes off that stone out on the field. The boy dragged himself up finally. Even then Laeg seemed to stare through him to that stone. Why? Senchan shoved the screens further apart.

The whole picture was of a wide plateau decorated with a ring of standing stones. The cauldron and screens perched on a knoll above the stones. Beyond them the ground disappeared down into a valley; far away, small dark hills clustered, patchy with the grayness of limestone.

"Where are we?"

"This is Muirthemne Plain. I hadn't—" he had to clear his throat "—hadn't seen it since long ago, right after the Wars when the Sidhe assembled the ring." Like one possessed, he drifted past Senchan and down the hill. Once again the boy was reminded of a spirit, not a corporeal man. And Muirthemne Plain? He knew of such a place, in the southeastern part of Ulster Province. But was it possible they'd traveled that far north? How? The screens shifted slightly. Hinges groaned. He decided it might be wise to follow Laeg rather than have one of those things fall on him.

Laeg strode into the circle, straight to the immense black rock in the center. He pressed his whole body against it, ran his palm down its one smooth face as if caressing a lover. His fingers found and traced a wide gouge in the center. Senchan followed as far as the edge of the ring, but hesitated to enter the circle. Places like this were scattered all over Ireland and, the story was, they were haunted.

Eight stones composed the outer ring, some half his height and others higher than his head. None of them resembled any other, which seemed to Senchan very odd. Rings that he had seen before had always been composed of similar stones. He crept along the periphery, careful to stay outside the ring. The stones looked as if the centuries had not worn, had not even touched them.

When he finished the circuit, Senchan had discovered that the stones shared at least one trait. All of them bore peculiar indentations—lines scratched down one face, some horizontal, some diagonal. He wondered if perhaps the stonecutter was inexperienced with a chisel.

"Do you read Ogham?" asked Laeg, so close by that Senchan jumped at the sound of his voice.

"Read what?" the boy asked shakily.

Laeg pointed at the chiseled lines along the stone. "This. Ogham. Druids' alphabet."

"You mean this is writing?"

"Druids controlled written words for as long as they lived. Words were power, weapons that could penetrate deeper than any blade, imparting wounds that never healed. Druids kept writing a secret so that words would carry weight, the weight of truth. Such truth died on the day writing became known. Now it isn't your word, it's your signature, that carries that weight. Yes, it's writing."

"But we still have words."

"Empty words are all you have, flung by fools who lack the subtlety of mind to recognize the force of a *geis*, of a riddle or a threat. Druids knew all that. They made laws—"

"But they s-sacrificed *children*," stammered Senchan. "And worshiped the devil!"

Laeg laughed. "So rules the newest order. In truth they sacrificed no children of which I'm aware. Criminals, yes, but what do you do with a murderer? Teach him to fish? And your evil Prince of Darkness hadn't been invented yet so how could they worship him? Lies, boy, all lies—even if, perhaps, well-meaning ones." He stopped speaking then, remembering suddenly through a vision how he came to know so much of a life that did not come into being until after he had departed this life. He saw in his mind's eye a circle of women there in Magh Mell. The women were all speaking at once in their secret tongue, the words winding, weaving in and out. Now it was as if his brain was a loom and the patterns of their speech were becoming comprehensible. He reached up, touched his temples. They told him that a new order had arisen, one that wanted all the magic in the world to belong to its god. That order had devised stories to repudiate Druid knowledge. "This is not new," the women had told him. "It has happened since the first time a new people conquered an old. It happened to the Fomoiri, to the Fir Bolg, to us. Our secrets are hidden from the Druids just as their knowledge is forever lost to the Christians. The head is always cut off before the tongue can tell its tale."

He repeated this last statement for Senchan but the boy disappointed him once more by not comprehending, requiring further elucidation. "The new order hounded the Druids. Some were even tortured and burned. The new society opposed them, and it's society that's let the knowledge be lost. The few survivors remember scraps. No more." How odd he felt saying this, recalling the women chanting. He had thought them part of a drunkard's dream.

"Do you read it?" asked Senchan.

"Very little. But I know these *stones* as if I'd carved them."

"What do they mean?"

"I can't tell you that—I have to show you. Come." He got up and led Senchan to the highest point in the circle, and also the smallest stone. "This is the first *and* the last stone," he explained, "the beginning and end of the circle. It's called the Pigstone. You see how it's fissured down the center? How the two dissimilar halves fit together?"

"Yes."

"You must touch it. Here, like so." He took Senchan's hands and pressed them into the Ogham notches. "Close your eyes and clear your mind." Senchan obeyed, but warily. Then a moment later his eyes opened wide and he looked at Laeg with startlement and wonder. Laeg smiled. "You felt it, didn't you? The words have power still, provided one knows how to find it. Again, close your eyes."

Senchan wasn't sure he liked this, but he obeyed. Laeg began speaking to him, softly. "Your hands are on the hearts of two men who were not men." Senchan felt a dull throb, monotonous, rhythmic, like the pulsation of the earth. "Once those hearts were tissue and muscle, but two angry Sidhe kings turned them into stone."

"How is that possible?" Senchan could not say for sure if he had spoken aloud, or if the thought had just echoed loudly in his head. But Laeg answered him, voice very close now, hot upon his ear.

"I'll tell you. It happened in the following manner and because of it thousands of people died in combats and old enmities burned like sulphur. One hero was made and more unmade. And all because of pigs."

Senchan fell away from himself, entering another realm of time and place. Seasons swirled around him, through him. He saw himself as if he were someone else, standing on the hill slightly above the circle of stones. He saw Laeg take his arm and gently draw him forward. The stone that he hugged became soft, then misty, and he passed through it.

He became the beginning of the tale.

"There were once two pigkeepers..."

Part One

I.
THE PIGKEEPERS' TALE

1. The Mast

There were once two pigkeepers named Friuch and Rucht, charged with maintaining the pig herds of two Sidhe kings.

Rucht, whose name meant "the snort of a pig," was short and so stout that a rope tied above his belly was the only thing that would hold up his baggy woolen trousers. His hair, which was the color of oak leaves on a cloudy fall day, sprouted like a tangled bramble bush from his scalp. Seen from a distance or amidst his huge herd of pigs, Rucht looked like a bulbous primeval plant root animated by some mischievous spirit. His pouchy eyes never quite agreed on where they were looking and his broad lower lip jutted out as if he had stumbled into eternal cogitation.

Rucht's dearest friend in the world, Friuch, could not have been more unlike him. Friuch stood lanky like some overgrown corn dolly—an assemblage of twisted stalks and chaff, a being formed of husks. His large eyes were button-black and he had the gums and teeth of a horse.

In manner the two keepers were also completely polar: Rucht, the cogitator, was ponderously slow to take action, while Friuch leapt into it with hardly any thought at all. What allied them took root far deeper than such strong contrasts in appearance or action could reach: both keepers were the offspring of couplings between Sidhe women and mortal men, between the magical and the mundane.

Friuch and Rucht were only half-Sidhe.

Though they remained in the land of the Sidhe, they lived as conspicuous outcasts in that magical society. Nevertheless, by their own rules the Sidhe were responsible for the two half-breeds and so each had separately been charged with the task (an estimable and, to some, enviable task) of caring for the Sidhe pigs. In this role they could live alone, removed from all detractors and secure in the knowledge that in their segregation they served their masters well.

Their meeting had been a happy accident. Each found in the other a curious comfort. Over many reunions, this comfort changed to deep friendship that had abided throughout the long periods when the two were apart in the service of their masters. Their isolation recessed every fall as the first breath of winter drove the green souls of the trees into rooting hibernation and forsaken branches released their seed, burying the land in a mantle of nuts. This was the time of the *mast*, as this mantle was known to the pigkeepers. It was the *mast* that reunited them year after year.

In years when the winter winds shook harder in the north, Friuch closed up his house, gathered together his pigs, and headed north to Connacht, where Rucht awaited him. Other years the *mast* fell thickest in the south and Rucht would be the one hiking off with his herd, down into Munster where his good friend dwelled. Either way, one month a year, the two friends rejoiced in each other's company—talking and drinking and playing endless rounds of fidchell, a board game with which they passed long afternoons.

The year the trouble began, Rucht had taken his pigs south.

Pigs are peculiar animals. They are remarkably clean by nature and can be as attentive and affectionate as a fine hound, never mind that they are being raised and fattened only for slaughter. Sidhe pigs were even more alert and peculiar than most. For one thing, they could expand to at least twice the size of the largest mortal pig. For another, they knew *why* they were being fattened.

"And that," said Laeg, facing a cold, blustery fall wind, "is a tale in itself."

2. The People of the Mounds

"At a time before our people came to Ireland, there was a clash between two primordial races of beings for the right to dwell here. Their names are forgotten to us now save for those few heroes and kings whose stories became part of our legendry. Both sides might have lived on the isle, but neither could abide the other. After an eternity of wars producing a flow of blood so great that it raised the level of the seas, one tribe chose to abandon the isle with honor and dwell elsewhere. They knew that if the fight continued, both peoples would go on battling until no one was left, until the ground was no more than broken spears and shattered bodies. And so these people gathered together in small groups on designated hilltops—all at the same moment, for they could communicate over great distances like lightning across a stormy sky—and they passed down into the *side*, the pregnant bellies of the earth. For this reason, they are called the Sidhe, the people of the mounds. Their world is near invisible, like fortresses of glass, and only upon your entering one or their passing out from it can you see them. Because of their honorable sacrifice in the face of defeat, the god Manannan threw a great feast for them in Magh Mell, with meat carved from his enchanted pigs. One bite of this meat made each of the Sidhe immortal; that was Manannan's gift to them. In his honor every year, while mortals offer sacrifices to the Dagda on the Samain day, the Sidhe slaughter a pig and feast to remember Manannan, the Son of the Sea."

For a moment, Laeg paused, then added, "You'll hear more of Manannan another time, for, though he was a god, he had a blind side called Fand. She was his wife and she is part of this tale, too, but much later. . . ." Senchan, he could see, had stopped listening to him; instead, the boy was staring past Laeg along the rough path that cut through the woods behind them. Far up that path, a squat figure was waddling toward them. Like a pack of dogs, a herd of pigs surrounded the figure and trotted along with him. From the images that had dazzled him

17

while Laeg spoke, Senchan recognized that figure. A smile crept across his face. He and Laeg moved off into the brush to let the pigs and their keeper pass by, then set off after the milling herd into the darker depths of the forest.

3. The Aer

Rucht led his pigs along the murky forest path. Autumn wind drove the lower clouds like boats across the sky. The dense woodland oaks flailed naked branches sadly as if to grab the scudding clouds. Acorns clacked around the trundling pigs, who shoveled the path clean as they followed their squat master.

One pig, attracted by the smell from rotting piles of acorns nearby, went off toward the woods. Rucht saw her. "Legan!" he called, with a voice as rough and bubbly as a thick cooking stew, "the forest's full of frights for the likes of you." The pig ignored his warning. He shooed the rest of the herd on and went back for her. She had snuffled her way into a huge pyramid of *mast*. Rucht considered her for a few minutes; then he mumbled a brief chant and faded from view, like a rainbow after a rain. Where he had stood, a bright ball of light rode for a moment on the breezes. Then it sank into the layers of leaves and nuts on the ground. These bobbed up as the hidden ball of light moved beneath them. Legan remained hedonistically oblivious to this until the pile of nuts she was devouring suddenly exploded in every direction. Flying leaves sizzled and burst into flame. Legan skittered back, off-balance, and fell over on her side, but quickly stabbed her stubby feet into solid ground and pulled herself around. She took off, squealing, back to the safety of the herd, which had wandered far down the path by then.

A swirl of singed leaves drifted down around the bulky figure of the pigkeeper as he reappeared. Legan turned around to give him a resentful and wounded look. Rucht only smirked, "You'd rather be lost to us? To abandon you to your pleasure would mark me as more pig-headed than you, old darling." Legan snorted. Rucht guffawed from the belly; a sound that

TAIN 19

had been known to break up brawls.

He resumed his walk and, when he had caught up with the herd, lagged behind to ensure that no others tried Legan's trick. Who knew what fiendish, ravenous creatures dwelled in the depths of that dark forest? What invisible eyes watched from the shadows? In this state of unease, he drove his herd on to Munster.

Rucht's daily hikes always came to an end at a well-chosen *sid* where his pigs were treated like gold and he was accepted as an honored guest. Yet there were inevitably a few among the crowd who disdained their half-human cousin as the bastard product of their own queen's lustful peregrinations. These few envied Rucht his job and his close friendship with Friuch; and it was these few whose goal became to crack open a permanent rift between the two allies. Most of their jibes rolled off Rucht's back like water off a duck: "Rucht the Ruin, Seer over Sows, shifts his shape to hide his many mortal blemishes." That stung a little but he had no illusions about who or what he was. So they tried another: "The keepers of boars—boorish keepers both—Snort and Snout keep us bored." Well, that only set him laughing his infectious laugh, and the entire population of the *sid,* their faces glowing red from hidden fires, caught the hilarious contagion. Only the coldest of hearts, the wretchedest of minds, remained bent on their initial purpose. Again they tried, and again and again. Rucht, like any mortal man, had his weak spot, his one soft bruise of doubt. It was inevitable that, sooner or later, someone would stick a dagger there.

"Pride take you in your magic. So generous is Ochall Ochne with his gifts, and Boeve with his for Friuch. Tell us: which of you works the greater wonders?"

Like nasty children, once the detractors realized that this point of contention truly bothered Rucht, they focused on his pain. Who *was* the stronger of the two? they asked him. Which half-breed *could* beat the other in a contest? they demanded to know. Who had more *mother's* blood in him?

Their cruel queries sharpened off him like a knife off a whetstone. With each pass, the blade cut finer and closer to the bone.

Rucht began avoiding the mounds, sleeping instead in groves, sheltered by trees and chill winds. One night the pigkeeper spent with a deer-man, who had antlers tied to his head as he danced in his grove, celebrating the Dagda, and who starved himself into delirium. The deer-man babbled throughout the night, hopping in circles round the pigs. The sleepless keeper lay trapped in the deer-man's circles and struggled all night with the question that bored into him.

After that, Rucht resolved not to speak to anyone at all—but too late: the damage had been done the moment the question had been asked. He could not stop wondering, doubting, sizing himself up against his friend. Rucht in his distress could not realize then the extent of what had been done to him.

Friuch, on the other hand, could. He laughed at what his squat friend confessed to him. "Rucht," he replied placatively, "Can't you see what they're trying to do? They're envious of every grand thing we have, right down to the good leather on your feet. They hate us both—we're not like them. For years they've baited you, just as they've done to me every time I come to visit you—you never gave it a thought. Why now?" He leaned back against the stone wall of his hut.

"But who is *better?*"

"Who cares? Will it grind your grain better? Will it fatten the pigs?"

"I care."

Friuch eyed his friend and his apprehension dripped into the pit of his soul. Here before him stood a new man, one whom he had not previously encountered, and one Friuch did not care to be with just now.

He left and went off into the woods alone. Surrounding him were the herds of pigs, whuffling and devouring everything in sight. He sat down with them, spindle-thin amongst all those fat bodies. The afternoon drifted away as he pondered. His friend meant too much to him for this to divide them. It was bad enough that the Sidhe of Connacht and the Sidhe of Munster had had a falling out long ago and that the friendship he shared with Rucht defied a dozen ancient restrictions. Most of the people didn't care, anyway—the curse of the whole schism was that neither side could even recall where their differences lay. Perhaps it had been a dispute such as this. Ochall Ochne and Boeve might have vied for supremacy, their client-companions splitting into factions—sides that had remained long after the fires of the conflict flickered out. . . .

Friuch shook his head and returned to the problem at hand. How was he to salvage and patch up his friendship? How could he give Rucht back his self-assurance? He could let Rucht win a contest, he supposed. Just a simple contest—

Friuch sat up straight; pigs grunted and shuffled back from him. What a *wonderful* notion. Why not silence all the taunting tongues permanently for both of them? He climbed to his feet and ran. His gangly legs carried him in great leaps over the squealing clusters of panicked pigs.

"Rucht!" he cried. "Rucht, I've found the answer!" His friend waddled out from the round stone hut. Friuch put his hands on Rucht's shoulders and explained his plan. "What we have to do," he said, "is act out a contest of skill! We do the same thing, the same way at the same time, thereby proving to anyone who cares to know that we're of *equal* prowess. And I'll tell you just what, too." So Friuch explained the details of the idea that had burst upon him. Rucht listened, his baggy eyes lighting up as the plan unfolded. A brilliant scheme! Rucht excitedly dragged Friuch off to the middle of the forest, where, as Friuch had described it, the contest would take place.

Back to back on that gray and gloomy day, the keepers chanted their spells. Their incantations mingled and twined like curls down a woman's back. Mist drifted out of the trees and spun around the two sorcerers as they spoke. Mist enfolded the whole of the forest. Around them, sensing the clash of forces, their pigs squealed and ran about in panic until, at last, the chanting stopped. The mist rose, fading, as if chased away by sunlight.

Standing on the hillside above the two keepers, Senchan looked on, dismayed. Laeg sat beside him, against the bole of a tree, nonchalantly picking burrs off his trouser legs. "So," he said contemplatively, "you think the spells took? Think they will dazzle the Sidhe?"

Senchan's face scrunched up even more. "But nothing's changed!" he cried. "You made it seem as if something fantastic was going to happen."

Laeg cocked his head. "Oh, but it has. Look at those two poor creatures." He gestured to where Friuch and Rucht were dancing in circles. "They can't *see* anything more than you can, but they know it's happened. You, being a product of Selden's world, must needs see it or it isn't there. What is invisible does not exist, isn't that so?" He got up, brushing

leaves off his backside. "Such thinking spells inevitable doom
for the tale tellers before long. The loss of imagination." He
sighed. "Well, let's go."

Senchan glanced down at the two keepers again to hide the
look of pain on his face. He did not understand Laeg's ad-
monishment. It wasn't fair to pick on him for things he couldn't
help. Selden hadn't even taught him what he was *supposed* to
know, much less the code of life from some other time. And,
anyway, why should he consider it important? Sooner or later
he was going to be put back where Laeg had found him, and
what good would all of this be then? Frustrated, he turned away
from the scene below. "Where now?" he asked.

"Further onward." Laeg started up the hill. "By then the
charm will have taken fully, the *mast* will be consumed, the
forest denuded, and the pigkeepers parting. At which moment
in time, the feast of Manannan will be a fortnight away."

The two figures climbed until the sounds of celebration
faded away and the forest became silent and empty under a
stone-gray sky.

4. Banishment

By the time Rucht bid farewell to Friuch and set off for Connacht,
the full effect of Friuch's spell had unfolded for all to see.
Rucht herded his pigs into a *sid* every night at first, to show
off the spell. The reaction of the Sidhe was not, however, what
he had anticipated.

They laughed at him.

Word of what Friuch had done traveled no faster than Rucht,
and each night he shocked the inhabitants of a new *sid* and
was in turn mortified by their derisive welcome.

"You chose a sorry day to visit Friuch," they goaded him,
"for he's surely shown his superior skill, *old darling*."

"Not so!" cried Rucht. "I've done the same trick upon him!"

But the same Sidhe who had set gleefully upon him a month
before scoffed at that, and teased and prodded and bullied him.

By the time he reached Connacht's southern border, he had come to avoid the *side* again and spent his nights in groves, with pine needles for a blanket and pine nuts for his supper. Now he would have relished the company of an errant deer-man. It seemed that only someone mad from starvation would offer him any kindness. What he did not know, could not have known, was that word of his magic upon Friuch had followed after him like a skulking dog and that those who had mocked him now admitted, grudgingly, that the two keepers must have equal powers. Withdrawn from his herd, Rucht cursed Friuch's plan and Friuch along with it. When he made up his mind at last to undo the spell, he discovered to his alarm that he could not. No counterspell devised had any effect at all. Nearly hysterical, Rucht tried making spells up. Nothing happened. Nothing changed. Nothing.

The figure that drove his pigs into the Caves of Cruachan the day before Manannan's feast skulked glumly, head down, resigned to play the consummate fool. Awaiting him there at the mouth of the caves, his master, Ochall, stood like a pillar of shadow with piercing raven's eyes. The tale of the pig-keepers' duel had caught up with and preceded Rucht to Connacht. Ochall Ochne had doubted it, or at least had wanted to. But now fury consumed him as he stared silently at the herd of transformed pigs waddling forth—waddling as the redoubtable spell had wrought them. They were small, scrawny things without a trace of meat upon their bones. Their rough hairy hides hung so loosely on their ribs that, had it not been for their telltale snouts, they would have been unrecognizable as pigs.

"So this," growled Ochall Ochne the Sidhe king, "is what comes of breaking ancient *geisa* through leniency. This, my punishment for letting you commingle with our enemies!"

"I—I did the same thing to Friuch's herd," Rucht replied apathetically; he had said it so many times lately.

"Then at least we're not to be the laughingstock of Boeve's Sidhe—though that mitigates your position only one degree with me. Our feast is tomorrow. Everyone knows the tale: you're equals, how thrilling. Now change the pigs back."

"I would but I can't."

"You don't know Friuch's spell?"

"I thought . . . I *heard* him, but . . ."

"Well, then, move off," his king commanded. "I'll deal

with it." Ochall pushed past Rucht. The pigkeeper stumbled
to the side of the cave and covered his face.

The shadowy Sidhe king spun his magic around the pigs to
reveal the spell that bound them. It appeared before him as a
luminous cord, woven round the animals. Ochall Ochne hissed
and glared back at his pigkeeper. The enchantment had knots
tied all along it where Rucht's simultaneous spell had violated,
deformed, and melded to Friuch's as Friuch's had to his. A
master seaman could not have unraveled those knots in a thousand years of untying. For all his great powers, the Sidhe king
of Connacht had no hope that he could do better. The feast this
year was going to be grim, the sea god's gift shabbily celebrated.

Rucht saw that his master could not change back the pigs,
and his disgrace became a secondary concern, dwarfed by an
all-consuming fear for his life.

A chill wind swept over him. It froze him in an instant, and
he knew nothing again until Ochall lifted the numbness away.
Then Rucht discovered that he no longer stood in front of the
Sidhe Caves of Cruachan. A dark, incarnadine place surrounded him. It sparkled dimly as through smoke. This was
the *sid* on Femen Plain—the *sid* of Boeve in Munster. The
two kings faced each other like two tall black trees. They spoke
in an ancient tongue that Rucht did not understand though he
heard every word clearly—a language that has not been spoken
in daylight since the time of the Tuatha de Danann. Peering
into the shadows, Rucht spied Friuch standing paralyzed beyond the two kings. Friuch looked as fearful and helpless as
he felt. *We are doomed,* thought Rucht, and he found himself
unable to grieve for Friuch. It was as if the spell worked over
the pigs had also affected him, withering away that part of him
that had cared for his friend. Now he had no friends—not even
himself.

The voice of Ochall Ochne suddenly rang through the cavern, and the walls brightened and spat red sparks with each
sharp word. The immensity of The Punishment was revealed.

"We have decided. You are forever banished from us. The
simple task you both lived to fulfill proved too ambitious for
your human halves. You have shamed your teachers, but worse,
your own people: there can be no feast in our lands this year.
We are discredited in the eyes of Manannan—you've broken
our *geis* to him and can offer no fitting retribution. So we must
try to mollify the sea by playing havoc upon the land. This we

will do through you and that is your sentence. Seven times you will be shaped by us, seven destructive forms of our choosing. Our retribution." The two kings retreated into darkness. Rucht stared at Friuch staring at him: farewell in a glance.

The blood-red world blasted them away.

5. Shapes of the Sentence

Samain was the most awesome day of the year in the mortal realm. It existed between the end of the old year and the beginning of the new: a day removed from the harness of time and the natural order of things. On Samain eve, the forces that separated the dead from the living dwindled until those two planes merged. In the dark of that night, the dead emerged from their tumulus graves. Skulls kept as prizes of war began to chatter; demons sailed the skies on horses of sunset; Fomoiri— the ancient, banished race of giants—rose like mystical isles out of the sea. The three Daughters of Murder—Morrigan, Nemain, and the Badb, called collectively the Morrigu—ruled that time out of time as a triple threat of madness, terror, and battle-frenzy. The three sisters were said to appear, to those misfortunate enough to encounter them, as large ravens. So, when on Samain morning, the entire populace of Cruachan Fort awoke to the cries of two huge black birds, the people thought they saw their doom in the sky.

But they soon realized there were two birds only, and these birds were ugly and deformed.

The birds squawked and clawed at one another. Feathers fell like pieces of night, covering the crops. Blood sprinkled across the plain, and where it fell, whatever grew there withered, whatever stood there fell over and died. The people of Cruachan decided they did not like those birds very much.

Warriors, men and women both, charged out, bellowing, onto the field. They heaved their spears and cast sharp stones from their slings. Every shot went home; but though a hundred spears impaled them, the birds did not even falter in their combat.

For the next year, each morning, the birds returned at dawn, magically made whole again. Every dawn brought their squawking. Every sunset left Cruachan Plain decimated, empty of life, and littered with the corpses of cattle and pigs that had strayed there. The inhabitants of the fort had to transport their food from over the hills to the south. Meantime, they sacrificed to every god known to every person who dwelled there—and Cruachan contained people from all over the isle, who worshiped hundreds of individual and tribal gods. The myriad sacrifices went on and on, through winter, then spring and summer. When the calendar came round to Lugnasad Festival, the Druids doubled their traditional sacrifice to Tailtu, the goddess over all nature, in the hope that she had power over the demon creatures. The birds fought right through the offering, and no force of nature came to lay them low. In great distress, the Druids retired from the festivities, if festivities could be used to describe so subdued a gathering.

And then, one morning, the birds failed to appear. Warriors crept out and scanned the horizon for a sign of them. The birds had vanished. By the second day it became apparent that they would not return.

The people threw a feast.

On the same day that the two birds did not appear at Cruachan, two monstrous black birds showed up over Femen Plain in Munster and wrought similar havoc there. No one could harm *these* two creatures, either. Eventually, the story of the two northern birds trickled down to Munster and the people of both provinces came to regard them as the very same birds. This did not make anyone in Munster very happy.

When the second year ran to its end, Ochall Ochne sent his steward, Fuidell, to Femen Plain. At Fuidell's approach, the two birds changed back into two pigkeepers; although, to the eyes of the mortals, they simply ceased to be. The pigkeepers' naked bodies were torn and bleeding; their eyes had become hard and black. Fuidell was reminded of his master's glare. He went forward with small, reluctant steps. Friuch saw him first. "No greeting for us?" growled the spindly keeper. "Not for those who wage war in their spirits and feed from the live corpse of their companion in exile," said Rucht.

Fuidell did not know these men. He feared them but feared his master just that extra bit more; he made himself ask them the question that Ochall Ochne had sent him there to ask. "What have you done in your first term?"

"No good," both keepers replied.

Their apparent joy in this saddened Fuidell. He understood that such was magic that it encompassed dark and unforeseen consequences—unforeseen at least to him, though his master might have known well what the keepers had become. Fuidell addressed them again. "You know what you'll be next?"

"Water creatures," the keepers replied, "but kept, we know, from the seas lest we offend Manannan again. A year of fury we'll fight in the Shannon, then a further year in the Suir." Rucht added, "Best warn them not to wash their clothes on the days we come by."

"Done," said Fuidell, and the two vanished from Femen Plain.

When two more years had passed they were transformed into two stags that ravaged the forests with their battle for supremacy. By the end of that period of exile, they no longer remembered their first identities. Hatred of one another shaped their lives. They became two warriors and fought a year in the north, following it with a slaughter in the south. Rinn and Faebur—Point and Edge—the people named them. Their struggle leveled mountains just as their combat as water monsters had flooded lowlands and their time as stags had stripped forests. It seemed to the Sidhe who observed them that the two became more evil with each incarnation. Uncaring, the warriors fought on. One would cut off another's arm and that severed arm would continue to move, to try to kill without direction until magic reattached it at night. Sometimes the warriors were so eviscerated by then that their ribcages lay open and empty to the spine; but they fought on relentlessly through the two years.

Then they became phantoms and spent their time trying to terrorize each other, assuming demonic shapes with a hundred eyes or rotting, chittering corpses the height of a house. Whole towns fled in panic at their horrible approach.

Next they transformed into dragons—flying dragons, a sight never witnessed since in Eriu. They were made of ice and breathed such cold as to freeze fish into place in a lake with one pass. Winter came early and lasted through the summer those two years.

Then at last the time arrived for the pigkeepers' final transfiguration. The Sidhe kings chose to turn them into something that would no longer terrify anyone. The change took place in an instant. Two dragons winging across frozen countryside

burst open; blood and meat sprinkled down like red rain and,
within this rain, fell two tiny yellow maggots. One of these
fell into a river—the Cronn—in a part of Ulster Province called
Cuailnge. The Cronn is a major source of water there, feeding
hundreds of springs. The maggot drifted helplessly into one of
these springs and from there to a feed trough where it was
devoured by a cow. The cow belonged to a farmer named Daire
mac Fiachna. The other maggot plunged into a well in Connacht, where it was unknowingly removed in a bucket and fed
also to a cow—one belonging to the Queen of Connacht, Maeve.

The punishment had ended—the Sidhe had new pigkeepers
(both of whom were admonished not to repeat their predecessors' mistakes). What had not ended was the power of malice
steeped for so long in those two souls, a power greater than
the kings of the Sidhe realized.

The two cows that had eaten the two maggots became mysteriously pregnant. Each, on the same day, delivered up a bull.
The bull of Cruachan grew into a blood-red beast named Finnbennach after the whiteness of its pointed horns; the bull of
Cuailnge was its exact opposite: a dark brown with black horns
as shiny as iron. Daire mac Fiachna named it the Donn for
these dark traits. The owners learned, individually, to be wary
of the prize bulls. The monsters had nothing in their hearts
save anger and frustration at being kept apart from a decisive
confrontation. Their single relentless question pushed its way
into the world. *Who is more powerful? Who?*

Laeg and Senchan stood at the rail of the pen that held
Finnbennach and the rest of Cruachan's cattle. The bull stood
scant inches away, allowing them a rare view of its red eyes.
Senchan had never seen anything so full of malice. The eye
showed white at the edges and it rolled around in a frenzy of
pent-up hatred. The eye drew him into its bloody core; he began
to hear a shrieking, like the voices of souls in torment. He
thought he must be tumbling—the ground had tilted, the plain
rolling him along . . .

"Come along, boy—wake up!" Laeg's command cut off
the shrieking.

Senchan trembled, found himself pressed against the rail.
He avoided looking at the red bull again as he climbed down.

"Powerful, isn't it?" said Laeg. "And that's just what all of this is about. Who is more powerful? Friuch or Rucht, Faebur or Rinn, Finnbennach or the Donn? It is a question that thrives in the heart of every argument, every fight, every war, that man creates. The cause of every conflict that ever was. It's even at the core of your struggle with Selden."

Senchan twisted around to stare at Laeg. "But—but that's not so. He *knows* I can't do anything to him. He *knows* he's more powerful."

"Does he? True enough, he's more forceful, more violent. But not because he knows he's more powerful. No, no. Because he fears your coming of age. Selden's sure to lose what little power he has over you the moment you walk out of your manhood feast. Then you're his equal and he can no longer abuse you without risking dire consequences, even death. You're more clever and wiser than he'll ever be despite all the training he's withheld from you. You just don't know it yet. Soon, though, you'll defeat him. With your mind, with your wits."

"But—"

"Not now." He took Senchan's arm and turned him around.

There, in the middle of Cruachan Plain, stood the ring of stones from Muirthemne. Right in front of him, the Pigstone rose up. But now it was in two pieces. The top had cracked where the tiny fissure had been, and the sheared-off portion of it had slid off and impaled the ground beside it. A distance the width of his foot now divided the two parts.

"Powerful," Laeg repeated. "We'll come back to this stone again before your journey's done. You can be certain that the world did not leave those two alone for long. The next stone is ready now. It's time to go on." He led Senchan along to the second stone on the right. This one was a sharp and sinister-looking spire of rock. Near the tip, two sets of spiraling rings were carved. Senchan reached up and brushed his fingertips lightly over the indented circles.

Behind him, Laeg said, "The twin forts of Cruachan. The home of Maeve and Ailell. She is the rock, you might say."

"And Ailell?" asked Senchan, hardly aware that he had spoken. His fingers slid down from the spirals and lodged in the Ogham notches cut into the stone's edge.

"Ailell is the hard ground beneath."

Across the plain, the wooden walls of two fortresses rippled into view through the heat. Senchan's vision became dotted with black specks. The heat was wasting him. He tried to tell

this to Laeg but could not make any noise. "This tale begins
in bed . . ." One of the black specks swelled up and blotted out
the view of the fortresses. Somehow, miraculously, Laeg managed to remain. Senchan stumbled toward him and stepped
through the black disk into a wide, low room.

II.
THE TALE OF DOMINANCE

1. Pillow Talk

Not far from the caves in which the Sidhe of Ochall Ochne dwelled two large round fortresses stood. A great timbered wall enclosed them in a still larger circle, and the whole enormous ring was called the Rath Cruachan. It was here lived the King and Queen of Connacht Province.

The king, whose name was Ailell, lived in some discontent, and though he had the will to suppress his peevishness, it lurked in him at every waking moment.

Recognized as he was as king of all Connacht, Ailell knew himself to be a *fer for ban thincur*— "a man under a woman's thumb." This did not mean that he regarded his wife as an enemy—far from it; he loved Maeve as deeply and unselfishly as any man could love a woman. Nevertheless, her unremitting pursuit of supremacy did take its toll upon him. So much did it weigh upon him lately that it had seemed to Ailell almost as if another personality—a darkly ruminant personality—sometimes crept into his mind; sometimes a voice not his own whispered a cruel list of shortcomings to him. The voice could appear while he ate a meal or debated law or rode in his great chariot. First it shattered his tranquility, then it vanished, leaving the king dissatisfied and ill-tempered. But this morning, the loud presence had entered his thoughts, spoken its unwelcome message, and then, to his great horror, settled in like some abiding lodger. Now as he made love to his wife, Ailell

31

sensed vaguely the resurgence of that audacious presence. The
dark voice grew louder, stronger, but he was in the grip of lust,
too consumed by coition to hear it, much less blot it out. The
perverse thing waited until Ailell came to the crown of his
actions, till every bit of sense and awareness had raced from
his head to the tip of his member. At that instant he lay open
to unimpeded invasion, and the entity simply took control.

The king plumped down to catch his breath amidst the tangle
of his wife's white-bronze hair that flowed over the whole of
their bed like rills of ice. He looked at her over the one arm
she had tucked beneath her head.

Satisfaction swam in her eyes, eyes with irises as pale blue
as death. She waited for her husband to soothe her with his
voice, then to reawaken her passion like a sunbeam unfolding
a flower. He was known to her and the world as "Ailell of the
Honey Tongue" (though what that meant to her did not necessarily correspond to what the rest of the world thought of).

Tonight, however, no sweet words lay behind those beard-
enshrouded lips.

He leaned up on one elbow and stared at her like a stranger
witnessing her wondrous nakedness for the first time. A spark
like cruelty flickered in his eyes and his lean jaw had a hard
set to it; but his beard disguised some of this while the queen's
own languor blinded her to the fever on his brow that was not
lust. She turned her proud pale face to him. Her eyes rolled
up at the expectation of ecstasy that experience promised would
follow.

"Is it not the case," Ailell began gently, "that the wealthy
man's wife is a fortunate one? Would you agree that is so,
sweet flower?"

Maeve's entire countenance ossified. "Certainly," she answered, bewildered, "but why bring it up here, now?"

"I was thinking earlier of my brothers and their queens and
I came round to thinking about you, naturally, being that you're
superior to any one of them."

"That is undeniably true. Still, I fail to see—"

"And I realized in recognizing that superior design—" and
here he paused to pass his fingers lightly across her breasts
"—how much the better you surely are now than when we
contracted to marry."

The queen had now quite forgotten any interest in a second
coupling. "Better in what way, dear Ailell?"

"Why, in all ways, my treasure. Before our marriage, all that was heard of you was that here was a province run by a woman who was, like her kingdom, plundered by all her neighbors."

Maeve sat up, but forced down her anger in order to learn where this would lead. "How strange that I have never heard you mention this before. It seems to me that I wed you because you lack the meanness of a serf, the fear of a farmer, and the jealous nature of a warrior. You are a man of even temperament and unjealous heart, both of which I know to be true from a thousand repeated occasions where lesser men would have revealed their baseness. Not you, Ailell—which is why I married you." Then to add a sting of her own, she added, "And not Conchovor." She went on, "Far greater your aspects to me than any *coibche* of pigs and gold you paid my father for the honor of having me. It would have been criminal for a treacherous or cowardly or wicked man to have married so generous and kind a woman as you have."

"You see, by your own words—you've more to your credit just in my person than you had alone."

He left her no choice with that statement than to defy him. "It is a well-known fact: my father was High King—no possessor of some rocky piece of unwanted ground, but a true king. He had six daughters, and only *one*—the one they call Maeve—won a province by her great strength, ingenuity, and wisdom. If any plundering has been done ever, it has been my doing. Men from all over this isle tried to woo me. They recognized that I am sovereignty made corporeal. I had those I chose and have always done. You know very well, Ailell my dearest, that there has never been a time when I had finished with one warrior but that another stood eager and quaking in his shadow. So it will be for me always. Of all those—who would fill a dozen lists—I chose you for the reasons I've named. And who was it gave Ailell his wealth of clothing, his shining chariot, and that gold which he now holds up to me as proof of his ascendancy? It is to *me* the villain must answer when you are affronted. *You are mine*. If I am somehow better for that, I will accept it as so. What you need to remember is that you are no more than a single item among *my* many possessions."

"That's plainly absurd," growled the king. "I possess you as well in like manner. We can't count ourselves in this matter. At best we cancel each other. However, my fortune's still the greater. Until you can prove otherwise, it's Ailell still rules above you." He smiled a smile that said he had made his count already and knew the outcome. Goaded by this, Maeve leapt from the bed. The bed rested on a platform in the center of their fortress, a pillar at each corner, gauze curtains strung between. A silver wand on a thong hung from a central beam of copper that ran overhead between the pillars. Maeve pushed aside a curtain, grabbed the wand, and rapped it fiercely against the beam. A great echo as of a dozen invisible gongs rang through Cruachan.

Within minutes, servants of both parties filled the great chamber around the pedestal. Maeve waited until all were gathered. She scowled, and her arms were crossed beneath her naked breasts. Observing her, the servants were visibly moved.

"It is inventory time," she announced. "Every piece of jewelry, every cup, every cow and sheep and dog we own is to be counted today, and the ownership of each thing noted by putting them on an appropriate list. One for the king and one for me. Each of you take a Druid with you and count carefully, I warn you. Then bring me the results that I may see who it is rules highest in Connacht." She dismissed them, then returned to Ailell. But he lay sleeping like a carefree child.

The queen departed from the shared bed and marched to her own chamber, where she gave orders for a certain young warrior to be delivered to her. He was brought in as he had been found—naked and half-asleep. Then he saw Maeve in the fire's glow with her eyes like liquid coals and her long thin face a goddess's mask wreathed in a nimbus of silver hair aflame. The warrior came stiffly awake. Soon he gave himself over willingly to an ecstasy like no other waiting to greet him this side of death.

2. The Count

The queen had said "today," but the tally in fact took many days while servants rattled off items and Druids notched the ever-growing lists. Maeve kept to her chamber and her pleasures therein; Ailell slept an unnatural sleep as if under some spell.

When finally one of the queen's servants entered her private chamber to announce the completion of the inventory, her warrior had disappeared. Only his bracelets and belt remained, accompanied by the lingering perfume of sex in the air.

Maeve dressed in her purple robes, clasped at the shoulders by rampant gold birds. She went to the central room, found it empty. Ailell had awakened and gone out.

On the great walled plain of Magh Ai she found her husband among the Druids who had done the counting. He stood listening very intently to one of them, and, as Maeve walked quickly up beside him, she heard the Druid say, "In all things listed, smallest to largest, you *are* equal."

Ailell frowned. Maeve interjected, "Equals we have always been." She was triumphant.

The Druid scowled. "I had not finished," he said. "Equal, I said, save for a single exception that defies us to judge it fairly."

"Show us this exception now," demanded the two contenders.

The Druid and his peers led a procession across the plain to where two cattle herds gazed in distinct, fenced formations that men had forced upon them. Among the cows, the Druid's exception stood out like a mountain: a huge muscled bull the color of blood and with red eyes so angry that to catch their gaze actually stung. The bull's horns were white and sharp as spears.

"Finnbennach," the Druid announced. "He is a calf from the queen's cow—there." He pointed to the opposite pen.

"Well!" proclaimed Maeve with a sense of victory. Then she faltered. "But why, then, have you placed him with the king's herd, you fools?"

"We did no such thing," replied the incensed Druid. "In fact we tried to drive him across the plain, but he refused to go and his refusal was of such a nature that we've no intention of attempting to remove him again. Finnbennach has gone over to the king's herd because he refused to be led by a female, albeit his own mother. Thus we cannot yet decide in whose favor falls the bull."

The king clapped his hands, turned on his heel, and marched off, grinning. Maeve went the few steps forward to the wall of piled stones that surrounded the herd. She confronted the bull, wishing it dead and slaughtered. For an instant those smoldering red eyes met her cold stare, and she saw in them what she had seen in the eyes of her husband three nights past. When the bull looked away, Maeve convulsed as if suddenly released from some pull of gravity. Unsteadily she turned back and found a servant behind her, awaiting a command, anticipating from experience a riposte from her.

"That bull," she said, "has tipped the balance of my kingdom, and my fragile Ailell cannot bear such weight on his back." The servant nodded vigorously. "It is up to me to take back the load and put things in balance again." She mused silently for a time, then gestured with her head at the second fort of Cruachan. "Go and fetch MacRoth for me." The servant bowed. "Send him to my sunroom." As she said it, she felt the hot eyes of the bull, behind her, touch her again.

3. The Donn

The messenger MacRoth stepped warily into Maeve's sunroom. He was a short man with uncommonly swarthy features. Great strength hid in his spare frame, but his arms were of unequal lengths from a childhood accident in which a horse had fallen on him. Of all the men in Maeve's service, MacRoth ranked among the best. He was a magnet for news and information and possessed the instincts of a diplomat. Nevertheless, whenever summoned by Maeve, he broke out in a cold sweat—he knew too well her capricious tendencies, her climatic shifts of mood. He could not count the number of people who had vanished after being called to the *grianan*, the sunny parlor. A mortal dread consumed him when he heard that she waited for him there of all places.

Maeve's *grianan* was an immense chamber filled with beams and tricks of light. Trellises along which vines and ivies had been trained formed the ceiling. Portions of the roof had not been shingled but were filled instead with some translucent material of Druidic creation that reminded MacRoth of ice on a pond. The walls, likewise, were more flora than wood, and breezes set the ivies nodding as if announcing his arrival.

Maeve awaited him on a great spread of pillows behind gauze curtains sprinkled with gold. The fine curtains billowed sinuously in and out of the sunlight. It seemed to MacRoth that he had to enter a mystical realm of shimmer and smoke to reach her. Nor was this the first time he had thought that: secretly, he believed the queen had divine attributes. Certainly her lust was remarkable; unappeasable. What *did* happen to her lovers?

He drew back a sparkling veil and entered the circle of pillows. Reclining, Maeve looked up as if drawn out of deep thought. Then she smiled softly and asked, "Do you know of what has happened?"

"I've heard something of it, yes."

Her smile turned bitter. "I must find the equal of that bull, MacRoth. I must match him, put him in his place." He wondered, did she mean Finnbennach or Ailell? "You will go out," she said, "search the whole isle if need be for a bull the equal or superior of that blood-red demon."

MacRoth sat down. "That's unnecessary. I know of such a one already. Yes, and he's a little bigger by all accounts than the White Horn. In the province of Ulster—a farmer called Daire mac Fiachna owns a huge bull. Its color—how coincidental is your comparison—is said to be that of dried blood on iron. It's won a reputation as fierce as our own."

"This farmer, you know him?"

"Of him only," he replied humbly.

"Always." The queen smiled on him. "You must go there, then. Offer this Daire in return for a year's loan of his bull fifty yearlings picked—equally, of course—from our herds. Try to keep silence in your going there, but if the people of—where?"

"Cuailnge."

"If the people of Cuailnge should find out and they fear the loss of their bull, offer to give them a share of land on Magh Ai the size of this farmer's land. Also, if he will come here and care for the bull, I'll give him a place between my thighs with time enough to appreciate the gift."

Time enough to expend his life, thought MacRoth, at which point the gift stays given. He arose and left, thanking the Dagda that she had never offered to pay him in like coin.

The afternoon he spent in collecting the people he wanted in his entourage, then set out with them for the part of Ulster called Cuailnge—a peninsula of hilly land bordered by rivers, containing some of the best grazing land in all Eriu.

Several days later, they entered the region. Going ahead alone, MacRoth managed to learn the whereabouts of Daire mac Fiachna without arousing undue attention. He knew what his queen wanted.

The owner of the Donn had white hair unkempt and spread all across his brow. His white beard and eyebrows were prickly. His mad-looking eyes lit up when MacRoth identified himself.

"Such an honor," cried Daire. His voice was like a beehive. "Great messenger of the Connacht clans, heh. You *have* to come in. Why didn't someone run ahead and tell me, mmm? As it is, it's going to take some time to prepare a proper feast." He waved his hand at all ten of them to hurry in, at the same time screeching orders to his servants. MacRoth sent his retinue away and sat down alone with Daire.

"What's this?" asked the farmer. "Where's everybody gone? Well, the feast won't take half so long to prepare now." He scrounged some parasite from his beard and popped it between his nails. "So, why is it you've come to visit me, hmm?"

"The Donn."

Daire's whole body rocked as he nodded. "Word of the great gargantuan of beef has reached the ears of Cruachan, has it?"

"Obviously, but there's more to it than that. Queen Maeve would very much like you to loan her the bull. She has promised you fifty heifers in return—one for every week she has the Donn in her possession. Think of the herd you could start with the Donn and all those cattle."

"Can't start any herd with *that* bull. Tried once. He damn near ripped the cow in two. Just that first teensy poke. Oh, it was a mess, it was terrible. Poor cow. We had to eat her." He fell silent. As he contemplated the offer he became more crafty, a shift in attitude that was painted across his face. "Besides, the herd I have would spill into the sea if I added to it much more. Manannan needs none of my cattle to complement his pigs, heh?" He burst out laughing. "So, what are fifty heifers to me?"

"I see. You would not want this bull out of your sight, is that it?"

"Not out of my sight, yes. Yes. No, I would not want to let him go that way. Yes."

MacRoth leaned closer. "Then the queen proposes you come

with the bull to Cruachan. She promises that, in return for your trust, she will welcome you with open thighs."

Daire mac Fiachna trembled, just a little. He sat up rigidly to hide his excitement. His eyes started to water.

"Of course," MacRoth went on, "if you're worried about how the people of Cuailnge will react to losing their renowned Donn, we have an offer to placate them as well."

"Oh, *sod* the Ulstermen. When can we leave?"

MacRoth sighed. "Would you mind if we had our feast first?"

Daire mac Fiachna nodded, bright-eyed, stuffed his beard into his mouth with both hands, and began to chew.

4. The Best-Laid Plans

MacRoth ate his boiled beef slowly, savoring both the flavor of the meat and the taste of easy victory. He had captured the farmer without the least effort. Privately, he toasted the queen for her unquenchable desire, safe at this distance from it himself. She made it so easy to ensnare people, men and women alike; such was her ubiquitous reputation and sway. She was a heady drink that brought thirst to anyone offered the cup.

The feast lasted late into the night. Daire sat on MacRoth's left. He drank far too much, but hardly noticed, so busy was he in his imagined couplings with Maeve.

Meanwhile, the servants and attendants of both men had sampled various brews and fallen into drunken palaver. A Cruachan messenger proclaimed, "No better man lives than the owner of this house." He hoisted his mug and splashed his own leg, which set him to giggling.

"That isn't so at all," argued another. "His king, Conchovor, is a superior man. The best in Ulster, it's said. He's made the crops bountiful and the beef savory and the wine flowing. And it's good he doesn't know about our li'l p-p-peregrination, because he would certainly not let that bull leave here. Then we'd 'ave to contend with the whole country."

A woman in Daire's household overheard this and excused

herself from another conversation. She asked to what bull the
drunkards referred.

"Why, to the Doon."

"The Donn."

"Absolutely. Everyone's heard about it and MacRoth's con-
vinced old Daire-down—ha!—to cart it to Cruachan."

"Which is a good thing," added the other besotted Connachtman, "because we'd 've stormed in and snatched it from
your master otherwise. So, come join us in a drink to your
master. Here's to ol' Daire-down. May the cunning cunny of
the Queen not gobble him up too quickly." They laughed uproariously and collapsed against one another.

The concubine went straight to Daire, bidding him to leave
the feast. Once they were alone, she shoved away his grasping
hands and asked, "Is it true that you're taking the Donn to
Maeve?"

"Ah, Maeve," pined Daire. He clumsily wiped spittle from
his ragged beard. "Yes, it's true. What's it to concern you?"

"Are you aware that if you'd refused, that bunch out there
would have slain us all and stolen the bull?"

"What? No! Not MacRoth."

"Truly. I've heard two of the messengers with him speak
the plan just now. Those two, there." She pointed through the
doorway.

"They'd kill us for my Donn? What?"

"Indeed they would. And, so, dearest Daire, think now what
must without doubt await you in Cruachan. The thighs of Maeve
have teeth." The farmer's lust withered at the image his concubine painted, just as she had intended. They had called him
her *master,* how dare they? She was a legal concubine with a
contract that made her Daire's *ben urnadna:* his legal wife for
a year. Well, they would soon regret treating *her* like a common
slave.

In the morning the party from Cruachan awakened and prepared sluggishly to leave. MacRoth found himself with a
thumping headache that made his eyes water when he bent
down. Damn all wheaten beers, he cursed. One never should
mix them with wines, even Maeve's best imported. He stumbled about, through the smoky hall half-blind, unable to collect
his baggage or his thoughts. It was the dreadful hangover that
prevented him from noticing before everyone was ready that
no party of Ulstermen had been assembled to accompany them.

He considered at first that Daire might be going alone, but that
seemed so unlikely that MacRoth sent one of his people to
have the farmer come speak with him.

"Why aren't you ready?" he asked when Daire arrived. "Did
you drink too much? We should get the Donn and go. Remember Maeve's promise."

Daire envisioned a lichen-covered cave mouth lined with
razor teeth. "No bull leaves here today," he said shakily.

"I thought you were so impatient to go. Those creamy queenly
thighs await you hungrily, you know."

Daire felt himself shrivel up. "The bull leaves no day at all.
And if I weren't a fair man, there'd be no Connacht messengers
leaving here either, without their throats opened up." He made
a rasping sound and drew one finger sharply across his throat.

For a moment MacRoth suspected that the promise of sex
with Maeve had undone the man's wits. "Please explain this
to me," he said. By this point, the servants of both sides had
surrounded the two. The outer circle belonged to the farmer's
people and each of them held a weapon, quietly drawn.

"You said that if I did not come willingly to Cruachan your
queen would have come back and killed me, taken my Donn
away by force!"

"I never said any such thing."

"Not you personally, perhaps. But aren't you answerable
for all your people? I know I am for mine. Those two there—"
he pointed out the drunkards "—proclaimed that very thing
last night. What do you think of that, heh?"

MacRoth could not help but chuckle; he tried to disguise it
as a cough. "When did a man of your station," he asked, "listen
to the voice of too much food and drink?"

Daire misunderstood this as a slur upon his concubine. "Men
often murmur in their cups," he muttered angrily, "what they
dare not speak out loud, hmm? I've said all I'll say. The Donn
remains here. That's final. And you go home empty-handed,
though full-bellied, which is more than you deserve!" He swept
back his wild hair with one hand, tilted up his head, and strode
imperiously from the room.

MacRoth's lips were by then so tight that the blood had
been pressed out of them. He stared up from under his brows
at the two accused messengers. Their inability to meet his eyes
confirmed their guilt to him, but he found himself unable to
unlock his lips to lambaste them. He closed his eyes and lowered his throbbing head.

5. The Return

This time, when MacRoth entered Maeve's *grianan,* it lay dark and gloomy, contrary to its name. The thin curtains hung like a wall of mist or woven spider's webs; behind it, the queen's shadow had the wings of a raven. "You returned with nothing," she stated. Her voice echoed all around him.

He did not even attempt to part the veils, having no desire to prove the contours true. "That's right," he said, then went on to tell the whole story, frightened all the while for his life because he had selected the men who had fumbled away the Donn. Would she know that? And, if she did, what would be his punishment? The wings of the shadow flapped. The ivies nodded in the dark breeze; now they accused him. He swallowed, then said, "And the foolish farmer believed their drunken lies."

"Lies?" said Maeve softly. "Hardly. It is well-known here, although you would not know yet. I have already made plans to take the bull by force. What care I how I acquire it?"

"But all Ulster will rise up."

"Undoubtedly they shall. But we will find a way in and out, and if a few warriors are lost along the way, what care I so long as they belong to Ailell? Go now and tell Fergus mac Roich I wish to see him."

"Of course." She had let him off; he turned away, elated, but her sharp whisper froze his joy. "Before you do, however, MacRoth, I want some justice done." He stood petrified, breathless, awaiting her pronouncement of doom. The queen said, "Those two messengers, those drunkards—have their lips stitched together. And make the others who went with you watch."

"Yes. Immediately." He made a hasty bow, then hurried out of the parlor, breathing hard as if he had just run a race.

Senchan, like MacRoth, found the queen to be an object of terror. When MacRoth ran from the parlor, Senchan was close on his heels—or would have been if Laeg had not grabbed hold of him and jerked him up short. "There is no point in following *him* just now," Laeg explained. "What he's about to do will keep until you've been properly introduced to Fergus mac Roich. And that introduction cannot transpire here." Laeg let loose the boy, who, though listening, had been keeping his eye on the fluttering curtains across the room.

"Fergus is a unique man, Senchan," Laeg prodded him. "Pay attention, boy. I'm telling you something important. I said, Fergus is unique. His strength and courage are surpassed by Cu Chulainn alone. He's an Ulsterman, but he lives, as you now know, here in Cruachan, in the house of Ulster's bitterest enemy. The reasons for this are essential to your understanding of everything that's to follow." He shoved Senchan forward, out of the sunroom.

They moved along the corridors of dark wood, past rooms of every size and use: one a weaving room, one for baking, another an empty feast hall not unlike Selden's. A fortress, it seemed to Senchan, was just many houses fit together.

Laeg passed him and maintained a quick pace that forced Senchan to hurry. Senchan wondered why he always did this. Sometimes it seemed to him that Laeg forgot he was even there, like the times when Laeg drifted into his trances. Then his lips would move as if he were repeating a silent chant. Senchan would stare at him, leaning close to try to catch the words but hearing nothing other than the soft smacking of Laeg's lips. It was during those moments that time seemed to fly past. Senchan would turn from his guide and find himself in a new location or in the same place but at a different moment in the day. He wasn't honestly sure he knew why he allowed all this to go on, why he didn't run away. Except that he wasn't too sure there was any place familiar to run to. This was a world unknown to him, peopled with these incomprehensible, sinister creatures. That Maeve—she horrified him. What had she done to that poor soldier that left behind only jewelry? He shuddered to consider the possibilities. How to escape from the nightmare of it was what he most wanted to know; but it was the last question he would have dared put to Laeg.

The corridor turned suddenly. Laeg stepped aside. Ahead, Senchan could see the doorway leading out of the fort. It should have been a rectangle of daylight at the end of the hall. Instead, only specks of daylight showed—where the massive stone that had appeared in the doorway did not entirely fit the frame.

The stone was a pillar of dark greenish rock with pale lines swirled through it. The whole of the surface that crowded the doorway was covered with a relief of runes. More Ogham writing laced the edge, continuing over the phallic tip and, presumably, down the opposite side. The ground around the stone had been pushed up, as if it had erupted there.

"Do you know the word 'internecine,' Senchan?" Laeg asked.

Senchan shook his head.

"It refers to terrible conflict within a single body where both halves of the body suffer mutually, for which reason an inter-necine conflict is generally useless, pointless." He paused for a moment, watching Senchan watching the stone. Then, instead of explaining his remarks, he said, "This is Fergus mac Roich's stone." He went around the boy.

"Where will we come out?" Senchan glanced back along the corridors, wondering again about MacRoth and, especially, Maeve.

"I don't know *that*," answered Laeg impatiently. His voice sounded far off.

Senchan turned back to him, to no one at all. The hallway was empty, the stone like a giant's thumb pressed against the door. The walls of Cruachan creaked as if an unseen hand attached to that thumb had begun to squeeze the fort. Senchan could visualize it quite clearly. With a deep breath, he jumped forward and merged with the runes.

III.
THE TALE OF THE KINGSHIP
OF ULSTER

1. Talking Heads

On the hilly eastern horizon a swollen red crescent of dawn
inched into view and turned the white cowl of the Druid's robes
into molten orange. His hazel eyes glistened with the light,
eyes like those of a wolf, an impression further enhanced by
his long, prominent nose and by the short brown beard that
grew high on his cheeks. His curly hair swept back from a
shaved tonsure—a clean line from one ear to the other over
the top of his skull. His gold earrings glinted, his high forehead
shone with the dawn's light, which bled slowly down his body
until it embraced him from head to foot. At that moment he
might have been a statue of red-hot bronze.

The hazy plain below him still lay in shadow. Flickering
torches indicated a group of people gathered in the thin mist
around the massive figure of a boar fashioned out of wicker.
Inside it a bound man lay among small platters of wood on
which the Druid had inscribed messages that some of those
people down there wanted carried to their dead ancestors. Fire
would bind those epistles to the soul of the captive. In death,
he became their courier. He had been found guilty of rape,
caught as he was in the act. That crime made him a superb
choice for this sacrifice, a fertility rite. The people were, the
Druid considered, most fortunate to have caught him.

Soon the whole disk of the engorged sun had cleared the

distant hills. The plain below glowed pinkish as if heather had
suddenly blossomed there. The mists rose away. Torchlight
became redundant but remained.

The Druid Cathbad raised his arms, held his hazel wand
horizontally above his head; above it, the crescent of the moon
hung, tiny in the blue.

Loudly, he chanted, "The smiling eye of Belenos is open.
It sees your sorrow, lack and loss. In his sight send the sacrifice
across the plain. From red dawn to red isle, let blood be the
road. From dry to wet, barren to fecund, out of death emerges
a birth! Welcome, Belenos, and behold with what honor your
people greet you!"

He lowered one arm, pointed the wand down at the wicker
figure. The torches leaped into the air as if of their own will,
bright fires arcing to land on or under the figure.

The bound rapist began to scream. Cathbad listened carefully, counting each separate cry. After nine, the rapist fell
silent. A spout of greasy smoke appeared in the midst of the
burning wicker boar. The Druid nodded with satisfaction. Nine
was as good a number as could be asked for. No further divining
would be necessary. The woman for whom those people had
gathered would give birth now; she and her husband could
rejoice in that certainty. A babe blessed by the sun, kissed by
the moon. He drew signs of thankfulness to each of these
celestial objects with his wand. The crowd below, comprehending, cheered.

Cathbad pulled up the hood of his robe and walked up the
hill.

The cheers went up again, to him, but he did not respond;
they had fed him, which was all the payment he asked, and
the walk back to his tumulus, the mound enclosing his secret
dwelling, would take all day. There were two *nemetons* to visit
on the road, two sacred groves awaiting his blessing before
any rites could be performed there. The ritual of consecration
took hours and then he would have to wait while fronds of
mistletoe were tied to the trees ringing the grove. Only then
would it be a proper *nemeton;* only then could he walk on.
And then there was a disputation in Tailtiu awaiting his judgment, for which he would have to don his black robes again,
as he had while hearing the evidence against the rapist. He
hoped, this other matter would be as simple to decide. Oh, but
this area had too many novices, not enough priests. He would
be glad of a few more graduates to carry the load with him.

At the crest of the hill, the Druid paused and sniffed the air. He sensed something peculiar nearby and looked all around, but the two observers—the charioteer and the boy—were invisible to him, just a sense of warmth, a space where the wind divided and passed around. The hackles rose on his neck. Being a man of knowledge, he did not care for the things he knew nothing of. Finally, hefting his wand and the parcel containing his black robes, he moved on.

His thin hand, carrying the bundle, bore scars across the knuckles, recalling earlier times before Cathbad had devoted himself to the nineteen-year course of study that had brought him here. After a while his arm began to ache and he switched the bundle to his other hand, took the wand in his right. He held it out for a moment like a sword, and he smiled distantly.

In his youth, Cathbad had been a war-chief, representing his king on battlefields too numerous for memory to contain. He had *been* the king in time of war, carried the king's sword into battle. And it was that sword that had led him away from the field and into the arcane principles of the priesthood. Battle upon battle, he came to wonder why it was that common swords bent when they struck and had to be straightened again before a second strike, while weaponry manufactured by the Druids remained straight and sharp after repeated attacks. He had seen so many men and women die because their blades had curled up like a triskele at the first deflection, leaving them helpless until they could pry the blade back. More often they were killed first. The secret of Druid manufacture had drawn him in like a fish on a line until he could think of nothing else. Battle lost its meaning. Knowledge became more important, then all-consuming. To learn the reasons behind an act became more vital than to commit it. He gave himself over to Druid lore. His king found another champion.

However, in his quest for knowledge, he would go sixteen years before uncovering the mystery that had brought him to this brotherhood: that the Druid weapon-makers paid homage to Goibniu the Great Weapon Fashioner by pouring blood over each hot smoking tang. The God of Smiths, in reply to the offering, placed great strength in the blade through the blood. This revelation awed him, but as a Druid, never more as a warrior. "It is holier to believe than to know," he muttered absently. That was what he and the others told people outside the order. Certainly, that rule kept the secret safe within their grasp, and just as certainly no Druid believed it. But, then,

warriors had no reason to know why a sword held its shape.
For a warrior it was enough to know he could count on it. His
skill lay elsewhere; his training lived in muscle and sinew.
Druids stood between men and gods, a human bridge that kept
both sides safe.

As he crossed the hills of southern Ulster and smelled the
sea's breath far away, Cathbad pondered the choice he had
made so long ago. He wondered what he might have become
if curiosity had not compelled him to seek answers—if he had
just been a simple singleminded warrior. Then, laughing at his
own answer, he said, "A trophy."

Cathbad's mound lay in a forest near Loch Ramor; the oak
grove *nemeton* he presided over was half an hour's walk from
there. A huge boulder, apparently a natural formation, hid the
entrance to the tumulus completely from prying eyes. Only
when one stood adjacent to both the stone and the mound on
the right did the recess in the boulder appear and, within it,
the opening into the mound. The only remaining opening was
a smoke-hole in the crest of the tumulus, and the smoke rising
from it on cold days had been used as proof of more than one
tale of the Sidhe. That was just fine so far as Cathbad was
concerned: it kept the curious at a safe distance.

By the time Cathbad reached the tumulus, even the smoke
would have been invisible in the darkness. He wove his way
through the forest by memory, brushed the stone with his shoulder as he passed from view behind it. Inside, he went about
his business as purposefully as a blind man. A tallow lamp
awaited his hand just where he reached for it in the blackness.
He skimmed his hazel wand across it. The lamp flared up,
spitting and hissing like a contentious cat, and casting a hollow
light about the cavern.

The walls of Cathbad's temple were covered with carvings,
runes, and drawings. One set of spirals represented his nineteen-
year-cycle calendar. Another, the year divided into feast nights
and lunar equinoxes. The rough floor contained a small rec-
tangular hole in its center—a shaft that descended far below,
perhaps to the bowels of the earth. Into it, the Druid threw
sacrifices, old wands, and his garbage. Near the shaft stood a
great black cauldron. Flanking it as they flanked the inside of
the cave entrance behind him, two squared-off pillars rose up
to the low cavern ceiling. The pillars contained six niches
apiece. Each niche contained a severed human head.

As the tallow candle took life and illuminated the entire cavern, the heads opened their eyes and, yawning, looked at Cathbad. He ignored their gaze as he passed them. Setting down his bundle, he muttered, "Darker out than a Fomor's shit."

"Ooh," responded the head, "that's *dark*." They appreciated his occasional bits of description of the world outside that they no longer played a part in. These were Cathbad's *vathi*, his seers.

With some reluctance, Cathbad straightened and asked, "What have you for me?"

"Riddles," answered a head by the door, and the session began. "A big future," said another high up on the right of the cauldron.

Cathbad pinched his beak of a nose. He would have preferred to sleep before wading into their twisted truths, but the *vathi* would resent his napping after having awakened them and would babble all sorts of insults at him. He would have to put a spell of silence over them, and he was much too tired to do that. Then he was sure that, later, they would tangle their riddles that much more—they had done so before.

Groaning as he squatted down beside the cold cauldron, he said, "All right, unravel your riddles." Casually, he tapped his wand on the base of the cauldron. A small fire sprang up, catching the peat bricks laid around the pot. "Tell me whose immense future do we inspect tonight—" he rubbed his hands together before the fire "—and let's not waste our time with sniggering comments, please. I'm *very* tired. I'm doing this first only out of my deep regard for you. So, who are your conundrums about?"

The heads exchanged gleeful glances. In unison they proclaimed, "You!"

Cathbad coughed and stopped rubbing his hands together. *Me?*"

"Mmm."

"A future coming."

"A virgin dethroned."

"A king dethroned, too, yes."

"And a charmed child on his seat." Then, at some secret signal, the heads fell silent, waiting, watchful.

Cathbad drew himself back up on his feet, his vexation plain. "Is this some preposterous joke? I'm very near throwing the lot of you out into the night. I'll let the wolves have you, you trophies for ravens. You're fortunate I'm so weary or I'd do it this second, but don't try me further."

One of the heads giggled but stopped abruptly as the others glared at him. So what if the Druid had threatened to toss them out so many times it was ludicrous? This once he just might do it.

A female head stated, "A royal woman, daughter of the Saffron Heel and twelve foster fathers. She dwells on an isle not far but distant. Fierceness flows in her veins. Her army is full female, all fuliginous in fashion. You follow?"

"*Flu*ently, thank you," he answered, only slightly mollified by the disclosure.

Another head took up the chant. "She wears no man, nor has she ever, though she's worn out enough to have two daughters in tow. Yet it's the son of her womb who rules seven years hence from his birthnight."

"The father is a priest of great power with a nose to match. His wits are addled by half and he's quite forgot how to play crown and feathers—"

"*You* could be buried beneath a hill, my little wit," shouted Cathbad, "like Bran!"

The head pouted. "I say what I see, head-master. Don't blame me."

"Head-master," Cathbad grumbled. "You say I am to locate a specific warrior, convince her to lie with me? To make a king?"

"Ah, he sees to the very core."

"He does, he does."

"A regular riddle-master, a mage of mazes, a whit of a wit—"

"Hold your tongue!" bellowed the Druid.

"I would, great Cathbad, but I've no fingers to clasp it." The heads all burst into laughter at that. He had never seen them so audacious.

Frustrated, he marched out of the room. The laughter died quickly behind him as the heads speculated on what he meant to do. When he returned, they fell silent. He had changed his clothing, exchanging his robe for a white animal's skin—a bull's skin. He went to the cauldron again, but this time leaned over the edge and looked into it.

"Bull dream! Bull dream!" someone shouted.

"Hush!" admonished another; then, to him, "Wait, we'll tell you straight."

"Plain speaking," assured the head below that one.

The Druid paused to reply to the room at large, "Thank you, no. I'll find out for myself the truth of what you say without playing the fool for a bunch of horseless headmen."

"Well, I'll be damned."

"Not again in this life!" came the shouted rejoinder. The heads, as he had anticipated, began arguing and insulting one another. While they babbled like a feasting crowd, Cathbad set to work. He lit a torch from the cauldron fire, then went through an opening far back in the chamber that led deep into the caverns below. Here the walls were of cracked crystal, and stalactites hung down like rainbow ice. Here no wind had ever blown and the air smelled as old as the tales of the Tuatha de Danann. The bull-robed Druid went on, sure of his path, passing deeper into the earth's secret places. Creatures with blind, egg-yolk eyes skittered at his coming—things that had evolved without ever having felt the warmth of Belenos's eye. Some hissed and fled, others stood their ground, sensing the immensity of the being passing by. Their tiny hearts fluttered in their watery bodies, revealing them where they stood. He passed them by, going on until the air had turned arctic and the trickles of water solidified. There he found what he wanted—a small ice-encrusted pot much like his cauldron. It contained a dark, frozen substance. After first wrapping tatters of the bull's skin around each hand, he grasped the rings on the pot and pulled it free from where it had frozen to the cavern floor. Then, grunting from the effort but alert and revived by the cold, he carried it away with him back through the corridors of eternal night, around and out like a small sea creature escaping from a nautilus. The torch, lying across the lip of the pot, rolled back and forth and threatened at any moment to set fire to his wrists.

The echoes of voices came to him first, long before he saw the light of the tallow. The heads were still slandering one another and, by the sound of it, tempers were flaring. It was no wonder, he thought, that they had led abbreviated lives. He entered among them again and set his cold burden into the center of the large cauldron.

The heads broke off their arguing. "What's that he's doing?" one of them asked the group in general.

"Tarbfeis," replied another, helmeted, head.

"What's that?"

"Well, you must be new here," answered a head from below.

"He does it now and again. His *bull* dream—reveals the identity of kings, the whim of the weather, the boils on a squatter's backside." The head snickered.

"Yes, but what's the secret?"

"Ah, well, now," began the helmeted head mysteriously, "that would be telling."

"You mean you don't know," accused the one.

"I don't know," admitted the other.

Cathbad touched his wand once to the large cauldron. The iron began to glow, at first in a circle around the tip of the stick but soon spreading to ring the lower half of the container. The color rose by degrees until the whole cauldron glowed red.

Watching, he looked as he had at dawn—a figure cast in flame, his deep-set eyes molten in carmine shadow.

Steam rose out of the cauldron, then a burping, bubbling sound. The glow began to fade. As quickly as it had heated, the cauldron cooled to black. Moving nearer, Cathbad accidentally touched his wand against the metal again. The wand turned to ash and sprinkled out of his hand. It had run out of power. He sighed. A new one would have to be made. These days he seemed to be fashioning wands every other week. Pretty soon he was going to run out of hazel trees nearby. Maybe he could make do with willow for a while.

Leaning over the edge of the cauldron, he lifted out the smaller pot. The liquid in it had thawed and now had the consistency of porridge. He set it down, then sat beside it. The heads watched, enraptured.

The thick reddish liquid continued to smoke as Cathbad took a thimble-cup and filled it from the pot. He then chanted over the cup, so softly that the heads could not make out a word of it. No one knows what words put prophecy into the bull's blood.

Cathbad drank the thimble dry. A thin trail of warmth ran down inside him, soon branched out through his limbs, into his head. The blood in the pot started to swirl. A whirlpool appeared in its center. Cathbad stared down into the spinning pit.

The contents of the pot became translucent. Tiny figures appeared through it. The whirlpool rose up and expanded, sucking Cathbad down into the center of the vortex. He said a single word: *"Fuil."* Blood. One segment of the whirlpool slowed and began to spin counter to the rest. This was the point he sought, the stretch of time that concerned him. He released his hold on the present and allowed himself to fall into the riddle of the *vathi*.

They had not lied to him, his seers. She was there: the daughter of the Saffron Heel.

Nessa.

2. The Amazon Queen

Laeg and Senchan stood on a rocky cliff overlooking a crashing sea.

"Not long after she had turned the marriageable age of twelve," Laeg said, "Nessa's foster family was slain by a marauding band of Picts who had sailed into a nearby bay. They spared her, the strange girl of contrasts—of black hair and white skin. She looked an awful lot like their moon goddess, and the superstitious pillaging Picts decided she should be awarded to their chief. He waited with the rest of their party back on the beach. Nessa was led naked before him. When she finally stood before him and saw what a loathsome, spotty creature he was, she laughed at him so shamelessly that it was the Pictish chieftain who felt naked on that cold northern beach. His face purpled, which at least hid the splotchiness of his skin. He drew his sword to slay the insolent girl. Nessa turned to her captors and asked for a sword, that she might try to defend herself. That was her right, as in any combat. One of the men nearest her drew his weapon and handed it to her. The chieftain paused to watch Nessa struggle with the weapon, one hand then two, seeking for a balance that seemed lost to her, holding it in every possible way. It was obvious to the most obtuse among them that the girl had never picked up a sword in her life. The chieftain laughed at her idiocy in defying him. He strutted forward to deal with her. His head still wore that malicious grin as it hit the sand beside his jerking, blood-fountain of a body. One swift blow had done the job: a triumph that made clever Nessa the new chieftain. However, she had some different ideas on the tribal arrangement. She chose three of the women from the group to accompany her, but only one man—the one who had given her his sword, whose name was Fachtna Fathach. This group of five destroyed the shored boats save one. In that one they sailed out of the bay, leaving behind the confused marauders of whom nothing further is known.

"After a day's journey, Nessa and her crew arrived at an uninhabited boreal isle that she claimed as her own. It was so tiny they could walk its perimeter in half an hour. Bitter winds assailed its rocky face and few creatures dwelt there—mostly black seals, which became the group's staple for everything. They ate the meat, dressed in the slick black skins from head to foot. Against the cruel weather, they built sturdy stone huts. The remainder of their needs they filled by plundering the neighboring coastline. New women returned with them as often as not. Soon the whole northern coast was alive with tales of the isle of women warriors who gave no quarter and expected none. Fachtna became Nessa's husband. Other men joined occasionally, too—the women did not hate men, they just preferred the company they'd grown used to. Nessa bore two daughters, Deichtire and Findchoem, by Fachtna. But he grew restive over time, under her gracious yoke. He had a secret jealousy. To three of the newer arrivals he went, plotting to overthrow his wife, promising himself to each of the three conspirators in turn. In truth he intended to master them all. His plot was discovered at an incipient stage. Nessa cursed him: 'A shame upon your beard!' He covered his face in his hands at this cruelest of revilements. She had every right to level this upon him, too, for such scurrilous behavior deserves the harshest punishment. After that day no one who met him could overlook the disgrace that made a sigil of his face; he took to wearing a cowl. Nessa claimed the rights of a full divorce from him. As he had provoked it, his *coibche*—in this case, his share of all plunderings—remained with her, and Fachtna was sent off in his boat with the sword he had lent her, his clothes, and three bickering, tussling banshees.

"After that experience, Nessa took no other husbands. She got her pleasure from male concubines brought over for her or, more often, from one of the warriors she could trust. This, then, was the woman in the *tarbfeis*, Senchan. And this is where Cathbad came to find her."

They turned from the crashing waves and set off across the small, uninviting island.

3. What the Druid Knew

Rarely did the northern clime offer Nessa's isle either warmth or dryness, but a few days each year the summer air did heat up enough to make sealskin slick with sweat. On one such day, Nessa and some of her women doffed their black garments to lie idly outside her hut on wide slabs of stone hot from the sun. The naked women felt lazy and pleasant, like big, well-fed cats. They told stories and jokes and recounted old adventures to the newer members of their group, but fell finally into a drowsy silence. They did not hear any approaching footsteps; did not notice they had a visitor until he was almost upon them.

Nessa heard someone gasp. She opened one eye a crack and saw a Druid striding silently toward her. She sat up. The warriors looked first at their leader, then at the robed figure whose face was hidden deep in the shadows of his blindingly white robe. If he noticed these lazing observers, he did not act as if he had.

Nessa wondered if he were real. Her isle was virtually sacrosanct. No one had shouted out the sighting of a boat, which should have happened if a priest had journeyed to her isle; Druidry was not practiced here. They had their own priestess, their own god.

As the apparition passed her, she proclaimed loudly, "There are *no* Druids on this island," expecting the figure to pass right on by, deaf to her as a ghost would be. But the robed figure halted and turned his hidden face to her. "There are now," he said.

Nessa sat up straighter. "Why have you come here?"

"Because you require my service," he answered.

"I need nothing of a man whose life is a secret."

The bright cowl bobbed. "I was once a war-chief, too. I know as well as you when to lunge and when to withdraw my sword."

Nessa tried to ignore the ticklish sensation brought on by

55

his ambiguous riddling. She inhaled deeply and said, "This is a good day, isn't it?"

"It is a good day," answered the Druid, "for begetting a king upon a queen." With that he pushed back his hood and stared openly down upon her. His gold earrings sparkled, two suns. His shaved forehead glistened.

Nessa studied his face, the cryptic message held for her in his deep-set eyes. She had had little experience in dealing with Druids, but not one of the few she had met had affected her this strangely, this . . . lickerishly.

"Is your riddle true?" she asked.

"It is. A child conceived this day will become a great king, forever remembered."

Nessa arose from her stone. The other women looked at one another in wonder and confusion. "I should be interested to see you wield that sword of yours," said Nessa. "Come with me." She took his scarred hand and led him away. He made a strange backward gesture at the other women. At first they thought he had shaken his fist at them; but when they looked at the slab of stone where their queen had lain, they found a sprig of mistletoe lying within the perspiration shade of her, where the stain of her thighs met.

Nessa could not believe the Druid's prowess in making love. She thought she had tasted every flavor of coupling there was, but nothing in all her experience had prepared her for his fierce penetration. He made her wild, made her shed her human senses to take on those of some elemental being. She dreamed while he thrust into her of the touch of a god. The touch took her away from herself and that cold room, into warm, wet places. The dream burst in a pain that was exquisite. She came back from where he had driven her to find him staring down into her eyes with an alarming glare. But he was smiling. "Cathbad," she whispered.

"You know me?"

"I heard your name spoken just now in a dream of spinning blood."

His smile grew. "A Druid has little to offer in the way of _coibche_. Our riches are knowledge."

"I've no family for you to pay, so your _coibche_ would be mine in any case—and I feel you have an overwhelming treasure for me. I should like to experience it regularly. You can pay a little at a time, as you come and go."

"I accept, provided the resting place for my wand is your dowry."

"We're of the same mind, I see," she said with an irony as heavy as his.

"Then we must be of the same body, too." He caressed her hips. His fingers glided, strayed like birds.

"Druids' studies include areas I never would have suspected," said Nessa. She reached down to stroke him up.

As Cathbad had foreseen, she became pregnant that day, though whether from the first or the fifteenth round it cannot be said. Nessa grew quiet and sedentary in her pregnancy. Her warriors attended to her and her new husband kept her pleased. Across the water the northern coast experienced a time of tranquility and plenty and did not ask questions.

The warriors had no idea what to make of the Druid. He came and went seemingly at will, disappearing from the small island whenever he had a mind to, while not so much as a dugout *currach* was ever seen sculling across the channel. Having no understanding of Druidry's deeper mysteries, they could not have conceived that Cathbad, through the *tarbfeis*, was existing in two segments of time at once and little by little was catching up to himself. The spin of the minor whirlpool slowed each day, coming nearer the clockwise whirl of time major. Few Druids could exist doubly. It was more a matter of abstraction than knowledge, and many who attempted the *tarbfeis* went mad. Countless novices had been lost in this way.

Sometimes knowledge is hidden for a good reason.

The pregnancy of Nessa continued past nine months. When a year had gone by, the women became concerned. None of this affected Nessa in the slightest. She remained phlegmatic no matter how worried they were. They finally brought in their own priestess; but, when presented with the facts, she merely gaped. So, at last, the women, led by the priestess of the isle, went before Cathbad and were finally let in on the secret: the queen carried a special child who required special circumstances for his birth. "He is being molded by magic; his creation takes time."

"But how long?" they asked.

Cathbad knew the answer exactly. "He will be born three years, three months, and three nights from the time of my arrival here." Some of the warriors who had borne children grimaced at the idea.

The priestess scratched her head thoughtfully, making her

calculations. She said, "This is most propitious. The birth date you predict is the Feast of Othar."

"And who might this Othar be?"

"Why, god of our island. The child *must* be very special."

"Yes. I said so," he replied, but seemed to have drifted off on some tangent.

"Then I'll go and ask Othar to give the child his blessing," she announced, but Cathbad didn't hear her.

Some time later, he asked one of the women what Othar's attributes were.

"Salt and stone," he was informed. Didn't everyone know that?

"It makes sense in a desolate place like this. But couldn't that also mean that your Othar is formed from tears and pitilessness?"

The woman could not say; she did not inquire into such matters. Perhaps he should address such questions to the priestess.

Intending to do just that, Cathbad went off in search of her. Yet, as he headed across the rocky ground, time's small spinoff was losing its last wisp of impetus, slowing, slowing, to a dead stop—a moment of no time at all. Then the larger whirlpool caught it up and flung it forward again. The Cathbad of Nessa's Isle snapped into the present out of which he had come. Flecks of memory shot away in the swift transition.

He awoke in the tumulus, face down beside the small pot. Above him a head murmured. "Takes a lot out of him, that bull-dreaming does." Cathbad got up on trembling legs, too weak to contend with the *vathi*. He pinched out the tallow wick and lumbered to his bed of straw in another, smaller chamber.

Two days later he awoke and headed off on his journey northward. He recalled vaguely that he needed a new wand and sought for the perfect hazel branch as he went. The matter of Othar was lost to him; the question he would never ask.

Nessa gave birth the night of Othar's Feast to a handsome boy. She named the babe after a brook in Crich Rois, where she was born: Conchovor. Cathbad and the warrior women held him up in the firelight and proclaimed him to be an auspicious child, born on Othar's Night. Far below them, an enormous surging wave shattered against the rocks. Thick salt spray stung the air and sprinkled like a sudden shower over the child. A frown crossed the baby's face, appeared and disappeared in an

instant, buried inside his soul like a worm within an apple
remains hidden until the fruit is cut apart. Many years later,
Cathbad would see that unnatural frown again and go cold
remembering the isle, the spray, and the attributes of Othar.
That night, though, he believed as did the warrior women that
the child, Conchovor, was flawless.

4. Parting

Nessa recovered slowly from the long trial of carrying and
birthing her son. She called for Cathbad and he came, held her
hands while she lay nursing the boy.

"You know," she said, "in the time I carried Conchovor,
my contract with you ran out. You said nothing."

"Surely you don't fear usucapion from me?"

Nessa smiled wearily, "No, I know I don't have to buy my
freedom from you, even if the contract has run these three
years. Who could divide our traded fortunes after all? How
can they be given back?"

He laughed.

"Cathbad, what happens now? What's our future?"

He knelt beside her on the furs. "Why is it that people always
beg to hear the future told when such knowledge inevitably
brings ruin? Everything you learn changes what you'll do, when
you'll do it. People who learn that they're doomed to die try
desperate means to escape their death and succeed thereby in
running straight onto death's spear."

Nessa grew alarmed. "I'm to die?"

"You? No! By the Dagda, no."

"But you said—"

"An example, that's all. An inappropriate one, I see. Death
is not in the future as far ahead as I've seen you. What I know
is that this child will be king after seven years. You are still
beside him then."

"Seven?"

"Yes. His fosterage will be different from any child's since
he has to learn twice as much in half the time, and then more

because we know already what he's destined to be."

"Who's chosen to foster him?"

"I am. When he's nursed, I'll take him away and teach him what he must know to be the king prophesied. Then, when it's time, we'll return to you."

"Then I'm involved in his kingship?"

"Oh, very much so," he assured her.

She gazed at him with life-weary eyes. "So much mystery. Knowing only scraps—it's like seeing a mountain through a mist. All you get are peeks at the face, or a bit of contour. You have to create your impression of a whole without ever seeing it. It's so frustrating."

"As I said, you can trap yourself with too much knowledge."

"How do you avoid it?"

"Me?" He let go of her hand. "I don't," he answered. His gaze wandered, eyes unfocused. "It's a Druid's curse to know too much. Time is a tree, you see. You cut it off at the stump and look at the rings within rings within rings. A tree's rings lead back to an infinitesimal beginning. Time's rings go on to an unseen end. My end—my own death—is unknowable to me. The curse is also that I find myself solely by the part I play in the futures of others. I could die in the midst of a bull-dream." He looked at Nessa. "That's how you and I came to meet, why we're here with this child. And I never hesitated, never considered the risk, once I knew what I had to do. Only sometimes, when I have time—" He smiled at the word and did not go on.

Nessa comprehended barely half what he said, but inferred from it that he could give no answers to satisfy her. On a less conscious level she realized, too, that their days of copulative bliss had ended forever. The child had stopped that just by existing. Without Cathbad's preknowledge of Conchovor, they could have made love forever; paradoxically, without that pre-knowledge, neither would have approached the other in the first place. She looked down at the suckling baby. Here was the part fate had planned for her. Hereafter, she must live in devotion to this child. She had gone from girl to warrior to lover to mother. And from there to what? Watcher? When would the time come? How am I to recognize the opportunity for Conchovor's greatness? she wanted to ask him. How can I be sure I do the right things to reach that point? She grasped then an inkling of the curse he carried: He could not tell her without destroying what he described.

* * *

A year later, after the man and child had vanished from her isle, Nessa knew no more about her future than he had told her that morning.

At first reluctantly, then with a renewed vigor, she returned to her old ways and led her glad warriors across the water once more. If, during this time, she ever doubted fate, she needn't have. Her victories had become legend, and it was the tales told of her that brought Nessa the warrior queen to the attention of Fergus mac Roich.

5. Invitations

The next several years passed slowly for Nessa, filled as they were with battle and adventures. She lived on her cunning alone. She spurned all former lovers and took no new ones, closing off that part of herself.

As time passed, she began to wonder if Cathbad had told her the truth—if she would ever see her son again. With no option to enduring, the warrior-queen maintained her unceasing watch for the Druid's promised return. In this she was not rewarded until the seven years were up.

At dawn one morning, a large sail-propelled *currach* approached the isle across the narrow channel off the mainland. The boat, containing three men, had not reached the shallows when the alarm went up and a force of warriors arrived on the strand. Dressed all in black, standing poised and ready for a skirmish, they looked to the three men in the boat like spirits of the dead.

One man jumped into the surf and dragged the *currach* forward with a rope, all the while squinting suspiciously at the sinister welcoming committee. He climbed back in the moment the craft was securely beached. The other two men got out then. The first of them wore a tunic of blue wool to his knees. The other, shorter man was dressed, like the women, all in black. Unlike them his darkness belonged to a robe: he wore

as well the tonsured skull of a Druid. The robe named his place
in Druidry: *brithem,* the class of judges.

The tall man in blue wool stepped reluctantly out of the
water. "I am Fergus the Messenger, servant of the king of
Ulster, the *fine* Fergus mac Roich. I've come here at the king's,
ah, request. Right. To offer marriage to Nessa, the infam—
renowned!—leader of this isle." He smiled broadly.

The women looked at one another, then moved aside so that
their queen could come forward. "That would be you?" the
Messenger asked her. She nodded once. "Yes, right, well, as
you have no family to placate—hmm?—the king offers his
coibche to you directly and sends that you should name what
you're worth."

Nessa's heart seemed to catch in her throat. She did not
know what to tell the Messenger, and in a moment of wordless
panic she fled from the beach. Some of the women chased
after her, disturbed that she had not given a characteristic and
pointed reply. "Others have made similar offers," they called
after her. "And you laughed at them and took their heads.
What's wrong here?" She made no reply, but gestured them to
stop, then continued on alone, reaching the opposite shore in
minutes.

A mist was rolling in there. Already it covered the shore
and drifted to the point on which she stood. This was what the
warriors called the "Dragon Mist," after the monsters of the
sea that sometimes arrived with it. Standing there, she could
hear their distant, high-pitched keens, and she shivered. As she
peered into the mist, two figures materialized in it—two people
walking on the surface of the water. One was a hawk-nosed
man dressed in a white robe. The other was a boy who clumsily
carried a spear, a shield, and a sword. The boy had fine features,
totally unlike his father.

Cathbad led the boy to land. Seeing Nessa, he drew back
his cowl. The years had left no mark upon him, she thought.
He might have been gone just a day. He raised his hand to her
and she reached forward and fit her fingers through his. He
said nothing, but turned toward Conchovor.

The child was a complete stranger to Nessa though he had
her mien, her cheeks and lips. His hair was brown, worn so
shaggy that he looked elfin. His eyes darted when they moved,
quick and knowing like Cathbad's. Mother and son observed
each other from a great distance. At last, Conchovor smiled

diffidently. Then Nessa knew him as part of herself. "Are you great?" she asked him.

"I will be," he replied, without any trace of haughtiness.

"Yes, I know," she answered proudly. To Cathbad, she asked, "What's to be my reply to the two Ferguses whose question I know you already know?"

Their eyes met again, but the warmth of his silent greeting had faded. "Tell them your price is the furtherance of your lineage. Your one desire is to have your son made king of Ulster for a year that his descendants may be recognized as children of noble status."

"But Cathbad, in a world stuffed with such self-styled 'royalty,' what good is that? He'll be nothing but a credential for some future fool to name!"

The Druid remained passive, expressionless. "Just tell them that. I testified once that you would play a part in his kingship. Now you will. He relies hereafter on *your* cleverness and invention to see him through."

She started to reply hotly: "Then why wasn't *I* educated for this task along with him?" But she stopped herself, recalling what he had said the day that Conchovor was born. She stared pensively at the Druid and her son for a moment. For so long she had counted the hours and nights till this time, till both had come back to her. Now that they were here, why did she want to fight? She had her son again.

Nessa turned and set off across the island, back to the beach where the Messenger and the Druid waited warily for her return. What they saw as she charged into view was something swift, black, and grim: one of the fiendish *Morrigu* come to devour their souls. "Right!" cried the Messenger. "That's it!" He dug in his heels and heaved the boat off the sand, then scrambled over the side. The Druid, seeing himself abandoned, fled into the boat as well.

From the safety of the shallows, they listened to the queen's most unusual terms.

Fergus the Messenger frowned at the price. The dark Druid, whose name was Morann and who was the great Judge of Ulster, saw the face of displeasure beside him and felt some judgment would be helpful. "Two cultures come together here," Morann explained. "What is fair to each is not necessarily fair to both." He sat down.

"Oh, thank you *so* much for your help," answered the Messenger. "You be sure and tell the king that. Fine. Fine."

The boatman leaned forward between them. "Does this mean we can go back now?"

The Messenger stood with an eye toward balancing, and he called to Nessa: "Word will be sent from Ard Macha on the king's decision. He will consider your offer carefully. I promise you that!" He sat down hard as the boat rocked suddenly. "Right. *Now* we can go back . . . though I don't know to what."

6. The Somber Warrior

"To describe so uncommon a warrior-king as Fergus mac Roich," said Laeg, "takes more than just a lengthy attributive citation. He was handsome. He was strong. But others were handsomer, others had more sinew." As he spoke, Laeg and Senchan passed unseen through the openings in the earthen walls surrounding the high hillfort of Ard Macha. "The essence of his remarkable character lay deep within him like a fish in a dark pool. As a youth it's possible his mettle was more shallow—that part of his history is unknown to me. I know that two years before he put the bit into Ulster's mouth, he had married; and that, simultaneous with his acquiring the kingship at nineteen, his wife succumbed to the disease that transforms the air in your lungs to water. She must have been an extraordinary person, certainly to him, and I think that forever after he believed that the goddess Macha had required her as a sacrifice in return for his triumphs. Later, he lost much more and won nothing for it, so his belief seems to me ungrounded . . . but, then, who knows what motivates those dark goddesses of nature? The wife left him a son, Fiacha, already fostered out by then. Fergus pared down his joy to circumscribe that single treasure. He awaited the distant day his son would come of age and be returned to him. Meantime, he proved himself a thoughtful if emotionless ruler. Nothing broke his calm; anger lived in him no more than laughter. So you doubtless wonder, my lad, why did such a man send out for another wife?

"All kinships had a patron god or, as in this instance, goddess, much as you have saints now. In Ulster a celebration took place each year to the Triple Macha that her fertile aspects might smile upon the land. The king ceremoniously 'wed' a mare and consummated his marriage to her. She was then butchered in sacrifice, her blood drained into a cauldron. The king bathed in and drank of the mare's blood. Through these acts he renewed his contract with the Horse Goddess. The night after his second such celebration, Fergus lay asleep. His body was dark still, with the dried mare's blood coating him like a sheath. In his dream that night, Macha appeared to him. She had a long, flaming snout and a white diamond embedded in her forehead. The Night Mare she is called in this guise. She told Fergus to find a wife and, as she spoke, he saw behind her a red mist and in it a dozen shadowy figures that took the shape of seals. Ocean waves crashed somewhere in the swirl of mist behind them. An odor like that of decaying fish assailed him. Macha lay down upon a thick slab of stone and spread wide her legs. 'Come into me,' she ordered him. She opened like a great whirlpool. Fergus fell into her. The red mist appeared within her; so, too, the black seals. A great warmth covered Fergus and he drifted into unconsciousness. When he awoke, the mare's blood had been washed away by a brine that now coated him. He could taste the salt of the sea in his mouth. Immediately he sent for his Druids and told them the dream. They conferred briefly and announced that these portents pointed in only one direction—to the warrior women who lived north of the Pictish coast. The leader of this band had lately become a popular subject of the *filid*. Yes, he had heard of her. 'They sing that she is beautiful,' he said, which was true.

"Fergus followed the Druids' advice in order to preserve the plenitude of Ulster, but his heart was never part of the bargain. He had long since forgotten such feelings. This was duty to his goddess and his people.

"When they returned to Ard Macha, the two men he had sent out went straight to him and told him of Nessa's extraordinary price. The king sensed something sinister in her demands, but couldn't fathom it. Morann was in agreement with him, having had much time on the way back to consider the *coibche*. Nevertheless, the Druid advised Fergus that 'You must get a judgment on it from the *tuatha*, all the tribes of the province.' It seemed not to be a matter for Druids to decide.

"Fergus invited his advisors—who each represented one

tuath—to a feast and had Morann outline the situation for them while they ate. Then the advisors pondered. I can tell you that no quieter feast ever took place in Ulster. In the end it was the fact that their king had no wife that swayed them. Advisors, Senchan, are always looking to marry off their kings in the name of fecundity. A fertile leader makes for good crops. 'You *should* have a queen,' they all agreed. 'It's important. So, accept her demands and fit a king's torc around the child's throat. We'll witness his ascension but we'll still call *you* king. What's a year, after all?' Fergus nodded silently. He could see no harm in it when proposed like that. A year was nothing. Perhaps, if he had asked his Druids to inspect the future anyway, matters would have gone otherwise. But I doubt it. After all, a bull-dreaming Druid had set off the whole chain of events.

"The next morning, Fergus the Messenger was sent off again at dawn, grumbling loudly about 'the spotty, disputative, smelly northern Picts' with whom he would have to contend again, and cursing the damned boatman who was surely going to cower in his *currach* to see the Messenger coming again, and bitching about his lot in life in general."

"He's a very irritable man, isn't he?" said Senchan.

"Perhaps. But the story goes that he had been performing great feats in bed with his wife when the king's servants had come to get him, to send him off. And they had refused to let him complete the affair before bringing him before the king. It is, you see, a fundamental aspect of fate that while directed at one or two individuals, it inevitably disrupts the lives of many in the bargain."

They entered a round wooden fortress perched in the middle of the broad hilltop of Ard Macha. Inside, the building was divided into four concentric parts.

Near the doorway, an old man sat, surrounded by piles of clay and small wedge-shaped tools. As they stood over him, watching, he fashioned one lump of the wet gray stuff into a long, flat strip with a wide groove down the center.

"He's making a sword mold," explained Laeg. "He must have been the caster in Fergus's reign. There was a different one by the time I arrived. Neither one probably made a decent sword, either. For us now, the trick is to unravel the path to the center of this place. The king will be there." He and Senchan left the old man at his work.

7. The Winning of Fergus mac Roich

Nessa came to Ard Macha. She brought with her the warriors who were willing to give themselves over to Ulster's rule, her slaves, her son, and Cathbad. Conchovor received foster parents, but as he was also the "king" the foster parents lived in Ard Macha with him rather than the customary opposite.

At first, Nessa found herself quite taken with Fergus mac Roich. There was about him some hidden force that set him apart from all other men. And he was attractive to look on. His linen tunics were all bright checkered patterns. He wore his lime-dyed, light brown hair drawn straight back, gathered like a horse's tail at his neck. His nostrils turned up at the edges so that he always appeared aroused or angered, and she thought for the first few days that her presence excited him. However, he hardly spoke three words to her in the first week and their initial session of lovemaking after the wedding feast was mechanical and all too brief. Fergus made no pretense that the marriage arrangement had been his idea.

Through gossip Nessa soon discovered what separated Fergus mac Roich from everyone else. It did not take her long to realize that any attempts to entice this man would only widen that gap. She dismissed him from her mind then. She had lived without men before; she could easily do so again. And there was far more pressing business to attend to.

Conchovor remained oblivious to her machinations. The Fergus mac Roich he encountered was an entirely different man from the one his mother knew. His mac Roich took him out hunting, spent endless hours training him with the spear and sword that Cathbad had awarded him on his seventh birthday. They rode out in Fergus's war chariot across the great plain below Ard Macha, taking turns as chariot driver or armed warrior, steering the course or flinging death's point. Fergus told Conchovor of ancient deeds and of battles he had known. Nights, the two of them dwelled in the feast hall, listening to *filid* sing intricate rhymes of the great heroes of the Tuatha de

Danann, those hero-gods who had fought impossible battles
across the land long before the *filid* or Fergus had been born.
Of Nuada, the great king who had lost his kingship when his
arm was cut off in battle, and who gained back his kingdom
when a remarkable silver arm had been fashioned to replace
it. Of Balor, whose Evil Eye was so huge that it took great
machines to pull back the lid that covered its deadly glare. Of
the battle-frenzies of a thousand divine heroes.

One evening, Morann the Judge went to see Fergus on the
matter of certain omens he and the other Druids had recently
encountered. He had been keeping watch for signs of some
treachery from Nessa, and what he had seen that night in the
steaming entrails of a rabbit had been the first hint of disaster
for the king. Upon entering the central room of Ard Macha,
the Druid judge found Fergus and Conchovor seated opposite
one another around the huge stump that stood in the center of
the fortress. On the stump was a *fidchell* board; but what astonished Morann was that his king was doubled over in laughter.

Seeing the Druid in the doorway, Fergus pointed at Conchovor
and tired to speak, but could not stop laughing enough to do
so. The boy gave Morann a puckish little grin, then lowered
his head. "What is this? What is going on?" asked Morann.
He was not sure if he should share in the humor.

"He beat me!" gasped Fergus. "The . . . impious little imp—
who taught him this game?"

"I—I really haven't a clue," said Morann. Then he fell
silent. He had never seen Fergus mac Roich smile, much less
laugh. And now here, over a game of *fidchell?* Thoroughly
befuddled, he turned away and left the matter of omens behind.

While the virtuous child had done what his mother could
not, she in turn was hatching a plot to win him what he could
not himself achieve.

8. Divide and Conquer

During the latter part of that year, a bizarre conspiracy unfolded
gradually under Nessa's direction. She began to meet from time
to time most casually with members of a select group. This

group consisted of her women warriors, servants, and Conchovor's foster parents. They sometimes came to her private chambers—never more than one or two at a time—but more often met on a designated hill, where Nessa would give them a task to undertake.

Conchovor's foster parents she sent out weekly among the people of Ulster, always to the west of Ard Macha. Each day they visited a different household. They demanded from each a tithe in the name of Fergus mac Roich. Their connection to him was widely known, and it was his right to demand anything from the people as all property was communally owned and he the head of the collected Ulidian *tuatha*—all the *derbfines*, or extended families, that together comprised Ulster. By the time the year of Conchovor's "reign" had ended, the foster parents had acquired a tithe from exactly one half of the citizens of the province. They still had no idea as to why or where these things went.

They would have been surprised to find that every treasure they brought in, Nessa gave to her warrior women and servants, who also made a journey into the countryside every week, but always east of the great hillfort. Loaded up with bags of treasure from gold coins to brass buckets, this group spent the year visiting the remaining half of Ulster. At each house they bestowed one of the items upon the family, saying, "This gift to you is the will of Conchovor mac Nessa, your wise new king."

When they had run out of gifts, they returned home to meet again with Nessa. Miraculously, she always had more treasures for them to distribute. Like the collectors, the distributors had no understanding of what was happening here. Not even Morann, who watched her suspiciously in every spare moment, had an inkling of Nessa's diabolically simple scheme.

When the year was up, Fergus mac Roich threw a great feast in Ard Macha to celebrate Conchovor's time as king. The boy celebrated joyously with Fergus, tasting his first wine, and was honored to sit among the great warriors of the province: such names as Sencha the Sage who judged all combats and had seen young Conchovor triumph over boys twice his age; Menn, the famous spearman, whose weapon, Bratach, arced through the sky like a rainbow because bright pennoncels tied along the shaft magically imbued the air with color; and Nuada, whose shield, Cainnel, glowed at night like a full moon.

Soon, however, the time came for Fergus to take back his

king's torc from the boy. Conchovor stood up and started to
take it off. "Hold!" cried a dozen voices from around the large
room. Fergus and Conchovor gaped at the crowd.

A handful of men came forward in a single file past the
cooking fire in the center of the hall. Conchovor recognized
the men as the representatives of the Ulster *tuatha* who advised
the king. He turned to watch Fergus, but mac Roich's face now
revealed nothing more than idle curiosity; however, his hand
rested on the carved hilt of his sword, Leochain. Conchovor
moved inconspicuously away a few paces. He also considered
his weapon.

The advisors grouped together in front of Fergus. "We want
you to know at this time that the people resent being treated
like your dowry." A pudgy man in front turned to face the
crowd. "It is our ruling that what was given up by Fergus mac
Roich should stay given, and what was won by Conchovor
should remain his." In the instant he finished speaking, his
head split in two down to his chin. His body stumbled forward,
came up against the huge vat of boiled beef that hung above
the fire, and folded over the edge of it. His sandals caught fire
but nobody moved to put them out.

Fergus mac Roich stood grimly holding his delicate, leaf-
thin sword. Blood dripped like a dark sap from its needle-tip.
His eyes shifted to the other advisors. It was at this point that
Cathbad and Morann entered the room.

"Slay no more, Fergus mac Roich," ordered Morann, "or
I'll circle your sword with a satire such that you'll never wield
sweet Leochain again."

"Did you hear what he said?"

"I did. And I've seen abundant signs before he uttered a
word. The ruling stands as pronounced. You have given up
kingship by choice and it has come to Conchovor freely. It's
the will of Macha and her people that he remain our leader."

"Morann—"

"Would you challenge the goddess?"

Fergus glowered at the boy beside him but saw at once that
Conchovor was innocent of complicity. Behind the boy stood
Nessa in a gown of red that hung from a large gold brooch
below her shoulder. She met his gaze with defiance. He knew
then the agent of his demission. Without taking his eyes off
her, he asked the two Druids, "What say those signs you've
seen regarding *how* the exchange has come about?"

"Precisely what are you asking?" queried Morann.

"Has this boy's mother employed treachery of some sort to steal away my torc?" He moved past Conchovor; Nessa held her ground. "Has she discredited our contract?"

Morann and Cathbad eyed one another. The judge was deferring to Cathbad, thinking Cathbad the better man to reply, unaware of the entanglements this created. Cathbad faced Nessa. "She has," he said, "to both questions."

Nessa shot him a wide-eyed look of betrayal.

"This feast," he continued abjectly, "marks the end of your first year in marriage. It can be taken as a legal terminal from which to nullify your arrangement if you so choose." He turned and quickly pushed his way out of the hall.

Leochain flashed between Fergus and Nessa. Two halves of a ruined gold brooch flipped up and dropped in the fire behind Fergus. The red gown pooled like blood around Nessa's feet. The only sound in the room was that of the dead advisor boiling in the pot. Fergus's eyes of torment looked the naked woman over one final time. Then he proclaimed, "Great shame upon your beard!"

Sword held ahead of him, parting the crowd, Fergus strode away. Nessa covered her mouth with one hand; the other had gone to shield the calyx of her thighs. The crowd stared at her in some confusion—no man had ever used that well-known curse before on a woman. The double edge of its meaning was barely dawning upon them.

The silence became too intense. One of the advisors turned to Morann and, pointing at the cooking cauldron, asked, "What's to be done about him?"

Morann scowled at the body. "Take him out. He's surely done by now."

9. The Geis of mac Roich

Any who thought they had seen Fergus mac Roich at his most withdrawn and silent before that night found that they had seen nothing yet. He continued to live among them in the fortress of Ard Macha, but he might have been a ghost. He retreated so deeply inside himself that he was alone even in a crowded feast hall—or would have been, since he no longer frequented them. Warriors who had taught him or been his friends avoided him entirely. To speak with Fergus was to have to look upon his empty face. Some people speculated that the curse he had laid upon Nessa had in fact infected him. Such speculation was quickly scuttled.

While Nessa remained facially unblemished, the insides of her thighs turned red from a rash so excruciating that she had to be carried from chamber to chamber. In spite of her infirmity she insisted on participating in all discussions on policy and matters of state from the couch on which she lay. She had a mind for tactics and, with close-mouthed Fergus no longer assisting them, the *tuatha* of Ulster needed her kind of help. Nevertheless, as time went by and her pain increased, Nessa came to the discussions less and less. By the time of the spring thaw, she had all but ceased to exist.

Cathbad ministered to her pain and soon became the only person she saw regularly. She called him her betrayer and spent her sleepless nights in bitter contemplation of other things to call him. He returned to her every morning without fail, deaf to her curses. His guilt stemmed from not having known the outcome of her plot. Not even a sign of it had been revealed in the *tarbfeis,* as if the bull's blood had masked what mattered most to him. He had not heard even an echo of Fergus's damning curse. For these reasons, Cathbad believed he had lied to Nessa all those years ago.

He became Conchovor's personal Druid, but Morann remained the chief judge in Ard Macha. The two of them seemed to get on well and quickly established their personal territories to each other's satisfaction.

The new king himself became a figure of awe to the people he governed. With the combined wisdom of Nessa and the two Druids to guide him, he ruled wisely and judged as fairly as any elder statesman. Because of the training received from Fergus, he handled weapons with the skill of any bearded warrior, winning every game, every combat. Yet, for all these overwhelming attributes, he had not an arrogant or vainglorious bone in his body. His soft-spoken modesty became the subject of a hundred tales and songs.

The first year he took true kingship, the crops produced the greatest bounty Ulster had ever seen. The Druids proclaimed that "this boy has powers over growth and fertility unmatched by any of his predecessors." In his role as leader, he presided over all marriages, but his advisors decided this was not sufficiently in keeping with his newly discovered talents. They passed a rule that hereafter Conchovor was to sleep with every bride on the night of the wedding feast, thereby assuring her fertility. "The king," they said, "should be 'first' in every family."

"And this is what drove Fergus mac Roich away to that horrible witch, Maeve?" asked Senchan.

Laeg turned from watching young Conchovor lying in his bed beside some girl twice his age, who regarded her king with great reverent cow-eyes. Darkness swelled in behind Laeg and the scene receded as though along a tunnel. Even as it winked out, the tunnel grew with smells and sounds and, finally, light of its own. Laeg stood with his back to the cooking pot at another feast.

Senchan blinked and swallowed, glancing around himself warily. Conchovor presided here, seated at the head of two rows of men who were shouting, laughing, cursing, and—it seemed to Senchan in one case—actually trying to throttle one another.

"No." Laeg's voice cut through the cacophony of the feasting. "That isn't what sent Fergus off at all. As you can see here—" He gestured to where a brooding, haggard figure sat cross-legged, away from the two rows. Fergus was pulling strings of meat from a large slice of beef in his wooden bowl. He seemed oblivious of all that was going on around him. "Fergus, or the shell of him, remained. It takes more than that to make *him* pack up and go." As Laeg said this, the Druid Cathbad got to his feet beside Conchovor. The smoky, crowded feast hall became breathlessly quiet.

"Here, now," whispered Laeg. "Watch how the clever Cathbad reroutes Fergus's path to self-destruction."

The Druid called out, "Fergus mac Roich!"

Fergus hardly glanced at him and went on eating in self-imposed insularity. "Your king, Fergus, wants you for his right-hand man. For his champion." Cathbad paused to let that sink in. "But no champion can act the way you do. No champion can be allowed to take his own life by slow degrees away from the battlefield, wedging mortar in all his mortal cracks. I'm aware of your misfortune. So is every warrior in this room. Morann and I have determined that you deserve no other fate than the one I hold for you. And it is this.

"I place upon you this night, Fergus mac Roich, my *geis!*"

The peril of his situation became clear to Fergus then. He stopped pretending not to hear. He leaped to his feet and tried to escape, but a solid wall of warriors rose up and held him back. He turned; they were behind him. On every side. He hammered them with his huge fists; a nose broke, a rib cracked, blood spouted and flowed. No one gave way and no one returned his blows. No one budged an inch to let him through.

Cathbad continued to shout at him. "You have no other *geis* upon you before this, do you?"

"No!" cried Fergus. "Let me through, you hairless chins!"

"This, then, shall be your *geis* of primacy. It takes precedence over any other put upon you ever after."

"No!" the warrior cried again. The Druid left him no choice now. He reached unwillingly for his sword. His hand closed on empty air. In his blanket of self-pity he had come to the feast unarmed.

"My *geis* on you, Fergus mac Roich, is a *glam dicin* in form, because you're as guilty of a crime as any thief, having stolen yourself from us. A satire then for him who has killed and buried his own soul." He began to turn as he spoke, directing his wand at the crowd, but deliberately starting with his back to Fergus. "What man eschews his people when they're faultless? Who fasts while others feast? And refuses the repast though he sits insubordinately amidst the sea of sustenance? The one who drowns the sound of merriment with the drone of his solipsistic musing. Let him who is such a one suffer all the cooking fires of Eriu, a sop at a time, never to turn from a proffered feast till every table sees him sated." The wand came to rest. The ring of men drew back, revealing wretched Fergus. Cathbad continued, "Whether foul pork or fair fowl, you'll not open your mouth but to fill it full from now till the night that no day follows."

He tucked the wand into his belt, drew up his cowl, and, with a bow to Conchovor, strode away. Passing near Laeg, he slowed and turned in the unseen warrior's direction; sniffed the air.

"Hello, Druid," said Laeg. "You who attempted to hold Cú Chulainn from his great battle. Your clever *geisa* couldn't save him, could they? Still, as Druids go . . . you're a matchless man."

Cathbad's high brow creased with exasperation. Was there something there, shaped by the smoke, or not? Finally, he shook his head frustratedly and continued out.

Fergus mac Roich had fallen to his knees. The blood drawn on the men surrounding him dripped now into his own hair, down his own face.

The *geis* could have gone either way for him: the Druid could as easily have constrained him from ever taking part in battle again—which is what he had feared he would hear, as punishment for killing that scurrilous advisor. This was not much better; death was what he had almost hoped for. The murder must have been admissible. That counselor must have offended someone's local god. Inadvertently, justice was served and it mattered nothing to him. To the Morrigu with justice!

A moment later the reverberating din of the feast began again. The men around him shuffled away, but he sensed someone still near. He raised his head and found that the warriors he had pummeled were lining up. As he stared up at the first in line, that man knelt down beside him and invited him to attend a feast in three weeks. Fergus closed his eyes and nodded. The warrior got up. Another took his place. Behind him, the line continued to grow.

"Before the night is through," said Laeg, "every warrior present will require Fergus's appearance at a feast. His calendar will clog up for the coming six months. A feast every single night. By the time that ordeal is over, he will have buried his bitterness and accepted, as does the rest of Ulster, that Conchovor was installed by Macha. Probably, he fancies that his dream set the whole thing in motion, so he's played a crucial role. What else should he think, after all? The gods were in on this one.

"He will come through the gauntlet of gluttony with revived joy in living. When he returns once more to Ard Macha—after that last feast—Conchovor comes out, embraces him, and the two of them go inside to where the *fidchell* board is already set up on the stump."

The images described flicked past Senchan; every time he blinked there seemed to be a new picture before him, around him.

"In winning that game, Fergus accepts the role of Conchovor's champion, for a time at least. The embodiment of the king. You see, as with that tale of Nuada, the king is no longer judged fit to rule if he is seriously wounded. The champion becomes the king so that the king will always survive intact."

Laeg took Senchan by the elbow and turned him away from the two men crouched over the silver board. *"Fidchell,* by the way, means 'wooden wisdom.'"

They walked back through the corridors of Ard Macha, past the feast hall where, seemingly a few moments ago, a crowd had been shouting. The hall was dark and silent, the fire a heap of ash.

The weapon maker was gone from the outer doorway and that exit was covered by a large fur. Laeg lifted it up and stepped out . . . into bright daylight, on the stone-ringed plateau of Muirthemne Plain.

Blinded at first, Senchan shielded his eyes and peered around. Fergus's stone had canted to one side, its base now partially visible, resting on the flat surface of a new stone, one sharp as a needle, that had erupted from the ground below and now jutted obliquely. The two stones formed a great v.

"What—?"

"Conchovor's stone," Laeg interjected. "'The Stone of Kingship.' Whereas Fergus's is 'The Stone of Honor.'"

"And Honor rests on Kingship," guessed Senchan.

"Clever boy. You're a born poet."

"But what are the others? Maeve's stone?"

"Sovereignty."

"The Pigstone?"

"Dominance. But now we've another to deal with. This one," and he pointed to the fifth in the circle. A small stone, its tip was jagged as if the top had been shattered.

"You see, Senchan, things might have gone on nicely forever in Ard Macha—except for the birth of a girl, and a curse."

IV.
THE SORROW OF DERDRIU

1. The "Troubler"

In the house of Fedlimid mac Daill the Harpist, everything was quiet. A low and unattended fire threw shadows of dancing giants up the walls, across the thatched ceiling, across the shapes of sleeping, snoring feasters.

One group of these figures slumbered in a protective circle around Conchovor. Firelight softened his round cheeks, caressed his beauty. He was ten years old this day: the feast had been a birthday party.

Behind him and all around the edges of the room stood harps of every size, some just empty frames, others polished and strung, in the light of the fire, with strands of scintillation. Deeper in the house, the fire picked up the varnished curve of a four-foot harp that stood beside Fedlimid, who lay awake, listening. Not far from him, his wife moaned softly. He could just make out the profile of her large distended belly. In the dimness of this recess, her belly looked like an overturned cauldron.

Fedlimid thought to get up and lie beside her but stopped himself and stayed where he was. If she wanted him, she would call to him. She was like that, and Fedlimid could not help fearing the one day she would die and not so much as utter a word. He sat up then and did the only thing he could to soothe her and to solace his troubled mind. He tilted back the tall harp and began to strum a soft *suantraige*, the most delicate of lullabies. His playing was like that of the Dagda, whose pure-toned harp was fashioned of gold. Listening to Fedlimid, one could hear echoes of the god gently plucking the soft notes that changed summer into fall and passed the world to sleep.

When his own eyes grew heavy, Fedlimid abruptly ended his plucking. He listened to his wife's breathing until assured that she had fallen asleep. Then he lay back and folded his arms across his chest, let out a great weary sigh and drifted off at last. Silence reigned in the house of the harpist once more. The peat burned down to glowing ash.

One hour before dawn, the silence cracked apart with a wild shriek that shook the walls. The warriors leaped up, clutching their rattling weapons, wiping hard at the sleep still upon their eyes and searching the darkness for the fiend that had howled. As they peered around them, the scream pierced the night again, high and shrill, as if a malicious sprite had tumbled into their fire. This second wail issued from the darkness where Fedlimid slept with his wife.

"It's got our harpist!" cried Menn the Spearman. He bounded forward and slammed into the shadowy warriors ahead of him, who in turn sprawled onto others—a great mass of flailing arms and legs that growled and cursed with a dozen voices. Menn jumped across them, and others pushed around them or tried to drag some of the topmost bodies to their feet.

At first Menn and the others could see nothing in the recess because their bulk blocked what little light the fire gave off. Then a torch was passed over those who still struggled to get up. It reached the front line and illuminated the recess.

Fedlimid knelt beside his wife. She lay unconscious in his arms. Even as they took in this scene, the scream came once more and those nearest the front realized it had issued from the woman's belly, which had seemed to flex.

Conchovor climbed through and went up beside his harpist. "Go and fetch me a Druid," he yelled at his warriors over the din they were making. He should have selected one of them but could not turn around, could not look away from the wife of Fedlimid. She had dark circles under her eyes and sweat-stuck hair on her brow and cheeks, but Conchovor felt as if he were looking through her. His eyes would not focus properly. For a moment he thought he smelled the sea. Behind him, the bickering died suddenly. From the rear forward, the warriors began to move apart, opening a corridor through to him. A white specter drifted down the channel and drew up at his back.

A scarred hand came to rest upon his shoulder. "There's death in that wail," the whisper of the Druid warned. "Get away from here before it hooks into you like a tapeworm." Conchovor glanced back, saw Cathbad's eyes so wide that the whites showed all around. But Conchovor could not leave.

Cathbad came past the king. He pressed one splayed hand over the face of Fedlimid's unconscious wife, then chanted, "Woman, what terror erupts from your womb that awoke these warriors as if the Nemain herself had settled upon their backs?" He felt movement—a twitch of her lips—and released her.

The woman sat straight up out of Fedlimid's embrace. Her eyes opened but saw nothing. She spoke in a monotone, the voice of a corpse reanimated. "Cathbad, conjurer, take these words from me. My man's gentle and pure, no mere 'fly' whose music buzzes. Ours should be a child of soft passions, so what, then, howls in here? No living woman knows what form life takes in the hollow of her womb. You must tell *me*." Her glassy eyes closed. She slumped back in her husband's arms.

Frustrated, the Druid drew his hazel wand and touched it to the woman's belly. The warriors could see his mouth moving but could not hear the words. They crowded forward, straining to burst upon him. From the belly of Fedlimid's wife the scream cracked again, and the warriors jumped back. Those at the rear, who had finally climbed from the tangle, were sent sprawling once more. The air filled with dust from their angry scrabbling. Cathbad turned and glared back at them. As if his stare were a mallet, the warriors reacted as if struck and unknotted carefully, quietly, like civilized men.

"Hear me, you lumbering protectors of peace," he ordered. His wand swung back and forth across their path, driving them back another step. "A woman lies within this womb, a woman such as you've never seen. Her hair a mist of gold and her eyes so green that grass is envious. No cloth woven matches the softness of her cheek, and her lips never need paint they're so very red and full. Red also will be the color of Ulster should she see the day her childhood's torn away. It's death her beauty offers. She knows your nearness, your fierceness. If she ever lays eyes on one warrior among you, all of you will be lost. The face of Ard Macha will shrivel like a hag's. Her name is Derdriu, and trouble is all she brings with her into this world."

"Kill the child!" the warrior Furbaide shouted. "To save us, we have to," argued someone in the back. The room churned again, this time with a call for death to the unborn child.

Weapons clattered impatiently.

In a daze, Fedlimid clutched his wife to him. Although he could not accept the Druid's forecast, he had heard his own wife speak: Who knew what demon she would bear?

"Silence! You'll do nothing of the sort!" cried Conchovor.

The warriors stopped their clamoring. Their faces turned hot with embarrassment and confusion.

"Conchovor, child—"

"No, Father Druid, don't interrupt me." The boy fixed a hard stare on him. "Your right is to speak *before* the king, that's the law. But the law says nothing about interruption." He turned away. "He calls *me* child, but I feel older and wiser than the whole lot of you here who quake fearfully at a baby not even born. Well, so long as *this* child stands between you and her, you won't kill that baby—not any of you. As I'm first in every family, this Derdriu is *my* daughter as much as Fedlimid's. Harm her and you attack me."

Cathbad peered at Conchovor's face, at the hard, obsessed look of the eyes. When had he seen that look before? The boy said to Fedlimid, "You'll foster your daughter to me, to protect her." The harpist agreed with reluctance but also with gratitude.

"I'll have her raised away from Ard Macha," Conchovor said, "to protect us from the cruel fate my Druid foretells. Then she'll meet no warriors. None of them will look upon her beauty. From the moment she's born, she is mine." His warriors fidgeted and lowered their heads as he swung around and took them all in, slowly. No one could find words to speak against Conchovor, not even Fergus mac Roich, who knew him better than any there. This person, though, was a stranger to Fergus, and the warrior sheathed Leochain and backed silently out of the house, retreating into shadows, full of foreboding.

"Good," said the young king when no one objected. "Then in Othar's name, let's leave this woman in peace so she can produce my Derdriu."

Othar! Cathbad stumbled back and banged up against Fedlimid's large harp. It sounded a loud discord at him. "Salt and stone," he mumbled at the bewildered harpist. "That's what he is, what he's become."

Now the wife of Fedlimid began to moan anew.

2. The Satirist's Pleasure

Derdriu was fostered on a secluded farm away from Ard Macha. She grew up seeing no one except her new parents, hearing no other voices than theirs. However, Conchovor did arrange to see her. The need to do so came in urgent fits, allied with phases of the moon, the pull of the tides. He would come there at night and peer in through a space between stones in the wall of the house. "Just to look at my prize," was what he told everyone, and they could see the obsession in his eyes. Cathbad charted the sequence of his fits, which helped in arranging events so as not to coincide with the king's evenings spent peeping in at Derdriu.

His warriors reconciled themselves to his behavior with the argument that when the girl reached her fourteenth year she would be eligible for marriage and the king would have her. Once Derdriu became his wife, the warriors assured one another, then his fits of madness would taper off. Meanwhile they arranged year-contract marriages for him, but none of these produced an heir.

Nessa and the *brithem* Druids saw to it that Ulster did not suffer for the king's inattention, although Nessa, too, fell into periods of madness. On one such occasion, as she drifted through the corridors of the fortress, she came upon her son. Sweat covered his face and his whole body shook. It was a full moon and the ocean waves tore at him. In their frenzy, they returned to his room and made love. This mad mutual seduction would have gone unheard of had Conchovor's seed not ripened in her. When Nessa discovered this, she went to Cathbad and babbled a confession, blaming herself. Cathbad calmed her and, once she had fallen asleep, went to Morann and the other *brithemain* and told them that they could no longer depend on Nessa's help in guiding the province. The efficient Druids carried on without her then during Conchovor's periodic withdrawals; Nessa gave birth to a male child she named Cormac, and Cathbad looked after him, fostering him to a family within Ard Macha.

More years passed. Nessa withdrew further into herself, but Ulster remained strong and fertile. The hopes of everyone involved might yet have been fulfilled had it not been for the arrival of the satirist, Levarcham.

She was a spindly and bent-backed creature, and she came to Ulster out of boredom with the southern lands. Her reputation preceded her, and the less distinguished people stayed out of her way for fear of becoming the object of her wicked lampoons. It was claimed that she could cause blindness or palsy, or even make one's hair fall out.

A sane, calm Conchovor gave her a good feast upon arrival, which Levarcham repaid with verses that extolled him and his warriors while making fools of every other province, especially neighboring Connacht: "A Connacht champion can be easily spotted, which is not to suggest he isn't spotted already; you can recognize him by this everyman's trait—the bush on his lip is so meager that he wears pebbles tied to his nose hairs to entice them, you see, over his mouth."

Eventually, it had to happen that Levarcham got wind of Conchovor's secret preoccupation; if satirists were good at anything it was ferreting out embarrassing secrets. She could easily have devised a vicious account of the young king's nocturnal forays, but she wanted to know the cause.

One night she followed Conchovor to the house where Derdriu was kept. She hid in a clump of high grass, watching the king watching the house. The air became colder as the night wore on. Owls called to one another and bats flitted on the air. The king huddled against the house as if frozen there in place. More like a dolmen than a man, thought Levarcham as she exhaled silent curses at the standing-stone king for keeping her here.

Hours passed before he finally left. Levarcham sat with her face pressed to her knees, using the trapped warmth of her breath to keep her warm. She did not see him go, but looked up, sniffling, and found his place vacant and no sign of him anywhere. She flexed her stiff fingers and rubbed her cheeks. Her mouth had petrified into a hard scowl. Rising, she slunk past the high wall that isolated the front of the house from view, creeping on creaky legs to the place where Conchovor had been. Light from within revealed a hole in the wall there. The hole fit around her eye like an extension of the orbit.

Through the smoke from the fire, sleeping Derdriu's beauty blazed forth like moonlight. The sight of her banished all thoughts of the cold night from Levarcham. Seeing Derdriu the satirist

became aware of her own shortcomings: of her crooked back
and skeletal body; of her acerbic temperament, which had arisen
out of her deformities as a weapon against their exhibition by
others; and of the gulf separating her from Derdriu more in-
flexibly than the stone wall at her cheek. She reeled back from
the vision and fled into the night.

Upon reaching Ard Macha, Levarcham hid in her rooms,
trembling, lost. She had seen herself revealed as if Derdriu
were a tall and perfect mirror reflecting her abominable soul.
But the mirror was of such overpowering beauty that the most
hideous creature would have endured its own naked wretched-
ness to look into the glass. Tomorrow she must return to Derdriu.
And, as she was Levarcham the Satirist and a woman, no one
could stop her.

She was waiting in the yard outside the stone house when
Derdriu's foster parents came out the next morning. Recognizing her, they tried to drive her away until she began: "I
know two farmers who till no soil, hidden by high walls, eating
fat and lean alike without one 'Welcome' in their soup . . ."
They left off assaulting her then. The mother fled back inside
to keep Derdriu in; the father rode off in a panic to Ard Macha.

No one knew just how Levarcham had learned of Derdriu;
likewise, no one knew how to make her leave now that she
was there. Conchovor assumed, as did all his advisors, that if
the satirist knew where Derdriu was kept, she must know the
whole tale. They decided that leaving her alone might be the
safest course, and such was their final ruling to Derdriu's father.

The reluctant parents made a place for their uninvited guest
to stay, as was proper hospitality to anyone. Once inside, she
could not be kept from meeting their daughter.

When Derdriu entered the room, Levarcham saw the dark,
cramped house swell with light, the walls stretch back to contain
all the beauty. *This girl is soon to be Conchovor's.* Levarcham
could not tolerate the thought of such innocent bloom being
locked away from the world. She knew of the rumored curse
but rejected it. Such loveliness—to be imprisoned, *that* was
the curse upon Derdriu. Levarcham decided then and there to
meddle in the king's affair.

Through the fall she remained at the farm. Conchovor took
to meeting her in a field of cornstalks nearby. His questions
were all about Derdriu: about her voice, her desires, every

aspect of her body from the arch of her eyebrow to the lacquer on the nails of her toes. Levarcham derived cruel pleasure from answering accurately in every detail. Through the satirist, the king sent gifts to Derdriu but forbade Levarcham to tell her where they originated. That was to be his surprise when at last they met, and he wanted his prize bursting with curiosity about him. One of his gifts—a hammered gold lunula—Derdriu liked so much, she wore it at her throat every waking moment. As to her interest in her secret admirer, she had practically none. Having seen no admirers, she could not conceive of any. The gifts, to Derdriu's mind, came from the world in general, and that separate world became her obsession as she was the king's.

She spent hours with Levarcham every day. She wanted to know how other girls dressed, what forts looked like and how the people in them lived. Were they all like Levarcham, thin and crooked? And did they grow up alone as she had?

Sometimes Levarcham was unable to answer and had to go off for a while before she could speak again.

One winter morning after a heavy snow, she sat beside Derdriu, watching the girl's father methodically skinning a calf. A flock of ravens was skimming the sky over the nearby woods, and one particularly venturesome bird, drawn by the smell, settled in the yard and began drinking from the pool of blood that lay beneath the hanging carcass.

Deirdru said dreamily, "If I could choose my man, I'd choose him from that scene." Levarcham followed her gaze but saw only a man at work. Derdriu explained, "I'd mold him from the things there: white snow for his skin, dark blood for his cheeks and lips, and the blackness of the raven for his hair. I'd be forever content with *him*." She laid her hand on Levarcham's wrist. "Tell me, is your king such a one as that?"

Levarcham trembled at her touch and with the excitement of knowing this to be the opportunity she had waited for. "The king . . . well, no—but I know one who fits your desires so well you might have shaped him just now. He is called Naise mac Uislenn. He's not too much older than you, but older enough to wed you, and bed you properly." She gnawed nervously at one knuckle.

Derdriu put her head down on her folded arms. "I'll be sick till I see him. Naise." Then, drawing the fur tightly around her shoulders, she stood up and walked away. Levarcham, after a quick glance at Derdriu's foster father, followed after her. The guts of the opened calf spilled steaming into the snow, spattering the raven, which screeched and flew off.

When Levarcham caught up with Derdriu, she said, "This fellow Naise is quite a renowned individual, dear. He is one of three brave brothers. In battle, they fight back to back like the hub of a wheel spoked with scythes. He chants and sings, too—having learned the art from the great Fedlimid, the king's own harpist."

"Fedlimid is my true father," Derdriu informed her.

"Well, then. They claim at Ard Macha that this Naise sits alone every night on the walls of earth around the hill and sings to the cattle grazing on the plain. His song floats out like a flock of doves, and each cow that hears him gives more milk than any two that don't."

"Alone," said Derdriu to herself, "on the earthen wall."

"Every night," Levarcham added. "At dusk. So they say."

Derdriu looked at her uncertainly. "And if he hates the sight of me?"

Levarcham replied, "That is exceedingly unlikely, child. But there's always the act of *flaying*, if you have doubts. You know of it?"

"My mother's spoken . . ." Her eyes had gone wide as if the idea were too huge to envision. A blush flooded her cheeks.

"I happen to know that the road west between here and Ard Macha passes many stones appropriate to that act."

Derdriu nodded. "I'll spit in his mouth to capture him," she said bravely.

Levarcham saw then how futile her attempt at liberation was. Where could a Derdriu hide from the world? Where was the place that contained no men who would be shaken, no women who would envy her? She would have to live among the dead in a burial chamber, and Levarcham was not certain *that* was safe. The satirist's plan could not succeed. Nevertheless, the girl now knew who she wanted and no one could stop her from seeking him out. Levarcham glanced back at the father roping the raw calf's carcass to a long spit. How had he endured his foster daughter's presence all these years? Was he perhaps castrated, wounded in battle so as to have no lust to fire? Or had he gone mad years ago without anyone having noticed?

Turning back, she found that Derdriu had gone. A line of footsteps in the snow led to where the high wall met the house. Levarcham dragged herself up there in time to catch a fleeting glimpse of the girl scurrying into the woods. How long would Derdriu's parents wait before reporting her disappearance to

Conchovor? Levarcham suspected it would be some time, while they first sought her in every direction on their own. To admit they had lost Derdriu might well prove fatal. Perhaps there was a chance for the girl after all. If the flaying magic took. If the tales of Naise's evening ritual proved true. Levarcham decided it was time to leave, before Derdriu's absence became obvious. Besides which, Levarcham wished to be on hand at Ard Macha when news of the girl's disappearance finally arrived.

She returned to the small house to fetch her belongings. Her hosts would not be sorry to see her go. No one ever missed a satirist.

3. Derdriu Flaying

"Flaying," explained Laeg, "involved stones like this one." He leaned back against a tall gray obelisk, triple his height and about the width of his shoulders. "You see the rounded cap at the top? You know what it represents, don't you? One needn't be obsessed with sex to recognize it. The world is absolutely chock-a-block with them, too—they stick up all over like the hairs of a two-day growth of beard. Of course, they serve purposes other than Derdriu's. As a matter of fact I'm not certain how the extraordinary notion of flaying did start—but never mind, Senchan, here she comes over that rise." He indicated direction with a shift of his cerulean eyes. Senchan got up from where he had been sitting in the snow at Laeg's feet.

Derdriu was a tiny black figure against the brightness of the snow. She walked down the gentle slope toward them with some difficulty, picking her way around all the rocks the snow had buried.

Senchan's throat constricted and his face tightened; though he was a mere observer, he was as smitten with Derdriu as was Levarcham or even Conchovor. Beside her pure beauty, Selden's dirty daughters really *were* bristled pigs. Laeg seemed totally immune to her charms and Senchan, with a young man's capacity for jealousy, was frankly glad of that. Besides which, he couldn't imagine devilish Laeg mooning for her attention anyway. He backed away from the immense stone phallus as she drew closer, forgetting in his awe that she could not detect him. Laeg almost moved off from the stone, perhaps out of reverence for the performance to come.

Derdriu approached the obelisk side-on, like a cat warily stalking a snake. It intimidated her, that much was obvious to both observers. Then determination set her features as rigid as the object of her intentions. The fur slipped from her shoulders. She withdrew from her tunic a gold fastener: a device like two small clam shells welded onto a curved gold stem, each "shell" fit through slits in the woven wool. She wrapped the bright tunic into a ball with the fastener safe in the center, laid the ball atop her fur to keep it dry. From the waist up now she was naked. The large nipples of her slight breasts were two ruby pegs supporting the shining lunula around her neck; rubies chiseled by the cold. Her tartan trousers, tucked into her fur boots, must be pulled out before she could stumble free of them. The boots she left on because, rite or not, that snow was freezing. She knelt, folded the last of the clothing, then spiraled as she rose to face the stone. And Senchan. This time she approached defiantly, untamed nymphet making a maiden stab at seductress. Her cold red fingertips caressed the pillar and she craned her head to see the tip with vague white clouds drifting by. Still watching the sky, she pressed her whole body against the stone. A shiver rippled up her back to be tossed from her shoulders, but she held her ground. She shifted to a splayed stance and began, awkwardly at first, to rub against the stone, rising up and down on the balls of her feet.

Senchan began to whine without knowing it.

Derdriu chanted: "Naise you must give me. Red, black, and white all over. Hard as stone, soft as snow. Naise in my ears, in my eyes and mouth. Poured in my breath, in the pores of my skin. You wet stone, whetstone, hone me till my sharp edge pierces him." She was breathing rapidly now; as rapidly as Senchan. "Naise," she said and repeated. Even after she had lost the ability to speak, her mouth formed and held his name.

Finally, spent, she lay against the stone on quivering legs. Senchan had sunk down upon his knees. Laeg drew him gently to his feet.

"And that is flaying. Not exactly in the same class of magic as setting fire to wicker baskets full of goats."

Unable to speak, Senchan shook his head. He finally got up the nerve to look Laeg in the face, to discover that no one was immune to the spell Derdriu cast. This failed to stir him; he no longer had the energy to be jealous. "It—it was barbaric," he said.

"Barbaric? To want her freedom? To select her lover by whatever means? What is so barbaric about freedom of choice?" Laeg looked him over as if reconsidering the wisdom of bringing him along. "I suppose that's the sort of attitude your new order has taught you: 'If we do it, it's fine and good; if someone else does it, it's barbaric.' Hmm?"

Senchan had no ready answer for that. He hadn't meant to criticize. He turned away to watch an enervated Derdriu rewrap and pin her tunic. "And she'll repeat that on every one of those stones?" he asked.

"From here to Ard Macha."

"I . . . don't think I can watch it again."

Derdriu shook the snow from her fur, then headed off purposefully toward the north.

"We won't follow her, then," Laeg said and shoved Senchan at the obelisk. The boy merged into it. Laeg took one step but stopped to give Derdriu a last forlorn glance before he passed through the stone, too.

4. The Brothers Uisliu

The strumming of a harp showed Derdriu the way on the final stretch of her journey to Ard Macha. She had walked for two days to get there. The front of her body from knees to breastbone were chafed and raw from all the erect stones she had flayed. And now at least she heard the sweet music Levarcham had promised and knew she was very near the one whose name had dominated her ordeal.

On the dark wall somewhere ahead, Naise unwittingly lured her in. She walked like a spirit on its journey to Tir na nOg, passing briefly through this nocturnal landscape, practically oblivious to the clusters of warm, round houses scattered on the plain around her, fires glittering through the doorways, catching her in their light and causing those people out in the cold to pause in their work and look up briefly. She did not see them. The only thing that held her attention was the huge bonfire on the top of Ard Macha and the music that seemed to issue from it.

Soon she could see figures reflected in the fire's light, and below them the dark lines that were the tops of the three ramparts protecting the hill. Distant voices sounded crisply on the air. Weaving through them, the harp continued its siren song. A huge boulder scuttled off to her left, drawing her attention for a moment, becoming a cow. She recalled what Levarcham had said about the milk cattle on the plain. Now she became aware of the populace around her—the many houses and fires, the low stone walls running in every direction to enclose countless herds of cattle and sheep. And in the huts, so many people, so close. The darkness hid their identities as it hid the shapes of the severed heads that hung as trophies beneath the thatched rooves. Then the music filled her mind again and all the people faded into the night.

Before long the fire atop Ard Macha passed from her view, became a smoky glow against the dark sky. The shape of the harpist became visible: a figure like a bear, he sat on the first snowy rampart. Nearer, she could see that he wore a thick fur with a hood. The harp he strummed hid in the shadow of him. How was she going to scale that wall?

He must have seen her approach but said nothing while he played. She stood directly beneath him, looking at his feet dangling overhead. When at last the sweet song ended, he leaned over and stared down at her, his face a cave circled in fur. For a second Derdriu feared that Levarcham had lied and that the harpist looked nothing like she imagined. But the voice that issued from the cave proved to be as pleasant as the music of his harp, if tinged with mockery. "You're the finest heifer of all the cows that have ever drifted here to listen," he told her. "And how uniquely high your shoulders sit for a heifer."

Her fear forgotten, Derdriu accepted the challenge in his words and replied, "The cows are always bigger where there's no bull in the yard."

The harpist wasted no time in setting aside his instrument and leaping from the wall. Dropping beside her, he somersaulted and came up on his feet. The hood had fallen back from his face and at last Derdriu saw him. Levarcham had not lied—Naise was the embodiment of the elements she had wished upon.

"I've never seen the like of you," he said as if picking up her thoughts. "Where have you come from that I've never seen you?"

"I've walked a million miles for you, my Naise. I want you. Now. Right here." She took off her fur and laid it over the snow. She settled herself down on it and removed the overused fastener from her tunic.

Naise had never seen anyone more beautiful. What or who she was did not matter to him. No one had ever offered herself to him like this; he could not even contemplate refusal. He got down beside her and spread open his fur above them to enfold their warmth.

They made love in the dark, on the ground beneath the wall, and it was not until they were lying united that Naise cared to know her name. When he heard it, he lurched up and stared at her with horror. "Derdriu! What have you done to me? You belong to the king!"

"So says he," she answered coolly. "I have chosen otherwise. I've chosen you."

More than that, she had found a path to his heart. Just being beside her made him burn with love. For himself, he saw that it was too late. But what of his family? Of Cathbad's prophecy? His desires could not be weighed against such things. He got up and started to put on his woolen trousers.

"Are you rejecting me?"

"I am. I—I *must.*"

She could not comprehend how the flaying magic might have failed her. And she had lain with him, crouched over him and spit into his mouth to bind him. How could he refuse her? She would not let anything force them apart now. She reached up and grabbed hold of his testicles and pulled him sharply down beside her. His scream split the night. The cold air carried it far.

In a hut on the plain two young men suddenly stopped in the midst of their supper. The older of the two, whose name was Ardan, looked at his younger brother, Ainle, and said, "Didn't that sound like Naise?"

Ainle nodded. "And I don't hear his harp."

Ardan set his bowl on the straw matting of the floor and reached for his fur cloak and spear. Seeing his intent, Ainle scurried up after him.

Naise tried to wrestle free of Derdriu's excruciating grip. He thought he was going to be sick. Her hand was like stone.

Derdriu was barely conscious of what she was doing. She began to chant to him, "Shame upon your manly parts like a withering fungus if you let anyone come between the woman who loves you and you if you love her, too."

Too late, Naise pressed his hands over his ears. He had heard it all, and he screamed out in worse agony than before. Derdriu had been cursed by a Druid and a *geis* of such consequences delivered by her had the power of a Druid's proclamation behind it. His second cry pierced the hearts of warriors in a hundred nearby houses. Derdriu released him in terror.

Doors were thrown back. Light spilled out in zig-zag patterns, and a horde of fur-covered figures charged into the night. Naise's brothers reached him first.

Ardan arrived beneath the wall and drew up short at what he found. Who was this half-naked girl crouched tenderly beside his half-naked younger brother? Had someone wounded him, knocked him from the wall? The girl looked up at Ardan with eyes that at first were distant but that quickly focused on him with fear.

"Naise," Ardan said. He knelt beside his brother. "Naise, what's happened to you?" Naise said nothing, but shook his head violently, refusing to look up from the snow. Ardan heard the thunder of many feet running toward them. He looked up to see Ainle and, behind him, warriors from many nearby houses.

Derdriu gathered her tunic around her and hid inside her fur.

Soon a ring of concerned faces surrounded the group of four. Ardan helped Naise to his feet. Naise seemed oblivious to his nakedness or the cold. He looked out over the crowd and hung his head, saying, "I love her, forgive me all but I do."

No one understood what he meant. Ardan grabbed his brother by the shoulders and shook him angrily, demanding to know what had happened. Obviously, he hadn't been wounded. If he had brought all these warriors from the warmth of their fires to learn that he was lovesick. . . .

Naise shouted, "No, you don't see!" then grabbed the fur hood around her head and pulled it back for all to see her face. "She's *Derdriu!*" he cried.

An urgent silence, like that before an eruption, followed. Each person there experienced his own admixture of reverence and revulsion.

Derdriu shrank from them, the press of eyes so charged with emotions, tongues licking lips or teeth bared in vulpine snarls, flared nostrils jetting steam like the snouts of a hundred horses. The rush of claustrophobia drove her back against the snow-covered wall. She read her doom in their final expressions.

Naise made an attempt to explain what had happened: She had come seeking him, by what mystical method he could not guess. Finding out who she was, he had tried to deny any ardor for her, and she had gone into a trance, putting upon him an incantation that required him to keep her with him and defend her, and there was just one way to do that. He had to leave Ard Macha.

"We're honor-bound to turn you in," said Fiachu mac Firaba, one of the warriors in the group, "if Conchovor comes to any among us. This is Cathbad's curse—it's begun. Still, it hardly seems just that you're trapped in it when you weren't even there to hear the curse laid out. That's not right."

"Naise is a good warrior," added someone further back. "How can we sentence him to death? Conchovor's lost his wits over this girl . . . not that I can't see why, but still . . ." There were murmurs of agreement with the implied injustice.

"I can't let my brother go on alone," Ardan said, "or be a part of his undoing. If he's to be cast out, then so must I be." He turned to Naise. "We'll go together, little brother. You and Ainle and I. We'll all protect Derdriu and your honor. There'll be no shame upon you while I live."

"And me," Ainle said with a child's determination.

To the crowd Ardan said, "Do what you must. Tell the king. We'll understand and forgive you."

"No," said a woman warrior named Errge. "The sons of Uisliu are friends to everyone here. If it's not on their heads punishment falls—and we seem to be in agreement this is so—then no one here can put it there. The only way to save honor all around is to go with them. There's no province in all Eriu would deny us a place in their hall. If you agree, then make haste so we can leave tonight, before the king gets word."

All attention fell again upon Derdriu. She still hung back from them, looking up with her chin pressed against the edge of the lunula. Naise went to her, touched her bare shoulder softly. "Come. We'll all of us go to protect you and save Ulster from the curse on you. Maybe if we go far enough, all our people will be spared. No one here thinks you're evil, you know." She searched his face for the love he had for her and, finding it, she hugged herself to him and burst into tears. She had never known of the curse upon her, had never thought herself different from anyone else. She was only a twelve-year-old girl who could not fathom how her love for one boy had snowballed into a monstrosity of one hundred and fifty warriors, their husbands, wives, children, and concubines—which was the size of the caravan that departed from Ulster that night.

Only one person saw them go. He stood on the earthen wall beneath Ard Macha in his white robe and watched them pass by with their hope, though he knew their flight would be in vain. He had warned them once and, had they listened to him then, there would have been far less trouble than what was to follow now. He looked up into the night sky and counted a star for every campfire those warriors would circle before they returned to Ulster.

5. Years of Exile

"They traveled all across Eriu that winter," said Laeg, "warriors without a province, *fiana*. Kings could always use skilled fighters and the *fiana* from Ulster always found a home. However, Senchan, most kings also owed debts or favors to someone— if not to Conchovor, then to someone who in turn owed him. Others could simply be bought outright. Soon enough, the exiles found their hosts plotting against them.

"In desperation, they left the isle and sailed to the land of Alba, where Conchovor's machinations could not touch them. What they forgot in this instance, though, was the affect that Derdriu's beauty could have: they were all honorable people, so their love for her, as it grew, was the love of foster parents for the child under their aegis. The king of Alba had a petty, greedy soul. When he saw Derdriu, he grew envious and tried to take her from them—first with offers of gold and cattle, and then with a promise of slaughter. The sullen, luckless exiles had no choice but to lade their *crannogs* and set sail again, back to Eriu.

"They landed on a bleak southern isle inhabited by a few goats, some rabbits, and hundreds of gulls. Dung spattered everything. Salt spray coated them with its grimy oil. They longed for nothing more than to go home, to find some means of reconciliation with Conchovor. They could think of none. Homeless, lost, barred it seemed even from the honor of death in battle, they lived that month in the deepest melancholy there is. For all they knew, they would live out their days on that chunk of rock until the ocean wore them away."

"But they were rescued," said Senchan hopefully.

"In one sense, yes," Laeg replied cryptically. "However, nothing, Senchan, is ever half so simple as it seems."

6. The Advent of the Curse

Tales of the tribulations of the fugitives in Alba had reached Ulster, exciting the populace and keeping the subject of amnesty alive. Groups of Conchovor's advisors took it upon themselves to approach him regarding the exiles' safe return. "Think how terrible it would be," they suggested, "if our friends should die in some foreign land, defending what isn't even theirs. They're not *fiana*. And it's all on account of that girl."

That girl, thought Conchovor, only the most beautiful woman in all the world. She belongs to me but Naise mac Uislenn has her. None of you has ever seen her—how could you idiots hope to understand? I've waited thirteen years!

The advisors disregarded the dark look recasting his face and put forth the rest of their argument. "Isn't it better to be magnanimous? Bring them home. Forgive—"

"Get out of my sight!"

The daunted advisors filed out. King Conchovor pulled at his short beard. His eyes were darkly ringed from sleepless nights, his temper grown short. Cathbad had ordered the Druids to avoid him, too; he could not even acquire a potion to help. Why had the Druid done this? Why? He realized he was drifting, his thoughts tumbling in all directions—another unfortunate result of poor sleeping habits. All because of *that girl*.

The solution, her return, ought to have been a simple matter. It *was* simple: either she and Naise would agree to Conchovor's wishes or she would become a widow. Forgive them?

Outside Ard Macha, a small crowd waited to hear the outcome of the advisors' adjuration. The men filed out shaking their heads. No, they had not found a way to move his petrified heart. He would do nothing. . . . At least, so everyone believed until two nights later when the king announced that he had sent off Fergus the Messenger to invite the fugitives home. Great rejoicing followed.

Cathbad did not celebrate, however. He continued to note every person who was called before Conchovor and, with other information gathered or inferred, to create a complete, interlocking framework around Conchovor's designs. Cathbad alone saw Levarcham the Satirist slip out of Ard Macha one night and set off to the south. He alone knew that one Eogan mac Durthact had been ordered to the fortress. Something evil was brewing. Cathbad smelled it.

Fergus the Messenger returned with the happy news that the fugitives wanted nothing in the world more than to come home. Their single stipulation was that they would return *only* if accompanied by Fergus mac Roich, as proof of Conchovor's good intentions. Fergus accepted readily to put an end to the strife.

The following day he set out for the shores of Leinster. He took with him his son, Fiacha, who had returned to him after graduating out of fosterage; two foster sons of his own whose names were Iollan and Buinne; the warrior Duffach the Dark, known widely as "the Beetle of Ulster," supposedly in reference to his thick, jutting eyebrows that shaded his glowering blue eyes with menace; and Cormac Connlongas, who was the yield of Nessa's incest with Conchovor, and who was only too glad to escape from the antinomy of those two authorities for any amount of time. It was felt that this larger band—especially with the king's son in their midst—would reassure the exiles all the more. Fergus also brought with him Conchovor's personal *geis* in the matter: that the Sons of Uisliu eat no food on their journey till they sat in Ard Macha with their king. This was not an unusual prohibition and added an extra note of honor to the proceedings.

That same evening, Cathbad watched from the shadows as the king ushered a secret visitor out of the hillfort. Cathbad could not see the face of the extremely tall visitor and caught only the king's final words to the man: "Remember, ask it of all. If you don't, everything will be lost—including you."

The following night, Levarcham the Satirist returned to Ard Macha. Cathbad intercepted her before she reached the center of the fortress. He dragged her back out into the night where no one could listen. "And where have *you* been, old acid-mouth?"

"Has ever a satire been written about a Druid?"

Cathbad replied drily, "What good would a satirist be with a *glam dicin* upon her never to speak except to . . . goats?"

"I've never met a Druid with a sense of humor yet. All right, I'll tell you what you want, cruel Cathbad. I've been to the Siuir's mouth, and I've spied there the face of Derdriu amongst the hundred and fifty, who, I might add, have grown somewhat from births and fosterage."

"But why did you go? Conchovor required it of you?"

"Oh, indeed. He pines for word of her—is she lovely? Has her beauty sloughed away through the rough two years with those 'conniving brothers'?"

"And?"

"She's as beautiful as always. You've seen her, too?"

"Not in the way you mean, no. In visions, in chants and dreams linked to carnage and destruction. Now the dream blood is murky, the answers hidden from me; yet in the center of the swirl I can see her face like a moon in a bloody sky."

Levarcham glanced away. "Well," she said, "it's time I went before the king." Cathbad moved to stop her but she silenced him with a crooked finger to his lips. "I won't be telling him what I've told you. She's grown bony and dry like a starved plowhorse. Eyes that once dominated the stars have turned to charred wicks in guttered lamps. I shall count the times he flinches. And I'll be gone from this place before she returns. Too many traps here for a satirist. Not enough good material."

Cathbad brought his hand out of his robe and suddenly flung something across Levarcham's shoulder—crystals of salt. "You'll need the luck against him," the Druid explained. "He's become more than Conchovor."

Levarcham went warily to see the king. She told him how pitiable Derdriu had become. Conchovor did not call her a liar. He listened attentively while she spoke, then dismissed her curtly and sent for another messenger. That night a second observer left for Leinster.

* * *

Eogan mac Durthact arrived the next morning, accompanied by his retinue of *fiana*. He had the face of a weasel and the habit of wringing his hands together as if in a constant state of agitation. His power extended over a region due south of Ard Macha called Fernmag. Experienced travelers were known to go far out of their way to avoid crossing through that region: Fernmag had a reputation for swallowing people.

Mac Durthact and Conchovor had been adversaries for years on various matters of policy—most notably those concerning demarcation. From the Fernmag lord's arrival, it seemed that their disputes were about to be parleyed.

Cathbad doubted this. The timing was too critical. He distrusted Eogan mac Durthact even more than the monster lurking in Conchovor, and he considered the man capable of any atrocity. In a state of confusion and helplessness, he turned at last for advice to Nessa.

She never left her chambers now. Cast off, she sang or hummed alone, sometimes erupting into fits of laughter or tears without apparent cause. She could no longer walk: after Cormac had arrived, the boils of Fergus's curse had erupted with renewed vigor. The skin of her excoriated thighs had grown leathery with scars.

Cathbad hoped she might climb out of her melancholia one more time. He sat beside her bed, where she lay awake, silent, staring into shadows. Quietly, he explained that the curse upon Derdriu might be coming true, but that all attempts at foretelling had proved fruitless. "What should I do?" he asked her. "How should I block him from destroying the province?" When she did not so much as acknowledge him, he added, "That harsh god of your isle is in this, too." Nessa suddenly grinned at him. He saw to his grief that she would never again conquer her miserable madness. He patted her shoulder, then got up to leave.

Nessa sang out suddenly, "It's a Druid's curse to know too much."

He stared back into her wild eyes and noticed for the first time a grayness about her, in her skin and hair. Had he grown old as well? He did not feel as if time had passed for him— but time was a jumble to Cathbad. Again he turned away.

Again she cried out. "History can be changed in a night!"

"Yes," he agreed, sick at heart, "yes, it can."

She tittered at him, or at some secret thought. He went out

and wandered alone through a seemingly deserted fortress. Fergus mac Roich remained his sole hope of fending off disaster. In a dark corridor the priest paused, closed his eyes and sought with his mind for the thread of Fergus's future among all the others. He heard a noise like a blade whipping past his head. He dropped into a crouch, his arm raised to fend off a blow. Out of his trance, he stared into the darkness, ready to face his foe.

The hallway was empty.

Fergus mac Roich led the fugitive army up into the heart of Leinster. He peered at the rolling landscape ahead, anticipating an ambush over every hillock, glanced back at the wide stretches of gentle valleys, expecting a force of warriors in pursuit.

At first he had trusted Conchovor, but things had happened to make him suspect the king's good intentions. First, as he and his group had crossed near the place called Dind Rig, he had seen a figure he believed to be Levarcham the Satirist hurrying away up a high, rock-strewn hill ahead. If it had been the crooked satirist, she could only be spying on them at Conchovor's command. Then, last night, as they rested from their day's journey in a hut near Rathangan, Derdriu had suddenly grabbed Naise's sleeve and whispered urgently to him. Surreptitiously, Naise had fit a stone to his sling, then had flung it at the window of the hut. Outside, someone had screamed. The members of the feast, in rushing out, had found no one there. Moonless, the black night shielded the spy, and the people had returned to their meals in tense silence. Naise, not allowed to eat, had tried to cheer them. "Whoever it was," he said, "they now share a common trait with Leinster's Eochaid Goll, the one-eyed sun god." Slight laughter answered the remark, and that died quickly. A heavy question hung over the matter: why should anyone be spying on them?

At midday Fergus and the forefront of the exiles climbed a high hill and were greeted with a beautiful view of the River Dub. More than that, between them and the river a huge house stood. Around the house a dozen spitted boars were roasting, servants worked, and a pot of wheaten beer stood steaming. The commingled odors of meat and beer reached the top of the hill, and a hundred stomachs growled as if in a paean.

Fergus led the way down toward the house, all the while considering how he would explain to their expectant host that they could not tarry with him.

The owner of the house appeared—a long, lanky man, so tall that he looked to be walking on stilts. He waved joyously at them. Fergus ducked out of sight behind Duffach the Dark. Duffach stared over his shoulder at Fergus cowering. "I don't believe it. The great mac Roich crouching behind me like some little boy behind his older brother."

"You're damned right I am. That tree of a man is a warrior named Borrach. He was present at the feast the night Cathbad bound me to my prime *geis*."

"So what? I was there, too, and you don't hide from me."

"Yes, but I don't still owe you a *feast*."

Duffach was not the swiftest of thinkers; nevertheless, even he comprehended what Fergus implied. More than that, in a rare burst of perception, he carried the thought further. "Odd, don't you think, then, that he has everything laid out for us? Beer has to be brewed for days. Those pigs weren't slaughtered just now, either."

"How can I escape this trap?"

"I can't guess," replied Duffach, "but you'd best find another rock to crawl under because that giant is heading straight for me." Fergus looked around frantically, but the majority of the crowd had passed him by and the hillside wore no cover wider than a blade of grass. He wondered how severely Morann would rule if he slew Borrach before the feast debt was discharged.

"Ah, it's 'the Beetle' himself," called Borrach. He reached out his long, lean arms and embraced Duffach. Though standing lower on the hillside, Borrach towered above Duffach. By hugging the thickset warrior, he was able to look over Duffach's shoulder and see Fergus mac Roich crouching down, pretending to pick burrs off Duffach's dragging cape. "Fergus mac Roich!" he shouted. He released Duffach and came charging around before Fergus could move. "I've waited years to have you wander across my land. What a golden opportunity—"

"Don't say it!"

"—for me to collect upon your *geis*."

Fergus stood up glumly. He stiffened at Borrach's resolute grip on his arm. Yes, he thought, Duffach had guessed rightly for once.

Borrach turned away from Fergus's accusing look, grinned at Duffach, clapped him on the back, and said, "Well, since Fergus is here to stay, why don't you *all* stay the night and enjoy the food I've got for you."

Duffach glanced uneasily at Fergus, then replied, "I wish we'd thought of that, we'd have sent a runner ahead to you so you could have had time to prepare us. I know Fergus doesn't care to eat alone, but I can see you've hardly enough food laid out for two."

Borrach's brow creased as he tried to determine how much sarcasm had just been poured on him.

"Unfortunately," said Fergus, "there are four among us who can't stay, as they've taken an oath to share their first meal with Conchovor. You didn't know about that, did you? He wouldn't *be* here, by chance, would he?"

"S-sorry, but he's not." Borrach turned red and went off quickly. "Must see to everyone else," he called back "Come down when you're ready."

"Fergus's sons came down the hill, accompanied by Cormac. "What's all this?" they asked. Fergus explained, adding that he was certain the situation was Conchovor's handiwork to get him out of the way.

"We can't let the brothers go alone from here," said Fiacha. "That has to be what he intends."

Iollan and Buinne said, "Listen, we'll go with them and protect them."

Then Cormac cleared his throat. "Honorable notions, but they probably aren't enough. If Fergus has been waylaid, then the way to protect the brothers is to send them along with someone whom none would dare harm. Me."

From the house below, Borrach called up, "Mac Roich, people are waiting for you to take the first slice."

"All right," Fergus replied to Cormac. "You and my sons I can trust. Duffach?"

"I'll stay, I think. I don't want all of us deserting you."

Fergus said, "I'm here among over three hundred people, Duffach."

The Beetle of Ulster only answered cryptically, "There are all different kinds of alone."

Rather than argue the matter, Fergus went down to the feast by himself, ahead of the others.

7. Borrach Recants

Borrach's feast seemed to drag on interminably. For every course devoured, his cooks appeared with two more. Fergus grew more exasperated with each idle hour. He imagined dozens of traps and ambushes set for his sons and not being among them made him frantic. Finally, he sought out his host and took him aside. "Your fine feast has found a place in my heart," he said.

"Really?" Borrach answered uncertainly.

"It's the leeks, I think." They both laughed over that. "But now," Fergus continued, "I think the conditions of my submittance have been fulfilled. It's time I went after Fiacha and my foster sons as I pledged to do."

"No, really, you *can't*," implored Borrach. "There's so much food left, and it will all *spoil* if—"

"Feed it to your dogs then!" Fergus snarled. He grabbed Borrach by the torc at his throat, bent him down like a green willow so that their eyes met. "I have some idea what the purpose of delaying me here might be. As the weight of a *geis* compounded your request, I was obliged to stay against my will. But you—you keep on like you've got the Dagda's cauldron that never empties in there, and I've begun to wonder how so much food came your way. Here, then, is my offer to you: that you and I go back and inform the exiles you're satisfied I've complied with the *geis*, in return for which I won't take any action against you regardless of how you're mixed up in this plot. If you choose not to agree to this and anything happens to the people I'm sworn to protect, then I swear to you, your servants will *need* the Dagda's cauldron to put all your severed parts in to bring you back to life."

Fergus released his grip on the torc. Borrach sprang upright like a birch tree and just as pale. He hurried off to where the majority of the feasters sat, and he announced abruptly that the *geis* on Fergus had been lifted. He added, "Perhaps all of you should think of going along with him. He's in a hurry."

Fergus mac Roich was certain that he had been deceived

and out-maneuvered. He and Duffach ferried across the Dub ahead of the exiles, who would be many hours in their crossing. He prayed that he might somehow overtake his sons and their charges in time.

8. Ill-Met on the Plain

The band of young expatriates led by Fiacha arrived below Ard Macha much sooner than Fergus could have anticipated. The reason for this was Derdriu: each time the group encountered settlements or travelers along the way, the people swarmed around them to see her. Somehow, everyone knew about her return. Her name had become ubiquitous.

To protect her and themselves, Naise, Ardan, and Ainle formed a tight triangle around her, keeping her from sight. All the curious onlookers got to see was the top of her head to her brow.

Fiacha kept up a swift, steady pace, with Cormac at the rear, flanked by Iollan and Buinne, who staved off all attempts to breach the barrier. The group raced to their destination.

They found the wide, green plain empty of cattle. A thin breeze blew steely clouds over the ridges. Outside the scatter of huts, whole families stood in doorways, silent, unmoving. Only unattended sheep moved on the plain. At the base of the hillfort, where Derdriu had first found Naise, a group of figures stood tightly clustered. Drawing nearer, Fiacha soon recognized the leader of this reception committee to be the red-haired king of Fernmag, Eogan mac Durthact. And from the neutral color of their tunics and cloaks, the group around him appeared to be members of his serving staff. Puzzled, Fiacha searched the hillside for Conchovor, found the king alone, near the top of the hill, with his hands around his face, probably trying to shield his eyes against the sun's glare.

Mac Durthact strode forward. His servants formed a ring around him, as if suspecting that the Sons of Uisliu meant to do Eogan some harm. It seemed to Fiacha that the king of Fernmag must have been brought here to act as an impartial go-between, to settle matters without letting emotions get high. Quite obviously, Conchovor was incapable of being impartial or forgiving. This seemed a wise course of action, and Fiacha assumed it must have been done on the advice of a Druid, maybe Cathbad. He looked forward to seeing that austere man of wisdom again.

Behind him, Ainle cried, "Look up there!" Fiacha looked and found the tops of the ramparts covered by the women of Ard Macha, all seated, watching, awaiting the first glimpse of a long-lost son or an expatriated lover.

He glanced again at the king of Fernmag coming toward him across the field. The servants in front of mac Durthact finally parted and Fiacha saw the wide smile on Eogan's vulpine face.

Eogan called to him, "Fiacha, let me greet first the young warrior called Naise. It's through him that both sides in this dispute are to be reunited." Brushing aside one edge of his enfolding purple cloak, he reached out his hand, palm up. The bracelets at his wrist clanked together like two spear tips meeting.

Naise broke from formation and moved ahead of Fiacha. He reached out to clasp Eogan's reconciling hand.

Eogan gripped Naise's hand, then yanked him forward, at the same instant throwing back the other edge of his cape. His free hand held a truncated, forked spear; he thrust the spear out in a fluid stroke. Fiacha could not see it—only an elbow bursting out of the cape as Naise floated into Eogan. Then Naise rose up on his toes and Fiacha heard a wet snap. Three shining metal points popped out of Naise's back. The tips withdrew and Naise recoiled, arms flung out as if to embrace his murderer.

Fiacha bellowed and charged forward. Swinging around Naise, he knuckled the nearest servant across the brow and, as the man fell back, jumped through the opening this created. He drew up defiantly between Eogan and Naise, who spoke out suddenly with chilling calmness: "Fiacha, my legs are all numb." Fiacha glanced back, saw the bewildered smile, the blood pumping out; saw as his vision swept the group that the "servants" were flinging off their cloaks, revealing on each back a forked spear strapped into place. Fiacha cuffed Eogan mac Durthact back. "Throw down that spear, assassin!" and drew his sword.

Naise stumbled up against his back. Fiacha shouted to the

others to protect themselves. His warning turned to a wail of
pain as the short three-pronged spear slammed into him with
all of Eogan's weight behind it. The prongs tore through his
back, plunged into Naise, pinned the two youths together. They
fell, Fiacha dying on top, Naise dead beneath him.

Fiacha heard the screech of a monstrous raven—Morrigan—somewhere very near. Night seemed to flood the sky and
the sun to turn into a red bead—the cold, hard Morrigan's
eye. He could not believe this treachery; he could not hear
Conchovor screaming from the hill.

Ardan and Ainle tried to catch Naise as he stumbled and
then righted himself. They heard Fiacha's cry but, ignorant of
the danger to themselves, did not have time to draw their swords
before Fiacha and Naise fell and mac Durthact's warriors closed
upon them. Three spears each cut free their souls.

Buinne, Iollan, and Cormac charged past Derdriu with their
weapons drawn. They slashed out against the Fernmag warriors, driving them back. Buinne became trapped between two
of them. He chopped one through the neck and took a spear
in his back. Iollan leaped in and killed that one. He trembled
in a berserk rage, began to spin his sword like a wheel around
him, slitting two more throats, opening up the bellies as well.
A low-flung spear caught him from the side, sent him flying
across Buinne. Growling, the warriors hacked his body to pieces.

Cormac last of all was left to defend Derdriu. "Get away,
get away!" he cried back to her. The remaining warriors turned
from Iollan and spread out, forcing him to increase his distance
from Derdriu if he wished to engage in combat. He was angry
enough to comply. Passing his comrades' bodies, he wrenched
the spear from Iollan and flung it at Eogan mac Durthact, a
sure shot; but one of the warriors leaped into its path to save
the villain. "No, you! You!" Cormac cried out in frustration.
He charged them, tears streaming down his face. They would
not engage him fairly, with honor: he was Conchovor's son
and they dared not kill him.

Cormac seemed to trip and sprawl. One of the warriors
laughed at him and bounded forward. Cormac, on his knees,
swept his blade around and cut the man's feet from under him.
Then Cormac leapt up at the two remaining warriors, but a
stone slung from behind him struck the back of his head, and
he pitched forward into the grass.

Eogan mac Durthact casually tucked away his sling as he
walked toward Derdriu. She had not moved during the swift

slaughter. Eogan stared at her with the eagerness of a rat encountering more cheese than it could contemplate. Derdriu reviled him with her eyes: "Kill me," they said, "finish what you've begun." She thought suddenly, *Naise is dead*. The phrase held no meaning, his body hidden from her, the vision of his dying already sealed off, memory's hermetic magic.

Mac Durthact grabbed her hands and tied them behind her. At that point Conchovor arrived. Anger poured from him like heat from a fire. He knelt and touched Fiacha, but the young man was obviously dead. Mac Durthact shoved Derdriu up to him.

Conchovor rose and stood over her. He could see that she wanted to spit in his face, and that made him want to strike her down, but he could not make himself do it. Unable to harm her, he willed her to wither, but even that impulse died, so much was he enthralled by the wonder of her nearness. Then, over her shoulder, he saw Eogan's lewd stare upon him. Conchovor took Derdriu by the hair and forced her back between himself and the Fernmag king.

The two surviving warriors appeared beside Eogan. One of them suddenly lifted Naise's severed head up inches from Derdriu's face and jiggled it at her. He wheezed laughter at her, but she did not seem to see or hear. Naise's blood spattered her.

Conchovor slapped the warrior's arm viciously, knocking the head away. "Enough!" he snarled. The warrior backed away. "Get from my sight," Conchovor told all three of them. "I'll keep my promise of good will, though not even Macha knows why after this—but you leave those trophies here and get away while I'm set in my purpose." Then he turned and dragged Derdriu with him across the field. She came sluggishly. Above them, the ramparts now lay empty.

Halfway back, the king slowed and called out, "Someone go and fetch Cormac!" He had forgotten his son. If Eogan had killed Cormac . . .

Two warriors came out of the first rampart and ran past him. When they returned, it was with the collection of heads that the Fernmag warriors had cut free. Cormac's body was nowhere to be found. An hour later, Conchovor learned that a horse was missing from a field nearby. He had no doubts what these two events meant. What he did not know was how soon word might reach the others, how soon they would return. He smelled disaster in the wind.

9. Retribution

In Conchovor's mind, hundreds of naked warriors surged across the plain, slapping spears against their shields and shouting to chill the bones of the defenders on the ramparts. The din he heard equaled the howl of the Nemain that could burst a man's heart with fear. He saw spittle flecking lips, madness glistering in eyes. He saw bodies swarm like ants over his walls. Certain this was a premonition, he lined the ramparts with guards to watch for the surging horde. Thus, no one even detected the stealthy invasion by three: Fergus, Duffach, and Cormac.

Three shadowy figures crossed the plain from three different directions, weaving in and out of the hushed settlement. They met within and climbed the hill together. People passed them in the dark without notice. At the top, they split up again to create three paths of havoc and death.

Fergus attacked two guards outside the circular fortress—two brothers who had been known to him but whom he slew now as if they were bitterest enemies. Duffach ducked around them as they fought and entered the fort. He came face to face with one of Conchovor's innumerable bastards, a child named Maine, and lopped off the child's head before Maine even saw that he was in peril. Duffach killed a second child as well, one that belonged to Conchovor's eldest daughter. He was thinking that Fergus would approve of this precise exactment of revenge. As he stood over his two victims, Duffach looked up to find a skinny messenger with a bloody bandage tied over one eye standing and gaping at his handiwork. Duffach raised his sword and the messenger shrieked.

From deeper in the fortress, the alarm sounded. The corridors echoed with running feet. Duffach slashed at two warriors but was forced to retreat. He backed outside, slammed up against Fergus, who ducked around him, spearing one of the two who pursued Duffach. The Beetle announced proudly, "Conchovor's *derbfine* is smaller by two thanks to me."

Fergus said nothing, glanced around to see Cormac being

driven back towards them. "It's time we made our escape. They'd like to hem us in." He yelled to Cormac. The three sped off down the hill, swiping at the few who tried to oppose them. Most of the warriors were racing to the fortress to protect the king.

As he ran, Duffach called out, "I thought you wanted to murder Conchovor."

"No," answered Fergus, ahead of him. "No, it's Eogan mac Durthact I want. Didn't you listen to Cormac's story?"

"Yes, but . . . I wish you'd said something on the way here, damn you. Mac Durthact's a rodent—I could have told you he wouldn't be here."

"All the same, we'll return with the others."

"What? Attack again? What at?"

Fergus glanced back at him and bellowed, "I hope one day I get to see *you* lose a vital part. Then you can show me how calmly you take it and how little you do about it."

They spoke no more to one another. On the plain, Cormac killed a charioteer and the three men rode off in the stolen vehicle.

Conchovor counted the dead—his child and grandchild among them—and sank down in the darkness outside. He had hoped to bargain with mac Roich before any slaughter began, promising to help avenge Fiacha's death. In truth, he had expected everyone but the Sons of Uisliu to fall into the feast trap he had laid. Mac Durthact was to have killed just the brothers. Why had he trusted that weasel after so many years of conflict? He knew better; he was not making the right choices anymore. His grip on his kingship seemed to be loosening. And now he had acquired an enemy that made mac Durthact look like a gadfly. The king stared into the heart of the conflict and saw one face there, one agent of his trouble, whom he could punish.

Derdriu.

He got up and returned to where he had her chained. He stripped her and shoved her along the corridors into his chamber. There he raped her. She let him crawl over her as if her spirit had abandoned her body, leaving nothing inside to protest. Her indifference fueled his anger. He whipped her, then placed a quivering knife against her cheek. "I might peel your face to the bone, here or here," he threatened, his voice trembling. The very act of saying it nearly made him sick. He became aware of what he had done to her—as though having performed

it in a trance—and reviled himself for it. Taking the knife, he
ran away to the room where the cedar-embalmed heads of
enemies were kept, found the unpreserved heads of the three
brothers, and dug out the eyes. He slashed and gouged the
dead, plastic skin, screamed until his voice failed and the spit
was dripping from his lips. The knife dropped from his fingers
and he followed it, still gasping and croaking his impotent
threats. He lay twitching, his legs drawn up to his chest and
his eyes rolled back in his head.

When the army of exiles swept down across the plain, no
one could find Conchovor. The fortress became a scene of
pandemonium with no leader to take charge. Three hundred
naked berserkers burst through defenses they knew by heart
and killed everything that got in their way. Duffach, refusing
to ascend the hill again, entered a house on the plain where
girls in warrior training lived. He stormed through alone,
swinging his sword with one hand, stabbing his spear with the
other, slaying everyone he encountered before setting fire to
the house. Above him, the hill looked incongruously festive
with the fires scattered across it.

Fergus and Cormac slew their way to the top. While those
with them cut down any defenders within reach, Fergus set
fires all around Ard Macha. The flames closed around the
timbers like fingers curling into a fist. Upon Fergus's signal,
the army turned and surged over the hill, down the opposite
side, collecting their strays, killing instinctively with animal
precision. Behind them lay a harvest of death.

As the fire consumed the fort, the survivors on the hill
braved the flames to drag out the wounded and unconscious.
Conchovor had been found almost last of all, still curled up
cataleptically. No one had gotten Nessa out: she had fought off
her rescuers.

The roof groaned as it collapsed. Conchovor came to his
senses with his mother's name on his lips. He tried to run into
the fire but was held back. Helplessly, he watched one wall
cave in and imagined Nessa burning like a sacrifice in a wicker
cage. The image would not leave him. He was left beside
Derdriu, who had been among the first saved. He would not
look at her, but suddenly lurched up, snarling, and struck her
to her knees.

He would have hit her again had not another hand clamped
over his wrist and twisted so hard that he was turned around.

Cathbad stood imperiously before him, the white hood of his robe cutting his face into light and dark halves. The Druid's bright eye accused him with the image of the fire. His teeth gleamed as he spoke. "Still striking down what you've worked so hard to acquire? Here is madness: a king who would dominate a child to her death. I will tell you this—that though you may succeed in impregnating this hapless girl as you have so many others, no offspring will come of it. No offspring of yours will ever rule here, Othar."

Conchovor's mouth fell open. His face took on an evil cast and tilted back from the fire.

"Yes," said Cathbad. "I know—how you've warped the soul I fashioned. I know. Reside in him as long as you like, but what I've said will be. Just as you'll find yourself required to let Fergus's Black Army of Exiles go free now. We have judged, Morann and I, and we find that they've merely offset your heinous acts of treachery. Sons on both sides lost forever, three sons of one mother, and the mother of a king. Whom I loved. Here is the end to it all, then. Count yourself lucky that the *brithem* didn't rule to take your head as a way of balancing the debt to Ulster." Abruptly, the Druid threw him aside and strode off into the wailing crowd.

"The army, as you've rightly surmised by now, went to the Rath Cruachan, where Ailell and Maeve welcomed them." Laeg tugged at his beard. "Cruachan could never become home for the expatriates, but Fergus and the others did have the assurance there that Maeve and Ailell would never side with Ulster against them."

"Yes, fine," Senchan said impatiently, "but what happened to Derdriu?"

"Well." Laeg bowed his head. "Conchovor kept her for a year. He never tried to assault her again, but he did chain her—first in a hut and then in his chamber, once the new fortress at Ard Macha was completed. She hardly ate or slept. Levarcham's false description of her became prophecy, then was surpassed. Day by day, as Conchovor looked on, the beautiful girl withered away. Her face thinned against her skull, the skin of her lips dried and cracked, her teeth turned brown and rotted. Those once-dazzling eyes, now ringed with darkness, never regained their luster. In desperation, Conchovor had people force-feed her and tried to cheer her with music. Each time the harpist—her own wretched father, no less—came to the chamber, she would request he play a *goltraige*, which is the saddest of all laments. Her father wept but could not refuse her. After he had strummed a verse, then Derdriu would begin her dirge, always the same words: 'You've taken from under the sun the one made from my desire, of snow and blood and raven's wing. I would gladly trade you all to have him back. My body knew him like it knows itself. I no longer sleep because the place beside me is empty and my body can't rest without him there. When I do slumber, he calls to me in my unhappy dreams, and I wake to find him dead and joy gone to worms—and I'll have none till I go to them, too. The husk of me will soon fall away, oh mighty king. As that's the part you coveted so, let it be bestowed to you. It will be your prize to remind you of this, motherless man—that there is something in the world overrules the sea and stone. Grief is stronger than both.'

"Conchovor endured this a few times, though her dirges choked him with self-disgust. Fedlimid finally went before Conchovor and implored him not to make him play for his daughter again. The dirges came to an end. For a year Conchovor tried to penetrate the wall of her indifference. Then, in a fit of anger, he screamed at her, 'How *much* do you hate me?' She answered without looking up that she hated him no more than she hated Eogan mac Durthact. Well, he said, then perhaps if she spent a year with Eogan, she would learn to hate Conchovor less. She met his eyes then and replied calmly, 'The two of you will never own me.' This infuriated him further, so he had her dressed and packed off to Fernmag." Laeg saw from the look on Senchan's face that the boy had already imagined what such a fiend as Eogan mac Durthact could do to her.

"Mac Durthact was sent for and promptly came to Ard Macha. He found three new structures barely begun there— just posts and thatch. Conchovor played on Eogan's vanity in offering Derdriu to him. You must remember that Eogan hadn't seen Derdriu since the day he dragged her over to watch her lover's body cut up. What he thought he was getting was a woman as enticing as a *Leanhaun Sidhe*, whose far-famed beauty drives all men mad. The offer had him salivating; that she hated him only made him more eager to bend her to his will.

"Conchovor had Derdriu dressed in layers of bright clothing

to hide her scraggy body and had a hooded cloak trimmed in gold put on to conceal her cadaverous face. He also rode in the four-wheeled chariot with mac Durthact to keep Eogan from discovering the truth too soon. Derdriu stood in the cart between and behind the two kings. Conchovor made a rude joke to Eogan about applying the girl between them as a way of linking their territories. Lubricious mac Durthact actually considered the idea.

"The road at that point ran through some very narrow passes cut from sheer rock. One of these was so cramped that the wheels of a royal chariot barely fit through the gap. They approached a place where a great block of granite jutted from the face of the sheer wall. The two kings and their driver moved to the right. Behind them, Derdriu cried out suddenly, 'Naise!' Then she leaned out over the side screens of the chariot. Before the three men could move, the outcropping stone smashed into her. The force of the blow snatched her body from the open cart. When they ran back to her, they found that her head had shattered inside the hood of her robe."

Senchan sat weeping over the girl's doom. Laeg told him, "You're not alone in your grief. All Ulster and the Black Army would mourn her passing. She had been the most beautiful in spirit of any woman. The *geis* upon her had ended as Cathbad had forewarned, in blood and slaughter, though even he had tried to defeat it. Mac Durthact fled the scene, unaware that he had been offered anything but a great beauty. Conchovor chose to walk back to Ard Macha alone. He returned home like a penitent prodigal and buried his Derdriu in all the work he had abandoned while she was alive. He had lost so much, he could not think of it. If Othar had indeed possessed the king before that, there was afterwards no sign of him. Conchovor became the quiet, forthright leader that Cathbad had promised Nessa. She and Derdriu were given great honor, by the way, and their remains placed in the same tumulus, side by side.

"Conchovor had his three new houses built to replace the fort of Ard Macha. Resplendent houses. One was called Crae-bruad, which is 'the Red Branch'—named for all the copper screens and red cedar panels that composed it. He lived in that house and held all his feasts and meetings there. The second house was called Tete Brec or 'the Twinkling Hoard.' The great and magical weaponry of Ulster was kept there. The third house, Craebderg, contained all the severed heads taken by the warriors of Ulster, which accounts for the meaning of its name—

'Branch of Blood.' The heads of the Sons of Uisliu lay in there, charred skulls without identity." Laeg turned away from the view across the plain of the great hill and the three tall houses like glittering red carbuncles upon it.

The image vanished abruptly.

Senchan looked up in surprise to find himself back beside the ring of stones on Muirthemne Plain. Until now, he had taken for granted that everything he had seen was real. Was it possible that he had never left here? No, he refused to accept that his love for Derdriu was an illusion. He looked at Laeg.

Laeg seemed utterly disinterested in clearing up the mystery. He said, "Now you know the history of Fergus mac Roich—how he lost his kingship and his sons and his home. Now you know the Sorrow of Derdriu.

"It's time to return to the parlor of Queen Maeve to see how Fergus answers her demands. Notwithstanding that his Black Army has dwelled in Cruachan for some years, this is the first time they've been required to prepare for any incursion into Ulster. Fergus . . . well, better you see for yourself."

Senchan got up somewhat reluctantly and left the Stone of Sorrow. He followed Laeg back around the perimeter to Maeve's stone. He drew up short at the sight of it. The great twin-ringed rock of Cruachan had somehow encased the lower half of Fergus's stone. He looked to where the latter stone had stood before. Conchovor's stone stood there, erect, alone. There was no evidence that Fergus's stone had ever been anywhere but right in the midst of Cruachan. He looked at them all, the entire ring, and wondered what the final shape of the circle would be.

The world returned to mist.

V.
THE PANGS OF ULSTER

1. Fergus the Fer Fognama

MacRoth accompanied Fergus mac Roich from the outer wall of Rath Cruachan to the doorway of Maeve's private chamber. Fergus had said nothing, asked no questions regarding why he had been summoned. MacRoth could not help but wonder if the warrior knew already. The queen had suggested that her plans to steal the bull were common knowledge in the Rath. For once, MacRoth felt uninformed, and the somber reticence of the Ulidian warrior served to chafe his wounded pride.

As they arrived outside the door, Maeve's voice echoed from the inner sanctum of her chamber, ordering MacRoth to leave Fergus there. He was only too happy to oblige.

Fergus entered the arboreal *grianan*. Sunlight dappled the dirt, sparkled on the gauze curtains ahead. Fergus speculated that light would spill into this room even while the rest of the world was bathed in rain. He drew back a curtain and stepped through into Maeve's round, tiled refuge of pillows.

She lay naked at his feet. Her shining hair surrounded her like braided sunbeams. Both her hands cradled her head, revealing the tufts of hair beneath her arms. One leg was drawn up halfway. He knew this was a pose for his benefit. "I am so glad you arrived at last," she said. "All this business of counting possessions has simply drained me to a state of languor."

"Sweet languor by the looks of it," he answered.

"It will be sweet—once you discard your tunic and come lie with me."

He obeyed her with a mechanical dispassion. She watched, becoming more hungry and eager because of his indifference. He fascinated her so. His skills at lovemaking delighted her, true; yet he never allowed himself to lose control, sharing the joy, perhaps, but never yielding to it. It intrigued her that any man could accept her charms without giving her dominion. Fergus mac Roich was a hermetic enigma—the only one she had ever encountered.

"There's so little for me to do these days," she complained as she lay down beside her. "I need something to rekindle my interest in life."

"Try drowning cats."

Maeve laughed at the suggestion and hooked her knees over Fergus's shoulders.

"I knew about her voracious . . . habitude long before we married," Ailell was explaining to his fool. The fool's name was Tamun the Stump. "Do you know, the first stories I ever heard about her told of how an endless line of swinish, greedy suitors went before her, one by one. They—all of them— came away broken, destitute. They had given her all that they had."

Tamun nodded, dripping grease from his chin back into the bowl of meat in his lap. He sucked at his fingers and encouraged Ailell with his wide, witless eyes.

"In the flesh she's disarming, more even than the tales convey. Seven sons and Finnabair—Maeve's brought them all into the world and it's not changed her one bit. Oh, perhaps—well, her breasts are heavier, the aureoles darker—but the body, the face, the appetite . . . all of a young woman.

"She means more to me than any other woman ever could, and I've been very satisfied in our arrangement here. How many men can say they've wed a goddess?"

The Stump scratched his slick chin, pursed his lips, finally shrugged.

Ailell shook his head at Tamun's obvious idiocy, then went on, as before, thinking out loud. "Did you know that those advisors in Ulster tried to wed her to Conchovor once? While I was arranging to pay her bride price. They heard about it and moved in quickly, secretly, with their promises to her family. She was packed off to Ard Macha to see if that was what she preferred. Left me bidding for empty air like some . . . simpleton. As if I was paying the bride price in radishes or rocks. Conchovor—a child. I might actually have lost her to him, to that little boy, but he was obsessed with his foster-girl—that Derdriu—and hadn't any interest in Maeve, or any other female, for that matter. Must have been possessed. And then some perverse advisor in Ulster actually suggested to her father that he give her to some enchanted Hound of Conchovor's that guarded the frontier of the whole province. And he was serious! Imagine, marry her off to some cur.

"I've sworn ever since then to pay them back for their rude treatment of her. And now I shall, even if it costs me the supremacy I've enjoyed over her till now. Even that isn't too high a price for a chance to reward their barbarity.

"That's the reason I keep the exiles off by themselves, because of their outrageous nature. I wouldn't want bestiality sweeping through Cruachan."

Tamun's brow knitted as he tried to follow the threads of this monologue.

"I know she's got Fergus mac Roich in her bed right now. I know that. He's better than some of them I suppose, but the reason I say nothing is that I know she's doing it just to keep him bound to us. It's not only justifiable, it's . . . necessary."

Tamun the Stump agreed. "Without doubt," the fool said. "I myself have made the same observation about shepherds and their sheep."

Ailell's jaw tightened. A tic developed in his cheek. He reached for the solid silver wand hanging overhead and started to get up. Sometimes he understood too well why his fool was called "the Stump." On the other hand, perhaps a good thrashing was just what he needed to release the anger in his thoughts.

"I am preparing an incursion into Ulster," Maeve said to Fergus. She looked with practiced unconcern to see his reaction. He showed no sign of surprise, not even of interest. "I have called upon forces through the rest of Eriu. My family has ties everywhere."

"So I've heard. But that ought to be expected of the daughter of a High King. Who didn't your father meet and manipulate?"

"He ought to have met you. I should have enjoyed that. You might actually have intimidated him. You knew of my plans, then?"

"Naturally."

She considered that he was probably lying, but she did not care. "I want you to lead the armies. I want Fergus mac Roich to take us into the tempestuous heart of Ulster."

"Is that all? Just take you in?"

"Of course not," she answered. "You—your men belong to me. I expect you to fight."

He folded his arms, drummed his fingers against his chest. "You'll need the armies of the other provinces to contend with Ulster."

"Possibly. But I think you may be surprised at how easily we slip across the border and how little resistance we encounter."

"It sounds as if you know something I don't."

Maeve sat up and leaned over his face. "Quite the contrary, my warrior of service. I am fairly certain you know exactly what I know." His dark eyes continued to withhold evidence; she would have been disappointed had it been otherwise. "I am going to tell you a story, Fergus. And when I finish it, I will ask you to corroborate or deny its veracity. Do you swear to do this, or must I bind you to me by making you *feast* on me again?"

"I'll answer you."

"Good." She eyed him over her shoulder as she drained her goblet of wine. "I may let you feast anyway." Then she rolled over, pressing up against his warm body. "I'm going to tell you the story of the rich landlord and his six sons. Do you know it?"

"You said, afterwards."

2. The Chariot Race

"In the great hills above the eastern coast of Ulster lived a man named Crunniuc mac Agnomain. Crunniuc was wealthy in terms of both money and offspring. He had six boys, all strong and favorable. His wife, poor thing, had died from giving birth to the last of these. I have borne septuplets, my little Maines, and I can tell you what excruciation that is. But then, you already have a widower's perspective on the subject. Forgive me.

"This Crunniuc had learned to live very comfortably without a wife. Surely he had concubines and slaves galore; he could afford them. But our tale concerns the day a different woman entered his life. She appeared among the mounds and hills outside his house. He caught sight of her but, as he was alone, he had no one to share this remarkable vision with. She came sauntering up the hill toward him, smiling a sweet smile. To his amazement, she passed right by him and walked into his house. By the time he ran up and entered it, the woman had begun preparing a feast for him and his boys, as if she had lived there her whole life. She knew where the two stones of his quern were, and which flagstones Crunniuc used for baking bread. Isn't that peculiar?

"Eventually all his sons returned from wherever they had gone off—hunting, or thieving—and each of them, as he set eyes on this gorgeous apparition, was smitten by her charms just as his father had been. They devoured the feast, those hungry boys, and proclaimed her a cook of great skill. Afterward, she retired to Crunniuc's bed. She stayed with them for a long time after that and . . . now, how shall I put this? They were all made content by her.

"While this nameless woman entertained Crunniuc's family—you Ulstermen, you are so quick off the mark that you ignore the simplest matters of protocol, like inquiring after who you're coiting. Where was I? Ah. While the time flowed by like honey for the family, down in Ard Macha a certain Fergus mac Roich and his Black Army of Exiles burned down the fortress and half the houses and slaughtered hundreds in the process. Not a happy time for Ard Macha. Crunniuc was fortunate to be so isolated.

"Conchovor and his warriors set about rebuilding their home: instead of one house, overbearing little Conchovor built three. They looked so nice, he decided to hold a fair on the plain below to celebrate his new and improved fortress. Everyone in Ulster was invited—even Crunniuc mac Agnomain and his boys." She cleared her throat. "Here, take that jug there and pour out a cup of wine.

"Apparently, Crunniuc wished not to go at first. The woman—whose name he still had not bothered to ask, if one is to believe the story—was very pregnant at this time. Crunniuc was paranoid about births; understandably so. However, his sons pestered him, and the woman sided with him. She wanted them all to enjoy themselves and not worry about her. She told them not to think of her at all. In fact, she went so far as to insist that Crunniuc not boast of her to anyone. I suppose she knew how you Ulstermen love to brag. And being that you *are* an Ulsterman, my darling, albeit an expatriated one, can you guess what happened?"

"Her husband went to the fair and boasted about her."

Maeve ran her hand along his spine. "You see?" she whispered, "you have heard this story." She sipped wine dark as blood from her hammered cup. "Yes, the landlord and his sons got themselves thrasonically drunk. Worse for them, they stumbled over to the area where a chariot race was to take place—and just as the king came riding out in his two-wheeled racing chariot. He was showing it off to the crowd, having his driver circle the field. But when he rolled past Crunniuc, the drunken and overweening fool proclaimed that his *wife* could outrun 'that jewel-encrusted ox-cart.' His wife no less. Conchovor heard him say it and we both know how much Conchovor likes being minimized. Look at that poor sweet girl, Derdriu. Such a waste.

"In a state of utmost dudgeon, Conchovor snatched the reins from his driver and rode back to the fort. There, he dispatched some guards onto the field.

"The next thing Crunniuc knew, he was kneeling in a pool of vomit in front of the king. One or two of his teeth had been bashed out. His sons hardly looked better. His king ordered him to substantiate his grandiose claim or else retract it and forfeit his life for lying. Naturally, as any man would do given such a choice, he swore to the truth of it. However, he experienced a little more difficulty convincing Conchovor of his sincerity than most others might; because, of course, he could not give them her name, this woman who was supposed to be his wife. Crunniuc whined and wheedled. Conchovor contemplated vivisection.

"He finally sent Fergus the Messenger to bring the fantastical woman to Ard Macha and extended the fair till her arrival. The prisoners were put in slave chains and kept in one of the less fashionable rooms of Craebderg. Wild rumors spread through the crowd, and no one left."

"So she came to the fair," Fergus interjected.

"She did, but not without much coaxing on the part of crusty Fergus. She refused at first. Honestly, she was well into the third term of her pregnancy; who could blame her? The Messenger explained that, if she did not return with him, her husband and children became available immediately for all Druidic sacrifices. In fact, they went to the head of the list. Had he told me that, I would have let them perish. Serve them right. But, then, you and I know there is more to this than has been revealed, don't we?

"The woman went back with the Messenger. The ride from the coast to the fair in a chariot covers, they tell me, some of the roughest terrain in Ulster. Promontories and rocks and one hill after another. For a pregnant woman, near delivering . . . By the time they arrived at Ard Macha, she was in labor.

"The Messenger took her right out to the field where Conchovor awaited them. By now, the crowd had swelled up like her belly. Even Crunniuc and the boys were hauled out on their leashes; all seven filthy, stupid beasts."

"Yes," murmured Fergus to the pillows beneath him.

"In stabbing anguish, the woman cried out to the crowd, begging someone to intercede on her behalf and delay the race until she could deliver. No one lifted a finger. No one so much as tried. They wanted to see this woman—about whom so many tales were woven—perform. She warned them, they would regret it.

"Conchovor insisted she race him right then. I suspect he sensed that things were out of hand; he may have feared he would lose the race otherwise. You know him better than I.

"With her man in chains and the king adamant, the woman had no choice but to submit, and she trudged to the starting point. Conchovor, showing more tact than her man—which is why he is a king—asked her what her name was. She looked him in the eye and told him that he should have known her name already. Conchovor made his driver stop lining up the chariot. 'It is upon your houses,' the woman said. 'We are married, you and I.' When he still failed to grasp the obvious answer to this riddle, she painted it in broad strokes for him: 'I am Macha.' Upon hearing that, Conchovor's blood probably turned to ice. I know he started to call off the race. The goddess hushed him. Now it was *she* who was challenging.

"He insisted then that she begin the race. Letting her win would hopefully have ameliorated the situation.

"She took off, much faster than any mortal can run. The chariot had no chance of overtaking her. Seeing that, Conchovor had his driver push the horses hard.

"To his amazement, as he followed the woman's path, she began to change form. Her body compacted. Her long skirts became too large for her and blew up and off, sailing over the chariot rail, barely clearing now-fearful Conchovor. Halfway across the field, the monstrous woman doubled over.

"She squatted and reached down to stretch herself wide. She gave birth in front of all Ulster to twins. In the midst of her pain, she screamed out in a voice like a raw wind a curse on everyone there. They had refused to help her in her pregnancy, so that would be the form her curse would take. In times of greatest peril, she proclaimed, all of them would be stricken with labor pains so severe that they would not be able to walk. The pains would last—"

"Nine days," Fergus interrupted grimly.

"One *noinden*, that is right. And the curse would linger through one *gens*. So Ulster—if we are to believe all this— is cursed for the next nine generations."

"Yes."

"The race never ended, you know. By the time Conchovor reached the spot where Macha bestraddled her discharged babies, she had changed into her evil aspect, the grinning Night Mare, her face stretched into a narrow horse's snout, her round eyes red like twin coals, and her hair a brown mane sprouting down her back. Conchovor sprang from his chariot and fled into Craebruad. Hideous Macha gathered up her babes and vanished in front of everyone, back to Int Ildathach, from whence she had come to the landlord. The fair ended on that less than cheery note. Crunniuc and his sons, all but forgotten, returned home in chains. I understand that the new hillfort and the plain have won a new name as a result of the occurrence: Emain Macha—the Twins of the Horse-Goddess. This is true?"

"Everyone calls it that now."

"It was because I inquired after that name that I learned this story." She climbed upon him and began nibbling at his neck. "You corroborate it all, then?"

"Macha's curse is real enough, as you knew. Only beardless children remain exempt."

"Then there will be no one to impede us."

Fergus said nothing.

"Even if it fails to affect the women warriors—and there is speculation that the women, knowing already the trial of labor, are exempt—we can handle the few who might meddle. What are these few against all the armies of all the other provinces? Should we sack Emain Macha while we're about it?"

"You'll have just nine days in and out."

"Yes, true. Wise counseling, my dear. I must not allow greed to ruin my plans. Equality with Ailell will yield dominant results. That will have to be enough for me."

"And how'll you motivate him to cut his own throat?"

"He yearns to go already. If you gave yourself over to pleasure, Fergus, you would know why. I am all there can be in a woman for you."

"And I'd wager you tell that to all your serviceable warriors."

Her pale eyes turned to ice. Slowly, she began to smile, then to laugh exquisitely. "Yes," she admitted. "Yes, I do. But, usually, it works."

Fergus rolled over then and let her take him inside her again.

VI.
THE TAIN BEGINS

1. The First Warning

Throughout the next two weeks Fergus mac Roich watched Maeve's army grow. Warriors gathered on Magh Ai from every province. Many of them were relatives to the queen or king; others, such as the entire tribe of the Galeoin, owed favors to someone or other but came along in pursuit of a good battle. Cormac Connlongas arrived with those of the Black Army who had settled in the south of Connacht with him. Fergus's men went out to meet them, and the reunion celebration lasted two days.

When Maeve's call had at last been answered from all directions Fergus counted thousands of people scattered like breeze-blown flowers across the plain. Clusters of purple, of yellow and red, frilled with gold, swayed and shifted and mingled. In one respect their number pleased him: The more massive the army, the more slowly it trundles. He hoped that things would not go well with these forces, that they would take too long and be caught in Ulster. If there was to be a battle, he wanted it fair. Most of all, he relied on a thing that no one there apparently knew about—one last secret in Ulster that he intended to keep a secret as long as possible. Many of the expatriates knew about the Hound, but they, like Fergus, preferred to keep such matters to themselves, to wait and see what would happen.

Maeve wanted to leave but her Druids advised her to wait

for some sign that the time was right. "Ridiculous," she told them. "How could the time be more right, when I have an army so great against a foe who will not even be able to stand up when the critical moment comes?" Nevertheless, she delayed two days while the robed men wandered in amongst the myriad camps in search of their sign. She, too, sought sporadically for something concrete—a flock of geese flying north or a moonrise dipped in blood—the kinds of things that would satisfy Druids. But the birds flew south and the crescent moon came up white in the chilly night sky. Finally, frustratedly, Maeve told them, "We leave today." The priests grumbled at her defiance, but they did not worry her half so much as did a gathering of hundreds upon hundreds of quarrelsome, unemployed warriors.

She ordered the army to gather itself up for a first day's march. Cheers shot across the field. The multicolored clusters swirled, then burst apart like dandelion heads. The army hurtled into action.

Maeve wove her chariot through the melee and up beside Ailell's to take her place with him at the head of the army. Ailell veered off unexpectedly and went to speak with his brothers. They had brought troops of their own to his army. Maeve quickly grew impatient with waiting for him and she resolved to lead them all by herself.

That south side of Magh Ai lay nearest to the Caves of Cruachan—the home of the Sidhe of Ochall Ochne. As Maeve raised her arm to order the armies forward, a bright red chariot led by two black stallions emerged suddenly from one of the Caves. The Druids began shouting and gesturing with their wands. Maeve reluctantly lowered her arm.

A young woman drove the red chariot. No one else occupied it. She drove straight across Maeve's path, blocking the way. She wore a red cloak speckled with green dye. Her hair looked like gold cast upon her head. Two tresses of it bound the rest tightly and a third hung as far down her back as could be seen. Her brows were black, no thicker than a fingernail; her eyes gray—exceptionally gray. Each one contained three irises. The Druids surrounded Maeve's chariot. They began to chant softly.

The woman from the Caves drew a sword from inside her chariot. It was a strange sword, made of hammered white bronze. The blade was round and circled by seven small, evenly spaced, red-gold rings. As the sword moved, the rings traced misty pastel trails, sprinkling the air with dewy rainbows that hovered in place until they faded away. The woman held the sword upright as she spoke.

"I am Fedelm," she announced, "come to fathom your fears of tomorrow."

"A prophetess?" said Maeve. "You have the gift of *imbas forasnai*, then?"

"The Light of Foresight dwells in these eyes, Queen Maeve. I learned and was transformed in the country of Albion, where I am known as Fedelm Bhanfil."

"Well, Seer and Poetess, tell us how we shall soon carry the day. Cast your inhuman eyes over this battle force and describe how you find them."

The woman looked past Maeve and scanned the whole teeming plain of Magh Ai before she answered. "I see you all crimson; I see you all red." There was sadness in her voice. The Druids ceased chanting.

"Absurd," snarled Maeve. "The King of Ulster and all his people will be in the grips of a goddess's curse by the time we arrive. I fear you have mistaken the sight of their blood upon these noble warriors. Reconsider with that in your mind, and look over my army again."

Fedelm Bhanfil looked gravely upon the expectant multitude and replied, "I see you all crimson; I see you all red."

"How can that be?" Maeve raged. "You should perhaps go back to Albion and review your craft before stumbling through more false visions. Your eyes are not right, young woman. With so many pupils, you see too much and are overwhelmed by it. I have half of Ulster with me—on my side. The bull I want resides in Cuailnge, where I can go and return easily in less than nine days. Who can obstruct me? I begin to think these robed retainers have brought you forth to mock me. Look once more, carefully, prophetess."

"I see you all crimson; I see you all red," Fedelm replied firmly.

"Damn you! Better you should stick to poetry—that is why they named you Bhanfil. If you *are* certain of your vision, then clarify it for me. How is it possible?"

Fedelm lowered the sword, pointed it levelly at Maeve, then began to gesture with it. The rings wove a strange web in the air. A bright red interlocking pattern soon emerged out of the colors, the rest of which faded as the red intensified. Maeve saw Fedelm's beautiful face through the pattern, her features become somehow part of it, Fedelm and the pattern merging. Her gentle voice floated out, rhythmically, like ocean waves.

> *"Here is the battle,*
> *One against you all.*
> *A light on spikes encircles his head,*
> *He is not very tall.*
>
> *More beauty rests*
> *Upon this favored child*
> *Than looks on any other son,*
> *But his heart is wild.*
>
> *Some brightness lives in him,*
> *A sinister, powerful thing.*
> *It Warps him this way, pops his eye,*
> *And makes his weapons sing.*
>
> *The host here yields collectively*
> *Its head to the skill of this scourge.*
> *Bodies' parts fill riverbeds,*
> *Victims of the Hound of the Forge."*

Abruptly, she fell silent. The floating tapestry blocked anyone's view of her. Maeve said nothing, biting back her anger. The pattern suddenly fell like rain, reddening the grass, revealing that Fedelm and her chariot had vanished.

Maeve snatched the reins from her driver and swung her chariot around. The Druids cried out and scattered from her path in every direction. She drove back to where Ailell awaited her.

"Who was that woman I saw you with?" he asked.

"It was a long-winded prophetess of the Sidhe."

"And did she have anything to foretell?"

"Yes, indeed," Maeve replied. "She said the only person to stand in our way will be a boy and his dog."

The king smiled. "Excellent. A propitious sign. Surely that satisfies our Druids. Well, then. I think we should go." He raised his arm and signaled the armies forward. The field echoed with cheering again. At last, everyone thought, they were heading off to victory. Only the Druids, like a ring of ravens, followed along morosely.

2. The Galeoin Problem

The army marched only as far as Carrcin Lake that first day. By the time Fedelm Bhanfil had written her riddle on the air, the sun had climbed to the top of the sky. The day was unseasonably warm and many of the warriors paused along the way to strip off their tunics and leggings. Those who had come prepared for immediate battle—arriving naked and already coated in splashes of war color—soon made the front ranks. This created dissension among the various tribes, all of whom, eager for conflict, vied for supremacy. It is the nature of all men to want to be first in long lines.

Ailell rode his chariot hard back to the clamor, and was shouting before he had drawn up at the thick of the skirmish. "This is a *raid!* Not a *race*. If you heard otherwise and came to show off your footwork and endurance, go home and return another time, when you'll see the rest of us celebrate our successes gained without you!" At that, the troublemakers separated in some embarrassment and Ailell returned to the front. Further disputes—if any occurred—were put down before the King and Queen of Connacht heard.

Shortly before reaching Carrcin Lake, Maeve ordered her driver to circle the army so that she might see who was quickest and who lagged behind. Watching the spin of her wheels, Ailell experienced a sense of foreboding that before the day was out she would have interposed once more where her authority was out of bounds. He said nothing of this to anyone, not even to his driver, Cuillius, with whom he discussed nearly everything in battle. He thought it might be more instructive to let Maeve intrude on the natural formation of the armies, if only to show her that she shared fallibilities with the rest of the race of men.

They camped at Cuil Silinne—a small nook of dry land pocketed between the rolling hills and claggy bogs that surrounded Carrcin Lake.

* * *

Ailell sat inside his tent, sharing a drink with three of the tribal leaders from Ulster: Fergus mac Roich, Cormac Connlongas, and Fiachu mac Firaba. Next to Fergus sat Flidais Foltchain, a handsome woman whose husband had died early that year. Flidais had recently married with Fergus. She knew full well of his unique relationship with Maeve, but that was no secret to anyone. A beautiful young woman reclined next to her. This was Finnabair, Maeve and Ailell's daughter.

The smell of basted meat drifted in, making stomachs growl. A huge cloud of smoke from the cooking fire rolled into the tent when Maeve flung back the linen curtain and stormed upon the scene.

Ailell busied himself with refilling his wine mug. Maeve stared at him suspiciously, certain that he had somehow foreseen a dispute and brought these people here to circumvent the scene she wished to make. For a moment she lingered in the doorway, holding back the linen, filling the tent with flavorsome smoke; then, her mind made up, she crossed over and sat in the center of the tent, facing Ailell. He looked up as if startled. "Well. And how did you find the armies? All in good order, I hope."

"Yes. There is, however, a problem, and I think it may be fortunate that all of you are here to hear this." She looked at each, one at a time, with significant solemnity. "We cannot continue our journey with the Galeoin of Leinster."

"Why, whatever can you be saying?" asked Ailell. "What's wrong with them?"

"Nothing. The problem lies in their being *too* efficient. At this moment, they are lying back and listening to a harpist they brought along—which is to say, they have already erected tents, caught game enough for all, and cooked and eaten it."

Ailell bowed his head to hide a sardonic smile. "I know that," he said. "That deer roasting on the spit outside was a gift from them. Said they'd caught one too many and would we honor them by accepting it for our meal."

Maeve's face pinched and puckered like a scar. "There it is—you see it for yourself. If they go on with us, they will always outdistance the rest. Every triumph will go to them. It will be the Galeoin presenting us with the Donn, taking all the trophies. Do we really want that?"

"Of course not. It's our invasion, our plan, and our bull. If you think their attendance is a problem, then go and tell them to stay behind."

"Stay behind! Really, Ailell. If they stay behind while we go on to Ulster, what will be left of our kingdom when we return?"

"I expect what's there now, but I won't debate the point with you. If you came here with the problem, you came with a solution as well—I know you. So what's to be done, hmm?"

"We have to kill them," she replied simply.

"That's what I love in you—calm, execrable thinking."

"Respectfully," Fergus mac Roich interjected, "these warriors are my friends. If you try to kill them, it'll have to be through me."

Maeve shot him a look that smoldered. "Like son, like father? Anyone under the command of my seven Maines would take pride in the opportunity if those sons of mine are too bored by the idea."

"And I," said Fergus, rising to his feet but keeping his voice level, "have a friendship of all Munster's warriors, who enlisted out of a bond to Cormac and his *tuath*, not from any debt owed you. Instead of a cattle raid, we can have a slaughter in Connacht."

"This achieves nothing, Fergus," Fiachu said softly. "The Galeoin came at your call, Queen Maeve. By invitation. Such treatment would engender a curse that even you could not withstand. Leinster's Druids would call the sky down on you."

Haughtily, Maeve asked, "Can anyone propose a viable alternative?"

"Why don't you just scatter them?" Fergus suggested.

"What, chase them off?" Maeve practically laughed at him.

"Divide them up," he explained pointedly. "You've seventeen troops here not counting the Galeoin. Why not reassign them, place them in with all the others? You could even tell them that you're in such a hurry that, by setting them at the head of every group, the others will see how they strain at the bit and will pick up their pace. Excitement is contagious."

Cormac added, "They'll believe that—they know their value."

Ailell nodded. Fergus sat down on the straw. The king said, "Well? Do you find that acceptable?"

Maeve crossed her arms over her breasts and pouted at the rear wall of the tent. "If it solves the problem, then I suppose I must."

"But she'd still prefer to kill them," Cormac whispered so that everyone could hear.

A moment later, Maeve had gone. Her daughter got up, not sure of what had happened, and went out after her. Finnabair was that rarest of flowers, a total innocent.

The following morning, Ailell redistributed the Galeoin in among the other tribes. The Leinster warriors took it as a great honor.

The army set off once more. That morning they crossed the moors of Moin Coltna, and the dust in their wake darkened the sky like thunderheads. Most of the afternoon was spent in ferrying troops across the wide Shannon, one cluster of men, horses, and chariots after another, while numerous naked fighters strapped their shields and spears to their backs and swam across the icy waters.

By day's end they had reached the plain of Magh Trego and camped along the reedy banks of a narrow river there.

That night, beneath a moonless sky, The Beetle of Ulster suddenly sat up in his tent. Duffach's eyes showed white all around. Perspiration glazed his body. He stared straight ahead out the doorway of the crude tent, his face a twisted mask, as if he saw some hideous creature prowling past. Without awakening the others near him, he stood and walked naked into the reeds, to where the cold water was ankle-deep. He sat down and, even though under a spell, sucked in his breath as the water froze his manly parts. His head snapped erect and he began to chant. It was not his voice that awoke the encampment. The voice issuing from him belonged to a speaker of inhuman proportions. It spoke high and sounded like wind skirling through a hole between two rocks.

"Now hear my vision!" it proclaimed. "The dark before the dawn. You think you're safe where you go, but numbers don't always ensure safety. In darkness, death will find you, slung from a single hand, while we hide the treasure you seek from you and your days dwindle to hours, flight-felling. The Warped One awaits at the cave mouth to the dark realm. We three daughters of Ernmas will accompany you hereafter!" Upon finishing, Duffach the Dark toppled over with a splash, unconscious, in view of those who had pushed forward through the reeds. They plashed toward him. Maeve shouted: "Do not touch that one!" but no one heeded her wisdom, and a dozen hands clamped hold and righted Duffach out of the icy water.

In that instant, the night came alive.

Colors pulsed out of the black sky, bright auroras shooting up like fountains. The temperature plunged so quickly that ice crackled on mustaches and beards between one breath and the next.

A vicious wind whipped down the river channel from the north, driving the smooth surface ahead of it. It burst upon them like a gale. The sky began to scream. The armies ran about in pandemonium at the sound of that scream—those who had never heard it knew what it must be and those who had heard the cry before tried to bury their heads under bundled-up cloaks and blankets. The Nemain, the war-spirit of terror, had found them. Later, when they had time to sort things out, the survivors would realize that it was she who had taken possession of Duffach; but while she remained, no one could think at all. Frenzy seized them. Some warriors ran around in circles, others took their swords and hacked at themselves as if they were their own enemies. A few green youths died of fright, pitching over as they ran, their hearts bursting from the intense pressure of such dread. Across the island, many mothers awoke that night to hear their departed sons cry out a faint farewell before the Nemain swept away their spirits. Instinctively, the mothers understood what had distantly occurred. They wept in solitude, for who else would have understood their sorrow?

Maeve shouted over the cacophony of fear, "This spot is haunted, we have to move! Those who can still reason, gather up whom you can and strike out for Granaird. We will regroup and learn our losses there!" She climbed aboard her chariot but had to take the reins from her cringing driver. Behind her, the Druids, in a line, moved through the camp, flinging salt across the ground to keep the evil of the otherworld from seeping out.

Fergus mac Roich was among the earliest to escape from the invisible spirit. He made his way on foot until his chariot, driven by Duffach's driver and containing the warrior's unconscious body, caught up with him. Many of the Ulster contingent were passing by at that point. Fergus called out to a boy in that group. The child ran to him, still quivering from the encounter. Fergus said, "Come with me," and led the boy away a few yards. Then Fergus laid his hand on the boy's shoulder. "I've a grave mission for you," he said. "If Maeve has her way, we'll be sneaking up on our own people and, though I hate what's been between us, I won't treat them that

way. I want you to run north of Lough Sheelin, north of Lough
Ramor, then due east to Muirthemne. This pandemonium will
cover your tracks. Warn every Ulsterman along that border that
all Eriu is come calling to kill them. You'll have honor for this
if you love our people."

The boy swallowed, then nodded rapidly. "All right, go
then." The young messenger turned and ran off into the night.
Fergus went back to his chariot, where Duffach sat, conscious
but babbling like a drunkard. He took the reins and drove on.
They passed hundreds of others, some burdened with weaponry,
some naked, and some tormented with madness, not long to
live.

The Nemain did not follow them. The Druids were satisfied
that they had sealed off the forces controlled by the three dark
sisters of fate for the time being. The Nemain might return,
however. The Terror of War gave no warning when it struck.
It was not prejudiced—it would take anyone it could get.

Everyone who survived counted himself lucky. But the Morrigu were far from done with tampering in the cattle raid upon
Cuailnge.

3. The Messenger's Encounter

Fergus's young forerunner followed the outlined course and
headed east into Muirthemne. Every person in every settlement
he came to heard his message. He stuck to the lowlands as
much as possible, going on so swiftly across the shriveled
winter landscape that he had no notion of how his warning
affected people; of how, in his wake, he was leaving the defenders of Ulster prostrate with pain and swelling. His words
could not have been more pestilential had his breath blown
plague.

Heading south to avoid the heights of Oriel, the boy followed
the Devlin River, skirting marshes where will-o-the-wisps danced
in the darkness. Just prior to dawn, he came upon a figure
bathing at a ford in that stream.

The bather stood in the middle of the water, where it was

no deeper than his knees. He was short, but that and the sharp cut of musculature from shoulder to waist were all the messenger could determine of the bather in the vague crepuscular light. The bather scooped up a great handful of water and poured it over his head. He yelled and cursed in good humor at the cold that made his whole body twitch.

As the messenger watched this, he considered that he had to cross that river. His loyalty to his cause required that he not delay any further. He crept down to the shoal and tried to make enough noise so as to announce himself.

The bather, hearing the scraping of his feet, came about suddenly. The messenger stopped dead. Although the glow of the rising sun was at the bather's back, his eyes flashed with an unnatural light as if they were prisms reflecting a sunbeam. For a split second, the smooth features of that face appeared. Then the lights in the eyes vanished and the silhouette returned, a silhouette with sharply spiked hair.

"How do you find me?" the bather called out. "Am I worth creeping up on?"

The messenger blushed and took a step back. He did not know how to answer the bather's arch tone. Then he remembered why he was there and repeated the warning that, after so many repetitions, he had refined into a single sentence.

Upon hearing Fergus mac Roich's message, the bather sprang out of the water like a salmon. He landed on the opposite bank, beside a pile of clothes. As he dressed, he told the awed messenger to hurry across so they could set off together at once to warn the rest of Ulster.

They headed north—straight for the heights that the boy had intended to avoid. He ran at the swift, steady pace that had carried him this far in so short a time. Even so, the bather quickly left him behind and was lost to view in the hilly landscape ahead. Then, just as suddenly, the dark figure reappeared, racing at the messenger. "You're fast but not enough for this day's work," he called as he neared. "I've no time to waste waiting." Without breaking stride, he swept the messenger up off his feet as if he weighed no more than a rabbit. The boy had covered his face at their apparent collision; now he opened one eye and nearly became ill. The landscape sped by in a blur. He closed his eye and gritted his teeth and listened to the thunder of the bather's heels slapping the ground in such close succession that the noise seemed like one endless rumble.

Soon they were ascending from the river valley, but the

young man did not even slow down. The messenger bounced up and down on his shoulder and thought: This is what it's like to be a sack of grain. They made impossible leaps over boulders and across waterfalls. Sometimes the boy was sure they were upside down, racing along the bellies of clouds instead of on the ground, but he did not dare look then.

At last they topped a ridge and dashed across a wide plateau, toward where a single stone hut stood near a twisted, stunted tree.

The bather called out, and an old man emerged from the hut. "Sualdam, my father," the young man cried, "this messenger I hold informs me that Queen Maeve is bringing a huge host into Ulster for the purpose of stealing the prize bull of Daire mac Fiachna."

"They'll smash the landscape flat, and that's for sure," answered Sualdam. "We must warn all of Ulster, and right away!"

"That's what . . . I've been . . . doing," the messenger said as they drew up before the hut. "Can you put me down now, please?"

Once settled unsteadily on his feet, he continued, "Fergus mac Roich gave me this information, saying that he didn't want to see Ulster treated unfairly—"

"Fergus is an honorable man," agreed old Sualdam. "But the fates don't much like him."

"Father, you must go warn Conchovor while this boy carries his message east as Fergus told him."

"What about you, Setanta?"

"Me, I'll go greet the invaders. Someone should be on hand to welcome them properly, and it's my duty." Saying that, he dashed inside the hut. The messenger turned to watch him pass but only glimpsed a pale blur with dark hair. Setanta returned a moment later with a cloak and a spear. The messenger squinted at him, but the light from the hut had turned him into a silhouette again. "Where's Laeg, father?"

"Gone to visit the bondmaid of Fedelm Noichride. He thought you were coming along, too, for Fedelm."

"And so I will perhaps," replied Setanta, "after I've shown the foreign armies that they'd do better to invade Leinster." He drew on his cloak, pulled up the hood. "Good luck, boy," he said to the messenger, and then to his father, "Farewell, Sualdam. You've raised me well. If this is the time that cuts me shorter, tell Emer that I thought of her at the last." He flung his spear up into the sky and raced off after it, a white ghost.

In a moment he vanished over the ridge.

"He's incredible," said the boy.

"And a half at least," answered Sualdam. "Now, come, take some food for your journey, and I'll take some for mine."

"I've told many people already. Word must be spreading."

"So we can hope, but it's best not to assume what you don't know."

They went inside, ate bread and beer. Then Sualdam doused the fire and the two went off on their separate journeys. The boy continued toward the coast. Old Sualdam hurried toward the River Dee. He made it as far as the sharp slopes of Slieve Cuilinn before the Pangs caught up with him and dragged him down. The warning reached no further either—the Pangs had outdistanced it at last. At Emain Macha the entire settlement was struck down without a clue as to why.

By midnight the entire province had been felled, and not a single sword-blow struck.

4. Setanta's Greeting

After Maeve's invaders regrouped at Granaird, they assigned the lead to Fergus mac Roich. He accepted the honor with the obvious disinclination of a man who would rather see anyone else lead.

Under a gloomy, overcast sky, he took the army first northeast, then gradually cut south between the two lakes of Sheelin and Kinale, but closer to Kinale so that the army, glimpsing its smooth surface far off on the right, thought they were seeing Lough Sheelin's northern shore. This detour was all Fergus could legitimately do to give Ulster the time to prepare its defense. If the Pangs of Macha did strike . . . well, that he could not forfend.

The weather aided him until midafternoon, when the heavy clouds blew away on a stiff wind and the position of the sun was revealed.

Maeve rode up beside Ailell and pointed to the west. "Do you see that?" she asked him. "Does that tell you anything?"

"Well, we're going south," he replied. "I'd like to know why."

"I intend to find out." She rode her chariot through the middle of the marchers, her driver blowing his horse-headed carynx horn to warn them all out of the way. Its eerie call warned Fergus long before Maeve reached him. He looked back to see the face of the carynx rising like a sea-serpent's head above the sea of soldiers and knew who pursued him.

Maeve drew up beside him, but he did not even look at her, pretending to be deeply immersed in watching the landscape ahead. "Fergus," she shouted, "it appears that you have led us nearly into Lough Lene, and there is absolutely no excuse I can see save treachery! If your allegiance is to old enemies over me, then give up the lead to one I can trust."

"It's no deceit," he answered flatly. "Didn't you hear Duffach's chant last night? That was the Badb warning us of doom on Muirthemne Plain. I know enough not to doubt *her*, so I took the liberty of detouring us south that we can come up at another point, bypassing the treacherous plain. I've warned and warned: There are darker forces here at work than you know."

"If that's so, you are one of them, Fergus mac Roich. My knowledge of the geography of Ulster is keener than you suppose. Your detour takes us right *into* Muirthemne. There remains hardly a way to get into Cuailnge now that misses it. I congratulate you. Now turn us back upon a proper course or I will cut off your head myself, no matter *how* many warriors side with you. Is that clear?"

He stared straight ahead, masking the smile that played on his lips. "Transparent," he said.

"Which is what you are to me, my dear." She leaned over the rails and scraped his cheek with her fingertips. "Had you been in search of me before Ailell, oh, what a stormy union that would have been, however brief. But what a meeting of thunderheads." She retreated abruptly and her chariot veered off.

Fergus altered their course, putting the sun at their backs as they made their way through the wet lowlands between Loughs Lene and Bane. The new course took them on toward the heights of Iraird Cuillen. The warriors could see it rising out of the distant horizon, and all of them understood how their path had been changed. Fergus was the first to see the tall obelisk that had been raised on the height. He waved two

chariots up to him and sent the warriors, Err and Innel, and
their drivers up to see what the tall, unexplained object was.

Upon their return, the two men carried a hoop between their
chariots. Seeing them approach, Fergus ordered the army to a
halt. Err and Innel set the hoop on the ground.

It had been made from the branch of a tree, its ends twisted
together. In all respects it resembled a spancel hoop, the sort
used to hobble the back legs of cattle and pigs, but this was
huge, looped for an animal of enormous proportion. There were
notches cut all around it, some straight, others at an angle or
slashing through others. "It had been formed around a pillar—
that was what we see from here," Err explained to Fergus.
"There are no trees up there."

Maeve and Ailell arrived. Maeve called out, "What trick is
it now, Fergus?" She looked weary of him.

"There's no trick. Look for yourselves." He moved aside
to let them see the spancel hoop. "Your own scouts brought it
back from Iraird Cuillen."

Ailell climbed down. He handled the hoop. "Not very prac-
tical unless it's meant for the likes of Finnbennach. Look here,
there's ogham on it." He glanced up at the pillar on the height.
"It's a warning to us, isn't it?"

"Yes, I expect so," agreed Fergus. "You'd best get your
Druids for this."

The robed ones arrived on foot, their tonsured skulls bright
with sweat. Fergus passed the hoop to them. Two held it while
the third read the pattern, then switched positions until all three
had deftly traced the notches with their fingers. Then they stood
together and conferred. One Druid left the others and came
forward. "It issues from an individual of enormous powers.
It's been made especially for your passing. The message reads:
'Enter my district at your peril unless you can find a man to
make the like of this loop and using just one hand as I have
done. I exclude Fergus mac Roich from this challenge.' We
advise you to take another route. Who made this can elicit a
great price for any defiance."

"I warned you—"

"Silence, Fergus," Maeve ordered. "Did you not listen? You
are excluded."

"Someone's survived the Pangs," Ailell pointed out. "And
where there's one, there are likely more. If we don't change
course, Maeve, you'll have everyone killed before we even *see*
your cow. I suggest we turn south again, into the forest of Fid

Duin, then make for Cuil Sibrille on the Blackwater when we come out. If our opponent is watching us, that ought to convince him he's succeeded."

Maeve tried to argue against this—she wanted to force the enemy's hand—but no one would listen to her. The army changed course as Ailell recommended.

Fid Duin was a vast forest of straight, slender ash trees. The first line of Connacht's armies to reach it began to cut a swath toward its heart wide enough for their chariots, and soon the air was thick with the spinning, winged berries from the felled trees. The Druids rushed about at the forefront, chanting blessings over the fallen, sacred trees, marking those from which they would later make wands. The lowest boughs brushed at Maeve's head as she scanned the forest depths. Far back in the trees, in a pool of sunlight, something flashed. Maeve leaned over the chariot screen for a better look, but the forest had swallowed up the view. It had looked like a chariot, the thing she had glimpsed. She wondered if she had been witness to a relic of the Partraige—an ancient tribe who had purportedly vanished into the depths of Fid Duin hundreds of years ago.

Then, moments later, the chariot appeared again. This time Maeve saw it plainly, and she saw the driver within: Fedelm, the Sidhe prophetess. Above Fedelm's shining head a woven red mist hung like a leaf-filled branch. The girl's voice rang in her ears as plainly as if Fedelm were beside her. "I see you all crimson; I see you all red." Maeve whipped around. The rear of the chariot was empty. Had her driver heard that voice? No, he replied, he had heard nothing at all. She searched for Fedelm again, but the hundreds of straight, narrow trees closed off her view.

She called the army behind her to a halt. As she climbed down, she called out for all the warriors to cut a path for her, and she pointed to where she wanted it.

The warriors set to work, confounded and reluctant by way of knowing that every moment they worked here the major part of the forces pulled farther away. They worked all the more fiercely in order to get out of Fid Duin's sepulchral depths.

When everything had been leveled from the "road" to the spot as the queen had directed, she pushed in past them. There was no chariot nor any sign that a chariot had ever been there. No path save the fresh one led away from the place where Fedelm had been. Maeve shouted in frustration, then railed at the swordsmen, calling them deceivers and conspirators with the Sidhe or with Fergus mac Roich. They had no idea what she meant. Their silent denial sent her raging beyond words. Moon-white hair streaming out behind her like a cape, she marched back to her chariot and slapped her driver into action. She heard Fedelm's whispered words again and extracted them from her mind. "We shall see," she said, "who is painted in blood."

Her driver eyed her askance but kept his mouth shut.

The forces camped at Cuil Sibrille, some arriving much later than others, and these latecomers entertained their brothers with a tale about a madness that had possessed their queen and the clearing that appeared in the depths of Fid Duin as a result of that seizure. Forever after that night, the clearing would be referred to as *Maeve Sleachtadh:* the Felling of Maeve.

5. The Four-Pronged Fork

It snowed that night hard enough to smother the cook-fires. Most of the army went hungry. They slept pressed together for warmth in tents or under chariots. In the morning they arose in the smoky light of predawn and headed out once more. Their bellies grumbled but at least the dry snow allowed the chariots to roll without trouble.

For most of the morning the armies headed south again in order to reach the Dub, as the confluence of the Blackwater and the Boyne was called in Connacht. There they intended to cross and then follow the Boyne along into the south of Muirthemne. They might have crossed earlier but the first ford would have led them through the middle of Tailtiu, which was the burial center for all of Ulster and bore the name of a goddess. No one wanted to go there for fear of unleashing an army of Ulidian spirit warriors. As it was, they would still have to deal with the more ancient burial site of Brug na Boyne, where the Dagda had once dwelled. In midafternoon they passed that place. The Druids left the army then to go off among the *cromlechs* and the mounds of the dead. They raised chants to

Eochaid Ollathair the All-Father, who was also the Dagda. This was his ground. The army passed by quickly without needing to honor or sacrifice to the ancient graves—the Druids would catch up later. Nevertheless, the proximity of the mounds and the mushrooms of stone scattered across the northern horizon painted the afternoon with grimness. The snow-covered craggy hills looked as if some unseen force preceding them had hacked the world to pieces. Tales of the giant monopedal Fomoiri mingled with the speculations raised by the spancel hoop found the day before. Had the Ulidians found a way to resurrect those one-legged monsters? Were the Fomoiri even now lurking beneath those gravesites? Imaginations churned with terror.

Err and Innel and their two drivers continued to ride ahead of the host. Fergus kept to their tracks in the snow. Still visible on his right, the wide Boyne flowed like black blood across the snow. The armies followed him around the hill of Slane and crossed over the Devlin River, ascending into drier, colder heights. Fergus would have liked to camp on the heights just south of Oriel, but Maeve insisted they push on.

In the settlements they passed, no one came out to challenge them, or even to watch them ride by. Maeve glimpsed few faces in doorways, and those few were female. In the entire journey so far, she had not seen a single Ulster male over the age of twelve. She would have preferred to pillage the settlements they passed but such luxuries would have to wait for another time—on the return journey, if they were left alone hereafter. *Damn the three sisters and Fedelm as well,* she thought, *we will leave here with the Donn.*

They came down from the heights through a gray ceiling of clouds. As those in the lead spread out across the lowland plain again, they were surprised to see the two chariots of Err and Innel racing back toward them. Fergus, sensing trouble, drove his team forward, ahead of the rest. Others followed his lead, but by then he had managed to bring to a stand both teams.

The chariots were empty of either drivers or warriors. The carts' interiors were smeared slick with blood. Blood coated the boards and the bronze sides. Blood dripped from the axles and speckled the snow below. Blood striped one white stallion as if its side had been ripped open.

The warriors snarled and shouted in a collective fury. Some tore off their clothing and rolled naked in the snow. They screamed and beat their wet red chests. Others took out their spears and called the charge, slapping spearheads against their shields in great cacophony. A mass of berserk fighters set off running to follow the tracks of the empty chariots back to the scene of carnage. Everyone expected to engage in a major battle with a vast defending force. More and more warriors charged past the empty chariots. The air rang with chants, shouts, and the bellow of the curved horns.

At a ford on the Mattock River, the trail ended in a muddy, blood-soaked mess. There the enraged warriors found their comrades.

An enormous forked tree-branch had been planted in the center of the stream. The thick bole split into four smaller branches as big around as a man's thigh. On each of these four, the head of one of the missing men had been impaled. Seeing these, the warriors stamped and hammered their spears more loudly still against their shields, and they called for the cowardly Ulstermen to come out and fight fairly. Then one amongst them shouted them to silence with the discovery that only one set of wheels led away from the scene of death. The army fell into confusion.

Ailell stood in their midst in his chariot, and stared with regret at the four heads. "Those were among our best," he commented to no one in particular.

"Of yours," Maeve corrected from her chariot beside him. The tally had begun.

The Druids arrived last of all, from Brug na Boyne. They studied the tree and discovered more Ogham letters carved into the black bole. They conferred, then presented themselves to the king and queen. Shouting down the din, many others gathered to hear.

"This is the work of the same one as before," said the Druids. "He alone did all this and again he warns of your passing this point unless one of you other than Fergus mac Roich can duplicate his feat. We could, perhaps, select four men for sacrifice if you desire it—that might placate him."

Ailell shook his head and gestured them away. "I can't believe one man did all this." He heard the muttering among his army, the murmurs of doubt and fantasy. He could not accept that Ulster had a Fomoiri defender.

Fergus mac Roich approached him, dripping wet. "It may surprise you to learn that this branch before us was severed from among that stand way over there and with a single stroke.

And if you care to repeat what I've just done and dive into the stream, you'll find as well that half again its length is buried in the silt, suggesting that it was thrown down there—I'd guess from the back of a chariot."

"Is that all you can say about it?"

"It's also smack in the middle of the ford and no one will be able to go further today, feat or no feat, until we pull it out. And that's all I have to say." He threw off a shiver.

"Get rid of it, then, Fergus," ordered Maeve.

"Give me my chariot, then."

He roped the tree to the rear of his chariot and hauled it by degrees out of the water, cutting a new stream as he went, all the way to the stand of trees from which it had come. The four heads were put with the four recovered bodies and given to the Druids, who solemnly took them away.

A dozen large fires had been started by the time the burial rites had begun. The ford of Ath Gabla would be the campsite for the night. Ailell had his feast with the Ulstermen again, Maeve sitting between him and Fergus at the fire, with Finnabair in front of her, curled up with her head in her mother's lap.

As they ate their meal of boiled pork and leeks, Ailell talked to them. "It appears that we have to address ourselves to what sort of person we've encountered." He pointed his long meat fork at the group of exiles. "And I suspect the lot of you know what we, with all our messengers and spies, do not. So, tell me, Fergus mac Roich, did Conchovor do this deed?"

"How could he? And even if he could, think, Ailell—would Ulster allow him to come here by himself, unprotected?"

"True. Celtchar mac Uthidir, then."

"By now he's laid low in Lethglas with the Pangs."

"Eogan mac Durthact?"

"Are you spitting on me? His like could never accomplish such a deed. Nor would he ever dare come out against us alone, knowing how I yearn to pare the flesh off his white bones."

"Then who, brave men all? You've kept your mystery long enough. I won't tolerate any further reticence on it. We know by now that our plans fall incomplete, and that something out there awaits us in the night like the Terror itself."

"Yes," replied Fergus, "I suspect he does."

"Who?"

"The one responsible for this is named Setanta. But he's

won a great title in Ulster, which has become his foremost
name. You've heard it, both of you; they call him
Cú Chulainn."

"Hound of Culann?" Ailell gaped.

Finnabair yelped and jumped up. Wine ran from her hair
and chin—wine spilled when her mother had dropped the cup
she was holding. Maeve hardly noticed her daughter's outrage;
the words of Fedelm the Prophetess were drowning out the
scene, ringing like a tocsin bell in her mind.

Ailell called his daughter to him, gestured a servant to come
and clean her off. Then, to give himself time to think, he leaned
forward, stabbed his long fork into the bubbling water of the
cooking trough in the center of the group, and flung a bit of
boiled pork to a beagle that stood near the entrance to his tent.
"We sit at feast," he said as he continued to stir the greasy
water, "and there's meat enough for all of us still here and
drink enough for half the army. So I think we'll all spend this
night getting better acquainted with your controvertible Hound.
No one objects, surely." He leaned back against his pillows,
then lifted his cup to his lips but paused before drinking. "Re-
gale me with his deeds," he said, then closed his eyes and
drank long to calm himself.

In the corner of the tent, warm despite the chill surroundings
of the night, Laeg and Senchan sat as well. In the pause that
followed, Laeg whispered, "Now you'll hear the story of the
greatest hero, my boy, that ever was, how he came to be and
what he did to earn his reputation. Listen to every detail the
Ulstermen give tonight—these tales are the legacy you carry
from here. When all else is gone, and this history you see
before you has been swept back into eternity, and me with it,
only conjuring words will remain."

Senchan nodded absently. He could not have argued had he
even wished to. The interior of the tent was altering for him,
becoming so sharply defined that he could feel every edge,
breathe every shade of color, smell every morsel of food. All
this stirred some eagerness in him and he leaned forward in
anticipation, hungry for their words.

"Listen, then," said Laeg, "to the story of Cú Chulainn."

VII.

THE BIRTH OF ULSTER'S ONE SON

1. The Interrupted Wedding

"There must have been hundreds of people from all over Ulster," began Fergus mac Roich, "at the feast young Conchovor held the night he gave his sister, Deichtire, to Sualdam mac Roig. It took place outdoors, the feast did, on the height of Ard Macha. This was just a formality, really. Deichtire loved Sualdam and they'd been intimate for over a year. Whether or not our eight-year-old king was aware of that, I couldn't say.

"Everyone was dancing around a great bonfire, and now and again couples wandered off into the darkness. A pleasant, unseasonably warm evening. A *crossan* appeared at some point and began hopping around Deichtire. It was Bricriu Nemthenga dressed in the obscene straw costume that night. Conchovor had submitted him especially to Cathbad for the performance because Bricriu has such a nasty, fractious way with words and, of course, *crossans* can't speak during their part in celebrating. I suppose Conchovor didn't yet comprehend fully Bricriu's skill at goading people. Just because Bricriu's sobriquet is 'the Bitter Tongue' doesn't mean he required words to annoy. And, dressed in that straw and wicker wrapper with its great pregnant belly, and wearing a leather phallus the size of my forearm, well, he had little trouble expressing himself.

"He started on Conchovor but soon made Deichtire his prime target. He chased her around the rings of dancers, over those

143

seated at feast, in and out of the fortress, till the obscene
pantomime had become obviously supererogatory, even to the
drunkest among us. Every time the *crossan* caught Deichtire,
he pulled up her skirts and jabbed her from behind with that
huge prosthetic pizzle, then she'd struggle free and the whole
chase would begin again. Most everyone laughed, but after a
while the sound was of embarrassment. Sualdam finally got
up and stormed off from the celebration, livid, but Bricriu didn't
stop. Then Sualdam reappeared out of the darkness from the
side opposite where he had left. Bricriu had, meantime, caught
Deichtire again from behind and was showing off her anatomy
to the crowd. His bull's pizzle jutted out from between her
thighs. Sualdam crept up from behind the *crossan*. He had a
lighted taper in one hand. He reached around Bricriu and pried
up the distended belly just long enough to toss in that taper.
Immediately, the straw torso began to smoke.

"Bricriu let go of Deichtire all of a sudden. He tore away
from her so fast that his pizzle wrenched free and remained
between her legs. He dashed like a greyhound, knocking over
dancers and scrambling over the seated crowd, and dove head-
first into the nearest cauldron, which, as it happened, contained
the next morning's cold stirabout. I nearly choked to death
from laughing. Deichtire joined the nearest ring of dancers,
waving her stolen prize in the air. Finally, she broke away,
went over to the cauldron and solemnly pushed the leather
monster into the gray paste with Bricriu.

"She returned to Sualdam then, everybody cheering and
toasting her as having 'unsexed' the *crossan*. She laughed with
them till she was out of breath. Gaily, Sualdam called out for
a cup of wine for his victorious bride. 'I wouldn't want her to
get mad and repeat that act on *me!*' he shouted, and the laughing
started all over again. The wine was duly brought. But, as
Sualdam passed the cup to her, a small white mayfly flew into
the drink. Deichtire was so thirsty she drank it all down. She
felt the mayfly in her throat, coughed and gasped, but by then
it was too late to do anything but swallow it. They gave her
more wine immediately.

"After awhile, whether from the wine or the chase or some
property of the mayfly, she grew sleepy and left the festivities
to take a nap. Conchovor ordered Deichtire's fifty female attendants to go with her to be sure she was all right. A moment
later, everyone had forgotten about her, because they were off
in a new course of laughter, watching an ungainly *crossan*

smothered in stirabout trying to pull himself free from the suction of that pudding's stringy grasp.

"Left alone inside the fortress, Deichtire fell asleep and began immediately to dream that a strange man approached her. He had radiant eyes and skin so bright she could not long look upon him. This man told her that he was Lugh Long-Arm. He had come to her disguised as the mayfly so no one would know him. Lugh wanted Deichtire to come away with him because she had such a gentleness about her that she brightened any place she went. He held out his hands to her and she reached out and touched him. She saw herself transform then into a bird. Her attending maidens, who had been nearby as she dreamt, also turned to birds. Lugh became a bird, too, but a huge orange one. His arm that she had held became a silver chain linking them together. The birds rose up, right through the ceiling of Ard Macha. Then, led by the bird-Lugh, they all flew off across the landscape of Ulster and into a *sid* near the coast.

"All a dream, as I said. Yet, when someone later thought to check on her and the maidens, they found that she and the maidens had vanished without a trace. The wedding feast ended in disruption. Searchers scoured the fortress and every hut on Emain Macha for her. We found no one. Poor Sualdam was nearly out of his head. He attacked dripping Bricriu, accusing the Bitter Tongue of stealing her away. Of course, that was preposterous. We kept the two of them apart till Sualdam regained his wits. But by then the search was over, and even the Druids could not discern her location. All they could say was that, from reading the entrails of a rabbit, they had learned that a god had passed nearby that night. That hardly consoled Sualdam, since even the unspecified god had failed to protect his bride.

"A year passed without any further sign of her. Then one day, a flock of enormous red birds appeared over Emain Macha. They swooped down to ravage the crops. Rampart guards sounded the alarm, and little Conchovor and the rest of us who were near set off down the hill after the flock. Before we got close enough to kill them, though, the birds took wing again. We gave pursuit but they managed to keep just far enough ahead that no weapon flung could touch them. We never lost sight of them, either, and our chase lasted all day.

"By the time evening set in, we still had not closed on the birds. The clouds of the night sky drank them up. Snow started

to fall, much as it did on this army at Cuil Sibrille. We were
caught too far from Ard Macha to turn back. Conchovor sent
some men out to search for shelter while the rest of us huddled
together to stay warm. Among those who went out were Fergus
the Messenger and Bricriu Bitter-Tongue.

"The Messenger returned first. He had found nothing but a
rundown farmhouse that lacked even a roof. Part of one wall
had caved in as well. He didn't think we should bother with
it. He joined us and we waited for the others to return. Last
of them was Bricriu.

"He also had chanced upon a house, but not like the one
the Messenger found. This house had a thickly thatched roof
and wide high walls and a chimney spout blowing smoke.
Bricriu had smelled food cooking—his stomach led him to the
door. Without the slightest hesitation, he went straight inside.
As if he owned the place."

2. The Farmhouse

"We must have waited hours for Bricriu to return. When he
finally did, he found few friends to greet him. We were all
freezing in the open when we could at least have gone to the
Messenger's inadequate shelter and made a fire. Three walls
were better than none, that was the general consensus.

"Bricriu informed us that he had found a great house where
the men could rest. Inside it, there was plenty of food and,
more than that, any number of willing women. Momentarily,
he was absolved of every treachery he had ever performed and
we pursued him perfervidly across the hills to the huge farmhouse. The door opened and a tall man came out. He bid us
welcome and invited us to share his humble feast. 'Humble'
it was not. He could not have done better if he had been given
as much time as Borrach had for the Sons of Uisliu. Dozens
of women waited on us in that warm place. We sat on sheepskins
on his wood floor. Drink was passed around by the bucketful.
After that fruitless chase, we needed little excuse to indulge
our tastes to excess. Soon, we were regaling our host with our

brave deeds and grabbing for the women when they went past. Conchovor alone had the sense to ask if one of the women was the fellow's wife. The man replied that his wife could not attend as she was pregnant and near to giving birth. That announcement stripped away our last sense of restraint. We made plain our intentions to the women, but they failed to respond one way or the other and continued serving food and drink as if deaf and blind. The warriors—even I—grew angered at this kind of rejection. Fighting broke out.

"Our host came to Bricriu of all people and demanded to know what kind of men we were that we lacked respect or awe of things greater than ourselves. He called Bricriu 'Foul-Mouth.' The whole building shook with his voice, his anger. I remember looking up at him between blows and thinking he'd doubled in size. The room had gone all smoke-filled, as though the chimney were blocked. The host's eyes suddenly cut through the smoke like two suns. I was coughing and tried to stand, but fell over on my side. Bricriu was howling like a dog. I passed out then, the world whirling around over me as if I'd drunk three times what I *had* drunk. And then it was the next morning.

"We all awoke at the same moment, buried in snow, some of us numb from the cold. The snow had fallen through the space that had long ago been a roof, piled in drifts where the one wall had collapsed."

"But how was it you awoke at *that* farmhouse?" asked Ailell.

"Because we'd been there all along. Bricriu's farmhouse was the Messenger's. The only difference lay in what we saw. The story came out then, because we had Bricriu penned in and none of us feeling sympathetic. He told us that the 'man' had really been Lugh Lamfada the god. The women, as we now saw, were the fifty servants to Deichtire. Had Bricriu shared this information with us, then the spells over them would not have blinded us; as it was, we saw what was in our minds: a brace of royal whores and a simple farmer. We had shamed ourselves before the god. That was Bricriu's revenge upon Deichtire and Sualdam, that he had waited a year to take.

"We found Deichtire not far away, in a second hut that had served as a stable once. She was the 'wife' Lugh had spoken of. During the night she had given birth to a child, a boy. In the remains of a stall beside her, a mare had given birth, too. A pair of foals stood on weak legs beside their mother. We got the rest of the story from Deichtire.

"The boy at her breast was the son of Lugh with her. He was to be named Setanta. She had gone willingly to . . . Int Ildathach with Lugh but had at once begun to miss Sualdam. Lugh, seeing her sadness, agreed to return her to the world, where his son would be a hero. Conchovor rejoiced at this fortune—to have the son of a god for a nephew! He gave the two foals to little Setanta as a gift. Who could doubt that their presence was more than mere coincidence? It was Macha giving her blessing to the event. The warriors and the maidens made ready to return home. All, that is, save Bricriu.

"Conchovor decided that Bricriu, for his omissions, should stay behind and rebuild the delapidated farmhouse into what Lugh had made of it. He could take as long as he liked, but he would not be invited again to Emain Macha until he had completed the task. His wife and effects would be delivered there. When the house was completed, he was to send word to Conchovor and a great feast would take place there, after which time Bricriu's house would be open for feasts and celebrations of every kind. Bitter-Tongue demanded a ruling on such a heavy proclamation, and in due course he got one. The Druids sided with Conchovor: Bricriu had offended the god with his deceitfulness and some extraordinary punishment must be served. Reluctantly, he set to work then. But Bricriu's a lazy man, and he's still at it from what I've heard.

"A feast night was set for Sualdam and Deichtire to complete what they had begun a year before. In the meantime, all sorts of stories scattered around Ulster about the baby Setanta. Most of these suggested that Conchovor had hidden his sister away after he learned that she was pregnant. The baby, so the story went, really belonged to him. Utterly preposterous, but how strangely premonitory, since a little more than a year later he was seduced by . . . by his mother, who subsequently gave birth to our luckless friend, Cormac. But loud calumny always finds a large and willing audience. So, when the *crossan* danced again—it wasn't Bricriu this time, of course—the hill and plain looked like a serried multitude had come to answer a call to war. In the midst of it all, Deichtire brought forth Setanta and told them all the story of how Lugh had taken her away in order to give Ulster a hero. Nearly true. The crowd cheered her, whatever lay truly in their hearts. Conchovor named Findchoem, his other sister, to be Setanta's foster-mother. Her husband, Amargin, swelled with pride. Then the arguing started.

Other warriors strode forward, bellowing. Sencha, who'd been with us on the bird chase, shouted to drown all the noise. 'I should be his foster-father. I'm as worthy as any!' He then listed his many deeds and strengths, and, truly, Sencha is a clever man to be the judge at all combats held in Ulster.

"Then Blai Bruga came up and more or less repeated what Sencha had said. *He* should have the boy: he had greater land and possessions than anyone else there save the king. The boy, given to him, would have the best of everything. More came out of the crowd after that. Pretty soon you couldn't hear yourself. The noise brought old Morann on his spindly legs from rites that the bickering had interrupted.

"'Silence!' he shouted in a voice louder than Sencha's. He pushed his way into the middle of the conflict. The crowd fell silent while he stood staring keenly at Setanta. Finally, he addressed the crowd. Since the child was unique, he said, it deserved special care: Setanta should be given over to *all* of Ulster. As Conchovor rules, he is naturally first in every family, but the family in this instance was the entire province. So, to simplify matters, the boy would live with Findchoem and Amargin, but all those present would be responsible for his upbringing. 'You,' Morann said to Sencha, 'you will teach him judgment and wisdom in combat. Blai Bruga, frugality. His parents, the duties that parents should teach. Their natural son, Conall Cernach, will be his brother.' The others, all of us, would go at some point to Imrith Fort on Muirthemne Plain and teach what we best knew to this boy. He would be the son of the widest *tuath* in the world, and all of us were his relatives because—to Morann—we all bickered like a family.

"He shoved his way out of the crowd to go back to his rites, muttering on the way that we were nothing but a herd of 'raging bulls lacking enough brains to coexist peacefully with dirt clods.'"

"So," said Ailell, stretching the syllable out, "this enemy of ours is the son of Lugh the All-Talented. Thus, the Pangs have no effect upon him."

"Also, he wasn't present in Ulster when Macha laid down the curse."

"But the name? The other name. How did he come by that?"

"That was another time," explained Fiachu mac Firaba.

"Well? Tell us of it," ordered Maeve.

Fiachu pursed his lips. The others in the group—Ferbaeth,

Duffach, Cormac, and Fergus—nodded their accordance that he tell the next tale. He sighed, tugged at his beard, and started his story.

VIII.
CHILDHOOD TALES OF
CÚ CHULAINN

1. The Blacksmith's Feast

"In Ulster, there's a smith called Culann. Not a very great smith—by which I mean not wealthy from his work."

"*You* mean that of everyone who hasn't founded a kingdom," joked Ferbaeth.

Fiachu took a drink; then, unruffled, he continued his tale. "This poor smith owed Conchovor a feast debt. That's what this is all about—the collection of that debt. One day when Setanta was still a fostering child—only six, he was—the king decided to call in Culann's debt. He picked fifty warriors to accompany him, including me and Celtchar and Duffach and, oh, yes, Cathbad. Very important, his coming, as you'll see. Conchovor brought only fifty because he didn't want to overburden Culann. Some of the warriors were out on the playing fields of Emain Macha—of course this happened before that plain had that name hung on it. On the fields the warriors practice javelin and sling, and play games like hurling. The children were there, too, performing their own versions of the same. Now, his abilities being what they are, Setanta had taken on the rest of the children that morning in a kick-ball game called Shoot-the-Goal—you must know it. Every time the other nestlings shot their goal, he blocked it or knocked them all flat, stole the ball away, and dunked it into their hole for points. The lot of them couldn't thwart him. A lot of the warriors had

suspended their practice to watch, and you could see from the
looks of some that they were damn glad not to be taking him
on themselves."

"Oh, really," disparaged Maeve.

"Yes," said Fiachu. "Really. I was there. So were some of
these other good men. Conchovor was so impressed at his
nephew's doings that he invited the boy to come with us.
Setanta didn't know the proprieties of addressing the king—
or, if he did, they'd gotten confused in the implicit understanding that he was talking to his uncle. He called back that he
hadn't had his fill of playing yet and that he'd come along
when he had finished off his playmates. Conchovor found this
hilarious and waved the boy off. Setanta went back to his game.
We gathered up the rest of our party and set off, at about which
time, here came the whole horde of screaming children, running
stark naked around our chariots. Behind them, little Setanta
carrying their clothes in a huge ball over his head. They'd
played the old Stripping Game and he'd stolen the apparel off
every one of them, while not a single grimy little handprint
had smudged his tunic.

"We drove our chariots and shouted to one another and made
races all the way to Culann's feast. You can smell his house
before you get there if the wind is right. All that fire and coal
and metal. The stink of slag in the air. The black smoke of his
fire like the dark arm of Goibniu pointing out his hill. He lives
inside a small *cathair*, although the stone wall round his huts
is only about waist high. He could have built it up, I reckon,
but he had got himself a guard dog instead—a great wolfhound.
The back of the dog stood level with the wall most places. It
took three good chains latched to its collar to hold that animal
back, and I'm telling you, if Culann had let it loose, that hound
could've bowled over a chariot."

"He means it was a large dog," Duffach interjected.

"See if I don't interrupt your tale, Beetle," Fiachu replied.
"Well, Culann offered us drink. Offered Conchovor a bath—
they had a tub of water ready for him. He accepted, being a
clean sort. We drew our chariots inside the stone wall and
Culann closed up the gate and loosed the hound. It circled the
cathair wall, ensuring that no cattle or pigs scuttled over the
stones, and guarding against trespassers. No one remembered
about Setanta by then—too busy drinking and bragging. It'd
been a long ride.

"The boy came along as he had said he would, late—early

in the twilight. He had followed our trail on foot, no less. All the way there, he performed exercises and skillful feats to amuse himself. He had one of the balls from the Shoot-the-Goal game, a hurling stick, and a practice javelin—all made of wood. He drove the ball with the stick and while it rolled he tossed the javelin up. Then he'd smack the ball again and skillfully catch the javelin before it hit. The hound saw him way before we did. It barked harshly, then tore across the hillside at its sighted prey. Somebody clambered up on the wall to see what had provoked the hound—the next thing I remember was hearing the cry: 'Setanta!' Then we were all climbing over the wall. Culann dragged back the gate. A few chariots went wheeling out, but the hound had halved the distance by then—no one was going to catch it. Culann tried to call it back, but he'd trained it too well. We watched helplessly, knowing that in a few moments Ulster's favorite child would become the dog's dinner.

"The wolfhound was all grace as it sprang. Setanta, he seemed oblivious to this monster. He caught his javelin, stuck it in the ground, then flicked up the ball on the end of the hurling stick. At the top of its leap, the hound's jaws opened to rip Setanta's throat. In that instant, he faced the hound and, with the hurling stick, slapped that hard ball. The crack echoed all over the hill. The ball shot right down the hound's gullet and burst out from under its tail, trailing that poor beast's insides.

"We raced out to him. The others ahead had already surrounded him and were tossing him up like a pig in a sheepskin. I think our reaction surprised him—*he* had never doubted that he would best the dog. Culann, though—he went to his house and sat off alone. We carried Setanta in to greet him, our host. The smith welcomed him perfunctorily, listlessly offered him a bath. 'But,' he said, 'I confess no joy in seeing you. You've robbed me of my greatest treasure. My heart is hollow, my hound is dead. Who will guard my cattle now? Who will be companion to me and my family?' He got up to leave us.

"The boy blocked his way, placing his sticks at Culann's feet. 'Sir, I will take his place,' he said, 'while I find and raise you another such hound as strong and loyal.'

"'My hound could guard the whole of Muirthemne Plain,' complained Culann. Setanta answered, 'Then so will I. My home, after all, is at Imrith. I'll be your hound.'

"Culann agreed to this arrangement. The warriors honored

the boy for his willingness to accept responsibility when it was his. A lesser one might have blamed them for forgetting him and allowing the hound to be set free in the first place.

"Cathbad came up to the boy and touched him with his wand. 'Henceforth,' said the Druid, 'you shall bear two names, and though Setanta be your name of primacy, your new name will carry the strength of your honor and fairness. Cú Chulainn you shall be called henceforth: the Hound of Culann.' He's a Druid—he talks like that. A joke contest started after that. 'He's a *dogged* warrior!' somebody shouted. 'No one can muzzle him,' yelled someone else. 'He *hounds* his enemies!' 'And if you trap him, you'll face his *doggery!*' And so on, until the round came to Conchovor and all fell silent to see what he would say. The king just shook his head disobligingly. 'Not from me,' he told us, 'I wouldn't dare invest in your . . . doggerel.' That suitably closed the contest of puns. At least, we thought so.

"Cathbad had endured this lengthy punishment with a bleak smile. Now he addressed blushing Cú Chulainn again. 'There is a *geis* goes with your title—that you never eat dog meat. If you ever do it will portend your death.' The boy swore never to forget this. 'Good,' answered Cathbad. Then he covered his mouth as if to hide a yawn and said, 'So here's an end to the episode finally—now this child has a new name and with it his personal dogma.'

"We all of us gaped, which seemed to satisfy Cathbad. He wandered off, fairly skipping, and humming in that deep voice of his. I don't think anyone moved till he had gone over the hill. Then the boy repeated his name to himself and said, 'It suits me.' Culann's wife came and said the feast was prepared and we followed her into the house. The Feast of Punmanship it ought to be called, from the word-play that began again once we sat down.

"Cú Chulainn stayed with Culann afterwards and performed as watchdog until he had trained another wolfhound. But he became the unremitting watchdog of all Ulster that day, at six years of age. And now he's seventeen. That's who you've to deal with."

"A ridiculous story," Maeve objected. "Anyone can kill a dog."

Fergus lowered his head. She would not listen so long as the Donn ran free, of this he was certain. Only Ailell might come to understand something of Cú Chulainn's force. Had he blotted out the sun with his greatness, Maeve would have belittled him.

"All right," said Cormac Connlongas with some bitterness. "Let me tell you how he got his weapons before his time."

"Before?" questioned Maeve. "So he is capable of dishonor, is he?"

Cormac refused to take the bait, but calmed himself before beginning his tale.

2. The Spear

"One afternoon when Cú Chulainn was seven, he went out playing on Emain Macha alone. Nearby, Cathbad held class for his novices. There were about a hundred of them in various stages of learning. Cú Chulainn liked to spy on them. All the children did. *I* did. Everyone wants to know secret things. None of the children ever understood what they saw, of course, because Cathbad would sense them watching and use his hand-sign alphabet; but that only made him more interesting to spy on.

"That day, Cú Chulainn did manage to sneak up on the Druid novices. He overheard one of them ask Cathbad what that day was lucky for. The tale of Cathbad and Nessa had become legend; everyone knew about how she had asked him that same question; his more advanced students used to do it just to tease him, and probably still do. I'm certain it annoys him no end, but he has to reply truthfully.

"He answered his student, saying, 'This would be *the* day for a child to receive his weapons. Most auspicious. He would become the best-known warrior in all Ulster.'

"The moment he heard that, Cú Chulainn scrambled away and back to Ard Macha.

"My father was teaching me fidchell that morning. Cú Chulainn came bursting into the king's chamber. He knelt on one knee and asked humbly if he could be granted his weapons that day. He hadn't reached the proper age, as I've said. Naturally, my father asked who had told him to come and request this so extraordinarily.

"'Cathbad,' Setanta replied.

"'Well,' said my father, 'his word has always been good enough for me.' And with that he left me seated at the board, went out, and returned with weapons—a sword, a spear, and a shield—for my cousin. They tried out a number of them. Cú Chulainn took practice swings against a section of the wall with his swords—I say *swords* because he kept breaking them and my father would grumble and go get him another one. Then they had me move the fidchell board—which was nearly as big as I—and Cú Chulainn practiced with his spear by chucking it into the stump. The tip bent and the haft snapped from the force of the throw. My father grumbled again and went out to get an armload of spears. He did not hide his concern that his storehouse of weaponry was diminishing right before his eyes.

"Finally, out of desperation more than anything else, Conchovor gave little Cú Chulainn his own kingly weapons, which were much stronger, having been fashioned by the Druids in their secret way. It was at that point Cathbad strode in.

"'What's this?' he cried out in real alarm. 'That boy's not ready for his shield. Woe to your mother, boy—put those down!'

"'What?' asked my father. 'Didn't you send him here?'

"'I most certainly did not,' the Druid swore. 'And surely not on *this* of all days.'

"My father became furious. He raged at Cú Chulainn, called him a little liar, and came very close to striking him. But my cousin pleaded his case. He had not lied, he said. He had overheard Cathbad tell a novice that a child given arms this day would win incalculable fame.

"'Then you ought to have lingered longer,' Cathbad informed him severely. 'You would have heard the *rest* of the prophecy: that the greatness of your name will bear direct relationship to the shortness of your life.'

"Conchovor studied my cousin. 'Well? And how do you feel about that?' he asked.

"Cú Chulainn stood proudly. 'For glory,' he proclaimed, 'I would gladly trade late years.'

"'A child's empty statement,' Cathbad caviled. 'How can you, who knows nothing of the fullness of a life well-lived, speak of this sacrifice so casually and hope we could listen to you?'

"Cú Chulainn replied directly, 'Good Druid, I was born to be a hero. The best of Ulster trains my body and my mind every day for this single purpose—to be the best of each teacher, the sum of all their better parts. I am all Ulster—the son of a warrior race, bred to battle, my duty to death.' He sank on both knees before the white robes of Cathbad. 'You know this to be true already,' he said with his head bowed. So grave.

"And Cathbad, too. I was too young then to understand that some secret ritual had been completed, some prophecy fulfilled. Cathbad's voice contained immeasurable weariness, as if . . . as if he'd had to climb a mountain to reach this place in time. I sensed through my father that he and I had become mere observers.

"Cathbad withdrew his hazel wand from a sleeve of his robe and laid it across Cú Chulainn's brow. As we looked on, the wand curved of its own will and circled my cousin's head like an oversized torc. The Druid began to chant: 'This, head of a champion, son of the light, perception and strength within. Hereafter, the Hound must have its Houndstooth. What weapon serves best the son of Lugh?'

"'The spear,' Cú Chulainn chose.

"'It is yours. Rise and carry the day.' He withdrew the wand. It had become straight again. Cú Chulainn stood up stiffly. Then the strange thing happened.

"Cathbad took my father's spear away from Cú Chulainn and handed him the wand in its place. Immediately Cú Chulainn gripped it with both hands, and the wand began to glow. It got so bright I couldn't look at it. The air crackled. Bursts of tiny lightning began to spark around him. He was glowing like a Water Sheerie over a night marsh. The glow rose over him and assumed the shape of a man, as bright as the sun. A clap of thunder rattled the whole fort; the fidchell pieces leaped off the board. The giant of light vanished.

"In his hand, Cú Chulainn no longer held Cathbad's wand. A spear had taken its place—a strange short spear, with a flat silver butt and a head like no other I've seen. It glowed as if heated white hot, and three of the four edges under the point curled out into hooked barbs. The other edge was solid, flat, and razor-sharp. Looking at it, you knew that if ever that spear entered the front, the only way to remove it would be out the back.

"'Behold,' chanted Cathbad, *'an tsleg boi ac Lugh:* the Gai Bulga, the lightning spear.'"

"And that is his weapon still. Forged no doubt by Goibniu and given him by Lugh himself while my father and I looked on no further from him than this."

A long silence followed.

Then Maeve said rudely, "It appears Ulstermen tell tales taller than a Fomor giant." She got up and left them.

Ailell was less skeptical. He considered it at least possible that they had come up against something unnatural. The four-headed tree had been real enough. . . . "Still, he's no god. Merely a god's son. Heroes bleed and fall. And this one's early demise has been forecast. *We* might validate the Druid's proclamation."

"What of his renown?" asserted Ferbaeth. "His fame has yet to spread beyond Ulster, Ailell."

"In answer to that, I advise you to recall what the Druid's exact words were—that is providing we can trust Cormac to have remembered them precisely. He mentioned nothing of this one's fame outside the province. And inside it, we'll give him fame enough. He will be one against a multitude."

"Perhaps if you heard of his training in arms," Fergus said, "you would understand him better."

"But Cormac has already—"

"I don't mean his training in Ulster. I'm referring to his training on the Isle of Women."

"Emain Ablach? He trained there?"

"He did."

"Then we'd best know of it." To a servant he gave orders for Maeve to return. When she did, she was carrying a small white dog in her arms. She went and sat next to Ailell, stroking the dog, ignoring the Ulstermen. Finally, with boredom heavy in her voice, she asked, "What now?"

"This you'd best hear for yourself, I think." Ailell nodded then to Fergus, who took up the tale again.

IX.
HOW CÚ CHULAINN
SOJOURNED
ON THE ISLE OF WOMEN

1. The Riddle Girl

"I've said before, and it was true, that Cú Chulainn was a beautiful boy. So much so, in fact, that practically all the women of Ulster adored him. And the older he grew, the more noticeable the women's attention to him became to their husbands and lovers. These men anticipated that, sooner or later, Cú Chulainn's beauty would bring trouble, and they had enough on their hands with Conchovor mooning almost constantly now over his budding Derdriu. So a group gathered together at a feast and elected to find the boy a wife. These men numbered among them the same ones who had urged me to seek out Nessa. Look what their meddling brought me; although they would argue that it had placed Conchovor on the throne, in harmony with the express desire of our goddess. Conall Cernach added another worry to the situation, fearing that, with Cathbad's prediction hanging over him now, Cú Chulainn might well die without issue and that it would be criminal for him not to give Ulster a son. 'Where else will the blood of Lugh come forth?' Conall asked me. I had to agree with that point, so we sent messengers out to the nine provinces to seek a woman for Cú Chulainn, soon to be thirteen.

"But as he bested us in sports and war, so this time he bested

159

us in our hunt. While we sought all over the isle, he found and
wooed a girl in Ulster. Her father was Forgall Monach, better
known to those here I think as Forgall the Wily.

"Her name was Emer.

"She's small, thin, and lithe like a cat. She has dark brown
hair, kinked and braided to her breasts, and when the sun
catches it, the hair flares red like a fox tail. She maintains about
her a puckish nature, so her eyes always promise mischief and
secrets that you know she wants you to know. For Cú Chulainn
no more perfect woman could exist.

"Their first meeting was in the great Gardens of Lugh, and
it happened by pure chance. She had gone there along with
her foster-sisters, of which she had dozens. They spent their
afternoons among the bushes of berries and the blooms of
flowers. All these girls were daughters of the families living
around Forgall's dun-fort nearby: since he had the fort and
much power locally, naturally all the families wanted to be
related to his line, to Emer.

"Passing near the gardens one day, Cú Chulainn heard Emer
laugh, and her voice floated sweetly like the sound of
Fedlimid's happiest *gentraige*. He left his chariot and approached the group of girls, greeted them each. Emer saw him
and loved him in that instant as he loved her. But, like him,
she was a cautious suitor. Also, her father was extremely pos-
sessive of her and she knew that her 'sisters,' to curry favor
with him, would tattle to Forgall about anything hinting of
courtship. So, Emer revealed her love to Cú Chulainn as if
creating a tapestry, one thread at a time.

"Emer answered his greeting: 'Straight be your road.'

"'It is, now I see this flowering garden.' He plucked a
blossom and tossed it at her feet. When she bent to retrieve it,
Cú Chulainn saw her breasts over the neckline of her gown.
'I see a country of gentle hills where I could rest my weapon,'
he said and hefted his spear idly.

"Emer looked up at him with an ironic smile. 'I know that
place pretty well,' she replied. 'But tell me, fair man, where
is your home that you've come from?'

"'I came down from *Epona* hill.' The girls eyed one another
perplexedly; they had not heard the hint of double meaning
and thought he had made a simple, if unhelpful, statement.
Only Emer caught the reference to the Horse Goddess of old,
the other and more ancient name for Macha. She alone grasped
its meaning. 'Where do you sleep on your long journey?' He

answered that he slept in the house of the man who tends the
cattle of Tethra.

"'What did you eat on your way here?'

"'A chariot-child.'

"'And where do you travel from?'

"'From the land under cover of the sea,' he answered.

"'Who are you, then?'

"'The nephew of he who passes into another, deep in the
wood of the Nemain. But now you've asked me enough and I
have as many questions for you. You know them, since you
asked them of me. Tell me of yourself.'

"'I, young sir, was raised in virtues both ancient and noble,'
Emer declared modestly, 'to be a queen of some small land.
But my sisters must go before I can marry, and no one can
have me who has not slain a hundred on each ford that circles
the dun of Forgall. Not only that, but a suitor of Emer must
kill three times nine, save one from each relative multiple.'

"'That's a hard line,' replied Cú Chulainn, 'but not impossible for one whose bark is loud.'

"Emer blushed and smiled. 'And what offer such a one
would make to me is accepted. It is taken. It is granted.' With
that, she stood and stretched and asked her sisters if they would
mind returning to the fort with her because she was tired,
leaving Cú Chulainn to fathom her riddles as she had done
his."

"And what, if I might ask, *is* the meaning of these riddles?"
queried Ailell.

"I'll explain. The first one I told you already. He told her
next that he slept in the house of Ronca, who was Conchovor's
fisherman—fish being the cattle of the sea, and Tethra, leader
of the displaced Fomoiri, being a lord of the sea."

"How clever," Maeve said admiringly in spite of herself.
She stroked her little dog as it slept.

"He and his driver had eaten a meal the night before of a
foal cooked on a spit. That is the chariot-child. And Muirthemne is the land under the cover of the sea because it was
under water once until the Dagda came there with his club and
sang the water away."

"And the other riddle?" asked Maeve. "He is the nephew
of the king, but I fail to see—"

"Conchovor was named by Nessa for the river Conchovor.
In Ross, that river flows through a dark forest called the Wood
of the Morrigu. Somewhere in that uninviting wood, it also

meets up with and pours into a second river, the Annalee—
hence his uncle *passing into another*. Cú Chulainn was testing
Emer, and he could see from the larksome light in her eyes
that she had solved every puzzle. By the time he asked her to
riddle him, he had lost his heart to her."

"And her riddles to him?"

"She said she'd been raised to be a queen of some small
land," Fergus iterated. "That, I think, meant Cú Chulainn himself. He's short of stature. She also told him, within her riddles,
that he would have to carry off her sisters and slay her four
guardians, who stood on four different fords around the home
of Forgall Monach. Each of the guardians reputedly had the
strength of a hundred. Emer had three brothers, too, named
Ibur, Seibur, and Catt. They each commanded a troop of eight
men, so the three times nine save one meant he would have to
slay the eight but save her brothers. I think the rest you can
figure out yourselves."

"The offer she accepted was of marriage?" asked Ailell.

"Naturally."

"To the Hound—the one with the loud bark."

Fergus nodded.

Maeve was scheming, seeking a weakness in their invisible
foe, but she needed more information. "Did Cú Chulainn win
Emer? Did he kill all those others?"

"That's an involved story. It wasn't as simple as all that."

She inhaled deeply to calm herself. "Well, Fergus, you seem
to have all the information. I, myself, am so wide awake—an
involved tale would be just the thing to hear now. You do agree,
of course."

"Fergus is always ready to tell a story," said Duffach somewhat drunkenly. Fergus contemplated him, but Duffach did not
see the look.

"Come, mac Roich," said Ailell, "you *did* promise to tell
us of the boy's training."

"True, I did. And so I will. Be patient, all."

2. Forgall's Treachery

"When his foster-daughters returned to the fort on the afternoon of the riddling, Forgall heard of Emer's encounter with the strange boy. He went ashen with the news, even though his girls got some of the specifics of the riddles wrong since they themselves didn't understand a word of it. But Forgall had stopped listening to them in any case. Fear clouded his mind and proposed to him his doom. The foster-daughters were certain he comprehended the riddles and, when he ignored them altogether, they marched off in a huff, complaining loudly and bitterly that Forgall always favored Emer over them. But those ill-tempered bitches were the least of his worries.

"Some years earlier, Forgall's Druid seers had predicted he would meet his end at the hands of one of his daughter's suitors. At that time, he had only sons, but his wife was pregnant and, as he feared, added a daughter to the brood. You might say that he ought to have killed her and solved all his problems then and there. I'd guess he considered it, too, but he wasn't cold enough of heart to commit such an act, and those same Druids would likely have condemned him as a criminal for trying to escape fate. What could he do? There was just one way out as he saw it: he used his wiles so that his three sons became overly protective of Emer and shielded her from outside contact. He hired four guards of great training and skill, whom he had train his sons as well as a select group of twenty-four others picked from among his fosters. This force became his great barrier; no one could get through that living wall. Forgall was confident of his safety.

"And now, with the girl barely turned twelve and marriageable, she had already threaded through his precautions to find herself a suitor and in such a way that no one had recognized what was happening to put a stop to it. Worse, if he guessed rightly, this hadn't been just any suitor, either, but the bloody, terrifying Hound of Ulster. Forgall determined that greater precautions were necessary. The first of these he undertook himself in secrecy."

"One morning on Emain Macha, Conchovor was watching a dog race. One of his servants came down the hill to him and announced he had a foreign visitor. Conchovor ordered the visitor be looked after in his chambers until the race had finished. His dog won, so he was in a cheerful mood to greet his guest. The visitor wore Gaulish clothes and bracelets, and he had the sharp features and dark complexion of a Gaul, too. In reply to Conchovor's welcome, he offered the king a small cask of Gaulish wine—a gift. 'Sweet is it and to the head, staggering,' he warned in that peculiar Gaulish way of turning simple speech around. Next he gave Conchovor a box of jewels. Then he explained, this was all a gift from his master across the sea who yearned for news of life here in Ulster. Young Conchovor swelled with pride but secretly considered that this unknown master might be contemplating an invasion. He studied his visitor carefully.

"They spent that morning in Conchovor's chambers. The old Gaul listened while the king went on about Ulster's great strength and energy, bragging of his house of warriors, listing us off: me, Conall Cernach the Victorious; Laegaire Buadach the Battle Winner; Cú Chulainn the Hound; the terrible trio of Naise, Ainle, and Ardan. The list went on and on.

"The Gallic messenger finally asked to see some of these warriors. Conchovor had been hoping for that. He obliged immediately, leading the Gaul out onto the sunny playing field. The Gaul insisted the king point out each warrior he had named. Conchovor complied until he came to Cú Chulainn. 'Ooh,' said the Gaul, 'that one has skill innate.' He watched the boy best a whole team of opponents. 'Benefit would your Cú Chulainn by a visit to the Isle of Apples, where Domnall Mildemail trains her students.'

"'Not many survive the rigorous training of the women warriors on that isle,' replied the king. 'There are, at present, three brothers named Id, Sedlang, and Laeg who went there seeking to improve their chariot skills. They've not been heard from since Lughnasad last. We would not care to lose Cú Chulainn's like as well.'

"'Ah, true,' agreed the Gaul. 'But survive, that one would. His talents would protect him. And I want—that is, I recommend only. Think you—a warrior greater than even now he is. Domnall. Perhaps Scathach even, or Aife. Is glory not work risks this big?' Then he added, 'But show me now the others you hold forth so boldly.' That being Conchovor's first duty to Ulster, he led the Gallic visitor away. No more was said about the Isle of Women—Isle of Apples, as the visitor had named it.

"While they toured, a feast was prepared for the Gaul. His own magnificent wine was opened, strained, and consumed. Conchovor and the warriors enjoyed his company all evening. He thanked them for their grand hospitality and, the next morning, set off on his journey again. Once over the hills east of Ard Macha, he paused at a stream, where he stripped and washed himself. The water turned rusty brown around him as the dye on his skin ran away with the current. He worked at his eyebrows, seemingly tearing the hair from his face; in fact, what he removed was horsehair that he had carefully plastered over his own eyebrows and cheeks. A piece of stained clay covered the bridge of his slender nose to make it sharp and pocked. He laughed all the while that he altered his appearance. No one had recognized him—not even the clever Druids.

"Forgall left the stream and hurried home, where he had to endure a long wait for news that his bait had been taken. He knew that hardly one warrior in a dozen returned from the Women's Isle. And, on the off-chance that the one became a two rather than the dozen a dozen and one, Forgall had a second plan, already brewing.

"Nevertheless, as he hoped, the matter of further training stuck in Conchovor's head until at last he mentioned it to Cú Chulainn. And Cú Chulainn, certain of himself in all things, agreed to go. 'I see how this fits in Cathbad's prediction,' he said. 'Greater will be my fame for it.' After making his good-byes to somewhat alarmed friends and family, he took his spear and set off for the coast. On the way, he detoured to the Garden of Lugh and waited there for Emer to come again. He did not have to wait long.

"Learning of her father's plans, Emer had taken to sneaking off early every morning to the garden. She found Cú Chulainn sleeping there in a bed of cresses. She knelt beside him and stroked his smooth cheek. He opened his strange eyes and smiled up at her. They spoke, freely this time, of their love for one another. Then Emer surprised Cú Chulainn by revealing that she knew his intentions. When he asked how she knew so much, she replied, her father had played a trick upon him and

the king. 'He fears you,' she said, 'and hopes you'll die in
Emain Ablach.'

"'I should kill him for this trick he's played on my uncle,'
Cú Chulainn mused, 'but I won't. Know it or not, he's done
me a favor here. This training is just the thing I need to finish
me.' Emer took no joy in the double meaning she heard in this
phrase. She left him and went to the pool in the middle of the
vast garden. He followed her. She leaned over the pool, then
stood and held out her cupped hands filled with water. 'Here,'
she said. He knew that, had they been at feast, her gesture
would have signified she had chosen him as her husband. He
saw no reason why this symbolic act should not be valid here.
He immersed his hands in her palms. Water dribbled out and
splashed their feet. 'There's too much water in the bowl,' he
said lightly. Emer answered earnestly, 'Too much isn't possible,
even when it's over-full.'

"With this they were pledged to one another and swore that,
upon Cú Chulainn's return, they would join together properly.
He would have taken on the Eye of Balor for her: he loved her
utterly. As he got aboard his chariot again, she warned him to
be careful, for her father had not won his name through idle-
ness. Cú Chulainn replied, he relished the confrontation that
would eliminate all which stood between them. Then he set
off.

"Word had been sent ahead by our messenger Fergus, and
a sea-going *currach* awaited him at Ringfadh. He set out alone
next morning across the eastern sea."

3. The Isle of Apples

"The camp of Domnall Mildemail lay in deep seclusion, in a
grotto. A thick stand of hazels sealed the grotto off from the
rest of the island. How Cú Chulainn found her camp, I can't
say. Much of that isle remains a mystery, and those who have
climbed its cliffs often will not or cannot recall much of their
experience. Let us say fate ordained it.

"The mouth of the grotto contained two rows of huts in

which the students dwelled. Domnall lived elsewhere, deep in the caverns beyond the huts. Cú Chulainn arrived at the camp late one evening, announced who he was and why he'd come. Three young Ulstermen came up to him and introduced themselves, then asked for news of their home. He told them what he could and asked, in return, for information about the life here in the grotto. One of the three—who were, by the way, the brothers Conchovor had mentioned to Forgall the Gaul—explained: 'You will learn more than you thought possible about whatever craft is chosen for you, or else you'll die in the trying. When we came here, every hut was full from a new crop of students, male and female, with visions of great feats in mind. As you can see, only this handful remains. And none left the isle by mortal methods.' Nor would he. Yet none of them could tell Cú Chulainn how to find Domnall."

In the corner of the room, Laeg leaned close to Senchan as if the others might hear him. "He hasn't got it word for word, lad, but that does approximate what I told him that evening. In fact Fergus's put it somewhat more succinctly."

Startled, Senchan stared at him with wide eyes. "You?"

"What's so remarkable about that? I had to meet him sooner or later, didn't I?" Before Senchan could speak again, Laeg admonished him, "No more or we'll miss his description of Domnall."

"She appeared the following morning," Fergus was saying. "And she treated Cú Chulainn at first as if he had been one of her students all along, ignoring the fact that he stood off to one side and just watched her. And no wonder, either. She had skin so white, it seemed to contain no pigment at all—not a freckle or a blemish. Her hair, too, was white, and it stuck out in stiff spikes around her reptilian face. Bracelets and rings adorned her arms, chains her waist, and twin torcs her throat. Her eyes were milky, the pupils vertical slits. The lower half of her face projected forward, the nose and mouth blended into a single rounded feature.

"Her warrior students set about their tasks without a word from her. They took up whatever weapon she trained them in. Slings, spears, swords. Some battled their friends. Others sought to destroy stuffed targets. Those like Laeg and his brothers, who trained for the chariot, stood on a piece of sloping ground, holding each end of a long leather cord that had been looped around a great boulder. They moved the boulder by degrees, first to one side then the other, by tugging on the ends of the cords. They had already mastered the most obstinate horses Domnall had.

"She came to small Cú Chulainn last of all and ordered him to follow her back into the depths of the grotto. The students paused to watch him depart: some saw with eyes of envy; others, looking on in sympathy, had accompanied her into the caverns themselves and knew they might be looking on him for the last time.

"First off, Domnall took him to a strange formation of rock— a large round flagstone balanced on the tip of a tall stalagmite. Beneath this pointed pillar lay a hot, smoking coal pit and a large bellows of uncommon design. Stone steps cut into the cavern wall led to the flagstone. Domnall ordered Cú Chulainn to climb the steps, requiring of him also that he remove his shoes. He obeyed her and awaited her next command from the top step. The surface of the flagstone, he saw, gave off steam or smoke. Domnall worked the bellows until the coals lit the entire cavern red. 'What you must do, Cú Chulainn,' she told him, 'is leap onto the flagstone and then balance yourself from one foot to the other, back and forth, until I tell you to stop. Be careful not to lose balance, because the fall from there will drop you in the coals and you'll cook before I can get you out. Be aware—everything else I have to teach you depends on your learning this.'

"He waited, taking the measure of the stone, where he wanted to land, and guessing at how much it might tip. Then he jumped from the step onto the hot stone. It tilted up and he nearly fell, but he stamped one foot to force the other side down, then the other foot to bring it up, and so on, back and forth, just to stay on it. Domnall said nothing, watched and pumped the bellows.

"All morning he pranced in place, sweat pouring from him like seawater off a *merrow*. As he mastered his position, he managed to strip down and continue his dance naked. Below him, Domnal pumped steadfastly, a constant rhythm, although she too was slick with sweat. Eventually she stripped down as well. The glow of the fire reflected off her as off a figure of bronze. The coals hissed and spat with Cú Chulainn's sweat. His nostrils stung from the vinegary smell, but he hardly noticed this over the pain in his feet. They hurt as if a hundred knives stabbed into them each time he leapt, but he blocked the pain and jigged on until he thought he must faint. It seemed to him he had danced for days. Then Domnall called, 'Stop,' and Cú

Chulainn bounded immediately to the top step but could not
hold himself up and fell headlong. Anticipating such a reaction,
Domnall was already there. She caught him and carried him
like a child. He rested his head against her slick, pale breasts,
his eyes barely open. She took him further into the caverns,
to a pool filled from a waterfall. Strange colors lit the walls
there and seemed to pulse, though Cú Chulainn admits this
may have been a feverish impression.

"Domnall lowered him into the pool. The cool water revived
him. She let him float out under the waterfall, then dove in to
cleanse herself and swam with the grace of an eel around the
pool. When his eyes opened and a look of peace settled upon
his face, she lifted him out of the pool and carried him to her
own hut, not far from there in the cave. The floor was of soft
rushes and the wall of crushed crystal. She laid him down. He
could not feel his feet then. When he looked at them, he found
Domnall on her knees there, oiling them from a small brass
beaker. She glanced at him with her strange green eyes and
said, 'The soles are black and swollen, but not so much as to
stop you from training more tomorrow. You do not yet have
the inner peace to balance the flagstone without ill effect. This
is the secret that will allow you to go on: No fire can burn you
if you make it cold.'

"'How is that done without watering the fire?' he asked.

"Domnall oiled his calves. 'You can make sun into moon
or become hotter than the fire yourself.' It was all a riddle and
his mind drifted, trying to unravel it.

"When she oiled his thighs, he became aroused. He hid his
face in embarrassment. Domnall's eyes glittered and, in a sultry
tone, she said, 'Ah, you're ready for more teaching. Let us
see, little Hound, if you can balance me.' This was the second
phase of his training, and once again Domnall Mildemail pumped
the bellows."

Maeve laughed loudly at this. "How long did it continue?"

"Late into the night, as you might expect."

"No, fool—his training. How long?"

"One year he stayed there," answered Fergus, "while back
in Ulster a girl named Derdriu escaped her captor in a way that
cleaved the province in two. No word of that reached him.

"When he had mastered the flagstone and could dance all
around the tip of the stalagmite without scorching his soles,
Domnall took him elsewhere and taught him to walk along the
shaft of a spear and to stand on its tip without piercing his

foot. Next he learned to jump out of the grotto pool, as high
as the waterfall, or to flip up out of the water and land beside
the pool. This feat is called 'The Salmon Leap' and it serves
him well. Then Domnall combined all these things and taught
him how to lay the Gai Bulga on the surface of the water, then
to leap up, catch the butt of the spear between his toes and
skim it across the pool. He even learned to make it slide up
the waterfall."

"Preposterous!" cried Maeve. Her small dog yapped in re-
flex at the tone of her voice.

Fergus did not respond to her. "The point is, this spear was
given to him *before* Forgall schemed to send him away—which
meant that he had stumbled upon his destiny. Great Lugh's gift
served as proof.

"Domnall's training had ended. 'Every individual has his
own talents,' she told him on his last night with her as they
lay in the afterglow of coupling. 'It's my craft to know what
talents belong to what warrior and to develop them accordingly.
Many are the warriors who don't know themselves enough to
see that, and who perish. You have a binding tie to water, to
rivers and seas, and it's the water you've learned to be like.
Cú Chulainn flowing like a river; Cú Chulainn smooth as a
lake. Cú Chulainn, whose shape ripples when anger overtakes
him, the way water ripples when pushed by the wind.'

"The next morning, she led him into the grotto once more.
She took one of the three Ulster brothers and paired him with
Cú Chulainn. She told them they were destined to be together,
to work as two parts of one being. The charioteer, whose name
is Laeg mac Riangabra, became like Cú Chulainn's brother.
He is a tall, thin man, his tremendous strength hidden, covered
in freckles. Domnall gave him a chariot from her hoard, crafted
by another secret sect upon the island, and gave him also
directions to the camp of Scathach. There they were to learn
much more. They set out and reached the heights of that camp
before midafternoon." Fergus glanced up at a gesture of im-
patience from Ailell.

"Again you mention this Scathach," said the king, "teasing
us with the name. The name of Domnall Mildemail the Warlike
is known to me. But the only Scathach I've ever heard mentioned is from the ancient tales of the Tuatha de Danann. That
Scathach was a goddess of Scythian descent who is credited
with training Nuada himself. However, that took place before
the Sidhe went to ground. Long before."

Fergus nodded but added nothing. When Maeve saw that
he would elucidate no further, she invited him to continue with
his story. "I will," he said, "but first we must go back to Ulster
to hear of the second part of Forgall's wicked plan. I could
relate that tale, too, but by luck you have in your camp one
who knows it firsthand."

"And who might that be?"

"Lugaid mac Nois, son of Cu Roi and King of Munster."

"What?"

"Does everyone know of this Ulidian warrior save *us?!*"
bellowed Ailell.

Fergus shook his head. "No, that isn't the case. Send for
Lugaid and you'll see that he knows of him only indirectly.
It's a quite different matter he'll speak of."

So a messenger was dispatched to go wake the Munster king
and bring him along. Meanwhile, the others replenished their
drinks and went outside on stiff legs to relieve themselves.
Laeg and Senchan stood and stretched, watching the warriors
pass near. Laeg recognized in Senchan's covert glances a new
respect, and he thought that there was nothing improved one's
own reputation more than to have it from the mouth of someone
else.

4. Lugaid's Story

The king of Munster entered the Connacht tent in the company
of twelve attendants and his younger brother, Larene. He wore
a long linen tunic dyed yellow and sprinkled with gold; two
disk brooches gleamed on either shoulder. He looked almost
as if he had been expecting their call. Only the red edges to
his alert eyes indicated his recent awakening. He hailed each
person amiably, then took his place between Ailell and Fergus,
who moved to give him the superior position.

Once his servants brought him a full mug and he had taken
a sip to clear his throat, Lugaid said, "Now, what matter of
campaign is it drags me from bed to this—" he paused to look
around "—this rare meeting?"

"Tales of brave Cú Chulainn," replied Ailell.

Lugaid arched one brow. "Then you woke the wrong man. The better tellers are all present. What can I add?"

"Fergus indicated you'd say that. It is about Forgall Monach and his daughter, Emer, you're to speak."

Lugaid's eyes half-closed and he nodded slowly. "Oh, yes. Our wedding."

Even Maeve registered surprise. "You? And Emer?"

"A handsome couple, wouldn't you agree?" When Maeve remained silent, he lifted his mug and toasted Emer: "that most delicate of pincers." His brother laughed into his wine and began to choke. Lugaid paused until Larene had composed himself; then, clearing his throat once more, he said, "Here, then, is my tale.

"A messenger of most oily Forgall Monach—his son, Ibur, I recall—came unannounced to Munster one afternoon. When shown before me, he proclaimed that it was his father's fervent hope that I, who had no wife and was, ostensibly, seeking one, would accept in marriage his daughter, Emer. Ibur explained that matters being what they were—I being a newly empowered king and Forgall's daughter the daughter of a lesser Ulster king, for that's how he saw himself—our stations in life suited one another perfectly, and I should have a grand, glorious girl of great beauty and sexual awareness. You don't get descriptions like that every day, and even when you question them you're inclined to consider them. Thing of it was, I knew a bit about Forgall's well-deserved reputation, the which suggests he was descended from eels. To protect myself, I proposed that I ought to meet this perfect girl first and at least let one of us go through the motions of courtship. 'Regrettably impossible,' I was informed. It seemed there was an army of suitors already suing for her body, making any delay in the matter out of the question. She was for me, you might say, unsuitable.

"They had put the onus on me to make the decision. Ibur continued to push, mentioning how his father wanted me above all the others out of deep respect for Munster's goddess, Anu, not to mention *my* reputation. I made some off-hand reply, and Ibur came back that the thought of our two lines linking up stirred his father greatly. 'Ah-ha,' I thought, 'so that's the game, is it, old Wily? Improve the line for your family?' Still, as I pondered it, I could see no harm in that kind of wish. Looking over Ibur, I found him to be reasonably intelligent and sound enough to hold his own in battle. Most likely his brothers shared these traits. Then I asked about dowries and such and Ibur related to me Emer's price of face and the anticipated amount of her *tinnscra*—a sizable dowry, that. Her relatives wanted to impress me. I asked what Forgall expected for a *coibche* from me, and Ibur named a price ridiculously small. Forgall was making it impossible to refuse, and still I could see no treachery in it. So I said yes. Ibur and I set a feast night and off he went.

"As soon as he was gone, I called in Druids and told them I needed a forecast on the marriage. Two groups of them went out and climbed the heights of the Paps of Anu. They made sacrifices atop the twin mounds. The answer was not long in coming, as very soon they came racing back to inform me that the reading of the entrails had foretold absolutely *nothing*. As if, one of them expressed to me, they'd sought the goddess with nonce words and she had ignored them like they were children. It was all too odd for words. I couldn't fathom it.

"Ibur returned on the appointed evening with a sizable wedding party. He and his two brothers formed a tight triangle around their sister, guarding her from sight until they had entered the feasthall in my fort. Such a beauty they protected. Rich sienna hair, and dark lustrous eyes. You can't tell what Emer is thinking. I knew upon meeting her gaze that marriage to her would be an endless string of surprises—not necessarily all pleasant ones, either. There was a good deal of anger smoldering under those enchanting lashes.

"I had rows of woven pads laid out for the guests to sit on. A cauldron of mead. Four kinds of meats. Loaves of bread. And a whole night's entertainment: *filid* singing new verses to treble Brigid, a dance performance of the Second Battle of Magh Turad, and much more."

"So you married the girl," said Ailell.

Lugaid grinned, a wide white smile. "You think so? Well, let's see.

"I had a large copper couch set at the head of the arrangement, and I wanted Emer to sit there with me, away from the rest of her family. I understand that, in Ulster, she's expected to remain with her father until the moment he's handed her *coibche*. My request defied the rule, but the last thing Forgall wanted was a commotion of any sort, so he gave the girl a severe look that said a great deal, then let her go. Her brothers tried to stick with her but she shoved her way through them and ordered them to stay away. She sat down beside me demurely, the picture of grace, with one foot tucked beneath her.

"I gave her my flashing smile that's won me more concubines across the isle than I can count. And what does she do? Does she flutter her eyes or flare her nostrils like a wild mare? No, she does not.

"Emer grabs hold of me by both cheeks and pulls our two faces close enough to kiss, then says, 'I am pledged to Cú Chulainn, whom I love and wait for. He has washed his hands from me, which no other man shall ever do. He would be here now except for my father's treachery that has taken him away. If you marry me, you'll *compound* that treachery.' By this point, her father's screaming blue fire to try and drown out her words. He clambers across the food pallets, squashing bread under his knees, splashing jugs of mead over everyone. He reaches up and grabs her by the hair and yanks her away before she can say more, then wrestles his way onto the couch beside me, still kicking his daughter away. Grips me by the shoulders, too— and I'll tell you, close up, Forgall Monach stinks like something a ram would disdain. He starts babbling then that I should forgive his daughter her ridiculous crush on the young warrior of Ulster. 'She saw him ride by *one* time,' says Forgall, 'and in her girlish way, gave her heart to him. Well, *he* doesn't even know she exists, how could he? He's off somewhere learning skills and improving his technique. Does that sound like a warrior lost in love? Of course not. You're a rational man, Lugaid,' he says. 'You understand the way women's fickle hearts skip like stones across the stream of comely warriors,' he says.

"I looked past him at Emer, struggling with her brothers, at the fierce look in her eyes when she glanced over at me. I knew then that old Wily was lying. What she had said explained what the seers had failed to find. Forgall, gripping my arm till it tingled, was waxing his casuistry, no doubt about it.

"So, what do I do? I look him in the eye, give him a wink and say, 'You're very likely right, Forgall. She's young and inexperienced in the ways of warriors, how our heads bob up at a sultry sidelong glance from a winsome vessel like her; never means nothing.' And he's nodding like a woodpecker at a tree bole by now. Oh yes indeed. 'There's just one small matter to clarify,' I add casual as you please, 'and then I'm sure we can get on with this.' I put my arm around him and draw him close, ignoring the stench. 'You see,' I tell him, 'I was fostered by the Ulidians, and that makes me a brother to

Cú Chulainn. Which, in turn, puts upon me the *geis* that I treat him in all things with good conscience. Now, if her story is tarradiddle—and I'm not doubting you for a moment when you say it is—then let's set to this feast so I can get off alone with my bride as soon as possible, right?' I give him a nudge and a wink. 'However, if there's truth in her claim to have traded vows with my foster brother—and it turns out you've deceived me into interfering with that—then in all fairness I have to tell you that when he returns from wherever you've sent him, both he and I are going to contest this union and we will without doubt resolve it by divvying up fundamental parts of your person.'"

The whole group of Ulstermen were laughing by this point. Duffach fell onto his back from the force of it and did not get up.

"I drew him closer, until my breath must have shot up his hairy nostrils. 'For instance,' I whispered to him, 'I should very much like your *head* for a wine goblet, seeing as how I can't drink too much of the stuff at once.'

"His face had lost all its color and a look of horror transfixed him. I leaned back then, crossed my legs and said, 'So, when do we marry, Emer and I—*father,* huh?' in a clarion voice that stopped the commotion around us. Everybody looked at old Wily. And he got up, polite as you please, moved his boys out of the way, took Emer by the hand, and walked right out of that hall without a backward glance or a farewell, with his babbling attendants and sons following him like a wake. And that's how Emer stayed single. She became known as the daughter Forgall Monach couldn't marry off, a reputation I feel personally responsible for—to my credit.

"The tale spread, I expect, to all the kings seeking wives, that the Wily One had tried to fob off a girl already betrothed by her own hand. And nobody would have her, not surprisingly. He was still trying to give her away when Cú Chulainn returned."

"And when did that occur?" asked Maeve.

"Oh, three or—"

"Hold!" demanded Ailell. "That would be the end of the tale coming before the middle."

"And you would hear of Scathach's teachings as I promised," added Fergus. "Those took place at the same time Lugaid was devastating Forgall's scheme."

Lugaid bowed lightly at the compliment paid him. He and

Fergus knew each other fairly well: Fergus had been king when Lugaid was first fostered into Ulster. Their familial ties ran close.

Maeve looked exasperated. "Very well," she said. "But I would rather not spend a week here listening to the inglorious deeds of your prize pup. Let us try to sum him up before the cock crows, shall we?"

"Naturally," replied Fergus. Behind him Duffach the Dark snorted in light sleep. Fergus looked down the line of warriors, the rest of whom were awake. He offered someone else the opportunity to take up the tale. They all deferred to him. Fergus took a sip from his mug. "I'll tell it straight, then," he said to the room in general, but he looked at Maeve as he spoke.

X.
THE FINAL SHAPING OF CÚ CHULAINN

1. Bridging the Gap

"The student camp of Scathach lay secluded in a grove of apples—the very grove that gives the Isle of Women its alternate name. The students lived there in a ring of thatched huts. Cú Chulainn and Laeg arrived in the grove at midday. The students all stopped what they were doing and came to see the remarkable chariot and its contents. Visitors to this camp were even more rare than in Domnall's grotto. Laeg and Cú Chulainn remained apart from the group until one of the students came forward. This was FerDiad.

"He was a bold youth, older than Cú Chulainn by a few years. His face was lean and handsome; already a light fuzz sparkled on his tanned cheeks, over his cleft chin. For the rest of him—his body remained hidden underneath a peculiar layer of horn. This is FerDiad's armor, but there's some contention as to whether it's a layer of protective clothing he always wears or the result of Scathach's magic that's transformed his skin into a polished, impregnable surface—like the body of a lobster, flexible but as hard as petrified wood. I've yet to meet him, for he lives at Irris Head on the sea. During their training, he and Cú Chulainn grew close. Some there are, say more than close."

"Oh? And what does Fergus say?" asked Maeve.

"I, madam, never say either way unless I know. And all I

177

know for fact is, they became friendly opponents in every combat exercise, constantly testing each other's strengths and searching for weaknesses."

"What did he mean: more than close?" Senchan asked Laeg.

"He meant they were lovers. And that is certainly true to a limited extent. Other circumstances shortly prevented its continuance."

"Lovers?" Senchan repeated, looking dismayed and ill-at-ease.

"Is there something wrong again?" asked Laeg. "Honestly."

Fergus mac Roich continued, "The other students soon gathered round Cú Chulainn. He asked where he could find Scathach and they took him out of the grove to the bridge that led to Scathach's house. The Pupil Bridge it was called.

"The bridge spanned a wide, deep ravine not far from the grove—spanned it at a point where the ravine carved a complete circle out of the earth. On the piece of land in the center, Scathach had built her house. To become her pupil, as the students explained to Cú Chulainn and Laeg, one had to find a way across the craggy ravine to the house. The only obvious path was the Pupil Bridge, a construction of ropes and slats of wood. FerDiad warned them—getting across that bridge was not so simple a task as it appeared. One had to use skill and cunning to get to Scathach's house. This proved to her satisfaction that the individual had learned enough to qualify for her training before coming here. What the secret of the bridge was, no one would tell. All the students had sworn to reveal nothing.

"Cú Chulainn saw no point in wasting time. If he was to become Scathach's pupil, as Domnall had advised, he had to perform this task. He and Laeg got back aboard the chariot and drove to the edge of the chasm. Cú Chulainn took his spear and jumped down. For a time he stood and listened to the wind, sniffed the breeze, and watched the bridge. Nothing seemed odd or out of place. He started across. Nothing happened. Expecting an attack at every step forward, he continued on. He came to the middle and turned back to Laeg with a befuddled shake of his head. At the other end, the bridge suddenly rippled, throwing out a great swelling that rolled swiftly at Cú Chulainn. The ropes creaked and wood cracked. He sprang forward to escape. Ahead, on the bank, Laeg hopped and gestured, shouting him on.

"He was fast but the bridge was faster. Its swell caught and tossed him off like a dog shakes water from its back. He smacked into the ground beside the chariot hard enough to leave a dent; but he rolled right over, leaning against a wheel hub, to see the ripple return to the opposite bank and the bridge become absolutely still again.

"Laeg cried out that the thing was alive. Cú Chulainn answered, 'Well, it's certainly willful.' He climbed to his feet and remained beside Laeg a while. 'Crossing this is going to take some thought,' he said finally, 'but these others have done it, so we know it can be done.' They tried to puzzle it out.

"While this was going on, Scathach was watching from inside her house. Her daughter squatted beside her between two piles of yarn, weaving on a loom. Scathach informed her that a new student had arrived; but Uathach, her daughter, merely shrugged and went on weaving. She didn't care much for the students, many of whom she had found to be brash and self-seeking.

"Scathach watched Cú Chulainn start across the bridge a second time. He walked with his feet wide apart, stepping on the ropes along both sides of the bridge, never touching the boards. She smiled ruefully at his ploy, closed her eyes slowly, and shook her head once.

"The bridge rose up again. In the midst of taking a step, Cú Chulainn tumbled to one side. The bridge snapped up and flipped him over the ropes. He vanished from sight.

"Scathach clucked her tongue sadly. Knowing the meaning of this sound, Uathach moved around to the other side of the long red blanket she was weaving, where she could see the empty bridge. Now she was sorry she hadn't taken a look at the student; she had assumed, you see, he would survive."

"Laeg, meantime, had gone quite wild. He ran about, calling for help, and finally dashed onto the bridge without any thought for his own safety. Leaning perilously over the ropes, he peered into the chasm but saw no sign of his friend's broken body. Then, right beneath him, the barbed tip of the Gai Bulga appeared. Laeg got down on his knees and craned out over the edge of the planks. There was Cú Chulainn, hanging from a guide rope that ran under the wood. He stared mutely at Laeg with great relief. Mute, as I said, because he carried the Gai Bulga in his clenched teeth. Laeg lay flat and hung his hands down to where Cú Chulainn could reach them. Removing one hand at a time from the rope, Cú Chulainn grabbed hold of his charioteer and climbed up him as if Laeg were a ladder. As they got to their feet, the bridge fluttered at the other end, warning against any attempt to go further. They went back to the chariot, defeated.

"Laeg sought a solution for his friend but could devise nothing against that spirited bridge. He shook his head sadly and confessed as much to Cú Chulainn. 'That thing is like water, like a stormy wave,' he said. Cú Chulainn's head went up at this, like a hound pricking its ears. Yes, he agreed wholeheartedly, it was *just* like water. He embraced Laeg, then took his spear and bounded out onto the bridge again. Uncomprehending, Laeg shouted new admonitions after him, but Cú Chulainn didn't listen now that he had his plan.

"The moment he reached the center of the bridge, it rolled up, snakelike, straight for him as he had expected. He crouched down, watching the boards rise up, one after the other, as the wave bore down on him. Then, at the last instant, he gave his Salmon Leap, soaring high above the bridge, which, like a frog at a fly, snapped up at him furiously—so hard that it wrenched loose its pegs from the inner wall of the ravine and slipped from sight.

"A great crash shook the whole grove so that fruit dropped from the trees. Dust in a huge cloud blossomed out of the crevasse. Cú Chulainn came down on Scathach's island in a somersault, then peered down at the undone bridge. 'You're no match for the likes of me!' he shouted down at it. He set off for Scathach's house.

"Both women had watched aghast as Cú Chulainn defeated the Pupil Bridge. Uathach had continued mechanically to weave while she watched. Scathach gave her a glance now and discovered, in the middle of the red blanket, two jagged rows of yellow yarn. She observed her daughter with growing amusement. 'I do believe this young man has bested *your* bridge, too,' she said. Uathach blinked, then looked awkwardly at her mother. The warmth of a blush came to her cheeks. Scathach invited her to go and meet this new student, to see what he was like. If she desired him as much as Scathach suspected, then they might find some time together before he began his training. Scathach would go off to Cat and Cuar, her two sons, to continue with their edification until the new recruit was ready.

"Cú Chulainn arrived at the house. An old woman came out to meet him. She had a hideous face that looked the very soul of evil. Her voice was like the screech of a flock of crows. She claimed to be a servant of Scathach's. He followed her inside. They passed Uathach's loom, and Cú Chulainn began to laugh when he saw the uneven yellow weave in it. 'Someone here has a jumbled sense of design,' he commented. The old woman grew angry at this and struck him. He grabbed her and she cried out as if in pain from his grip. The sound of running footsteps then echoed through the house, coming closer. Cú Chulainn shoved the crone away as an armed warrior charged into the room. The large warrior drew up, seeing him, and lovingly brought up his sword. Cú Chulainn backed against the loom; the rocks weighing down the gathered strands of wool clacked together. The warrior whipped the air with his blade, swung to take off a head. Cú Chulainn ducked the blade, grabbed up the weighted strands, and spun them over his head. He snapped them hard and the rocks broke free and flew at the warrior, who had the speed to dodge the first but was too close to escape them all. One broke his knee; another caught him above the eye, punching a dent in his skull that killed him.

"The gruesome old woman howled at Cú Chulainn, but he silenced her. He said, 'I've no sympathy with the way I've been treated here so far. What sort of servant are you?' He asked for food and drink. The old woman shuffled out of the room. Cú Chulainn dragged the warrior's body outside.

"In one corner of the room lay a soft pile of blankets from the loom. Feeling suddenly tired, he lay down on them to rest. He'd hardly dozed off when the old woman returned. Without opening his eyes, he identified each sound she made: the setting down of the tray, pouring of drink, rustling of her clothes as she brought it to him. This was what he pictured. But then the blankets moved, and Cú Chulainn opened one eye to find this woman lying beside him, her hideous face pressed close to his, her stale breath on him. He sat up and tried to push her away, but she showed remarkable strength and held him while she said, 'Destruction upon you if you refuse me. Ten times terrible things to ruin your future with Emer.'

"At the mention of Emer's name, he stopped struggling. He asked where a serving woman got the power to pronounce a *geis*. 'The gods of all the Druids will burst the heart of anyone who is not of magic blood,' he said. The old woman did not explain, but said, 'You killed my guard. There's no one to replace him save his slayer.' Cú Chulainn replied, 'If she sees it as fair, I'll take his place while I'm Scathach's student. But now I think I'll rest, alone.' He lay back, his eyes closed.

"'There's more to it than that,' she said. This vexed him. He cursed the old woman and sat up again . . . and there beside him was a beautiful naked girl. 'What sorcery is this, and which is the real you?' he asked.

"She told him, 'This is me as I am truly, Uathach, your teacher's daughter. I saw your feat that defeated the bridge and I think you're glorious. Now you've replaced him who guarded me, who was also my lover. I no longer need a disguise for you.' Her hands traveled the country of him. 'You've honor. I can show you how to get my mother's promise to teach you everything she knows. But you must give me what *I* want first.'

"He knew well what she wanted, which by now he wanted, too. And that's how Cú Chulainn came to be a member of Scathach's house. As you'll shortly see, this led to his meeting Aife.

"Uathach told him that her mother was out training her younger brothers and that Scathach rested nights in the boughs of a particular yew tree. She described to him precisely what he must do to secure all he wanted.

"He went that night to the yew tree and he could see the sleeping form of Scathach overhead. With his spear held close to his side, he did his leap into the tree. Up he somersaulted, hooking the hollows of his knees over a thick branch so that he swung upside down above Scathach. He put the tip of his spear between her breasts as Uathach had instructed. His voice a whisper, he said, 'Death hangs over you, woman.' Scathach opened one eye and observed the barbed spear nicking the valley between her breasts. She opened the other eye and looked up at her captor. 'That leap has served you well, twice now,' she commented. She asked what services he demanded of her. 'Full training,' he answered, 'plus a dowry for my Emer and a forecast of my future.' Scathach consented to all three things.

"Cú Chulainn continued to live with Uathach, serving as her guard and lover, but he spent most of his time with her mother. He learned to juggle nine apples at once; to balance on the rim of a spinning shield; to hammer the ground in a way to send thunder into the nearby hills; to leap over a slashing sword and kill the wielder without a weapon *and* before his feet touched the ground again; and, with Laeg, how to crouch and balance without support in a moving chariot, how to exchange places with the driver and still wield a spear. Other things, too, he learned. Often his training went in tandem with

FerDiad's. Laeg also practiced with FerDiad, but FerDiad preferred to fight alone and on foot. As I said, the three of them
became fast friends." He paused and drank again.

Senchan leaned against Laeg. "If she taught you, too, then
you had to have gotten across that bridge as well as Cú
Chulainn."

Laeg's eyes sparkled as if from intoxication. "Certainly."

"Well?"

For a moment he said nothing. His expression went from
that of exasperation to mild amusement. "I climbed down the
bridge while it was still hanging into the ravine. The contraption
served nicely as a ladder. Once down, I waded the stream, then
picked my way up the other side, which was not so formidable
as the outer cliff."

Senchan looked for all the world as if he had just lost his
dearest friend.

"Well, you're the one who had to know. Mind you, the
bridge was alive and kicking the whole time I was descending.
The thing was raging—it even twisted around at one point and
tried to slap me against the cliff face."

"It did?" Senchan asked with reviving adoration.

"I'd prefer to take on the whole of the Fir Bolg any day.
Yes, I know you don't know who the Fir Bolg are. Now, be
quiet and listen to Fergus."

". . . got into a conflict with another of her kind: Aife. Aife
is said to be a daughter of ancient Partholon, whose wife com-
mitted the first adultery in Eriu. That makes her as ancient as
Scathach. Their contention was over disputed territories. Cú
Chulainn and Laeg might easily have ended up *her* students
instead of Scathach's and history would have rolled out in a
much different shape. They might not have been involved in
this conflict at all.

"While Scathach and her sons prepared to battle Aife's forces,
Cú Chulainn came to his teacher and demanded the right to
join the fight. Scathach tried to persuade him he was only a
student and not part of it, but he had a ready answer to that—
namely, that he was her daughter's guard, not just any student.
This fact notwithstanding, Scathach preferred not to have him
along, perhaps *because* he was close to her daughter. Whatever
her motives, she put a sleeping draught in his drink to make
him sleep a whole day, by which time the combats between
her trio and Aife's appointed champions would be over. She
watched to be sure he drank it all. For a moment, she thought

the potion had not taken effect. Cú Chulainn continued to argue as fiercely as before. Then, quite abruptly, he toppled over. Scathach left him and harnessed her chariot.

"However, an hour later, as she stepped across the body, Cú Chulainn's hand suddenly reached out and clutched her ankle.

"'Let go!' she shouted.

"'Not until you let me go with you,' he replied, then twisted her off her feet.

"Uathach entered the room in time to hear this, and she cried out, 'No, don't let him have his way!'

"Cú Chulainn gave her a dark look. 'You've just ended all that lay between you and me. Find a new log to warm your bed,' he told her. Then he returned to his argument with Scathach, demanding the right to be her champion, which neither son could legitimately do, lacking enough skill. Scathach agreed grudgingly. After all, he had somehow overcome her potion; to deny him what he wanted at this point might have been a denial of the gods. Uathach fled the room."

2. Rope Tricks

"The tradition on the Isle of Women is the same as ours where warfare is concerned," Fergus explained. "They let single combats decide their victories. Aife counted Scathach's retinue and selected three of her own warriors to represent her. Theirs was the right to choose the form of combat, and they chose the Rope Feat. Aife's group led Scathach's to a wide clearing. Her three champions set about stringing a thick rope overhead, each end of which they tied around the bole of an oak. While they were thus engaged, Cú Chulainn went to Scathach and asked to be the first to represent her, as balance of this sort was the first skill Domnall had taught. Scathach accepted. Her own sons were able climbers but had learned few other of his feats.

"Aife's three champions now introduced themselves: Ciri, Biri, and Blaicne, the three sons of the witch, Eis Enchenn. They had her looks, to be sure. When they removed their helmets, they revealed three wicked faces, all feathered black, with the dead onyx eyes of birds. They replaced their helmets and asked to know who opposed them. Scathach's sons introduced themselves: Cat and Cuar. Cú Chulainn did the same. One of the bird brothers remarked derisively that he resented having to take on three boys instead of three men but would kill whomever Scathach chose. Once this decrial had been voiced, the three feathered fiends marched off across the clearing. At the other side, where the mysterious Aife waited, they stripped off their clothing save for the intricately worked helmets, climbed up the tree they had chosen for their terminal, and stepped out onto the rope.

"Cat and Cuar shimmied up their tree. Cú Chulainn jumped straight up, naked, and landed on the rope as if he did this sort of thing each day, which he probably did. Before the two sons of Scathach had reached the rope, he bounded forward, running on it as if it were a path. He did not yet unsheathe the sword his teacher had given him for this fight. The three champions walked lightly forward like one creature with six legs. Their weapons came up like hackles. The first of them, Ciri, crouched low and prepared to open Cú Chulainn's middle. His sharp bird's tongue flicked out of his bronze helmet. The shrillness of his cry made the oak leaves shiver.

"Both parties rushed quickly toward one another now. Their feet whipped along the rope. Ciri lunged to spit his target. His blade cut only air.

"In the instant of the bird-brother's thrust, Cú Chulainn sprang up off the rope. He spun upside down in an arc above the three, his sword drawn; the blade swung like a pendulum. It cut a straight thin slice through all three helmets. He landed on the rope behind them, his bounce flinging the bodies free. They flew in every direction."

Ailell laughed and clapped his hands. *"Very* nice," he said.

"Cú Chulainn jumped down. He observed the bodies, nudged them with his foot. 'Well,' he proclaimed, 'I won't take any heads here and that's for sure. I don't trust these birds.'

"Aife called out angrily from where she stood, demanding single combat with 'that clever boy,' as she called him. He agreed to it, then went back to his starting place on the rope. Scathach awaited him there. 'You've done a great thing here, but don't let it swell your head now,' she warned. 'Aife's worth a hundred of Ciri and his brothers. You jump over her and she'll spit you down your throat and out your arse.'

"'Then I need to know her weakness. Tell me what she values most in life.'

"That Scathach answered easily: Aife loved her chariot and all its trappings. Armed with this knowledge, Cú Chulainn took his place again on the rope. Aife hung back, unlike her students, while he danced to the middle of the rope and waited. His opponent came forward one step at a time, curling her toes tightly around the cord to keep from sliding. Up till now, Cú Chulainn had thought she wore a brown cloak, but he saw here that the cloak was hair, hanging to her knees. Her arms protruded from it. Her eyes were rose-red, her cheeks painted in woad-purple stripes. Where the hair occasionally parted, he could see her flesh beneath. Aife wore no armor, and the hardness of her musculature carved her features sharp and proud. She quite caught Cú Chulainn's eye.

"The moment they met, he pretended to perform his leap again. Aife jumped up, too; and, as Scathach had warned, if he had tried his trick again, she would have had him. But he went straight up instead, meeting her in the air. Their swords clashed once, the force of it tossing them apart. The rope dipped and vibrated like a harp string when they landed. Cú Chulainn crouched low to ride out the vibration, one leg straight out ahead of him, balancing on his heel. Aife had more experience on the rope. She flipped herself forward immediately, throwing the force of her somersault behind the blow she now struck. Cú Chulainn brought up his sword edge-on to block her and she sheared right through it, leaving it a useless stub.

"He flung it away. Then his face took on a look of surprise and he pointed excitedly past her. 'Look!' he cried, 'your driver's got so involved watching us, he's driven your chariot over the edge of the hill and toppled it!'

"Aife dared to look. In a split second, Cú Chulainn had leapt inside her sword range. He grabbed her wrist and pulled her off balance. To catch herself, she reached straight out and he tore the sword from her grasp, but also stopping her fall. He grabbed onto her hair and flipped himself like a wave right over her head. Now they were back to back. One sharp tug on her tan hair and Cú Chulainn had Aife teetering backwards. He dropped onto one knee and caught her over his shoulder, quickly rocking to keep his balance. Then he reached back and plunged both hands into her hair, grabbed onto her breasts, and hoisted her up on his back so she couldn't struggle. In this fashion he took her back to Scathach.

"Laeg met him where he jumped down, offered him the Gai Bulga. Cú Chulainn dropped Aife and took the spear. She rolled over only to have the tip of his spear prod between her breasts. Angrily, she charged, 'Your conduct is unfair.' He replied that he did not recall any establishment of terms between them. Nevertheless, he inquired after what she thought just. 'A life for a life,' was her answer.

"'To that I agree,' he said. 'I shouldn't want to harm so fine a teacher as yourself. But you must agree to my three terms first.' He removed the spear, let her sit up while he listed them. 'First, an end to your fight with Scathach and never attack her again. Next, you take me into your house and train me as Domnall and Scathach have done before you.'

"Aife complied with both of these terms. She asked what the third condition was. He replied, 'That you bear me a son, so that our blood may mingle and create an even greater warrior than the two of us combined.'

"She climbed to her feet—a full head taller than young Cú Chulainn. Beside her, Laeg was grinning. Aife studied the Hound's parts, his skill and bravery. 'Agreed,' she said.

"So, Cú Chulainn left the house of Scathach where his friend FerDiad stayed on to take his place. Aife gave him the last of his training on that misty isle, and he slept with her every night throughout."

"And did the woman bear a son for him?" asked Maeve.

"No one knows that, just as none, save possibly Laeg mac Riangabra, knows what secrets he may have learned from her. But he gave her a gold ring that had been his from Deichtire, with instructions to pass it on to their child when his training was complete and Aife sent him out to seek his fortune. And they agreed on a name: the boy was to be called Connla.

"Before leaving the isle, Cú Chulainn returned one last time to Scathach's house. She still owed him on two points of his contract with her. She anticipated him, too—she had the *imbas forasnai* of seers and Sidhe; after all, she's older than both. His dowry was there in a box. Scathach awaited him on her knees. He knelt before her, Uathach looking on fecklessly. Scathach gripped his shoulders. Her eyes rolled up and she began to chant to him:

> 'Salute the unvanquished,
> Though short his life from now till death.
> In that span, many foes will fade.

Red blood is spilled, red are wives' eyes.
Twisting, bending, your body swells.
Swells from fury, hot as Lugh's light.
But for the rest you'll fight alone
And pay a great toll in your person's flesh.

Be wary of ravens and predatory kites,
Beware of Maeve and Ailell's niggardly honor,
Win in water every day
And collect your heads by the star-blanket's light.
Show no mercy when Maeve's time comes,
Or else sacrifice your life on some other day.
Your future would kill ten different men
So keep Emer close and avoid Morrigan.'

"She slumped over against him, her wicked face etched with weariness, drained of color. Her thin lips were bluish, as if she'd got ague. Uathach told him softly that he must go. Cú Chulainn chose not to press his grudge against her. He wished her well, then went out, across the restrung Pupil Bridge, which did not so much as flutter underfoot. In the students' camp, he spent his last evening on the isle with Laeg and FerDiad.

"The following morning, he sent Laeg off ahead to the coast to have their chariot loaded aboard the *currach*. His farewell to FerDiad went unwitnessed. Cú Chulainn set off on foot, the Gai Bulga sheathed on his back. He followed the ravine that flowed beneath the Pupil Bridge. The ravine became a gorge, and Cú Chulainn's path wove the heights of cliffs. He smelled sea on the breeze, tasted salt on the air.

"At one point as he walked the tortuous path, an old woman approached from the opposite direction, hobbling along with the aid of a staff. She had just one eye beneath her brow, to the left of her nose. The eye was shiny black like a huge bead. The ledge there was extremely narrow—barely enough room for one person between the sheer rock face above and the straight drop below. Cú Chulainn offered to lead her back down the path to a wider point where they could cross; he was in no hurry now. The crone insisted he move aside and let her pass right there. She said, 'I don't care for you one whit and wouldn't follow anywhere.' He stifled his annoyance at the choleric hag as he went to the edge of the cliff and made room for her to pass by standing right at the brink of the precipice. His toes dug into the rock; his heels hung out into space. He

half-bowed mockingly and spread his arms wide as if in reverence of her, all the while shifting to maintain his balance.

"The old woman shuffled up the path. He looked up at her
from under his brow, watching as his own image grew within
her glossy black eye, smelling her breath as she neared—an
odor of turned earth and worms. That eye, he knew that eye
. . . In a flash he sprang off his toes just as the old woman
stamped her staff where his feet had been, and a chunk of cliff-
face exploded. Had he hesitated an instant, she would have
sent him plummeting to his death.

"She cried out shrilly in exasperation. Cú Chulainn landed
on the path where she had climbed. Her false face was gone
when she swung around to meet him. He saw her as she truly
was: a great beaked head of oily black feathers. Her pincer-
like mouth clacked in irritation. He knew her because her sons
had been so much like her. 'Eis Enchenn,' he said, 'I defeated
your sons fairly on their own rope.'

"She squawked and stalked toward him. 'Killed them, all
the same,' she screeched, then swung her staff with surprising
speed to knock him off the cliff. He flipped up and landed
agilely on the staff as it whipped beneath him. His added weight
drove the staff down, against a rock, where it split in two. Eis
Enchenn stumbled off-balance. She tottered on the verge of
the cliff. The Gai Bulga spun out of its sheath in Cú Chulainn's
hands. Its razor edge severed the witch's head as her feet slid
over the brink. Her spouting body dropped; the feathered head
rolled down the path, screeching 'Raaa!' like a kite, until the
path turned. The head rolled over the edge, its fierce cry trailing
away. Where her blood had spilled out, the rock face was eaten
away, smoking and hissing. Sections of the path broke free and
clattered into the chasm, but Cú Chulainn bounded over them
all.

"That was his final deed on the Isle of Women."

In the corner, Laeg nodded. "An accurate and reasonably
unembellished tale, if I may say so. That encounter with Eis
Enchenn continued to disturb him ever after, though. His dreams
were often haunted by that malicious black eye; he was forever
after paranoid of ravens, crows, kites. Which turned out to be
to his advantage, as you'll see, Senchan, once Murder's Daughters meet up with us again."

3. The Besting of Forgall's Host

"Someone else must take over the telling," complained Fergus. "I've exhausted my voice. Any more and I won't be able to call out my warriors this morning."

Beside him, Duffach the Dark rose up suddenly. Beneath his beetling brows, his blue eyes were hard and remarkably clear for a man who had passed out not long before from drinking. His thin mouth, though smiling slightly in insolence, was drawn into a scowl from the scar at the left corner of his lips. "I'll finish the tale for you," he announced, then looked around to deny any objection; there was none.

"Fine," he said. Then, peering into his mug as he swirled the dark brown sediment from the bottom, he began to speak in his murmurous voice. His audience leaned toward him without realizing it.

"Forgall Monach heard that Cú Chulainn had survived the ordeal of training. He knew his time had come. This was the foretold adversary. Nevertheless, he tried to defy the stroke of fate one final time.

"When Cú Chulainn reached the domain that Forgall ruled, he found Emer held captive from him by an endless array of guards. Forgall's domain is called Luglochta Logo—something no one else has bothered to tell you, by the way. Once he had arrived, Cú Chulainn spent a full year before he got close enough to Forgall's earthen ramparts to even *see* Emer. All he got then was a glimpse of her from Laeg's chariot during a lull in the fight."

"Fight?" asked Ailell.

"Indeed. Forgall had fitted the landscape with a forest of warriors. He promised his daughter to every one of the soldiers he hired—whoever brought him Cú Chulainn's head."

"That is a ploy with some merit," commented Maeve. She glanced thoughtfully at her own daughter, Finnabair, curled up asleep beside watchful Flidais.

"It would seem so," Duffach replied. "The fools believed

him. With Cú Chulainn dead, they thought the curse would be off Emer. I shouldn't have to tell you the outcome."

Maeve looked up from her abstraction. "But you do, dear Duffach, you must."

He bowed with impudent formality. "Of course. For the great spread-legged queen, anything." He drained the last of his drink while his audience expressed their individual responses to his comment, all of which he ignored as he continued. "Cú Chulainn whittled away Forgall's *whole force*. Row upon row of warriors. One at a time, in challenges. By the time he finally caught that glimpse of Emer on the ramparts, he had already begun to fulfill the terms of her riddles. Her guardians, who stood outside the fortress, who had the reputation of being as strong as a hundred men each—Cú Chulainn cut them down. Wheat to the sickle. Then's the time he looked up and saw her. She was the sun to him. His strength doubled just to see her.

"Emer's brothers charged out with their three troops. Remembering the riddle, Cú Chulainn took on each troop separately. They were on foot so he jumped out of the chariot and faced them on foot. Dust swirled and blood sprayed in all directions. Grass turned red that day. What happened in the center of that maelstrom, I don't know, but I'd guess he took on his wild aspect they call the Warp Spasm in Ulster. I've never seen in him the Warped One. I hope to the gods of my people that I never do, now we're on opposite sides. It served him well that day, I know. He slew every troop except for the brothers at the lead. He trussed them up and deposited them beside his chariot, what's called the Sickle Chariot—that also hasn't been mentioned before, but it's the chariot Domnall gave them.

"Now the fortress lay unguarded. Cú Chulainn sprang up, hurdling the ramparts. Forgall stood right below him, watching him sail overhead like a minor sun on its journey. The twisted visage of the Warped One may have terrified old Wily, or maybe the certainty of doom painted across his plain. We can't ask him to tell us because, whatever the cause of his panic, Forgall Monach cried out and careered blindly across the rampart. On earthen walls there are no rails, as you know, and he stepped off and fell into the yard. Again there are tales of this: that he died of a broken neck; others, with an eye to the original prophecy, claim he impaled himself on the Gai Bulga. Anyway, he died.

"Cú Chulainn captured Emer's foster sisters and planted them beside her brothers. He made all present swear allegiance to him, then released them. After that, he and Emer were husband and wife." Duffach raised his cup and drank till it was empty.

"And there the matter rests," said Ailell, clapping his hands. "It's a wonderful tale you've all shared. I thank you."

Fergus became dismayed. "It's not just *any* crock we've spilt here; these are stories—*true* stories—about the one man who will oppose our intentions to steal the Donn. One man like a whole army."

Ailell nodded. "Oh, I no longer doubt the reality of him. You've drawn him for me: I can see the little two-legged whirl-wind quite distinctly now. None of which alters one simple fact."

"Which is?" asked Cormac, also embittered by Ailell's flip-pant reaction.

"Which is," answered Maeve for her husband, "that your Hound has won his fame already by deeds that have filled the night and could, I do not doubt, fill another; that Cathbad's prediction will come true by my hand—Cú Chulainn will now go to his tomb a young man."

In the corner, Laeg chuckled. He climbed stiffly to his feet, then stretched. "She's rather headstrong, that Maeve. And somewhat premature in her assessment of how things stand."

Senchan got up and followed Laeg out the door of the tent. "You mean, he doesn't die a young man?"

"Ah, now, I didn't say that. But youth, you see, is a relative matter. Look at me—I'm past six hundred years old and I might be thirty. How old am I, then?" He inhaled the wet predawn air and observed the hint of rose in the sky. "But it's no good my telling you. All that is for you to see. Come, let's stretch our legs before the army awakens. Hungry?"

"No. No, not at all."

Laeg smiled. "Odd, isn't it?" He strolled past a string of tied horses. They rolled their eyes and shied away. A few nickered. "You can sense me, can't you?" Laeg said to the horses. "What grown wise men can't perceive, you animals know. It's what man traded in order to think for himself, that gift for touching upon the *other* world. Still, I wouldn't desire to be a grub."

"Laeg," said Senchan. "I've a question."

"Yes."

"Well, Emer was of Ulster, wasn't she? And she and Cú Chulainn were ... that is, they contracted a marriage, didn't they?"

"Not all marriages were contracts as such, lad. Not every man and woman started fresh every year. But, in answer to your question, yes. Conchovor himself threw the feast to celebrate their vow."

"But, then, didn't she have to sleep with him? With Conchovor, I mean?"

Laeg halted and looked at Senchan with admiration, then began to laugh. "Very, very perceptive. Indeed, that was so. And it had the poor bastard in a sweat, too. He'd already lost half his camp to the Black Army of Exile, and he didn't care to give up the rest to the destruction of the Warped One. But it was also the law, which he had enjoyed the fruits of till now. Can you guess what happened? No? Well, actually, as before, it was the two Druids, Morann and Cathbad, who resolved things. They made their announcement before the king spoke at the feast, that the king would sleep with Emer that night. All eyes turned to Cú Chulainn—you could feel peoples' souls backing away. But he just sat happily on his uncle's right, moon-faced, delighted and drunk."

"I can't believe it."

"Oh, well, you see, Conchovor would sleep with Emer, to maintain harmony with Macha. To maintain order and harmony with Cú Chulainn, Cathbad and Fergus the Messenger spent the night *between* the bride and the king. Fortunately, because of all the wives he'd entertained thus, Conchovor's bed was uncommonly broad."

They walked on some way in silence. Around them, in the mists of dawn, the army began to gather itself together for another day's trek. Naked warriors bent and stretched to get their blood flowing. Some hacked and spit. Others went into the stream at Ath Gabla and poured chill water over themselves, rubbed it across their goosepimpled flesh, hissing, cursing. Up and down the lines, colors blossomed like flowers as clothed warriors came out, gathered, prepared to depart. From woods nearby, men and women shouted and laughed, making rude jokes about the people of Ulster, jokes no self-respecting satirist would have repeated. Laeg frowned at some of these as he went along. To turn the boy's attention away from such talk, he asked, "How have you liked the tales thus far?"

"Glorious, Laeg. And this camp. I never imagined anything

like this." Senchan chewed his lip for a time, then said hesitantly, "I think I know why you brought me this far now."

"You should."

"I think so. You want to teach me a different way of life, of seeing things. Of thinking."

Laeg grinned widely. "That's *absolutely* right, Senchan. You've uncovered the plot, then."

"Yes," replied Senchan, more self-assured now.

They continued on up the hill after that, neither saying anything further. At last, unable to wait any longer, Laeg turned and blocked the way. "Well," he cried expectantly, "what is it I'm training you for? What are you going to be?"

Senchan drew himself up proudly, the vast army below him, and said, "I'm going to be a *warrior!*"

Part Two

XI.

STRIFE AMID DISHONOR

1. Vocational Guidance

"A warrior?" Laeg had gone stiff. His neck grew blotchy red. "A *warrior*?!"

Senchan tried to shrink away. He could not find voice to reply, to protest his good intentions.

"And who, if you'd be so kind to tell me, will you be doing battle with? Old Selden the Master of the Farting Cows? His scabby children? I seem to recall you foreswore that for fear of tackling the whole *tuath*."

Senchan would have addressed that point but he remembered the rationalization only as something he had thought, not spoken. Laeg had heard it? Impossible. Or was Laeg overhearing his thoughts right now? Senchan stared hard at his guide and thought with all his might: "Answer me if you can hear this."

Laeg's brows knitted. His expression became perplexed. Behind him, a wagon rolled past, up the hill. Finally, when Senchan was satisfied that Laeg could hear him, Laeg made an exasperated burr and turned away. He began shouting— apparently at a stand of trees on the hill. "A warrior! Are you pleased with yourselves now, you pop-eyed pixies? Does this turn of events delight you? What more proof do you need to know this world's had done with us? Leave it at that, can't we? We mean nothing to them now. Look at him. Look! Nothing!" He grabbed Senchan by the jaw. "You don't, do you? Not a clue. See? See him? All right, you feel some weighty debt to us for loosing those keepers upon the world. Well, I absolve you all of your guilt: it wasn't your fault. Me, I quit! Now for pity's sake send this poor bastard back home and let him get on with mucking up his life!"

The nearby stand of trees suddenly bowed toward them. A stiff breeze knocked Senchan back a step. Senchan heard a voice in the wind, a whispery, scratchy sort of voice—the sound of branches clacking and rubbing together.

"Ssh," said the trees. "Laeg, don't treat the c-c-center of your journey as if it were the destination. Don't utter threats-s-s. You'll return to us-s-s yet. . . ." The wind died.

Laeg doubled up and tipped over. Senchan ran to him. Laeg's thin face was paler than ever. He allowed himself to be hoisted up.

"We'd better listen to them, huh?" said Senchan. "Do we go with the army?"

Laeg nodded weakly. He said, "For now." After pausing to draw his breath, he added, "Soon the time comes when I enter the tale actively and you must become your own guide."

Senchan bit his lip to hide his fear. To be abandoned in the midst of these evil creatures . . . Laeg again seemed to hear his thoughts, snapping at him, "A minute ago you wanted to *join* them. Are you so sure you've picked a proper vocation? Such matters deny haste." Laeg suddenly moved off under his own steam, up the hill. "Come on now," he called, "we mustn't lose sight of the mercenaries." He broke into a run and Senchan, sprinting to catch him, lost his chance to decide if he wanted to follow.

2. The New Challenge

The combined armies of Connacht rolled ahead once more, but the last of them had not left Ath Gabla when those in the lead— the mercenary *fiana*—encountered a new obstacle in the ford near Ballymakenny. The small stream bed there had been filled by the bole of a huge oak tree lying on its side. Its naked roots dangled with clods of dirt and grass like the hair of the Badb.

Notches cut along it required Maeve's Druids be sent for again.

Dressed in their white robes, the Druids wedged through the muttering, anxious army, which eyed them warily and grumbled louder still. On finding the king and queen near the tree, one Druid informed them, "Your forces grow restless and irritable and, if you don't do something about these interruptions, they'll soon be cutting each other up."

Maeve told him to deal with his task and to let her deal with hers. The Druid went ahead a dozen steps, then sank up to his knees in the mushy ground; by redirecting the flow of the stream around itself, the tree had turned the banks to muck. Crying out, the Druid hiked up his robes and sank lower. One of the warriors, named Fraech mac Fidaig, caricatured the priest's panic while wading in but reached out and tugged the Druid free. The salvaged, dripping priest stomped up to Ailell. "If you want that tree deciphered, then you'd better find a chariot to bring it to me or me to it!"

Ailell patiently summoned a chariot—one belonging to his son, Orlam—for the Druid, who went and took Orlam's place on the open platform. The driver led the horses in a tight circle, then walked them backward; they took the chariot down the bank and into the muck, where it sank over its axle, near enough to the tree for the Druid to span the remaining distance and run his fingers over the letters. He called out to his group as he read: "No better route . . . can you find than here . . . no change of course . . . can avail you . . . I watch unseen, defying your continuance . . . till one of your two-wheeled team can jump the bole first time . . . Soon I think we will know one another."

The challenge floated back through the army, passed from one row to the next, until the last of them, still at Ath Gabla, had heard it. Dozens of chariots rumbled out from the body of the army, eager warriors ready to hurl themselves at the tree, while Orlam and his driver pushed their chariot out of the mud and out of the way, snapping the axle in the process.

Before long, Ailell controlled a line of carts stretching to the horizon. As he looked over the ready champions, he told Maeve, "I don't believe this will take long."

The queen did not argue with him but had ideas of her own. She called the warrior Fraech mac Fidaig out of the line and said to him, "I have a deed needs performing."

He held up his fist as was the way with his people. "I'm the one for it."

"My sentiments exactly. While I trust my husband's judgment that these brave men will have no trouble, still I would not care to miss the opportunity to hunt down this scourge, Cú Chulainn, while he dawdles. I want you to find him. Circle around our gathering and—" She broke off speaking as the first chariot in the line went rumbling past, picking up speed, the driver whipping his horses, the beasts wild-eyed. Dirt sprayed up behind the wheels; the chariot bounced over the lip and down the bank. The horses made their leap. Their forelegs sank into the muck but the force of their run threw their bodies further ahead in a sprawl that jerked the driver off his feet. The chariot tongue stabbed into the muck between the beasts, pulling their heads into it. They slid on their necks into the water. The chariot and driver flipped up over them and catapulted into the side of the huge tree. No one moved. The broken boards, rails, and one twisted wheel tottered back slowly with a plop into the mud. Most of the driver remained plastered to the tree.

With a plaintive glance skyward, Maeve turned back to Fraech. "Circle around us, as I said, wade the stream if necessary, but see if you can catch him off guard while he enjoys our display here, which I'm certain will continue long enough for you to slay him. Bring me his head and your reward will be uncountable riches and unspeakable pleasures."

Fraech flexed his hand to show her his strength. "This will solve all our problems."

Maeve returned to Ailell's side. The debris of the first chariot had been removed. "This won't take long at all," she said.

"Next!" cried Ailell.

3. In the Stream

The crash of chariot against immovable tree echoed through the hills to Fraech. He glanced back into the distance but the army could not be seen from this ridge. Fraech had counted fifteen such crashes so far. Maeve had been right—they would never surmount that tree; but, of course, that had been the intention of this warrior Cú Chulainn, whom Fraech had ex-

pected to encounter long before now. Apparently, the Hound
had no interest in seeing his trap do its work.

Fraech crept along toward the stream. It lay beneath him,
the banks describing promontories. Here the stream was a river,
full of depth and current.

A voice carried to him from beyond the bank, somebody
singing. Fraech dropped flat. The singer spluttered and splashed
in the water. Up on his knees, Fraech drew his sword and then
loped ahead in a crouch. The river below came into view a
little at a time, and he stopped the moment he could see the
bather.

The man below was not large. He appeared to be well-
muscled, and his hair was black. This had to be the one Fraech
sought: all other *fir Ulaid* would be helpless from the Pangs
of Macha for days to come.

Fraech took a minute to sort out a plan. Then he edged
further upstream. Not far from there, the river curved. Past the
bend, Fraech stripped off his clothing and, leaving behind his
sword, slid down the bank and entered the water. It was so
cold that he whimpered in spite of himself when the water
reached his hips. He forced himself deeper, over his head.
Then, stretched out like a log, muscles taut, he let the current
take him. As he rounded the bend, he changed his position and
floated silently on. The bather continued to splash about carelessly. Fraech tensed as he neared, took a deep breath, and
dove down out of sight.

The bottom was more solid than he would have thought. It
allowed him to kick off upward with force enough to pound
Cú Chulainn's back and toss him up out of the water. The
Hound splashed back down; Fraech grappled for his throat from
behind. He caught it with both hands and shoved the Ulsterman
under him. His thumbs jabbed to crush the larynx. Beneath
him, Cú Chulainn sank like a stone and Fraech had to follow.

In the utter darkness of the river depths, something like a
cincture gripped Fraech by the ribs. For an instant he envisioned
some monster that had awakened at the sound of combat. Then,
whatever it was sent him shooting up to the surface, water
tearing at his eyes. He burst from the depths, tumbled into the
air, rising as high as the bank where he had hidden. Then he
dropped. He cried out and water jetted into his mouth as he
hit. He knew he would drown. Something caught his hair. It
suddenly pulled his head up. He choked and sucked in what
air he could get. A gentle voice near his ear said, "Let me

spare you, brave wrestler. You're defeated now."

"That's not . . . allowed me. I'd be shamed before Maeve."

"Honor's a hard thing when you aren't winning. I must accept your choice."

Fraech drew one last deep breath and twisted to break free as his head was shoved into darkness again.

Thirty chariots lay in a heap beside the stream. Nearly as many drivers lay there, too—most of them in pieces. Maeve had stopped bothering to watch. She sat in one of her tents, holding her dog and waiting impatiently for Fraech's return, which would end the need for this bathetic redundancy. How many chariots would they lose by then? She hardly dared imagine.

Ailell entered the tent. "It's not going to work, this jump," he said.

Maeve stroked her dog. "And it only took *thirty* failures for you to recognize it. Men are so quick to grasp a situation."

"Fergus mac Roich has agreed finally to put an end to it."

"He has? How?"

"He wouldn't say but rode off somewhere. We're waiting on his return now."

The queen cocked her head. "I wonder. . . . There are times I distrust him utterly and times . . . He does not take prodding well."

"You care little for his wife, I think."

"Flidais? I never even consider her. She knew of my arrangements many years before she married him. In fact, I should expect her presence is a boon to us. After all, she is a Connacht woman. But if your comment means to imply that I should reinforce the bond with Fergus, perhaps I can find some time along this road."

Before Ailell could reply, the crowd outside the tent began to shout. "Fraech!" they cried. "It's Fraech—look!"

Maeve hurried past Ailell, shoving her little dog into his hands. The crowd had gathered at the stream bank. *Now*, thought Maeve, *I'll be rid of this gadfly Hound and on to my reward.* She pushed through the throng. They parted to let her pass.

In the water, his head resting up against the tree bole as if listening to the roots, Fraech mac Fidaig lay. His arms rolled with the light current. His mouth was dark with the water brought up from his lungs.

Defeated, Maeve lunged away as members of Fraech's *tuath*

arrived to retrieve him. The nine of them waded in and dragged him to shore, then hoisted him up and bore him off past the queen, who stood by disjointedly, her mind adrift in speculation on the nature of the Hound of Culann. Her displeasure contained a kernel of arousal, a sensuous curiosity about what that man might perform within the fur. She could not repress her nature in this regard even though she wished him dead on the spot.

The nine bearers carried Fraech toward their bivouac, far down the line. They had not covered half the distance when they were stopped by a bright red light that burst upon them. It colored every tree, every blade of grass, like a sunset. The light spilled from a hillside and, momentarily, a cluster of figures emerged out of it: nine women dressed in green tunics. Behind the bearers, the whole army had stopped to watch.

The women wore torcs on their brows, sparkling gold around their red hair. They looked as much alike as sisters. The light, like a ramp, held them up. They came to the body of Fraech and took it gently from his people without a word or a glance. Then they lifted him high and bore him back with measured steps up into the ruby light. Once the women had passed through it, the light faded like a rainbow, retreating into the hill. Brown, then green, returned to the earth, color to tunics, sheen to metal. Those faces that had dared look into the light were flushed as from a slight sunburn.

"What time is it?" someone queried.

"About midday," came the reply.

"I thought so. The veil between the two worlds is thin today. I take it to be midday at the third of Macha's *noinden*."

"And that's a *sid*. We don't want to be here come nightfall."

"Well, someone had better jump that tree or we will be." Murmurs of worried agreement passed along the line.

As if in answer to the request for delivery, Fergus mac Roich returned, on foot and leading his team of horses by their bridles. He could not have stood in the car behind them; it was filled with rocks and dirt. This seemed far more strange to the warriors than what they had just seen and they followed as if on a string. Near the bank, he turned his horses around and, as Orlam's charioteer had done, walked them backward until the end of his car lay right above the wreckage and gore of the muck.

Cormac and others from the Ulster camp came up and began to help him as he unloaded first the stones, which they piled up into a short platform out over the muck, and then the dirt, scooped out and patted down using boards from the wrecks around them, which, last of all, they laid down over the dirt. Fergus walked up the boards when they had finished. He jumped up and down to test the firmness of his ramp. Satisfied, he got into the chariot and drove his team back to where Maeve had her tent. Other chariots in the line moved out of his way. He continued back as far as the *sid* before turning. Then he waited for the moment when everything was right.

With a snap of the reins and a bellow at his horses, Fergus rode the chariot forward. It lurched and bounced over the ruts dug by his forerunners. As he steered, he leaned over the rail to line up his wheel.

The two steeds pounded up the short ramp. Boards cracked, splinters of wood spat into the water. The chariot caromed off the first shattered boards as the horses made their leap. They cleared the tree by scant inches. Fergus and the chariot bobbed up high behind them. The wheels skidded across the bark with a shriek. The car bounced up, then vanished from sight. The crash that followed shook the ground all the way down the line. A great cloud of debris burst up above the tree. The army stood stock still. They did not know whether to wade the stream and see what was left or to just send the next chariot out.

Two hands reached up from behind the tree, and Fergus mac Roich pulled himself up on top of it and stood there, coated with muck, his hands on his hips. "Well," he shouted at them, "if everyone's satisfied that we've honored the challenge, I suggest we move on!"

The whole army burst into cheering as one massive body with thousands of mouths. Maeve smiled at Ailell and said, "Sometimes I trust him."

Within the hour, the tree had been roped and dragged out of the way by two dozen drivers. This created a dam across the stream for a short while. The warriors kicked down Fergus's ramp into a roadway across the muck. They plunged ahead hurriedly, but they gave the *sid* a wide berth.

Maeve took her little dog and cradled him in her arms as she climbed aboard her chariot. Ailell reached up to squeeze her hand. In that moment the head of her dog burst apart, splattering them both with its brains. Maeve flung the dog down and whined deep in her throat. Ailell bounded over the rail to shield her with his body. He scanned the terrain until he spotted a lone white figure atop the *sid*. The figure raised one arm as if in greeting, then leaped out of sight behind the mound.

"He tried to kill me," Maeve said in a shaky voice.

Ailell bent down and picked up the bloody stone that had killed her dog. "No," he said, "he did what he intended, I think. From where he stood, such prodigious aim could have slain us both."

Color returned to Maeve's cheeks like heat to embers. "That hero has cost me more than I am willing to spend. Now he throws death in my face. I have done with honoring his delaying jests, do you hear? Send out as many as we can spare into those hills. If they have to level the land, I want his head hanging from my bridle. I want that above all else. Cú Chulainn and the Donn—both those bulls are mine!"

Ailell saw that their calculated foray into Ulster had become tangled and dangerous, but this was not the time to argue. He wished to protect his wife from harm. He would slaughter the manhood of the entire province while they lay helpless if anything happened to his Maeve. He jumped down and called for warriors. Those nearest turned from crossing and came to him. His son, Orlam, would have gone, too, but Orlam's driver was still sifting through the debris of the jump in search of an axle. Orlam raged over this inconvenience, accusing his charioteer of disgracing him. Helplessly, he watched nine other warriors charge out naked on foot to scour the hills to the north. Ailell came up to Orlam and gripped his shoulder. "There'll be other battles, other feats for you. Don't be petty in your treatment of your driver. And don't pout, boy—there's no skill in that." Ailell left him then and went ahead with the army.

4. Cú Chulainn Amends a Rule

So busy was the charioteer wrestling free an axle shaft that he neither heard anyone approach nor sensed a presence nearby until a shadow fell across him. As he assumed this to be Orlam, he glanced around without rising, preferring to appear too involved with his muddy work to get up, thereby avoiding more insults or a beating from Ailell's hot-headed son. But the silhouette behind him did not belong to Orlam. This figure, with the sun cutting like a crown around its head, stood a full head shorter than even the charioteer himself and wore a robe with a hood. The man squinted and shielded his eyes from the glare. He gasped, let go the axle, and pressed back against the rubble. The figure must be headless! At each proposed eye socket, the depths of the cowl were pierced through by cylinders of sunlight.

The figure spoke gently, a soft amiable voice. "What is it you're doing here, man?"

The charioteer stammered, "Trying to replace the shaft for my chariot that broke in this bog."

The stranger placed his hand on the upright axle the charioteer had been prying at. "This one?" he asked.

"Yes. But it's—it's stuck, wedged by that wheel." His voice failed him as the stranger set down an odd, barbed spear, took the axle below the spokes of its top wheel, and tore it loose from its couplings and collars and the wheel that had wedged it, which lodged in the mud below. From the remaining wheel, the stranger pried off the cap. He spun the wheel free and flung it casually over his shoulder. The wheel sailed over the top of the north ridge and out of sight. After inspecting the shaft for damage, the hooded stranger leaned it to where the driver could brace it up against himself.

The driver began to drag the axle up the bank. He glanced nervously at the figure as he went, and saw it now merely as someone in a long white cloak. The sunbeams—surely they had been a trick of the light. "This isn't your normal line work, is it?" he said.

The stranger shrugged in reply. "Whose driver are you?"

"Orlam's. Son of Ailell, King of Connacht. Who are you, arriving so late?"

"Cú Chulainn," came the soft reply.

The driver dropped the shaft and clutched his throat. "Ah, I'm dead," he wailed.

"Nonsense. I've no quarrel with charioteers. It's a rule of mine not to fight them. My own will join me soon enough— if he can untwine himself from the thighs of the *cumal* he's in love with. Where is your partner now?"

"Partner?" asked the driver; he had never regarded his relationship with the overbearing Orlam in those terms. "He's sitting on the other side of that tree you laid down."

"I must visit with him. You stay here now." He stepped over the axle where it had fallen. The charioteer saw the tip of his profile passing, then his back with a sun-spiral woven in gold thread between the shoulders.

Cú Chulainn bounded up from the debris to the tree bole. The driver thought he rode the air like a bird, and he watched as Cú Chulainn leaned over the tree and dropped from sight. Utter silence followed. The driver shifted his stance and slapped at a bee on his arm.

The cloaked figure sailed up into view onto the tree once more, jumping from there over the driver, landing behind him on the makeshift road. "Turn around now, face the tree," he ordered the charioteer, who readily obeyed. "Lower your head a little, like you're bowing to the king." Trembling, the driver complied. Something wet and warm was placed on the back of his neck. "Now," the gentle voice continued, "you must go all the way to where the army is with that prize upon your shoulders. But don't tarry, I warn you, before you reach the camp. I'll be watching."

The charioteer nodded, the weight shifted, and Cú Chulainn warned, "Ah, ah! Careful with your prize. Off you go. By the time you come back I'll have your cart repaired for you. Mind the stream."

Low to the ground, the charioteer edged off. Blood began to drip from his neck. He could guess what it was he carried and knew better than to stop. His back soon began to ache.

The army signaled his approach to the king and queen once his identity had been discerned. He had not reached the army when those two stopped him but obedience to them required him to linger. Ailell's face drained of blood and Maeve's eyes narrowed. The charioteer leaned further to let the weight fall forward. The severed head of Orlam spilled to the ground beside him. He stretched up, flexing his shoulders. Quickly, he explained how the hooded creature had come upon him, what they had said to each other, and what amazing things the Hound had done. He scooped up Orlam's head, relating how Cú Chulainn had ordered him not to stop before reaching the body of the army. Before he had replaced Orlam's head, a slingstone cracked open his own head and flung him to the ground between the two monarchs. They jumped apart. Maeve shielded her face.

A white-cloaked figure vanished into the woods to the southwest. "It would seem," Ailell said, "that he's amended his rule regarding charioteers."

"You find this amusing? We have lost a close fosterling."

Ailell did not answer. He called out to the nearest warriors and sent them off to the woods. Fists hammering their shields, bellows and screams of ferocity echoing after them, the men and women sprinted for the trees.

They did not catch him for all their zealous effort, but they did manage to drive him into a trap.

5. More Than You Can Chew

Ailell's nine warriors had scoured the hills around Ballymakenny all afternoon to no avail. They had returned to the ford where the chariots lay in piles and, finding Orlam's chariot rebuilt but unattended, they had searched the area until one of them came upon his headless corpse. Cú Chulainn's trail from there was easy to follow and they charged off again, two of them in the borrowed chariot. The trail led them through a glen from which they could smell the campfires of the army. They wove in and out of the trees and finally lost all trace of the Hound at a ford there. This final vanishing act dashed their hopes and they dropped down on the banks. They had not rested five minutes when the sound of many roaring voices brought them to their feet. "What is it? What's going on?" they asked one another. One of the nine, named Lon, splashed through the stream and climbed up the high bank on the other side. He saw through the trees a single white-cloaked figure racing across the landscape. He could not believe the speed with which the figure ran, and he understood with a weary admiration why they had never caught sight of the Hound before this. Far behind this figure, Lon saw warriors in vain pursuit. "It's Cú Chulainn," he told his comrades, "and he's coming this way!"

The others jumped up. "Get rid of that chariot. Drive it off. Hide yourselves." Lon hissed, "Up here!" and waved them across. The swift padding of feet could soon be heard, growing louder every second. Then the pace slowed and the sound of a splash occurred below them.

The nine jumped out as one, dropping down into the stream. The figure in white had a bare moment to look up. Lon glimpsed the face beneath the cowl and he thought, "This is just a boy." Then the weight of all nine men fell upon Cú Chulainn and buried him in the streambed. They lay, all nine of them, shifting around to catch their breaths and to keep all parts of their prey under the surface. They would have gouged and chopped him but their own pressing weight kept their weapons trapped, unusable. Minutes passed, the cacophony of the pursuing warriors increased. Then the water began to boil.

Those nearest the bottom of the pile cried out. They felt the body beneath them wriggling, shifting, changing shape. Panic seized them and they wrestled to get free. A massive, gnarled hand shot out where no hand should have been. It waved about with reptilian grace. Suddenly it clutched one of them by the face and lifted him from the pile till he stood on his head. The hand flung him across the stream where he smashed against the bank. Lon tried to slash the hand with his dagger. The point stuck in the palm, the twisted fingers caught the blade and snapped it in two. Lon tumbled back into the stream. The whole mass of warriors began to rise as if a mystical isle were ascending beneath them. Another man spun from the pile and crashed into the bank beside the first, then two more skimmed the stream, dead. Lon bobbed up to see the emergence of the monster. The sight froze the blood in his veins. The water hissed and bubbled all around it. He might have fled if he could have thought to move. The hideous thing of knots crushed the last man clinging to it, then reached out for Lon.

Beating at their dented shields, shouting their hoarse threats, the trailing warriors pounded Cú Chulainn's path, emerging beside the stream in time to see something enormous dive beneath the surface, which began bubbling fiercely. Behind, it had left nine bodies implanted in the opposite bank. The warriors eyed one another: no one of them would cross the stream. Soon the bubbling stopped. The threads of steam on the glassy surface faded. The warriors walked along the bank, their weapons raised, but nothing presented itself. Finally, as night set in, they trudged back to their camp to inform the king that his group of nine had been destroyed by that most horrible of water-beasts, the half-fish, half-dragon thing called the *wurrum*. As for Cú Chulainn, maybe the *wurrum* had gotten him, too.

Upon hearing this supposition, a jester from Ailell's retinue jumped up. The thought that the Hound might have perished inspired him and, beside the central bonfire of Ailell's troops, the jester invented his dance and song. "I know no man, no boaster, who killed what vexes while those who vex and swear to kill sat by and hoisted their boasting. If I were a warrior instead of me, no boast, I'd have taken his head before the beastie did. But that's how it always goes: the *wurrums* feast last of all, nibble, nibble."

Though his words nettled some, most of the men and women slapped their legs and laughed. The jester capered and bowed to each, then suddenly in mid-leap spun forward and fell on his face in someone's lap. Still believing this part of his act, the warriors to each side shoved him back on his feet. Their gaiety died in their throats as they saw the blood spilling out from around a stone embedded above his ear.

Ailell knelt beside the jester. "By the god of our people, is there any doubt left he's still out there? His toll today is twelve. I wonder how many of them mocked him. There was no *wurrum!* Now, douse the fires, quick—there are plenty more stones in the fields below."

"I don't understand this at all," said Senchan.

"You don't? What could be more obvious? Their conduct has been remarkably derisive. If they treated him with due respect, they'd offer a single combat between him and their champion. That is the proper conduct in these situations—divination by battle. They ought to expect no better than his random assaults. Ailell is barely beginning to appreciate this."

From where they stood, below the ridge of encampment, they watched the fires flicker out, heard the faint hissing, and saw the golden figures bleed into the dark sky.

Off to their left a figure in white jumped up where, to Senchan's eye, no one had been. The figure ran to a pile of small rocks and dropped down there. "What's he doing now?"

"Waiting," Laeg replied, "for the army to settle in. That way they won't know of his successes before dawn."

"Successes? What can he do? The fires are out."

"The fires, yes. But, lad, they can't put out the stars. Look again at the line of the ridge, select yourself a cluster of stars and stare at it for a while."

Senchan obeyed, choosing a grouping of four large stars. He refused to blink even though his eyes began to ache with the strain and tears flooded them. His effort was rewarded finally: one by one, each star disappeared, only to reappear momentarily as the one beside it vanished. He rubbed his eyes and stared again. "The warriors," he exclaimed, "when they stand or move about, their bodies block the starlight."

"Just so."

"And in the morning . . ."

"In the morning many will have expired, by first appearances from a mysterious malady, but soon enough identified as the work of the Hound—a stone for a trademark. Not so soon, however, to quell the superstitious tales from starting about Morrigu's nocturnal slaughters. In truth, the three sisters have quite a different plan for confounding Maeve and Ailell."

"Which is where we're off to next."

Laeg ruffled his hair. "Bright lad," he said. The two of them faded away, leaving Cú Chulainn to his long night's work.

6. The Raven and the Bull

In the part of Cuailnge called Temair—the area where Daire mac Fiachna resided—the great bull called the Donn stood placidly chewing long grass from around the base of a slender standing stone. Now and then the bull would raise his massive head and scan the open, sloping field to Daire mac Fiachna's house. He would wonder vaguely why no one had come to tend him these past three days . . . ever since that runner had arrived. The Donn remembered the runner well enough, linked as he had been to a chill of prescience. The Donn could not carry the connection further than that because no deeper intelligence lingered in the beast.

He had seen women emerge from the house time and again, to gather water and then return. They would no more have set foot in the bull's field than he would have let them live had they tried. Tainted through his incarnations by furious stupidity, the Donn embodied the most hateful bigotry and prejudice.

Something—a fluttering sound—drew his attention away from the house of his keeper. He looked around but saw nothing. He sniffed but smelled nothing. The shadow of the standing stone stretched bulbously in front of him. The fluttering came again and something at the tip of the shadow unfurled.

Above, perched on the top of the stone, an enormous raven sat. Even the dim-witted bull could tell that this bird was not of the normal breed. Its wings stretched out easily as long as a fence post. Its beady eyes were full of blood. Seeing them, the Donn became agitated, recalling that somewhere beyond the visible landscape lurked an old enemy that color. He pawed the ground, at first digging a trench around the stone, finally knocking it askew.

The bird flapped, then began to speak in the language of the bull. The Donn hesitated in amazement and listened to the chant.

> "*Wise you are to be restless so,*
> *When time draws near that you should go.*
> *For coming this day across your land*
> *Is the plague called Cruachan and her* fiana *bands.*
> *This raven speaks the truth to you*
> *In telling that death is all they'll do.*
> *Death of man, of horse and stream,*
> *Death of the Donn lies within their scheme.*
> *Escape the snare before it's sprung*
> *And follow me to Slieve Cuilliun.*
> *No time to dawdle, nor women to mock,*
> *Else the Donn never slaughters Finnbennach.*"

The raven flapped its wings again, breaking the trance it had woven. The bull had bellowed then, his voice resounding from the hills. His herd came running, always obedient, and followed as he lowered his head to charge the low stone wall that hemmed the field.

Stone flew through the sky, crushed to gravel from the impact. Women ran from the house in time to see the Donn escape over the hill with all his cows. The women could do nothing to bring him back; but even if they had thought of a way, they would not have interfered, because they also saw the giant black bird that perched on the bull's horns. Daire's *ben urnadna* muttered, "Morrigan," and the others nodded to themselves and whispered for protection to various gods. Back inside, Daire mac Fiachna whimpered in pain. The women drew back into the safety of the house.

7. Maeve's Shield

All that day the army pushed hard and watched the endless hills for any sign of Cú Chulainn. Shouts of "There he is!" burst sporadically from over-eager or tired and red-eyed warriors. The thing spied would suffer attack, and the blind ferocity of some led them to strike at the object before realizing it was a sheep or a pale standing stone.

The army proceeded to the place called Es Ruaid, where the mouths of three rivers formed a wide waterfall. Behind the fall lived magical beings known as the Harpers of Cain Bile, who were older than the most ancient invaders of the isle—than the lost warriors of the woman Cessair—but who might easily have been children by appearance. The Harpers had learned their art from a nameless race much older than themselves and had offered it first to the tribe of Nemed when that people sailed onto the beaches a millennium before. No mortal had ever sung as sweetly or played with as much grace as the Harpers of Cain Bile, and whenever someone came near their cataract, they emerged from the water, their skin as pale as the moon, their eyes like the blue flowers of bugloss; with their silver harps, they would play music to banish all cares.

The clamorous approach of the Connacht force brought the Harpers out to soothe with their art. They rose up out of the water and floated through the wood. Their leader went out ahead. When he finally saw the army, he raised his harp to play, but before he could strum a single note, members of that massive force cried out, "There he is!" and broke formation to charge, howling, at the harper. Spears shot up, forcing him to dodge back into the trees. He called to the others to flee for their lives. The leader and most of those nearest at hand made it safely back beneath their waterfall. Others, cut off from that retreat, changed into deer and escaped in that way by out-distancing their pursuers.

Much later, after all the luminous musicians had returned beneath the cataract, the Harpers exclaimed that these new invaders were insane and apparently opposed to the idea of music. This saddened the Harpers greatly, but they reasoned that the ways of men had become too perilous and incomprehensible to penetrate. They resolved not to go out and play for the like of such barbarians again. And they never have, though the waterfall of Es Ruaid remains.

"Late that same day the army entered Cuailnge. They crossed the wide strand of Ath Lethan directly, having reached it while the tide was out. The high cliffs seemed to forbid them entry, which served merely to churn their pugnacity so that they began hacking away at the ground on the way up from the shoals, and they chanted their discordant war chants, rhythmic petitions to numerous tribal gods, gods who would have clashed under other circumstances but who now, in belief, would be allied in a thirst for our blood. The warriors began to kill everything in sight, slaughtering innocent beasts and fowl, leveling copses, all the time challenging Cú Chulainn, becoming petulant when he did not answer the invitation."

"Where was he all this time?" asked Senchan.

"Here on the heights of Slieve Cuinciu with me and his wife. He raved all day at the treacheries performed by and for Maeve and Ailell, but mostly at Maeve. In his mind, she bore responsibility for everything that had happened. He swore to me that he would kill her if he ever got a clear shot. That became his obsession finally, to kill Maeve. Emer tried to talk him out of it. She warned him that a woman's heart could retain the yearning for vengeance an eternity, the way a lake can hold onto warmth long after the sun has set. Poor Emer."

Laeg went up to the hut where she now pleaded with her husband. Senchan came up beside him to peer in. He still found it hard to believe that this man who sat there holding his wife's hands and shaking his head in gentle refusal was the same one who had embedded nine men in a hillside. What kind of being was a hero? How much god and how much man? And, because of the godness of him, how much of humanity did he lack?

"Emer," said Laeg, "knew the futility of reasoning with Cú Chulainn, but she had the precognitive intelligence to sense that their future would be tainted by this conflict. She worked her argument every way to warn him that making an enemy of Maeve would prove both futile and jeopardous; but, well, men often fail to listen to what they themselves haven't thought of, their hate blinkering their reason. Especially warriors do this.

"Maeve had traits similar to Emer's—more incisive, too. She could feel Cú Chulainn's threat, almost as if she could hear him all that distance away. That day she selected a brace of tall warriors from the various *fiana* and had them encircle her, with their shields kept up before them to create a solid, impenetrable wall around her. She never left her tent after that without first assembling these men, and to speak with her anywhere in the open, Ailell had to pry his way through them. At first, he worried at her delusion. Maeve insisted, 'The White Hound wants my head and, each time he kills someone else, he grows more eager to have it.'

"Finally, after being pressed to see Emer's wisdom too long, Cú Chulainn stormed away from Slieve Cuinciu to the invaders' camp. That they had penetrated so deeply into Ulster riled him further. He called himself belittling names to goad himself into the Warp Spasm, but it wouldn't come. He paced and circled the encampment for hours, stomped the ground, seeking one sight, one clear shot at Maeve. He failed to see her at all. He had marked her tent but no one came from it.

"Then, at last, the tent opened and the woman came out alone, barefoot, and carrying a cup of wine. Her torc gleamed in her white hair. Cú Chulainn spun his sling and snapped a stone. It shot through the camp so hard that the blast of its passing bowled warriors aside. The stone sailed true and the queen was dead by the third step she took. Cú Chulainn jumped in glee, astonished at the simplicity of it. At that moment, the tent parted again and a group of shielded warriors emerged. They marched in a circular formation directly over the fallen woman, but not with the urgency that should have compelled them. Something moved in their midst. Abruptly, they turned around and chugged back into the tent. Two servants came over and picked up the body, which Cú Chulainn now saw was naked and was not that of Maeve at all. The servants dragged her off toward Ailell's tent.

"He had slain a *cumal* dressed in Maeve's clothing, carrying the queen's cup, her hair powdered white. He understood now that the real Maeve had been inside that ring of shields and that his haste in acting had probably cost him any further opportunity to attack Maeve directly. He mourned the slavegirl, detesting the killing of innocents. Emer had been right in telling him to wait. Now his anger could no longer be so easily satisfied."

"What happened then?" asked Senchan.

Laeg only replied, "Come and see."

8. The Split

Inside her wide tent, Maeve sat upon pillows, a fur cloak drawn around her shoulders for warmth. Her white hair lay piled like a cloud around her head, held in place by a gold ribbon torc. In a brazier nearby, a fire burned, and one of her bondsmen tended it to infuse the tent with a little heat. The bondsman heard the tent open and looked up; as quickly he averted his glance. Three Druids entered.

The three wore animal skins in the form of heavy robes: two were furred like Maeve's; the third skin was sleek and dark, the man inside it had antlers strapped to his head. Maeve nodded to him. "Lothar," she said by way of greeting. The horned Druid bowed. He sat down with the other two behind him, a triumvirate.

"You wish to know where the Donn can be found," he said flatly, "with no time to waste in search if it's hidden away."

Maeve said nothing.

Lothar removed a two-headed spike from his robe and stuck it into the ground between himself and the queen. He reached back to one of his companions, who gave him a trussed rabbit that might have been conjured out of thin air. Lothar took the struggling rabbit and held it up over the two points of the spike. He stared into the rabbit's eyes, muttered a chant for the rabbit to hear. The animal stopped its squirming, soon went slack in his hands. It closed its eyes, asleep.

Lothar impaled the rabbit on the spikes. With great care, he then pried open the carcass and drew out a string of wet entrails, laying them across the palm of his other hand. He lowered his head and narrowed his eyes, seeking the magical pattern in the slimy intestines. His eyelids fluttered.

The rabbit's carcass jerked suddenly, violently. Then it rose up on the spikes, swelling and rippling from within.

The bondsman gaped at what he was forbidden to watch. He covered his eyes and crawled away into the shadows. Maeve's eyes glittered with the fire in the brazier.

Out of the hole where Lothar had drawn the entrails, a black needle stuck up. The needle rocked back and forth, forcing its way out. More of it appeared, becoming wider until, quite suddenly, it split down the middle and let out a raucous churr. It wrestled further out. The carcass stretched up on the spike until Maeve was certain it must burst. She checked her belief against the Druid, but he continued to lean over the guts he held up. Blood dripped from between his fingers into the black beak struggling to break free. The hole widened and the head attached to the beak popped through. Then the tissue of the carcass gave way and the entire body erupted out of it.

For a moment the bird stood on the carcass, its body spotted with bits of fur, gleaming with blood. Then it squawked again and flew up to escape.

Lothar's whole torso twisted and dipped suddenly. The bird in its desperation did not even see the point of the antler that pierced and impaled it. Briefly, it squawked and flapped, then it hung like a garland of moss from Lothar's headpiece. Still with an eye to the rabbit in case of a further revelation, the Druid reached up and plucked the raven from his horn and stuck it on the spike.

His eyes rolled back and his hands opened, spilling the slick intestines in the dirt. He shook, his teeth chattering. His right arm shout out stiffly, fingers splayed as if trying to reach Maeve. She instinctively leaned away but saw immediately that he had not been trying to grab her. As quickly as his arm shot out, it dropped. The double spike skewered Lothar's hand. Instead of trying to pull free of it, he pushed down inexorably until the body of the spike protruded through his wrist. His fingers dug into the two corpses.

Maeve concentrated on his face—the pure white of his eyeballs; the stricture that seemed to combine terrible pain with glee. She watched to see the moment of insight when it arrived. Druid magic had always captivated her. As a child she witnessed their rites and over the years had developed a theory that something incalculably ancient and huge fed them its power in spurts, in fitful bursts. At some point she had divined that this ancient force was female and that it could be opened for her as well. Listening, extending her senses, she had brushed against that feminine force in its dark, enchanted lair; she had drawn from it like any Druid; also like them, she had not found the way to harness more, to make it see her or give her all she wanted. She lacked Lothar's training but she had a trenchant intuition. To "hear" the opening of the path between this Druid herdsman and the bull—that mattered, that was important.

Lothar's face relaxed. He drew a deep breath like a new-born's first. Maeve drew breath with him, in tune to the changing rhythm of the powers at play. Lothar leaned up and wiped the sweat from his face with the hand that had been impaled. It revealed no marks to show that the spike had pierced it. On the ground, just a few loose feathers and tufts of fur remained.

Something thumped in the shadows behind Maeve and she turned to find her bondsman lying on his side in a faint.

Lothar announced, "The Donn has fled Temair Cuailnge. One of the three Morrigu has warned him of our coming and opposes us by telling the bull that we mean to kill him. Gone to Glen Gat, hidden with his heifers in the Black Cauldron. Trapped there—the Cauldron's a bowl between mountains with nowhere to run. Morrigan taunts the bull as well as us." He tore the spike from the ground as he hissed the last word. The divination had ended. Stiffly, the triumvirate filed out and left Maeve alone.

Fergus and his Ulster companions would surely know the location of the Black Cauldron. But the Morrigu might as easily drag the bull somewhere else in an attempt to stretch the conflict out past the *noinden*. Maeve needed a way to deceive the three sisters. A way to trick and slay that faceless murderer, Cú Chulainn, as well. Her husband desired to deal with *that* singular curse; she would let him. They would split up their forces. His would continue into the heart of Cuailnge as if nothing had changed. Her army would steal north along the highroad of Midluachair and take the bull. Then she and hers would drive their prize ahead while he and his protected their back against the spectral sling expert.

The thought of her coming triumph sped her heartbeat. She would find time for Fergus, too.

9. Disarming mac Roich

Ailell stood by as his wife's portion of the army rolled north, glazed by the light of dawn. She had with her a herd of captured cattle, driven out in front of her army by herdsmen under the guidance of the Druid Lothar—in this way to disguise their purpose and identity from the Donn until they had sealed off the Cauldron. With her she kept the warriors of Munster and their king, Lugaid mac Nois, and the Black Army of Fergus mac Roich.

This last troubled Ailell. Servants in his pay had overheard conversation in which Maeve wished that Fergus were mated to her. Such talk might easily have been something spoken in passion—as Ailell truly knew it to be—but he could not afford to dismiss it completely. It indicated that Maeve might at some point overlook a casual treachery by Fergus, one that could lead to Ailell losing more warriors. Lose too many and Maeve would indeed gain the upper hand over him. What Ailell needed was a whip hand over Fergus. As the last of Maeve's force moved out of sight, Ailell called to his charioteer, Cuillius.

In quilted leather breeches, bare-chested and cold, Cuillius came running up. Ailell told him, "Today, I'll drive the chariot. For you I've another task of more value to me. I want you to join that army along the highroad, but stay out of Maeve's sight. Watch her and Fergus, find out what they say, what they plan. Follow Fergus's activities closely. But, Cuillius, above all, find me power over him."

Cuillius grasped the torc at this throat. "I'll see it done," he said. He rushed off to exchange his leathers for a brown tunic and robe, dull colors to suggest a low caste. He would blend in with the herdsmen and no one would give him a second glance.

When he reached the highroad, Cuillius stood for a moment on a ridge from where he could look in two directions and see the two armies, the one pushing north, and the other, the one he had left behind, moving northeast to cross the Cronn. For

an intense moment he experienced complete freedom. The torc
at this throat weighed against his neck. He remembered himself
and ran over the ridge and down the slope.

Maeve had her tent pitched on cold dry ground near enough
the Gatlaig River to hear its torrents. Her herdsmen had already
set out for the Black Cauldron while she and most of her
warriors waited here for word of the capture. She had not been
in the tent more than a few minutes when a steady rain began
to fall. She invited Fergus to come in and keep warm and, she
said, to discuss tactics, an offer she had often used before when
she wished his company in bed.

He saw to his own men first, and he found Maeve screened
off at the rear of the tent. He peered around the red linen screen.
She had shed her heavy tunics and cloaks to snuggle between
blankets of fur. She told him to come in and sit. "Where would
you like me?" he asked.

"On *my* fur, of course," she replied as she flung back the
top blankets. Fergus unfastened his wet cloak, watching her
taciturnly, revealing no hint of the thrill that ran like icewater
through his chest at the sight of her. Whatever he said of her
anywhere else, however much he disagreed with her mad methods of warfare, he knew that no other woman anywhere matched
her. Any attempt to refute so obvious a fact would have proved
futile; Fergus had never bothered to try. He loosened his belt,
lowering his sword to the ground. Naked, he slid into the
warmth she held open for him.

Outside the tent, soaked, shivering, dripping, Cuillius sat
amidst Maeve's servants and slaves, awaiting her call. He and
the others huddled as tightly as interlocking swirls in carved
design, but gained precious little warmth. Cuillius had thieved
a hostage chain earlier; its collar, attached round his throat, hid
his torc.

The tent opened and a face stuck out of the slit like a baby's
head protruding from the womb. "The queen calls for wine!"
yelled the bondsman and he thrust out two goblets. "One of
you go and strain—"

Cuillius snatched the cups and scurried, splashing, across
the yard. The wine casks stood off beside a wagon, where they
had been lowered to the ground. A perforated bronze strainer
hung by its handle on the hook of one cask that was in use.
Cuillius raised the lid, then leaned his head against it to keep
it up while he fit the strainer in one of the cups and dipped the

cup into the green pine barrel. Next he took out the strainer and flipped its gritty contents over his shoulder. He repeated this for the second cup, then let the lid slam down into place. With his hands over the tops to keep out the rain, he carefully wove his way back to Maeve's tent, the hostage chain dragging after him. The household bondsman, watching for him, parted the opening and let him in.

The heap of Fergus's clothing with the sword laid on top drew Cuillius's attention briefly as he looked around—he had never been inside this tent before. His gaze returned to the sword again.

The servant took the wine from him and went to the rear of the tent where linen draperies formed little chambers, the way some larger farmers' huts were cordoned off by hangings. Cuillius heard Maeve's voice, muffled by the drapes. Quite suddenly he knew what to do.

Before the bondsman returned, he had emptied the scabbard, thrown off his false collar, and dissolved into the sheets of rain.

Ailell could not stop laughing. HIs charioteer found the humor infectious but could only shake his head in appreciation, having laughed himself out on the run back from Maeve's tent.

He had not shown his prize to the king until after describing how he had played his part: his cleverness grew in the telling. Then he had hauled out and presented Ailell with the blade that Fergus called Leochain. "It's so delicate in weight and balance," he had said, "that it's a wonder it hasn't broken in battle."

Ailell sat down on a low table. "Take the sword and place it in our four-wheeled cart, under the boards of your chariot seat. Wrap it carefully, though, tie it securely—we wouldn't want to unman Fergus utterly." This engendered a new fit of laughing from him. "I can't . . . I can't imagine, can you, what pleasure she'll elicit from him now he's deprived of his point!"

Cuillius carried off the sword, tears of joy running down his face.

Ailell dispatched a runner to Maeve's encampment to invite Fergus back for a friendly game of *buanbach* and a "tactical discussion." By now, the king felt certain, Fergus would have discovered his loss. Ailell instructed his household servant to set up his fidchell board instead of *buanbach,* then sent for a wood-carver. This was going to be a sweet lampoon, he thought.

The runner met Fergus returning on the highroad. The invitation—notably the reference to a tactical discussion—provoked the warrior, eliminating any doubt in his mind as to the whereabouts of his sword. He lifted the runner aboard and drove more urgently than before, the runner shouting directions as though thinking that Fergus did not know the lay of the land.

Upon arriving, Fergus made his way through a throng of attendants straight to Ailell's tent. The moment their eyes met, Ailell cracked a smile but inhaled deeply to recover. Fergus glowed with embarrassment. "Odd," he growled, "that so overseeing a king should be laughing while his warriors face the unknown thing that Macha's Curse can't touch. Or are you, perhaps, a king who over*looks* instead?"

"I'll overlook your barb," replied the king, "out of modesty. Come, sit at the board. It's good to relax with a game while . . . chatting."

They took their places on furs piled around the raised board. Gold kings and queens stood at the center, the warrior pieces pegged in around them. Fergus raised one eyebrow. "This isn't *buanbach*."

"I changed my mind—a royal prerogative. Why should it matter which game we play? You know them both, and I like the look of this one better, the kings and queens forged in battle. And, speaking of things forged, am I wrong or do you seem to be lacking the filling for that crafted scabbard?"

"Play the game," Fergus replied flatly.

They began then, working in silence. Fergus outmaneuvered Ailell in the early moves, hemming in his center pieces, taking two of Ailell's warriors. The king leaned over the board, scrutinizing his position as a hawk might view a battle. Without looking at Fergus, he commented, "Even if you were to win a victory here, you couldn't take my place. That is all I wished you to know. Kings and queens are not the same as warriors—something I know far better than you, else you'd not be displaced from the command of Ulster. That stings your sensitive warrior's pride, even though you mask yourself well, and that serves to prove me right. Fondle and coit all you like, Fergus, but remember that those hills so sweet are only half the plot of land. The portion on which you do not lie is rocky, sharp and high. Ah, there's my move."

Fergus stared at the game board until the red blindness passed from his eyes and he could delineate each gleaming piece again. He took long to choose his next move.

The game continued on through the day while Ailell's army journeyed ahead without him. Word of the match reached Maeve as all things did. Late in the afternoon, she arrived with Finnabair in tow. She took her place adjacent to them and tried to discern the source of the undercurrent of stress. She thought at first it was simply a matter of men and their childish nature to dispute over games. Her presence put Ailell off his game briefly and he made a faulty move. Annoyed as Fergus took another of his pieces, he muttered, "It won't be the fault of mine if this gold king is impaled on the point of the silver monarch. The *queen* will have done it."

Then Maeve understood: *This contest comes off the board.* "Don't you find," she asked Ailell, "your devotion to this action incredibly stupid?"

Ailell closed his eyes and sighed. "You are incredibly distracting."

"So I have been told by many."

"I wouldn't dare try and count them. I haven't enough digits."

"Jealousy in you?" she asked, truly surprised.

"No. Merely concern over this one who is seeking openings in my defenses. Nothing more than that."

Fergus spoke up at last, tired of the tension. "It's in your defense I'm here. The warring that goes on is confined to this tent—and it's the same war as brought all of us out to this alien plain. While you bicker over me, the sleepers crawl back toward daylight. Before long they'll be up and we'll be the ones in the center of the board, ringed around by Ulster. There's my counsel you so distrust. Now let us get on with this," he snarled at Maeve, "and the sooner we'll get back to the game we're all of us playing."

Maeve sat dumbfounded. In the space of a few minutes she had seen jealousy in her husband and hot temper from Fergus mac Roich. Behind her, Finnabair looked from one to the other of them but gained no insight into the matter. Whatever the text of the argument, Finnabair lacked the gift for reading it.

In the early hours of the morning, Fergus managed to eliminate all the warriors of Ailell's and had separated the gold king and queen. He looked to win within five moves. However, with the warriors gone, Ailell's two crowning pieces gained new freedom to move. King took queen, then both ensnared the silver king, leaving the scattered silver warriors powerless to act. Fergus conceded the game.

"Bravely fought," remarked Ailell. He stood, his legs stiff. "And now, as you're going out to face the world again, you'd best take this to disguise your infirmity." He removed from under the furs a large wooden sword with a rough, knobby grip. "At least it will fill your sheath till the errant blade is recovered."

At last Maeve grasped the specifics of the game.

Fergus took the carved parody and wedged it into his scabbard. He said, "It's a fitting jest, but don't pass till you hear the last of it. Since I've nothing but a stick to display, you'll understand that I'm neither able nor willing to kill any more Ulstermen for you." Maeve started toward him but he put out a hand. "And you, madam, will have to entice another champion to take on the Hound. I'll speak with him, bargain with him, lead my army toward him; but hereafter I represent no one save me and mine on the field." He turned abruptly and tramped out.

The king and queen repressed their mutual recriminations. Finnabair blurted out, "Will somebody tell me what's happened?" When no one did, she shoved over the fidchell board and stormed into the dark.

Senchan picked up the silver king and inspected it as he leaned back on the furs where Fergus had sat. He had not fathomed the rules of the game he had just witnessed. Seeing his look of distraction, Laeg said, "Do you know much about folly, lad? About pursuing an idea, a goal, blindly and at overwhelming cost? It's an attitude that can take a game like that one and turn it into a massacre, and only skill can prevail. Sometimes skill can triumph over one's own folly. Sometimes."

"Whose folly was this?"

"All parties concerned, really—but mostly Ailell and Maeve's and it's a point you should take note of because hereafter it will guide everything. It's as follows: Ailell is seething with jealousy and a sense that Maeve is flaunting her sexual appetite at him, but he cannot admit this even to himself, because it would open grave doubts in him about his character. Maeve, likewise, cannot admit his jealousy either because she has held his tolerant nature up to the world. How can they be wrong, both of them? Impossible. And so they act as you've just seen. Mark that now, it will answer many questions that will arise. But back to the game off the board.

"Fergus's departure and Finnabair's indicate to the waiting messengers and servants that the king's tent is no longer inviolable. The first runner enters and informs Queen Maeve that the Donn has been taken, but not without some cost; specifically, the loss of Lothar. Upon seeing the Druid out front, the bull acted as if he had a grudge against Lothar, almost as if he perceived that Lothar had been the one to locate him. The bull stampeded the herd, Lothar fleeing for his life, but not fast enough to avoid those iron-black horns. With Lothar hoisted in agony, the Donn then circled the Cauldron, all the while shaking his head back and forth till he had literally shredded the Druid to bits. Maeve is regretful of this but too gladdened by the news of the capture to spend much sorrow. A brief discussion ensues, plans are drawn up. The runner departs to inform various troops to prepare for departure from Ulster.

"Then enters runner number two. Cú Chulainn has struck again, while the army marched ahead along the Cronn. Many more were slain as the board was played. Worst is that one of the king and queen's seven sons named Maine went up against the phantom warrior and died.

"No sooner has this sorry news been voiced than a third runner, out of breath, arrives in their midst to inform them that the Donn has escaped again, to Bernas Bo. It will require more force to take him and lead him out of the province. Things have not looked bleaker, which is to say, the direction of the game has shifted. They have the prize almost in their grasp but they can't get to it in order to get out. Now they have to call a truce. They have to talk with Cú Chulainn. And, as you saw, they've just royally screwed their go-between."

XII.
CÚ CHULAINN'S ONE-MAN STAND

1. The First Covenant

Cruachan's army camped that night near a ford on the Cronn River where the king and queen's son Maine had fallen. Atop one of the ridges separating the camp from the Cronn, Ailell watched as a *cromlech* was erected over his son's body. One of Ailell's foster sons named Etarcomol came up to him as he stood beside the raised stones. Excitedly, Etarcomol directed him to look down across the ford, where a fire could be seen. Maine's mourners grew agitated at this sight; they began howling and stamping and beating their chests. Two came up to Ailell and begged to be sent creeping down to kill Cú Chulainn in the night.

"What?" cried Ailell. "And add your heads to his collection? All you'd do is incite him against us again—slinging those sodballs of his all night long—any of you goes out: if *he* fails to kill you, I won't."

Overweening Etarcomol replied, "Well, Lugaid Allchomaig is already gone out seeking him."

Ailell glared at his wife. She stood in her protecting ring beside the *cromlech*. "Remember, when this is over, who invited the king of Munster." He gestured for the slaves to lower the capstone on the *cromlech*, then walked hurriedly away.

Etarcomol scurried up to Maeve and shoved his face through her guards. "Mother, I'll go and kill him if you like."

226

"Oh, shut up," she snapped. She and her guards turned and clattered after Ailell like an armored ouroboros.

Lugaid mac Nois Allchomaig tore a hunk of bread from the loaf Cú Chulainn held out to him. The bread was cold and doughy but all they had. In his haste, Lugaid had forgotten to bring something from his own ample stock of provisions. He tried to appear content with this meal although it tasted more like collected bird droppings than bread. He passed the loaf on to Laeg mac Riangabra. The young charioteer bit off a section, then threw the last pasty lump to Cú Chulainn. Laeg leaned back on his hands against the frosted hillside. The grass cracked beneath his palms.

Cú Chulainn said, "I've seen you in amongst the invaders, Lugaid. And once, at night, I recognized your form crossing the ridge to relieve yourself and held off casting my sling at you. Your whiskers are distinguishable even against the stars."

Lugaid scratched his thick red mutton-chop beard that left his dimpled chin naked. He had considered shaving off the beard, sporting just the heavy mustache. Perhaps that wasn't the best idea after all—at least not before he was back home in Munster. Lugaid dismissed this matter for now; the thing he had come to ask was far more pressing. He had intended to bring it up right away but, full of doubt, was more like to bring up some of his half-digested bread.

Cú Chulainn spoke up. "Did *they* send you?"

"They? No. They hadn't even arrived when I set out. They were off building a monument to one of their boys—one you struck down today. Probably camped by now, though." Peripherally, he spotted something glittering in the darkness and turned his head to peer past Laeg. The fire was reflecting off the rails of a chariot back behind them. Lugaid assumed it must be the one they called the "Sickle Chariot," although the fire did not reveal to him a cause for that agnomen. He noted that the rails of the chariot were bare of heads; Cú Chulainn had taken no trophies as yet. "I've seen a fair bit of your handiwork about. You know, it's amazing what grows on trees these days."

Cú Chulainn's face twitched with a slight smile. Laeg grinned openly. Cú Chulainn said, "I heard what happened between you and Emer. She speaks greatly of you. You're clever in your dealings and I must owe you something for the taunts upon Forgall the Late Obstacle."

Lugaid thanked his gods for the Hound's perceptiveness. "Well—if you feel like that—then I'd much appreciate it if you'd spare the rest of my men from your hand. We joined, you know, out of allegiance to a debt owed Maeve's father. All we've come for is the collecting of the bull, which is taken, so it's whispered about. We might be retreating if that's how it is. Ailell'd as soon be off before Ulster pops up out of the mists around him—at least, I'd think so."

Cú Chulainn nodded grimly. "So long as he abides by the codes. But no one's come to challenge me yet and I'm sure that's Maeve's doing. The whole world knows her worth."

"She's a great queen, my friend. I'm not saying nothin' against her."

"That's fair, Lugaid. You don't bend from your view and that's well with you. I'll spare your force with two provisions: First, that you point them out to me with signs—I can't be responsible for men I don't know; and second, that you and they leave off the battle if Connacht's force is still here when the Pangs let go."

"I've no quarrel with Ulster, either, now have I? That's all fair, ain't it? And I'll do this," he tugged on his whiskers, "to indicate my man."

"But you do that all the time," answered Laeg, "even when you're off alone, pissing in a stream. Are we to consider the stream under your command?"

"Only so long as I'm pissing in it."

"You were raised in Ulster, all right," Laeg mused. "And lucky for you, else the Cronn would rise up and drown you for your impertinence next time you piss."

Lugaid snorted. He stood, straightening his tunic and cape with a flourish that masked his toss of the dungy bread into the fire.

"Tell Fergus that I'll apply the same to him if he desires," Cú Chulainn said. "Plenty of his people are tied to me in some way, even arrogant Duffach. I've little care for such slaughter as Conchovor's brought home once already."

Lugaid turned back. "Oh, yes—about mac Roich. He's had a falling out with them. Word is, Ailell's charioteer stole his sword while he was off accommodating the queen. Looks as like that's true, too—he's got some ugly, knobby, blunt end sticking out his scabbard." He found himself unable to repress a smile and quickly turned to the darkness again. "Fergus says he told them right out that he'd have nothing more to do with killing Ulstermen—so he's halfway to your terms already."

"What base treatment of so fine a warrior!" exclaimed the Hound. He leaped up, grabbed up the stone he had been sitting on, and flung it angrily into the night sky. "Tell him I'll speak with him whenever he can."

Lugaid nodded. He hurried to his chariot and only when aboard did he glance back at the short figure standing menacingly beside the fire. Dealing with semi-divine beings was a dangerous and delicate thing. Nearness to godhood made people crazy.

2. Further Bargains

The Leinster camp was in a state of turmoil as Lugaid drove past it. One of their members had been brushing down his horse when a stone the size of a cask came shooting down from the heavens and killed him. Lugaid heard people crying out about this awful omen, about stars beginning to fall, a signal of the end of the world. Knowing the truth but guided by his hunger for a real meal, Lugaid drove past. He figured to make a cursory report to Ailell first, to get the indigestible work over with.

Outside Ailell's tent, Fergus mac Roich caught him and they began to discuss Cú Chulainn's offer.

Inside, Ailell could hear the murmurs of the two men—their voices carrying far in the cold, crisp air. He tried to pick out the gist of it, but succeeded only in identifying them. That they whispered infuriated him. He got up, tossing back his furs, and strode outside. "What are you keeping from me?" he demanded. "Are you in collusion now? Over what? Fergus's unmanning by his own hand?"

Fergus smiled ironically. "It wasn't my *hand* I was using."

The skin on Ailell's skull drew tight. "I don't care to have to be watching the both of you for tricks when it's the Hound of Culann who's my enemy."

"Let's go inside," Lugaid suggested.

In the tent, he told them both what had occurred at Cú Chulainn's camp, including the offer made to him and Fergus;

but he kept his "signal" to himself. "He thinks highly of you, Ailell, but he resents that no champion has been selected against him."

The king was thinking on other matters. He grabbed the two men by their sleeves. "What would you think of keeping the more select among my troops in with your own? That doesn't break your vow or even alter it. It would give you each a greater command also."

Fergus threw off Ailell's hand, his bracelets clanking. "You'd ask this of me? Lugaid, I couldn't debase myself to the degree that this man asks. Go back to Cú Chulainn for me and ask him if he accepts what Ailell proposes."

"Now, wait—"

"It's only right," agreed the King of Munster.

"Tell him for me also that my sign will be spikes."

"I'll go." He glanced inquiringly at Ailell.

"All right," Ailell conceded. "Tell him because it's honorable. I'll give you a salted pig and a cask of wine to offer him into the bargain." He had these delivered, then waited alone.

When Lugaid came back without the pig or the keg, Ailell grinned with delight. "He accepts," Lugaid assured him. "He says you can put your men anywhere you like—if he wants 'em, he'll find them anyway."

"Why, the cockscomb. Very well, we'll see what he can find."

During the night, the king planted over a hundred warriors of his own in amongst Fergus's and Lugaid's forces. In this way he anticipated getting them home again while Maeve's forces would suffer the greater losses. The men of Ulster and Munster built their central fires larger and expanded their rings to canton the new additions from Connacht; they shared their space, for the most part, with something less than enthusiasm. The plan shortly reached MacRoth and he reported it directly to Maeve. By morning, the entire army would know.

At dawn Ailell awakened to shouts and the clang of swords and spears against shields. Still wrapped in his heavy fur blanket, he ran out into the icy gray and pink landscape, following the clamor, which came from Fergus's Exiles. A throng of warriors circled that encampment; they were so intent upon the scene that Ailell had to pry his way through them to see.

Bodies lay scattered around the embers of the fire. Ice coated some of them, frosted the beards of others. "He went back on his word," Ailell mumbled to himself. He called out to Fergus, who was not to be seen. As he scanned the faces of the Ulstermen, Ailell realized that they had changed: all the exile warriors—Duffach, Cormac, even, he now saw, Fergus—had limed their hair, stiffening it into curled spikes. The spikes on Fergus's head had bleached nearly white at the tips and shone like metal in the early light. Fergus looked to Ailell like an avatar of a sun god: Belenos incarnate. Wherever he turned, he discovered the Ulidians, men and women, coiffed the same way. One or two—that would not have been uncommon; the warriors of Ulster often limed their hair; but all of them? In one night? He recalled suddenly Fergus's parting words to Lugaid last evening: "My sign will be *spikes*."

Glumly, the king roamed through Ulster's camp, kicking at the bodies, naming each of them, thirty dead in all and not one with spiked hair, every one of them belonging to his group.

Fergus came up to him. "Life's not improving much for you, is it?"

"Don't think for a moment I don't comprehend this deceitful scene."

"I should think an idiot could comprehend. The Hound's been barking again."

"I was referring to *your* treachery."

"My treachery? What would that be? You heard Lugaid say that Cú Chulainn wanted a sign from me and you heard my answer. You didn't ask what it meant, you were so deep in your plot, but you could have, and you'd have gotten an answer."

Defeated, Ailell shook his head. "At this rate, I won't have a warrior left to face him. We should have engaged him in single combats from the start. I could have sent the whole army north while a combat was waged on that eastern ford. But my wife insisted on her methods—on the efficacy of them. They've certainly been effective at reducing my numbers."

"And that's not the plan at all, is it?"

"Will you go and speak with Cú Chulainn for me?"

"I'll not. You've used me enough lately and—" Fergus stopped as a cry went up from the opposite end of the camp.

The call had come from one of the king's herdsmen. The man had discovered a naked body. He led them to it. It lay doubled over the hammered copper side-screen of Ailell's two-wheeled chariot. The king feared the worst and would not touch it. Fergus turned the body. Its skin peeled where it had frozen

to the metal rail. The stiff corpse belonged to Cuillius. A large
hole had been punched in his chest. One pointed facet of the
stone that had slain him shone with the blood that had crys-
tallized around it.

Fergus emitted a soft, sarcastic chuckle.

Ailell goggled at him. "You'll never be anything but a warrior, mac Roich, just as I told you."

"Yes, you seem to set great store by that fact, as though it
mattered to me that I'm not a king in Ulster. However, since
kings are above warriors, you could do one thing for me. You
could tell Cuillius—if your power can reach him—that he may
keep my sword a while longer, if he thinks it might assist him.
I'll look forward to his reply." He strolled off through the
crowd, chuckling to himself again. Duffach embraced him,
grinning like a wolf.

Ailell grabbed the herdsman who had brought him there.
"Go fetch MacRoth. Doubtless you'll find him near my wife's
tent. Tell him to sound the alarm to move—but not loudly
now. No carynx fanfares, no trumpeting at all. And north, we're
moving to Bernas Bo."

3. The King on the Field

Laeg was standing guard that morning on a rise above the camp
at the ford. He called out that someone approached now, coming
out of the hazel trees at the base of the ridge. Below, Cú
Chulainn threw off his furs, which tossed up a powder of snow.
A layer of snow covered the landscape all around and more
was falling. Dressed only in a loincloth, Cú Chulainn stood.
His breath rolled out like smoke. "Who is it?"

"A short man, dark as a sunburn, with a close beard and a
sharp beak. His brooches look bronze. He carries a hazel wand
in his broad left hand—"

"A Druid, is he?"

"And a sword with jeweled ivory hilt in his powerful right.
Sword and wand touch above his head."

"A herald, offering wisdom and war, some secret knowledge

there. I guess I won't prepare for battle yet." He squatted on the fur and started to rub snow over his chest, sucking his breath as the coldness charged his blood.

The herald, MacRoth, climbed the hill. He studied Laeg as he approached, noted the ends of trousers beneath the heavy fur that Laeg wore against the cold, and guessed that this must be somebody's driver. "Whom do you serve?" he called out.

"That man, there," answered Laeg, gesturing over the crest.

MacRoth nodded to him and continued down the slippery hillside that was devoid of footprints before his. He turned his head and looked at Laeg again. It disturbed him vaguely that Laeg had not left that rise all night.

The youth at the bottom of the hill rubbing snow all over his nearly naked body did nothing to steady MacRoth's nerves, either. This had to be the one he sought; surely no other Ulsterman could be about with the Pangs still at work. His brow knitted; he glanced up the hill again. Then, how was *that* one standing there? It was too much to dwell on just now.

The boy—MacRoth could not think what else to call him—stared up nonchalantly with snow melting down his blood-suffused face. It became obvious that he was waiting for MacRoth to speak.

MacRoth made a sound like a sheep bleating, then asked, "Can you tell me where to find the warrior called Cú Chulainn? Is he asleep?"

"Well, it's said that between the Monday after Samain feast and the midweek following Imbolc, Cú Chulainn never sleeps. He just rests his head against his spear from time to time. Mind you, I don't trust such things."

"Yes, well, do you know where he is?"

"Why?" the boy asked. He had such a mellifluous voice, thought MacRoth. "What would you wish of him?" He got up, standing no taller than the Messenger. From beneath the furs he took out a red tunic sprinkled with gold. It was sleeveless. The boy's arms were strangely muscled in tight ridges, as if he had been magically created from lengths of rope, his skin stretched tightly over the skeins. Whereas, thought MacRoth, his face was so...untroubled. Not a line showed there. The black brows arched as if painted on, in a perfection that many women might have envied. So, too, his long lashes and black eyes. The boy's mouth was wide and full, his nose small. It could have been a woman's face, and a beautiful woman at that. So smooth the cheek....

"What would you wish of him?" the boy repeated.

MacRoth jolted out of his reverie. "I've a message from the King of Connacht, an offer to Cú Chulainn to switch his allegiance to the lords of Cruachan—"

"Cave or Rath?"

"Cave—no, no—Rath, of course."

"It makes a difference. No doubt in return for wealth, land, and all the women he can eat."

The boy's mocking boldness flustered MacRoth. He stumbled through a few words, then shook his head and started again. "If he will pledge to Ailell rather than to the—" he refrained from calling Conchovor a "tyrant deluded by power" as Ailell had done "—the King of Ulster."

"Surely no man of honor could expect such a one as Cú Chulainn to sell off his foster-brothers so cheaply. He has a large family to support these days, you know."

"I'd heard, yes." He found himself moving into rhythm with the boy's offhand jesting. "Is there any agreement, then, you think he might make?"

"Concessions from Cú Chulainn? Let me see. Yes, there's one I can think of."

"What would that be?"

"Now, I can't very well answer for him. You have Ulstermen in your camp, don't you? Ask them if any knows what the fellow might require."

"I shall do that upon my return."

"Good luck to you, then, on your way home." He returned to dressing and drew on his white cloak and hood, thereby removing the last shred of doubt in MacRoth's mind as to whom he addressed. He climbed back up the hill with the easy gait of a youth, back to where Laeg squatted. If that other face had been as gentle as a girl's, this one contained the leanness of a fox. A fox that had seen the world and all its surprises.

"Enjoy your visit?" Laeg asked without looking away from the horizon. "He likes you, you know. You're an honored man, MacRoth."

"He knew who I was?" When the other did not reply, he asked, "Why should he respect me particularly?"

"Because it's told that you can cover all Eriu in a single day, on foot."

"I don't see—"

"You can outrun him. He respects your skill."

"Oh, I see."

MacRoth returned to camp, still refreshed by his conversation with the Hound. He told his story to Ailell and the Ulstermen. When asked to clarify the riddle, Fergus laughed at the king again. "You know already—he yearns for an honorable struggle. He's Ulster's champion, the king on the field. He wants acknowledgment, trophies."

"I'll give him the chance. If Fergus delivers the offer." He gave the gathered warriors an expectant look. Not all of them were on Fergus's Black force; he would not be outmaneuvered this time.

Etarcomol swaggered forward. "And I'll go with him."

"I don't want you," Fergus replied indignantly.

Etarcomol addressed the king. "How do you know this slaughterer can be trusted with the likes of Cú Chulainn? You need someone there to bend him to accuracy." He sneered at Fergus, who, in reply, clutched his sword—only to recall at the rough touch that he had no sword.

Ailell did not care to have his foster son pestering him all day, which was what would happen if he did not let the impertinent warrior go. "He's to be under your protection, Fergus. Swear a *geis* to that."

Fergus stared coldly into Etarcomol's eyes. "You can't force this on me. But I'll watch him, on the condition he makes no attempt to harass or provoke Cú Chulainn. He's too much like Bricriu for me."

"And who is Bricriu?" asked Etarcomol.

"A deceitful, bragging, petty, self-seeking creature whose father was a maggot and whose mother a dog's turd."

Etarcomol took a step toward Fergus, his hands balled into fists. The group of men around Fergus drew their swords part way, their teeth gleaming with eagerness. Etarcomol hesitated and reflected upon the wisdom of studying cloud formations.

Ailell waved them to put away their weapons. He grabbed his foster-son by the hair and dragged him away. "He's all you'll have between you and the Hound. Don't be flatheaded enough to provoke your sole protector."

They went out in separate chariots, Etarcomol with his driver, Fergus alone. When Laeg saw them emerge from the gap, he called down to Cú Chulainn again, first describing Fergus: "large man with a crannog's rudder stuck in his belt."

"Yes, riddler, I know who that is," Cú Chulainn called back. "Give me another."

"The second one's a thin man with a face damaged by malice."

"I don't know him but I don't much care for his looks."

"Understood." Laeg threw off his fur and took up a long spear. He waved Fergus over the rise with the spear but stepped out and blocked the way to Etarcomol, whose driver obediently reined in despite his passenger's snarls of contempt. Etarcomol jumped down and proceeded on foot, watching Laeg sidelong; Laeg addressed the other driver and did not attempt to hamper Etarcomol further.

Cú Chulainn embraced Fergus heartily. Fergus praised Emer's beauty. Cú Chulainn blushed and praised Fergus's integrity. He offered food and drink from the gifts Ailell had sent.

"Thank you, but that isn't why I—" he looked over his shoulder at the hill "—why we've come. It's in answer to your offer. Ailell's accepted, on the grounds he'll lose fewer men if he sends them out against you one at a time."

"No matter what he believes. Combat is more proper. The sling is useful, but I'd rather face a foe."

Footsteps approached from behind Fergus. He said, "In that case, I expect he'll start sending them out as soon as we return. Good luck to the gods of your household." He started to go. As he drew even with Etarcomol, he grabbed the other's upper arm. Etarcomol threw him off to continue forward. "Boy," growled Fergus, "I warn you, as I said, the moment I leave here, my guardianship over you ends. Come now or suffer the consequences."

Etarcomol's reply was to curl his lip at Cú Chulainn. "This is what all the quivering's about? I don't see anything here worth so much jelly. This is nothing but a pretty boy barely old enough to be off the nipple."

Cú Chulainn said to Fergus, "You had to swear to protect *him?*"

"I did. He's fostered to the king, though with no more joy than in my custody."

"Then I won't harm you," said the Hound to Etarcomol, "even though you whittle at me with that knife between your teeth."

"I'll be the first comes against you," Etarcomol boasted.

Fergus had heard all he could stand. He yanked Etarcomol off his feet, then twisted his arm up behind him and walked him to his chariot. "Take the viper home," he told the chari-oteer, then went to his own vehicle and drove off. Etarcomol's driver followed across the ford. Then the warrior snatched the reins and shoved him out of the way. "I can't wait longer to deal with that child."

Laeg called out that the second chariot had turned about with the warrior at the helm, his spear up and at the ready.

"I can't ignore the obvious statement being made there," Cú Chulainn mused. To Laeg he called, "Come take the reins and let's meet him at the water!" Laeg raced down the hill. He bounded to his place aboard the chariot. The twin horses picked up their heads and pranced in place, chomping their bronze snaffle bits. Cú Chulainn removed his white cloak as he got in behind Laeg, but he did not strip down for battle.

Etarcomol's chariot reached the river and, as the warrior saw the Sickle Chariot emerge from behind the rise, he turned his vehicle parallel and gave the reins back to the driver with a warning to obey him.

Laeg drew his chariot up broadside, barely a foot separating the wheels. In his red tunic, Cú Chulainn leaned on the rail. "It's your fault if this goes further."

"It has to go further, little boy, so I can take your skull home."

Cú Chulainn answered by swinging down over his rail, grabbing the top of Etarcomol's wheel, and tearing it off its axle. Etarcomol cried out. He slid across the boards, doubled over the rail, and fell onto the frozen bank. The terrified horses jerked ahead suddenly, dragging the chariot up the hill. It bounced off the axle, tossing the driver out.

Etarcomol clutched his spear and splashed into the shallow water toward Cú Chulainn, who tossed aside the wheel and drew a sword instead. Etarcomol made a threatening thrust with his spear and Cú Chulainn wove an intricate swirl around it with his blade. The warrior's tunic fell from his shoulders, sliced through.

"There," said Cú Chulainn, "is proof of my skill. Now go home alive."

"No."

"Oh, yes, you're right. I forgot." He swung down and took Etarcomol by the hair, lifting him off his feet. With a flick of the blade, he sheared off the warrior's hair along the scalp. Etarcomol fell back into the river. "There now," said Cú Chulainn. "You have a skull to show your friends. Go home alive."

Etarcomol screamed and, slipping, clambered to his feet. He gripped his spear close under the point and jumped onto the rear of the Sickle Chariot. With one hand on the rail, he jabbed madly at Cú Chulainn. The Hound danced over the wild thrusts twice, the second time stamping down the neck of the spear. He spun his sword and sliced through the top of Etarcomol's head, not stopping until he reached the navel. The body folded over and toppled back into the stream. "I have my limits," the Hound said to the corpse.

He heard the rumble of another chariot rebounding through the gap. The chariot emerged; it was Fergus mac Roich returning. Fergus had discovered the absence of his ward and come back to stop him, but too late as he now saw. He jumped from his chariot before it had stopped. On the way to the river he saw the broken chariot and the driver climbing to his feet in the snow.

The body and its internal parts floated amidst thin ice in the dark water. "Little dog," Fergus said, "this disgraces me." He drew his wooden weapon. "I've nothing but this against you, but I'll hammer you into the frozen ground if need be."

Cú Chulainn lay down his sword and leapt over the rail, onto the bank. He knelt before Fergus. "No disgrace can be got from dealing death to those deaf to good faith. This strutter bragged beyond the binding of a hundred *geisa*. What was I to do?"

"And what am I, who still lives and must now bear another flagstone of dead flesh upon my back—what do I say to them?"

"Ask his charioteer."

Fergus called the driver to clear the matter up. "Three times this youth tried to send him away and each time Etarcomol refused and tried to slay him. He left no choice, none."

Fergus went down to the gory body and began hauling it up. "I suppose not. His kind never do. I'll need two small spancel hoops with pointed ends, little Hound."

Cú Chulainn went off and returned a few minutes later with hazel branches fashioned as requested. Fergus took them and pierced the corpse's heels with them, then twisted the ends together. He tied a line to them from the rear of his chariot. After taking aboard the displaced driver, he bid Cú Chulainn farewell again and drove back to camp. Pieces of the body were flung off along the way, leaving a trail of odious markers to guide all future combatants.

The camp had been reduced significantly in size: Ailell had sent most of his people north. The circle of twelve who protected Maeve was chugging across the camp. The battered, vacated corpse scraped to a stop in front of them. Maeve peered out from between two shields. "Etarcomol. My, how you have diminished," she said scornfully. "You always were an empty boy." She withdrew back inside the wall and moved on.

A small *cromlech* was erected for the youth. The Druids came up to Ailell and asked what they should put on the letter he would carry with him into the next life. Ailell had nothing to say. Maeve shook her head, too, having no messages to send over and nothing kind to say about the deceased. The king offered the honor to anyone who wished it.

With his hot cup of wine, Fergus got to his feet and offered to give Etarcomol an epitaph. "For me, say that he goes to the Isle of Youth lacking any guts." Then he sat down unsteadily again.

4. Single Combat

Ailell stepped into his tent and found his wife seated near a brazier. She offered him a cup of wine and he sat beside her to take it. "It is Estremnidean wine, dear. I brought two kegs of it on my household wagon, since I knew you would forget it in your provisions."

"And you were right." He drank the sweet red wine. Maeve brushed her hand across his throat. Her nails clicked against his gold torc.

"We must decide who to send out against him. Which warrior do we want facing him first?"

"We've got plenty to select from. Although," he added, "none from Ulster or Munster will participate now." Slowly, in the ensuing silence, his face screwed up with anger. He set down his cup and slapped the ground. "Who *is* this pup? He's used fostering as an overwhelming obstacle. I know Fergus knew of his presence out there long before he told us—he had to. He could have warned us if he'd been honest."

Maeve refilled his cup as an adjuration toward calmness. "He is a warrior, Sweet Tongue, as you yourself have pointed up so clearly. His honesty takes its own form, requiring him to answer your questions but not to volunteer what you do not know to ask for. Stop treating him as an equal, Ailell. Remember as I do that he always speaks the truth but leaves it unfinished where possible. Ulster warriors are as protective of their knowledge as Connacht Druids. One day they will guard their tales so closely that the world will forget about them and remember only you and I. See him as I do and you will learn how to trust him."

She was right, of course. He studied her beautiful, genuine face and was reminded of the divineness surrounding her that he had perceived on their first meeting, just as she had seen the attributes of a king in him. "The Great Queen," his warriors called her, and indeed that suited. He admitted to himself that he had won his fame by uniting with her to the envy of every hopeful swain in Eriu, of all those Ulster advisors who had tried to marry her to that boy. If possession of the Donn increased her power, then it increased his by association. She would effectively unsex Ulster, spread the wings of her supremacy like the raven quills of the Morrigu over them, and he would be beside her. She was right, as always. He should not obsess himself with Fergus mac Roich when the real enemy was time. To gain more of it, they must pit someone against their unseen foe. He sipped his wine and pondered. "If we had time, I'd send for Cu Roi—pit dog against dog—but we haven't the luxury. What do you suggest? Give me a name." He touched her shoulder.

"What about Nad Crantail? He is among our best. His holly spears have such balance that he might well inflict death on the Ulster upstart from a great distance—before the boy realizes a combat has begun."

"What can we offer him to do it?"

Maeve slid against him. "I have given that much thought. It seems to me we should offer him Finnabair in marriage." Ailell glanced around and Maeve said, "She is not about. I sent her off earlier to my tent where she is now bathing and receiving a manicure." She kissed his neck. "Warriors will want more than a few cattle and some land. They would do anything to be tied to our line. That is why so many came, after all. That is the underlying and unspoken reason."

"Really?" he murmured distractedly. His hand had snaked up under Maeve's robe to cup her breast.

"I have researched it most thoroughly, my dear."

"Then . . . we should approach him with this offer."

"I have already sent out little Maine Andoe to ask him."
She unfastened his tunic belt.

"Have you? That's good," he whispered as he undid the
clasp at her shoulder and began to unwind the red cloth from
her. She was such a prize. How could he ever be at odds with
her?

Nad Crantail agreed to fight and kill Cú Chulainn in return
for Finnabair. She knew nothing of the plot and did not understand the lustful look he gave her when he passed her in the
doorway of her mother's tent.

Nad Crantail loaded his chariot with nine spears he had
carved himself, each one meeting his rigid specifications for
balance. The tip of each had been burned black over a fire,
then carved with a bronze-headed axe into a point like a long
black thorn. He placed a pointed helmet on his head and climbed
up beside his driver. Members of his *tuath* ran beside the chariot, shouting and cheering and beating on their oval wooden
shields. In response, Nad Crantail stepped out and danced on
the chariot yoke between his horses.

On the ridge to the east, not far from the grave of Maine,
three figures climbed to the snowy crest. These were three
selected Druids—one in white, one in brown, one in black
robes. The white one was Maeve's Seer, who would watch
over the combats and divine their outcome. The brown-robed
Druid was of the *filid* class and would watch in order to recount
the battle for others. The black Druid was the *brithem,* who
would rule on disputes and points of violated law. The three
sat on the side of the ridge with a clear view of the ford below.
The boy seated near them studied their hard, humorless profiles,
their shaved foreheads and squinting eyes. He thought them
eerie, not like Cathbad, who filled a warm spot in his heart;
but even with their untold secrets and divinations, they did not
disturb him half so much as Maeve did. He could not imagine
going alone into her tent, a warrior taking instructions, accepting her touch and more. Maybe Laeg was right, Senchan
thought. Maybe he ought to be thinking of some other occu-
pation. But how did that explain his being here?

The brown-robed Druid turned and looked straight at him
then. The priest got up and came toward him. Senchan thought
he would faint; his heart seemed to be rising in his throat. The
Druid came to a stop inches away, then leaned down over him.
Senchan fell flat against the hill. The Druid scooped up a

handful of snow and turned away.

"Look at this," he called to the others. "A flower, blooming out of season, right through the snow."

"Let me see it," said the white Druid. Once he held it, his expression clouded over. "Why, it's dog-bane."

"An omen, surely," said the judge.

"No question," agreed the one in brown, reseating himself. He glanced back at the sound of people approaching—members of Nad Crantail's *tuath* clambering up the hill. "There he is!" one of them cried. The Druids flung away the flower and watched the chariot come to a stop below.

Nad Crantail jumped down with his bundle of spears and weaved through the grove of trees to get a clear shot.

Across the ford, Cú Chulainn had been passing the time in the practice of bird catching. Laeg would toss up the Gai Bulga at a passing dove and Cú Chulainn would jump over the spear and, at the pinnacle of the jump, reach out and nab the bird. Upon landing, he spoke secretly to his prey, then released it; the bird always returned when called. It was a trick that Scathach had taught him.

Nad Crantail saw him and selected a spear from the bundle. He hefted it, then with a sudden dash, let it fly. He took up another.

"Look," cried Laeg as he saw the first spear sail out of the grove across the river.

"Marvelous!" said Cú Chulainn. He leapt high up, making his dove call and catching the shaft of the spear between his toes, so lightly that it carried him on up through the air. A dove flew to him and he placed it beneath his tunic. As the spear dropped away, another shot past and Cú Chulainn caught a ride on it. He made his call again and more doves flew to him. He stuffed them under his tunic with the first, at the same time somersaulting away from the second spear, snagging a third and then a fourth.

His clothes soon bulged with captured birds that did more to buoy him than the catena of spears. He laughed heartily at the great game. Across a brown, snow-dappled heath, Laeg raced along beneath him in the chariot. When one of the spears came down and stuck in the floorboard beside him, Laeg yelled in surprise. His voice frightened the doves both in and out of Cú Chulainn's red tunic, and the whole flock took flight. Cú Chulainn rose higher than any spear could touch and glided away on the wings of doves.

To the audience on the hillside, the picture was quite different. The people shouted and jeered: Cú Chulainn had run away! The tribunal did not know what to think but held to the omen of dog-bane as evidence that this was so.

Senchan knew they were all wrong and shouted at them, but they could not hear him any more than they could see him.

When the *tuath* and the Druids returned to camp they told their story and all the remaining troops save Fergus's hooted and derided Cú Chulainn.

"He's aptly named," went one squib, "because he certainly crawled off like a dog—with his tail curled under him."

"He belongs with the pigeons."

"Birds of a feather, eh? Except he's featherless—not even a man!"

"If Nad Crantail didn't exactly triumph over the Hound, at least he *winged* him."

The Black Army stood by and listened darkly to all this noise. Fergus said, "It would have been a better day had he not been there at all."

Among them, Fiachu was the first to give out. He disappeared in his chariot before anyone noticed his absence. From the river ford he followed the tracks of Laeg's chariot through the crackling scrub of the heath until he saw the two men sitting at a fire. They invited him to join them in an afternoon repast of the birds they had spitted. He refused bitterly.

Cú Chulainn set down his meal. "Why so harsh, brother? If they all saw it, didn't they find my sky-sailing feat worthwhile? You should thank that fellow, whoever he was—"

"Nad Crantail."

"—yes, thank him for his addition."

"Addition?" Fiachu yawped in disbelief. "He was trying to kill you."

Cú Chulainn exchanged glances with Laeg, who shrugged, not knowing what to say. With a sudden, unassured laugh, Cú Chulainn asked, "But why didn't he use real weapons? Did he think he could harm me with pointed sticks?"

"Of course he did, you little fool! And think how that 'great feat' of yours looked to the Druidic triumvirate—they're back in camp now, composing slurs against you. Nad Crantail says he can't fight you fair—you don't even have a beard. Lucky for you, most of them have gone off to fetch the bull."

"What?"

"What I'm trying to tell you. You've been treating this as

some game—some entertainment for your pleasure. While you're having fun, the enemy's run off. Taken the Donn again."

Cú Chulainn began to twitch. Laeg scrambled for a jug and flung its cold contents over Cú Chulainn's head. The water hissed and turned to steam against him.

Laeg advised Fiachu, "You have to learn patience with him. Calling him names and showing him discredited could—could— well, he might explode in every direction and tear us to pieces for lack of something appropriate to kill."

"What do we do?" asked Fiachu. He glanced at Cú Chulainn, who sat in seeming oblivion, still quivering, his eyes bulging.

"Go tell Nad Crantail that Cú Chulainn's preparing for a real combat to prove that he wasn't running away. I'll have him cooled by then and reasonable, but he'll want to set off after Maeve's army, so tell your champion to meet us at the next ford north, and to get there first if he wishes to prove himself."

Fiachu hurried back to his chariot and rumbled away. Laeg hoisted Cú Chulainn's broiling body onto the boards of the Sickle Chariot. "My poor friend," he said, "why must you suffer these fits? Sometimes I wish you were a bit less tainted with divineness and more like the rest of us." He tried to stand Cú Chulainn in place, but both legs had locked in a sitting position. In some way Laeg did not understand, his friend was caught in the middle of a transformation. He recalled the time that the women of Ard Macha had been forced to drop him in three separate tubs of cold water to bring him to his senses: he had caused the first two to burst.

Laeg finally roped him up against one rail, then draped the white cloak over him. Kneeling, Laeg waved a hand in front of him, but Cú Chulainn continued to stare, pop-eyed, at nothing.

"That will never do. You look postively ten years old with those big cow-eyes of yours, and that spear thrower wants a full-grown foe. Let's see what we can do."

He went back to their fire and heated some water, which he then poured on the ground beside the chariot, making a puddle of steaming mud. He scooped up a handful and slapped it on Cú Chulainn's chin, then tore up some brown grass and stuck it to the mud. The final effect was blotchy and uneven, but it would do from a distance. Then, placing the Gai Bulga in beside him, Laeg went off to yoke the horses.

*   *   *

The three Druids arrived first after Nad Crantail. Behind them, the din preceded the other audience by an hour.

Ulster's champion had reached the ford not long before Nad Crantail. Laeg had dragged Cú Chulainn out of the chariot but found him still paralyzed. Beside the ford there was a short standing stone commemorating some noble deed or warrior all but forgotten. Laeg dragged Cú Chulainn there and propped him upright against the stone while he roped him in place. The stone came to the top of his shoulders and would be obvious to anyone, Laeg saw at once, so he snatched up the white robe and draped it over the stone and warrior, completing his own transformation of the Hound.

The first clear view that Connacht's warriors and the Druids had of their opponent was of a deformed, hunchbacked figure rocking sluggishly from side to side.

Bemused by what he saw, Nad Crantail walked over to Fergus mac Roich. "Tell me the truth now," he demanded. "Is that Cú Chulainn?"

Fergus squinted. "I think so."

Nad Crantail shook his head, flustered. "I don't know. I was further away earlier, but I'd swear his face wasn't half so dark then. And he looked, well, smaller."

Fergus cleared his throat. "He's known to puff up when he's angry."

Nad Crantail mumbled to himself and wandered back to his chariot. He took a bronze-tipped spear, set it down, and removed his clothing except for the pointed helmet, his torc, and his leather belt. He waded into the ford. The water stung his feet. "Are you Cú Chulainn?" he shouted.

"What if I am?" came the reply from the deformed figure; it was actually Laeg, hidden behind the stone. Cú Chulainn moaned and raised his head. The presence of his enemy in his field of vision cleared some of the fog from his brain.

"If you are the Hound, then I'm here for you. This time I've brought a 'real' weapon." He waved his spear. "I hope it finds a place in your heart."

Cú Chulainn stiffened. Before Laeg could think of a reply, he yelled, "Let's hear the terms of your combat!" Laeg shook hands with himself and slunk back to the chariot.

Nad Crantail looked to the Druids, found them nodding in agreement. Good, he thought, here at last was a true combat with a true, manly, bearded opponent. Behind him, members of his *tuath* began to slap blades against shields.

In the Sickle Chariot, Laeg took out a scythe and started rapping it against the rails, a musical clanging that rang above the thunder of the wooden shields. Over the din, Nad Crantail called, "We throw our spears and no dodging. How does that suit?"

"No dodging," agreed the Hound, "but jumping up is allowed."

"Done!" the warrior cried and flung his spear with all his might. Cú Chulainn leaped over the shot so hard that he snapped the rope and tore free of his clothing. The spear cut between his feet and split the stone in two. Still afloat, Cú Chulainn chucked the Gai Bulga up into the clouds. He landed beside the stone, his naked form revealed to them all.

"He's just a boy—that's not a real beard!" someone shouted.

"He cheated!" cried another.

"Shut up!" ordered Nad Crantail. "He kept to the rules."

"Thank you," said Cú Chulainn. "You have my permission to dodge my spear by jumping straight up, too."

"Sure. Throw it, then."

"I did, already."

Nad Crantail had a presentiment of disaster but did not have a second to act on it before the Gai Bulga plunged down through the point of his splendid helmet. The shaft stuck out where the point had been, vibrating like a plucked string. Nad Crantail gasped, his eyes wide. He managed to keep his footing. "Let me say good-bye to my folk now," he asked. "I know it's my time."

"Go."

With blood like tears on his cheeks, he wove unsteadily back to his adherents, now silent and grim. Suddenly, he began to laugh wildly, but this changed into an uncontrollable fit of crying. The fit ended abruptly; the warrior stiffened up and said, "Some other will have to take his head." He began to giggle. "I've got his tooth in me, and it burns, I'll tell you, it's fire in my mind. No one—no one will take him till you pull that tooth." His people watched him go, slack-jawed in response to his erratic farewell. He had been such a controlled, impassive man; somehow, that spear had unhinged his mind.

Dragging his shield and sword across the river with him, Nad Crantail stumbled through rushes and scraped his way to Cú Chulainn. He held out the sword and said, "I'm yours." He was grinning but his eyes wept.

"I must tell you, brave man, that my spear is such that it

can't be drawn back out but must complete its journey."

Nad Crantail waved his hand as if this were a triviality. His grin sickened.

Cú Chulainn grasped the ferrule of his spear and shot it down with all his might. The point burst out under Nad Crantail's ribs and drove into the hard ground, its wicked barbs hung with flesh like strands of moss. A geyser of blood spouted from the helmet. Cú Chulainn took the tendered sword quickly and severed head from body before the body hit the ground. Removing the helmet, he handed the head to Laeg, who carried it back and tied it by its plaited hair to the chariot rail, the first prize.

Cú Chulainn laid down the sword and stood to go, but a call from the other side of the ford stopped him. The Druid in the brown robe had come forward.

"What is it?" asked Cú Chulainn. "The fight's ended."

The Druid held out his hand and started down to the water. "Give me your spear," he said. He had overheard Nad Crantail's warning to his fellows and thought to capture the "tooth" with guile.

"Name some other gift, I'm tired."

"Only that. It's a foul and grim device that no warrior ought to have. It abuses the rules of combat—"

"This brave man didn't think so and it was his place to rule it so, not yours. Ask the *brithem,* poet!"

"Give it me or I'll assemble such a satire about you as no one has ever heard. Give it me or I'll make you crawl under a rock and never show that smeared chin again, little muddy beard."

Cú Chulainn hung his head. "I shouldn't like that. Here, then. Take it." He threw the spear underhand. It skimmed the river. The Druid bent down to snatch it, splashing as he stepped out. The blade skipped on the ripple he made and jounced over his outstretched hand and into his forehead. He jerked up sideways and stood there, swaying.

"How do you like my gift?" inquired Cú Chulainn.

The Druid was cross-eyed trying to look at it. "It stuns," he said, then fell over on his side.

Cú Chulainn went and took his head also. He held it up and said to it, "Words may be dangerous, poet, but you can't hide behind them." He went to the chariot and tied that head beside Nad Crantail's. Laeg gripped his arm suddenly and pointed northward. A great chimney of smoke split the sky. "That'll be Maeve and company. See, the rest there are hurrying off to join her. They'll all have to cross somewhere further upriver."

"Then we'd best outstrip them." Laeg pulled him into the chariot and took up the reins.

"Laeg," said the Hound. "I felt as though I'd died, lashed to that stone, as if I were someplace else." He sighed. "But I hope you don't have to fill your jug too often on my account."

Laeg was grinning as he drove his team into the water.

The departing chariot seemed to drag the world away with it for Senchan. Darkness swallowed him. The pinpoint that was the world receded like the end of a tunnel, the mouth of a cave.

Laeg's disembodied voice echoed around him.

"The smoke comes from the house of Celtchar mac Uthidir. He, himself, is snarled in the Pangs, but his wife and her women aren't. His wife, named Finnmor, has slowed Maeve further.

"The queen's intention was to make Ulster suffer for all the trouble caused her. Also, she thought to cause enough conflagration that, should Ulster rise soon, it would be too busy stamping out fires to chase her down directly, for which reason she has rolled flat everything in her path. Her army's like boulders. Farms laid out, fences ungrounded, the cattle herded inevitably ahead of them. In keeping to the bargain made with Cú Chulainn, no cattle were to be moved from the ford where combat took place. Nothing, however, had been said governing cattle picked up along the way."

"His plans went for nothing, then," Senchan protested to the dark.

"It's never for nothing. He had slowed them down again, dispersed their forces. Between him and Finnmor, they cost Cruachan's army a day. When you emerge from this place between moments, it will be after the battle of Maeve and Finnmor. Celtchar's wife has been driven back, the house put to flame, and most of the women defending it killed or captured. It's a minor battle you needn't see. Someday, when you've time, go to a map and note all the place names with Maeve as part of them: Maeve's Hill, Maeve's Lash. You can follow the army by the places bearing her name."

"So where am I going to come out?"

"Gotten used to this sort of travel, have you? You'll come

out at the Flurry River. What happens there . . . I can't tell you."

A hazy outline appeared in the darkness.

"You look like a ghost, Laeg," Senchan marveled.

The hazy figure grinned mischievously and replied, "Boy, I've been nothing else since first we met."

XIII.
TALES OF FURTHER COMBATS

1. An Offer of Finnabair

Laeg and Cú Chulainn cut south below Maeve's force, then west across the Gatlaig River and into the narrow valley of Glenn Gat, skirting the Black Cauldron. The valley lay empty in its destruction, no longer of concern to anyone. Mists like a layer of gray stone buried the depths and it would have been all too easy to imagine the ghosts of Connacht's recent victims drifting through that land. Around their road the small trees grew wide apart, twisted black trunks taking on fantastic shapes in the fog.

The rushing horses spun the mist away and kicked up clods that sometimes struck the trees just below. The dead branches shook like angry fists at their passing. Cú Chulainn could smell the death in that valley and Laeg preferred not to view anything but the road ahead. Finally it plunged down to where a causeway—a short corduroy road—led them across the wide marsh where the mist took birth and then ascended once more to link with the high road of Midlauchair. The tightly packed logs of the causeway spoke like thunder beneath their wheels. The thunder retreated into the depths of haunted Glenn Gat like the war chorus of a dead army on the run.

They left the highroad and arrived at a ford along the Flurry River north of the Cauldron. There they made camp in a broad copse. The Flurry offered few fords; this, the widest and safest, would have to be the one that Connacht chose if they wished to get their cattle across quickly. They would have to come here.

Cú Chulainn asked Laeg how long it would be before Ulster rose up, but he could not say for sure. "As many hours as make up the time since that boy came to warn you. Less, perhaps, for those who heard his message before you. More for those in the north. Two days to four, I'd imagine."

"Then we should be thankful of the numerous fords between here and Crich Rois."

He had barely finished speaking when Laeg raised a hand to quiet him and strained to listen. They heard a distant rumble. "The army!" Cú Chulainn cried. He got up.

Laeg continued to listen, motionless. "Wait, Cucuc," he said a moment later. "It can't be the army. Whatever this is, it's coming at us from the northwest, and the army's over there." He pointed to the east.

"I hear cattle. Someone's driving a herd." He climbed up on the rails of the chariot. "I can see their mass now. Herdsmen in bright cloaks, and there's a huge black monster in their midst."

"That'll be the Donn." Laeg scrambled to his feet. "They're coming to meet Maeve and Ailell here."

Cú Chulainn dropped down onto the boards. "We ought to meet them first, I think." He pulled Laeg up past him and they sent the horses galloping anew. Across the shallows, they followed the road, but stopped and drew up broadside to the approaching herd where they could still see the Flurry in case the army cropped up.

One of the herdsmen on horseback rode ahead of the herd and came up to them. With some skepticism he eyed the youngster standing on the rail. From his angle there were no heads visible; those hung on the far side.

"How did you come by so many cattle?" Cú Chulainn asked appreciatively.

"We found them at Slieve Cuilinn."

"Stole them, more like. All the herdsmen of Ulster are struck down by Macha's Curse and their cattle have scattered these past days when there weren't any women to watch them."

"Is that a fact? All the men are laid low, you say? So what is that to me—only boys like you are left running free. Now move aside and let us pass."

"What's your name?"

"My name?" He nudged his horse closer and prepared to draw his sword. "Buide mac Bain—the name that'll be on your lips when you die, boy." He pulled the sword and swung it up across his horse, which bolted forward at his kick.

"Not swords, mac Bain. Let's fight with spears. Here's yours!" Cú Chulainn flung the Gai Bulga. The herdsman rode right into it. The spear pierced his side and the barbs severed his sword-arm cleanly. Cú Chulainn bounded off the rail with his own sword drawn and landed beside mac Bain where he fell. "Now," said the Hound, "let me tell you *my* name."

That name shaped Buide mac Bain's lips as braids of his hair were looped around the rail beside the other trophies. "Let's take that bull away," Cú Chulainn said to Laeg.

As they neared the Flurry River ford, the Cruachan forces sent runners ahead to seek the herdsmen. The runners returned shortly with the alarming news that Cú Chulainn had gotten there first and slaughtered their herdsmen. Soon the ford came into sight, with the cattle of Ulster, including the Donn, gathered together on the far side, hind legs bound by spancel hoops, and tended by a short figure in a white cloak. Maeve shook with such rage that half her press of shield bearers stumbled forward. She went to her husband as camp was officially declared. "What do we do now? He plagues us everywhere we go."

Ailell eyed her in some doubt: her fits of temper were growing more virulent; she had always been such an imperturbable woman. "I've had a thought. Fergus's tales have this boy training on Alba, correct? Then shouldn't we be seeking someone else who's passed the same rigorous course?"

"You have someone in mind?"

"Ferbaeth."

"But he's an Ulsterman," Maeve replied, "governed by Fergus."

"Yes, I know. But I also know he has intentions regarding Finnabair. If we plied him with wine, he just might shift his allegiance."

"Oh, wise Ailell." She embraced him. "You must go and get Finnabair and this warrior right away."

"I? And what will you be doing?"

"I have another idea, courtesy of your suggestion. I must

go and speak with MacRoth, then I shall join you." She kissed him.

Not much older than Cú Chulainn, Ferbaeth had been a friend of Naise's. He had not acquired many more friends since the episode of Derdriu, preferring, much as Cú Chulainn did, to keep to himself. One could speculate, from his example and that of FerDiad and others, that those who had gone to Alba had given something away in return for their skill, something that left them cut off from their fellows. It might have been that they recognized in themselves some danger to mankind, or perhaps in mankind a danger to themselves.

Ferbaeth had been courting Finnabair since before the cattle raid. She had more color in her hair and cheek than her mother— Ferbaeth would have said it was because she was more human. Where her gentle, soft-spoken naivete had come from, no one could say. Ailell sometimes claimed inebriously that she expressed his uncontaminated placidness. Whatever the truth, Finnabair had won Ferbaeth. He was with her when Ailell sought them out, and together they went with him to Maeve's tent.

The queen had laid out bread and cheese and silver cups of wine. Her household servant was trimming the mold from the slab of cheese as they came in. Maeve said, "We serve most warriors beer, but for one on whom our daughter dotes, only wine will suffice. Please sit upon the rushes, Ferbaeth, and you beside him, Finnabair." The girl did as she was bid, but she eyed her parents suspiciously.

"What a trial this whole expedition has been," lamented Ailell. He began to recount the tribulations he had personally endured. The tale was a long one and called for many toasts in honor of the numerous dead. When it became obvious that Ferbaeth had drunk his limit, Ailell patted his back and said, "We think of you, Ferbaeth, as our hope, our defender, our champion out of all the army."

"You do? I'm unprepared."

"Naturally," Maeve agreed, "but think nothing of it. We have considered this throughout the journey and it is our desire that you have Finnabair."

The girl hugged her warrior and gazed, starry-eyed, at him. She had grown as drunk on their praise as he had on their wine.

"You've had as much training as Cú Chulainn," stated the king.

"More, I should think," Maeve rejoined like a Greek chorus.

"You're as fierce."

"Fiercer."

"As strong."

"Much stronger."

"A slayer, a slaughterer, the champion of the armies combined."

"Say that you will kill Cú Chulainn for us. For Finnabair."

Caught up in her parents' chanting, the girl cried, "Oh, you must, you can!"

Ferbaeth set his cup down clumsily. He had trouble meeting the weight of all three expectancies. "C'hulinn's my fosser-brother, like ever'one. Sworn forever." He pounded his fist against his chest.

"Finnabair would be your wife forever. Surely that is more binding than this pledge of fosterage that is spread so thinly over an entire province."

Ferbaeth lowered his head, trying to crawl through their argument. "All right," he said. The beads in his plaited hair clacked as his head snapped up. "Tomorrow, I'll go cut off 'is head."

"Tomorrow!" Maeve cried. Ferbaeth belched and toppled like a stone into Finnabair's lap. "T'morrow," he muttered. The queen gestured at her daughter. "Take him back to his tent, dear. He won't be brave again until he has slept some."

The girl lifted him with the help of the household servant. They carried him between them out of the tent.

Ailell looked into his wine cup. "Marvelous viniculturists, those Estremnideans. Should we hold them responsible for this blunder, do you think?" Maeve stared at the doorway, refusing to look at him. "Maybe, if he had eaten more cheese. . . . So, dear wife, who *else* desires Finnabair?"

"Half the encampment," Maeve answered through her teeth.

"Could we possibly target someone in that rather expansive group, hmm?"

"That brother of Lugaid's."

"Larene? Yes, he does, doesn't he? Lugaid won't like it a bit, but Larene's full of himself, so there won't be a need to pour wine into him. He'll be easy to deceive—I know his cloth."

"Then go tailor him to suit before we lose the light."

Ailell paused to finish his cup of wine before leaving. True to his word, he had Larene back in the tent within half an hour.

Finnabair returned once Ferbaeth had been put to bed. The strong wine had made her sleepy, too. Ailell had her sit beside Larene. She greeted him with a moony smile. Soon she had laid her head against his shoulder and begun to snore softly.

"A perfect couple, you two are," whispered Maeve. "Why, what handsome children you could create."

Larene nodded thoughtfully, then put his arm around Finnabair's shoulder and gave her a squeeze. She nestled closer against him.

"We've decided to give her to the man who brings us Cú Chulainn's head. What do you think of that plan, Larene?"

For a moment the vainglorious warrior blanched, but as quickly he put on a steely look. "Is that all? Why, I could do that for you before the sun sets. For this beauty, I'd take his head twice."

Alone in the corner where he and Laeg had listened to the tales of Cú Chulainn's childhood, Senchan shouted at them, then rolled to his feet and bolted from the tent. He ran straight into Laeg outside. Tears dripped from Senchan's eyes and he looked away from Laeg in embarrassment and disgust.

"What's wrong? What is it?" The boy said nothing. He began chewing on his lip. "You've seen the new twist in the plot, haven't you?"

"They're stupid. You're all stupid."

"Who is?"

"You. The warriors. All of them."

"Why?"

"Because they are. Maeve can trick any of them into anything. They're all too dumb to see what she's doing. They're all too busy being clever and puffed."

"Does this mean you no longer care to be a warrior?"

"I hate them."

"What about Fergus? And Cú Chulainn? Or the female warriors, who are for the most part fortunately exempt from the tempting offer? What of me, and Lugaid and even Cathbad, who was a warrior in his time? Are they all petty, strutting swashes?"

Senchan pouted.

"You ought to have more wisdom than you're displaying

here. You're no lip-pushing infant who needs constant dusting off. You dislike treachery? Good for you. But it isn't being used on you. You think that all warriors—all brave heroes—are uniformly alike off the field, all brave, wise, and clever men who remain untarnished by more ignoble lusts? Balls. If she made the same offer you just heard to her whole army, they'd gather up and go after Cú Chulainn en masse. The only thing stopping her is that the Exiles and Munster and probably the women would take sides against her and there'd be a real bloodbath. We're men and women here, boy. We suffer from what all men suffer: infirmities of character as well as body. Don't confuse generality with individuality. Look at Ulster as a province, with a curse laid on it for a boast, because its character as a synthesis has been fashioned around that one thing—boasting. But Fergus is an Ulsterman. So, too, Cormac and Cathbad, whom you dearly admire. Reconcile that if you can without turning them into flesh."

Senchan stared up at the sky and gulped a deep breath.

"You're watching human beings."

"Except for Cú Chulainn," replied the boy with a quivering smile.

"Well, yes . . . of course."

Behind them the tent door parted and Larene swaggered past.

"I will agree with you on this, though," said Laeg. "That it's remarkable *he* has the strength in his neck to hold up a head that size. On the other hand, it makes him easier for us to follow."

2. Double Folly

Lugaid's heart stopped when he heard what his brother intended. Cold snow seemed to have filtered into his chest, encrusting his heart. He knew his brother well—knew the futility of trying to talk him out of his murderous plan. Left with just one avenue of hope, he took his chariot and rode across the ford.

He came upon the two defenders of Ulster in amongst the trees. Their embraces were warm, but Lugaid stepped back immediately. "I haven't much time, and I need an enormous favor of you." He then explained how his brother had been beguiled into committing himself with "a carrot called Finnabair that they're waving under every nose that pokes into their tent. They've duped Ferbaeth to take his oath to kill you, too, so's the story. He was, and still is, drunk, which is all that's saving him so far."

"Ferbaeth will change his mind when he sobers. We're too close for such combat. For you, old friend, I'll spare your brother. But I must incapacitate him at least or duty will require him to come at me again."

"I shouldn't care if you hammered the shit from him, so long as the remaining five percent survives." He hugged Cú Chulainn again. "You are a good friend." Reassured, he returned to the camp.

Before an hour had passed, the quiet of the copse was broken by the sound of chariot wheels rolling, hooves drumming on the cold ground. Cú Chulainn stood behind a tree and watched Larene urge his chariot on past. Cú Chulainn caught the rear rail and let the chariot yank him in.

When he heard the feet of his guest strike the boards, Larene swung around. He wore leather armor and a crested helmet, but even thus protected his nerve broke and he tried to flee over the rails. Cú Chulainn caught him in the air and spun him around to get a grip on his middle. Then, holding him out of the car, he began to squeeze Larene's ribs. Quite literally he produced the effect Lugaid had jokingly suggested, and he continued to squeeze with one arm and steer with the other, the end result being an evacuated trail that led across the ford and back to the edge of the army's camp, where Lugaid waited. As the chariot passed the Munster king, Cú Chulainn tossed his drained brother into his arms, then jumped out and ran off before anyone realized what had happened. "The Ford of Larene's Spoor," they called that place afterward.

Ferbaeth sat holding his head in his hands. He had blank spots in his memory—for instance, just how he had gotten back to his small tent—but he remembered all too clearly what he had promised Maeve and Ailell. His brain swelled against the inside of his skull when he stood, but he knew what he had to do and, under cover of the uproar over Larene's remodeling, he sneaked out of the camp and went into the trees across the river in search of Cú Chulainn. He found the Hound in conversation with Fiachu mac Firaba, but they spotted him slinking toward them and stopped talking. Cú Chulainn leaned toward Fiachu and said, "It may be good that you're here for this."

Ferbaeth steeled himself and came boldly the last part of his journey. "I've come to renounce my friendship to you," he informed Cú Chulainn.

"What?" Cú Chulainn was dumbfounded. "To *me?* I'm your foster-brother. We spent time on Alba together."

Ferbaeth rubbed at his eyes. "It can't be helped. I swore an oath. And I'd look a coward before Finnabair."

Cú Chulainn bit back his acid reply. He could see that Maeve had done this. She breathed evil on everyone who accompanied her. "Take your friendship with you when you go!" he snarled.

He flung curses among the trees as he stomped through the underbrush. A holly tree had been struck by lightning, snapped off low, leaving just a sliver of a trunk. Blind in his anger, Cú Chulainn slammed his foot down onto the sliver. It thrust through his heel, up inside the skin of his calf, popping out below his knee. In his angry state no pain touched him; he stared at the protruding needle as if the leg belonged to someone else, as if the dripping sliver were some unexplainable deformity. He bent down, took the shard beneath his heel and tore it out of the ground with part of its root. In an instant he had drawn it out of his leg; then he flung it away and clamped his hands over the wounds where blood had begun to gush.

Throwing off clods of dirt, the sliver spun back through the woods. Ferbaeth was walking away dejectedly, Fiachu remaining behind to avoid taking any side in the matter. A spray of dirt assaulted Fiachu as the jagged stump spun past. He cried out. Ferbaeth raised his head at the sound, and the sliver drove through the back of his neck and wedged out between his teeth.

Fiachu ran to him but the young man had died in that instant.

Cú Chulainn, having heard Fiachu, too, hobbled hurriedly back. He shut his eyes in anguish over this misadventure. "Probably this is better than if we had fought tomorrow, do you think? We could only have shamed each other and our province. If only he'd listened."

"I'd say your point was well taken."

Cú Chulainn hissed. "Don't try and cheer me with puns. Look at all I've done today. I took three heads when their

pointsman provoked a fight. One was Galeoin! I've no quarrel
with Galeoin. Then I gave up Larene to help Lugaid, and now
Ferbaeth's lost to the fit of temper he spurred. Wasted lives,
and still no combat here. It's Maeve, always Maeve, like a
worm in every bite of the apple."

Fiachu picked up the body. "I'll take him back and explain.
But choke the anger in your mind, Cú Chulainn—or Maeve'll
make you pay. Pay dearly."

"Many challenge me. My reputation reaches places I've
never been. The time must come for me to lose. So Cathbad
predicted and so I accepted. I'll pay when I have to, not before."

Fiachu did not try to argue further. As he tramped away, he
called back, "Who do you think will come out next?" His
question frightened a large crow from overhead. It cawed and
flapped away. Whatever Cú Chulainn answered, the crow
drowned it out.

3. The King of Buan's Daughter

When Cú Chulainn walked out the far side of the woods, he
found two figures approaching from the west. The first was a
woman in a small chariot. A grotesque, demonic horse with
round white eyes pulled the cart. The wheels did not appear
to meet the ground but this might have been an illusion in the
snow. The woman wore a bright red cloak that rode low across
her breasts and was gathered above her elbow. She had pale
skin and her hair was as red as the pleated cloak. Her brows
were this color, too, and were feathered oddly against her
forehead. To one side and behind her chariot, a man walked
along, driving a strange cow with him. Like the horse, the cow
had wide, blind eyes. Cú Chulainn felt he ought to have gleaned
something from this but his brain had gone numb to any memories. The herdsman, oddest of all, looked like a rough carving.
His body bore pock marks all over it like weathered stone. He
wore a squat conical cap and a rope belt around his naked torso.
At that distance his dusky face contained vague gouges for
eyes, a bulbous nose, and a wide, triangular lower lip. This

group stopped at some distance. The woman climbed down and approached him alone.

She saw the gash in his leg and her face clouded with concern. He stood rooted while she bent down and draped her cloak around the wound. His leg went as numb as his mind. The color of the cloth grew darker, a silhouette of his calf. The stain—if that was what it was—spread out and vanished into the redness of the whole cloth. When she withdrew it, the wound had healed. Cú Chulainn stared at it, trying to force one coagulated thought to the surface. He could not have said how much time had passed while she knelt.

A question jumped into his mind and he asked it. "Who are you to do such magic?"

"I'm the daughter of King Buan." She had a soft, scratchy voice that made him itch for her sexual favors. Her identity did not surprise him: the oddness of her had already pointed to the Sidhe. The cow and horse looked like nothing so much as creatures from Manannán's sea herd. The weird man was grinning foolishly—an open, black hole of a mouth, toothless.

"You've traveled far to be here," Cú Chulainn said. "Why?"

"Because stories of your greatness have reached even to us. And, hearing them, I fell in love with you. Come deep into the glen and lie with me for a while." She held out her hand.

Her pale fingers drew him as if she held a cord tied around his waist. He took two shaky steps, but resisted. The muscles stood out down his back. "You can't expect me to abandon the ford now. Surely if you love me as you claim, you won't threaten me with such disgrace."

"I want you, all of you."

"That much is evident." He managed to take a step back. "I've no time for you or any woman when the whole countryside stands open to these invaders. Go away if you love me."

Her fingers flexed. His heart thumped and his throat tightened. "I could help you," she suggested, "if only you'd come with me. Come away. Think of the reward for all you've done." She plucked a gold brooch from her cloak, which then slid down her milky body. Every thatch of hair on her shone like twilled copper.

Cú Chulainn dug in his heels. He fought to breathe, gasping, writhing in her clutch. He knew that she lied. No one friendly to him would have tortured him so. "None of what I've done," he hissed, "has been done so that I might part a woman's legs.

Take your help with you as you go." The mute herdsman frowned.

"If you don't help me, I'll hinder," she threatened. Her finger pointed accusingly at him. "In the moment when you need your abilities most, I'll wrap your legs to trip you and keep you from your leap. Locked in place, you'll be cleaved by your enemy's sword."

"No daughter of Buan ever concocted such a threat. If you interfere in my combat, I'll put a wound in you that no one else can erase."

The pointing hand began to reshape into a ribbed claw. "Then I'll drive the captured herd across the ford and trample you underfoot." Her body spread out and down. Her fine breasts inflated and sank onto the flesh of her mottled belly.

"Then I'll sling a stone from the stream into your eye and that socket will stay empty unless I make it otherwise."

The woman cackled. Her hair darkened to glossy black and sprouted more thickly on her scalp, condensing into feathers. Her beautiful face became a horror with bulging eyes and a great wide grin that stretched nearly to her ears.

"Then I'll become a lure to lead the Donn against you and he'll tear you down the middle." She splayed her spindly legs wider apart. From the feathered hair that curled from her navel to her thighs, a pink bulb emerged and descended to her knees. The brown talons of her feet dug into the cold ground.

"If I see your like in the herd, I'll hurl a stone to shatter your skinny legs. But tell me, pestilent thing, which terrible sister are you?"

"The Badb, Cú Chulainn, whom no man rejects except for death." Her eyes had become beads. She clawed at the ground and her enormous pudenda swung against her legs.

"Bilious bird-hag, my fate's formed already by Cathbad. I owe you nothing."

The Badb squawked like cloth ripping. Black feathers erupted down her body. She swept up at him and he flung himself onto his back. Her talons clicked past him.

When he rolled to his feet, the chariot, horse, and heifer were gone. The herdsman remained: a roughly carved stone figure planted in the ground, its member poised, its expression vacuous.

4. Battle with a Beard

While Fiachu and Cú Chulainn had spoken, Maeve and Ailell had plied another warrior with the offer of Finnabair. Contentious Loch mac Mofemis had drunk their wine and heard the list of his skills and rewards. The king and queen made one small error in judging Loch—to urge him into battle they described his opponent as a "mere child" and "a youth ripe for killing."

Loch climbed to his feet and tossed his cup away. "I don't fight children," he declared. He refused to be swayed.

When he had gone, Ailell said, "Marvelous. What now?"

"He has a brother."

"Naturally."

And so, as the Badb threatened Cú Chulainn, another mac Mofemis entered the king's tent—an older, quieter man called Long. He had no such qualms about his opponent. He would have fought an infant if he had done the things Cú Chulainn had. As to the matter of Finnabair, Long already had a wife, but not an *adaltrach*—a wife-mistress, subordinate to his wife. Not wishing to waste time, he refused a second cup of wine and, with a cursory salute to the gods of Connacht, who were not his gods, he went out to meet his fate.

In a nearby tent, younger Loch was still fuming over the idea of challenging a child to combat when he heard the women servants of his camp wailing in despair. He thought: So, some other fool has taken up the challenge and died; how many incompetents there are hereabouts, that one child can defeat them all.

He reached down to a chain clipped through a stake beside him. He yanked hard on the chain and a young girl tumbled into his tent. She was dirty, covered in rags and bites from sleeping in the hay with his dogs. Her slave collar was brass and had turned her neck green. Loch ordered her, "Go out and see which idiot's died now." He unfastened the chain from the stake and dropped it.

The girl reeled in the chain. She lived for moments such as these—the brief periods when she could run on any trivial task or errand. There had been a time, when she was very young, when no one had chained her; sometimes she had dreams about that time, but it would not come again. Hers was the slave's life, best survived by the pretense that serving was an honor. That way, one escaped at intervals, to fetch water or carry a message.

None of this was apparent to Loch, who considered all slaves to be an inferior breed, inferior even to his hounds. How often he had watched one of them scurry off, that look of idiot delight on the otherwise blank face. He could not imagine that a slave might surprise him.

The girl returned at a stumbling pace, her head—in fact, her whole filthy torso—swaying to and fro as if she were drunk. She shuffled up to him without raising her head. Loch saw that her face was striped where fresh tears had washed away some of the dirt. In that moment he had a vision—of something bright and spinning that scraped his throat with rime. He clamped his hands around his neck, then reluctantly viewed his palms, expecting blood.

The girl had gone to her knees in front of him.

Loch tried to shout at her but found his voice throttled. He coughed. "What's matter? Who's died?" He cleared his throat.

She sniffled and smeared her face with the back of one hand. "Begging muster's pardon. It's yer brother."

Loch mac Mofemis could not accept this. The girl was an idiot. She had seen a headless body and assumed it to be Long. Her meager tick's brain couldn't distinguish between two tartans, much less two similar shades of a cloak. What nonsense. He batted her aside as he went out to see for himself.

The crowd was carrying the body right to him. He stopped dead outside the tent. They brought the body to his feet. There were the rings and bracelets and silver bands of his brother. The torc had been taken with the head. Loch realized coldly that he was now the family leader—he must have that torc. Like it or not, he would have to confront what he had rejected not an hour ago.

Ailell had set a feast for him, knowing full well that he would have to come. Ailell repeated their offer to him in Finnabair's presence this time. She seemed to take no notice, however, sitting blankly beside them. Was she grieving over his brother, he wondered?

"We want to apologize," said Ailell. "We're sympathetic to your plight. After all, if we hadn't exaggerated Cú Chulainn's youthfulness to you, your brother would still be alive and you would be . . . be receiving so much honor right now for having slain him." Just then, Maeve came in behind Loch.

"I'd rather fight a man than a whelp," he persisted.

"Why?" Maeve asked. "Will you turn from him if he fails to meet your specifications? Your brother is slain, your family left without its head both literally and figuratively. Should I send out others before you so the Hound might age like a cask of wine? What do you want, mac Mofemis? He was old enough when he brought down Nad Crantail. He had a beard then."

"People say it was just mud and grass he'd smeared on."

"People chatter. He still owns your family."

He smashed his cup against the ground. "All right! I'll strike him down once and for all."

Before he could leave, Maeve reached out and grabbed his arm. "One request. Your brother fell already at this ford. Rather than fight where the waters are tainted, demand your confrontation at the next ford along."

Ailell fretted. When Loch had gone, he said, "I'm worried that he'll reject the battle when he sees Cú Chulainn at last."

"That is no longer a problem. Before he returned, I sent my bondsmaidens down to the water to taunt the Hound. They pretended to bathe and call out to one another how no one else will face Cú Chulainn because he lacks proof of his manhood. They suggested to each other loudly that he ought to smear his face with berries. Shortly after that, they were 'surprised' by his appearance on the banks above. He had purpled his chin with woad and, more than that, he held a patch of grass to his jaw while he addressed them."

"And while he's gone downstream to fight his new battle, we can steal across and take back the Donn, hmm? It breaks no rules since the bull's already on the other side of the ford."

"You concern yourself too much with your *fir fer* rules of combats. 'Fair play' decisions would not apply to this in any case because Loch's duel has nothing to do with our combats. He has gone out of personal revenge—a family matter meaning nothing to us."

"You have a fine interpretation of the law. What do you

think are the chances Loch might actually succeed?"

Finnabair sniffled. Maeve said, "What do you think are the chances of divine intervention on his behalf?"

5. The Badb's Promise

Duffach brought the news of Loch's impending combat to the Ulster camp. "Gone to demand back the torc mac Mofemis. Hot-blooded by all accounts."

"So it might do to have witnesses," Fergus concluded. He and Duffach set off together. They became confused upon finding the ford abandoned. Numerous chariot tracks led further downstream and the two men followed. They heard the shouting of a small crowd before they arrived at the second ford. Here were the Druid judges: as the two arrived, Gabran the *fili* made his way through a fen of rushes to the water's edge and proclaimed that there would be a great trampling in that place.

Cú Chulainn waded into the water. It reached just below his knee at that spot. Loch mac Mofemis came in. A shieldskin of carved horn covered his shoulders and chest. At this distance, Loch saw that the darkness on Cú Chulainn's chin was a stain like a rare birthmark. He colored with shame. Why had the boy done this, unless to make fun of Loch's pride? Angrily, the Connacht warrior waded in deeper and took the first swing at his enemy.

Cú Chulainn blocked the blow with his shield, then, using its raised umbos, battered Loch away. Loch stumbled, slid, but kept his footing. He splashed forward again. Cú Chulainn moved back for a better stance.

A huge black eel coiled suddenly up his leg. It stretched to his other leg and snarled his other foot, all with such lightning speed that Cú Chulainn was lashed off his feet.

Loch bounded forward, seeing his chance.

Cú Chulainn strained to keep his head above the water. The eel slithered up his body, its weight bearing him down. He managed to block the first of Loch's blows with his shield again and raised it blindly to take the next. The eel slid around his throat and dragged his head under the water.

Loch swung with all his might. The shield caught the force of his blow, but the blade slid off and bit into Cú Chulainn's arm.

The water shot up in great gouts as the Hound and eel wrestled. Loch might have killed him then but the violent thrashing and the slapping tail of the eel knocked him sideways time and again. Even so, he got in enough unfended blows to dye the water red.

"By Macha's Mane," Fergus exhorted Duffach, "he's going to die if we don't do something."

"You can't interfere in a combat and you know it." The black *brithem* glowered at Fergus. "All you can do is call to him." Then Duffach added softly, "Make him mad."

"Sometimes you amaze me." Fergus shoved his way forward to call out, "Look at that shrunken little dwarf out there. Even the fish can best him!" The crowd started to laugh, some to jeer. Fergus went on derisively, "What did that infant expect to gain against the likes of a real warrior like Loch? And with half of Maeve's army watching, what an embarrassment. I don't dare think of the nasty things that Gabran will say about him afterward." The crowd added their own ridicule. Fergus moved back through them.

"You couldn't have done more if you'd been Bricriu himself," Duffach assured him.

A huge geyser burst up in the middle of the Flurry, sending Loch sprawling, crushing flat the reeds. At the top of the spout, Cú Chulainn squeezed the eel's throat and slit its belly open. He plunged his hand into the gash and tore the slimy monster from its hold. With all his might, he flung it at the crowd. It flew past them and smashed against a boulder. Everyone turned in time to see the eel rupture into a dense black cloud.

Cú Chulainn plummeted back into the stream, seeming to push the geyser back down as he fell. A towering wave formed below and began to roll up the river.

At the previous ford, the Donn had been taken and the other cattle were being escorted back to the camp. The wave appeared without warning. Herdsmen screamed and ran for their lives. The cattle panicked and galloped in every direction. The wave caught many, sweeping men, horses, and cattle along with it. Part of the escaping herd stampeded into the Connacht encampment, ripping through tents and trampling dozens of hapless victims.

Cú Chulainn had terrible wounds on his legs and arms, but the eel had taken the slashes aimed at his belly and head. He wove forward again, up to his knees in blood as much as water. Loch waited for him, shifty in his stance.

Behind Cú Chulainn, the air clapped with thunder. Out of nowhere a small herd of cattle appeared. They hit the water in an instant and he dove for safety. He came up spitting. His fingers had found a good smooth stone under the water. He dropped his sword and pulled his sling from his belt. All that remained was to identify the Badb among the cattle.

He found her slinking behind them in the guise of a she-wolf. Before he could get a clear shot off, she had turned the herd away from the fleeing crowd and was driving them back at him again. Cú Chulainn flung the stone, then made a leap to carry him over the horns of the steers bearing down on him. The stone sailed true and burst the wolf's eye. The cattle slowed and began to wander aimlessly. He drove them out of the river, but the wolf had disappeared.

Loch hung back now. His opponent was obviously weakened but not to the extent that he couldn't fight; and getting close to him might prove fatal, too, if whatever these demons were tried another ploy against him. Loch scanned the riverbank.

Where the cattle milled about, one huge red heifer suddenly broke from the herd and charged down toward the shallows. The other cattle turned and followed, more like an army of ants than a herd of cows. Cú Chulainn swung about to see the heifer, her head down, coming straight at him. He tumbled out of her path into deeper water. Diving down, he collected another stone, fit it in his sling, then kicked back up. He burst from the surface in a somersault that carried him over the herd. Upside down, he located his target and snapped off his shot. The wide flat stone cut through the forelegs of the heifer and she crashed down on her knees. Her body sank out of sight as the water turned to red froth around her.

Silence fell upon the scene. The cattle had become bovinely sluggish once more. The crowd dared to edge back to the bank. Cú Chulainn dragged himself back into the middle of the stream. He began to shiver.

Fergus thought that he must be entering his Warp Spasm; instead, Cú Chulainn's eyes rolled up and he began to chant.

*"I stand in solitude
against all comers, even those
who are not human try my edge
to see how sharp I am.*

*Blades grow dull if not honed;
I take the challenge from these
Thieves of cattle and our courage.
But, Conchovor, come soon now, rise and challenge!*

*I am the only tree not knocked flat by the wind.
You others had better find your roots again.
No fortress wall is built of just one stick—
a barrier takes many many trunks.*

*Now I grow weary.
Laeg, send me my best
If I'm to challenge another fool
in this contumely contest!"*

He made clicking noises in his throat as he came out of the chant. His eyes opened wide and blazed like prisms catching the sunlight. He sought for his sword in the blood-muddy water and found nothing but Loch's shield floating there.

Loch realized that if he did not strike now he would have no other chance. He wrenched free of the muck and slogged at Cú Chulainn again.

Fergus stopped breathing. His belly became a knot.

6. The Old Woman's Cup

Loch swung a fierce blow in a roundhouse. Cú Chulainn scooped up the shield and fended him off. Loch swung again with all his might and the shield split in two. The blade slit across Cú Chulainn's arm.

Something flashed on the surface of the water. Members of the crowd skittered back, thinking some new monster was about to arise. Others observed the figure of Cú Chulainn's charioteer waist-deep further upstream. They watched what appeared to be a silver needle skim past the bank where they clustered.

Cú Chulainn flung the halves of shield at Loch and leaped out of the shallows. Loch fell back from the killing blow he had intended. He glimpsed something bright beneath Cú Chulainn's foot, something candescent that moored his attention. For a moment he forgot his purpose—long enough for the Gai Bulga to seek a space beneath his horned plating and snap out from the Hound's foot as if with a will of its own.

Loch tried to slash down at the mangling spear but he lacked the speed and cut the water behind it. By then his fingers were stiffening and pain had overtaken his thoughts. He slid down in the water and sat with it up to his armpits.

Cú Chulainn said, "Yield to me."

Loch said, "Done. The family mac Mofemis needs its torc no longer, now that it lacks the head for displaying."

"True words. You won something, anyway."

Loch mac Mofemis shuddered. His head sank against his chest. He might only have been sleeping in the water, but everyone knew he was dead. In leaning forward, he had brought the tip of the Gai Bulga out into view, where it showed like a hooked beak in his back.

The Druids declared the combat at an end and gave the ford to Cú Chulainn. The champion tottered toward Loch. He moved with mechanical purpose. The world grew dim in his eyes. The air buzzed in his ears.

Laeg helped Cú Chulainn sit in the back of the chariot, then hurried off to gather herbs for the seeping wounds that laced him. While Cú Chulainn sat there, a crippled old woman came hobbling, leading a cow along the edge of the water. He wondered if she were some peasant who had stolen one of the scattered herd. He smiled to himself as he watched her. His world had gone pale and dreamy.

Seeing him, the old woman limped up from the stream. She had one eye and squinted to hide the lack of the other. As she climbed the bank, she kept one hand pressed hard against her belly as though it troubled her. The cow plodded dully after her.

"Sir," she said to him, "you look turned inside out. I can see bone and muscle and vein where I'd be expecting skin. Would ye be dying?"

"Not, no," he wheezed. "Weary enough, though . . . to beg a cup of milk off you."

"That I'll gladly give." She drew a cup from beneath her ragged cloak, stepped back to the cow, and bent under it to squeeze a teat of its pendulous udder.

When the cup was full, she carried it to him. "Here's to ye, sir."

"And good health to you." He sipped the warm milk, savoring it as if it were the gift of life. "May you be blessed by all the gods of our province for the kindness of your cup."

The old woman straightened up and stopped pressing at her belly. "Let me refill it." She took it from his weak fingers, returning it to him full after squeezing from the cow's second teat.

Cú Chulainn drank, eyes closed, in ecstasy. "My blessing on you again," he sighed when he was done. Milk dripped from his chin.

The old woman raised her brows as if in alarm. The empty socket on the right of her nose filled up with an eye. "Here, here, now," she said, taking the cup away from his trembling grasp. His chin rested on his chest. She filled the cup from the cow's third teat and fitted it back into his hand. She had to place his other hand around it to keep him from spilling the milk. "You need drink one more cup to restore yourself, me lad. Just one more."

He wanted to fall back asleep in the chariot, but the woman sounded so fearful for his health that he mustered the strength to drink down the third cup. The milk was sweet and satisfying.

Dimly, he saw a hand reach under his nose to take the cup away. It was a slender, milky white hand with red lacquered nails. This troubled him enough to rouse himself from his lethargy. He forced his head up, whispering, "Emer?"

The illusion of Buan's daughter stood before him. She smiled in smug satisfaction. He understood how he had been tricked. "If I could," he gasped, "I'd repeat my work on you."

"But you can't now and you've done more than you imagined you would, for which I thank you. Three seems unlucky for you. Perhaps four would suit you better." She offered him the cup once more. "Drink this one and your wounds will heal up for a time."

"How long?"

"That's my secret. But if you wish any strength at all, then drink it."

"You're an evil bitch. Evil. You've lied to me before."

"Evil has no allegiance. I'll save you for my own reasons."

He saw clearly that she was telling the truth. He reached for the fourth cup. When he had finished it, he found the Badb was gone. The cup turned to dust in his fingers. He shook, then teetered back onto the rough boards and fell asleep.

In that sleep he dreamed that six more warriors came to collect his head. They glared at him with rodent eyes, rabid with the urge to slice up his life. He sprang up and swung his sword in a great arc that seemed to stretch for miles, lopping off treetops and hilltops as well as six heads. He saw himself from high above, the way Tuan watched the Battle of Magh Turad—saw the bodies spout their fountains, saw the rolling heads blink and lose sight; saw the sky turn black as if a raven as big as night had spread her wings over the earth. He tumbled out of the sky and sank into himself. The blackness followed.

When he awoke, Laeg sat with him, looking very grim. Behind Laeg a young boy appeared, all hazy like a ghost. Cú Chulainn closed his burning eyes and woke a second time, from the dream of having awakened.

XIV.
THE TREACHERIES OF
MAEVE AND AILELL

1. Cú Chulainn Meets Maeve

"By my reckoning," said the queen in the firelight, "the first Ulstermen will rise up in two nights. After that, the plague of pain will let go swiftly and we can expect to be confronted by an army that has the advantage of surrounding us. I say the time for your warrior ways is over. We have abided by rules of challenge invented by a barbaric caste who drink till they are drunk, then slaughter each other without regard for those selfsame rules."

Fergus mac Roich drew lines in the ground with a stick, seemingly deaf to her. Duffach started up angrily but was pulled down by his belt. The other warriors who filled the cramped tent muttered or made disagreeable faces. None contradicted her as yet. She obviously had more to say on the subject.

"These methods of arbitration—some of you have used them to Ulster's advantage—perhaps all of you. Well, I am neither a warrior nor some third-rate sovereign to be led onto the boar's tusks by such a pack of hounds, and I will have done with you and your challenges now. Go and complain to Ailell of your wounded pride—it means nothing to me. I have the Donn back now and will tolerate no attempt to slow my progress further. You are warned. Dilatory behavior hereafter will reap lethal reward."

Fergus stopped drawing in the dirt. He dropped the stick

and dusted his hands, all the while giving Maeve an up-from-under look. When she refused to meet his gaze, he turned it on her Druids in the hope they would rule against her. The priests lowered their eyes. Of course, he thought, they would see everything her way; they would side with her if only to defy the warrior class. Warriors preferred simple answers—life or death, black or white—while Druids demanded that codes be observed, laws enforced. Cathbad had told Fergus once, "Warriors are fires, blazing hot, and Druids simply the firetenders. We stoke in accordance with instructions from the gods. Much of the confusion that arises is due to the gods' being more fickle than any man, doubling our task. We must act often beyond our instructions to ensure that the blaze doesn't consume everything."

Fergus considered that Maeve's glaring error lay in her failure to recognize that the code of single combat always held sway, even in those drunken brawls she dragged into the dispute. It was so ingrained in a warrior's character that the code replaced instinct; ply him with drink, take away every shred of thinking and reasoning power—the warrior would still be left with that code.

He scraped the dirt with his stick again. There was no point arguing that with her. She could not see it from her position. Her needs dominated her thoughts. On the other hand, so did his. Deep down inside, Fergus knew what he wanted: a bloody confrontation between Ulster and Connacht, a battle so fierce that every hand in Ulster would answer the call, a clash that would put Eogan mac Durthact in front of him. That was what Fergus needed. Had he confessed this lust to Maeve, he was certain she would have understood, even sympathized with him; but she would not in any way have allowed it to sway her. Fergus resigned himself to doing nothing. Screaming at Ailell—and there were some set off now to do just that—would gain nothing, for Ailell was of that different caste, also. No, he told himself as he stabbed the stick into the dirt. The hopes of Fergus mac Roich rested with the Hound of Culann.

His wounds had receded within the hour of the Badb's promise, but Laeg kept him smothered in balms nevertheless, knowing that the magic of the weird sisters would lapse at the most treacherous moment. He intended to treat Cú Chulainn as if the healed wounds had festered.

The onset of night found them at Focherd, seated by their

fire, chewing tender slices of boiled beef. Cú Chulainn's arms and legs shone like milky quartz from the unguents smeared on him.

A messenger from Connacht emerged out of the darkness. His name was Traigthren, and the two warriors invited him to share their meal. Grateful, he squatted beside their fire and rubbed his arms. After a while, he said, "You know there are runners everywhere right now, out looking for your camp?"

"We've seen their torches," Laeg replied. "It's simple, really—we knew you'd retreat once you'd stolen the Donn. So we came here to Focherd to stop you. It's the most direct way, but wherever you went, it wouldn't have mattered much. It's all lowland around here. Anyplace else, you'd have to cross the Nith and its tributaries at least twice." All the while he chatted on, Laeg eyed the messenger scrutinizing Cú Chulainn. What tales would the armies have invented by now? And what would this fellow add when he returned? A description of some polished, gleaming creature with slicked-back hair and not a trace of a wound on him? That ought to set them all jabbering. "Why are you trying so hard to find us?"

Traigthren realized he was being asked a question. "Ah, well, to put it simply, the queen—Queen Maeve—would request a meeting with Cú Chulainn on the heights of Ard Aighnech this morning before dawn. He is to come unarmed and alone to her. She will come unarmed, too, with only her female attendants to protect her from him. This much trust is put forward."

"She could trust me with her life if I didn't want it so badly," Cú Chulainn said. "Go tell her . . . I'll come. And alone."

Warmed, Traigthren stood. With a final scrutiny of Cú Chulainn gnawing at a bone, he ran off into the darkness again.

"You must be mad to agree to it!" Laeg chided.

Cú Chulainn observed him over the bone. "Why?"

"Because her laws are above yours and mine. She holds to Druidic law and that law states that battle codes of equity apply to warriors alone."

"Where is the fault in that logic?"

"It isn't a fault, it's the specificity of the thing. Druids define a warrior as someone with a weapon. If you give up your weapons, you're governed instead by Coward's Law, by which legality you're fair game. Unarmed, you can be sliced as they see fit. The Connacht Druidry will support it by saying you renounced your rights."

Cú Chulainn tossed aside his bone. "That smells peculiarly of Maeve."

"It should. Sometimes, Cucuc, you astonish me. You tell me constantly that she's not to be trusted, that she reneges on every promise or else fills her offers like a meatpie with chunks of deception. Yet, here's an offer—obviously to destroy you—and you accept it with complete credulousness. In many ways, my dear friend, you are as innocent as Finnabair. If you insist on going alone, at least for your driver's peace of mind take a sword!"

"Very well. But I'll hide it under a leather shirt, strapped to my back. If she's straight with her offer, then I'll appear straight in my acceptance."

Not many hours later, while Laeg tried unsuccessfully to sleep, Cú Chulainn climbed the height of Ard Aighnech, guided by the light of a torch. At the top he found the queen awaiting him and encircled by fourteen cloaked bondsmaidens, their identities owned by the shadows. With their rigid postures, they reminded him of standing stones, a ring guarding an altar stone. All he could see of that "stone" was her feet. For days he had observed her concealment within her circle of shields. He found it hilarious that even here she feared him enough to hide behind her women. Then his eyes narrowed. There was something too martial in the positioning of those cowled *cumals*. Women warriors might stand that way, but not slaves.

"Maeve," he called out, "a *gift* for you." He flung his torch into the midst of the circle. The stones took life, scuttling like crabs away from the fire. Their hoods fell back. Fire revealed hard female faces, some painted for war, some scarred by it, all of them intent upon him. As they moved out, they bent down to pick up javelins hidden in the trampled brown grass and the patches of snow. Cú Chulainn scowled as he reached under his thick shirt and drew his sword.

Fourteen javelins shot across the height, flying towards one point. Cú Chulainn began to spin in place, his blade whipping up and down his body. This was the Windmill Feat, the Feat of *Cuilithe* that Aife had taught him. Faster than the eye could follow, he spun. Every spear point met his sword and snapped away at an oblique angle. The wide row of warriors found their neighbors' weapons shooting back at them. Without shields, they could only dive for cover. Ten of the women fell, impaled on their own steel. The remaining four turned to Maeve for orders, but she had fled. They drew their swords and advanced on Cú Chulainn. He still spun, blade whipping. Like a water spout he suddenly moved, skimming the grass. The warriors tried to unite, to encircle him, but he bobbed and whirled and lopped off all four heads.

Maeve had barely reached her tent when the call went up that something monstrous was descending upon them. Down from the height, the spinning pillar whisked, nearly transparent in its revolutions. Rocks sprang away from it. The thing passed from view into a stand of trees and holly shrubs and some of the nearer perimeter guards ran up to attack. Before the thing appeared again it was preceded by bits of bark, twigs and branches, all flung off the windmill with enough force to pass through other trees, rocks, and perimeter guards. The survivors abandoned their plan and scattered for their lives.

The whirlwind entered the camp, shredding tents, casks and wagons, throwing off burning peat from fires. The warriors learned quickly that the wind had a razor's edge. It blackened the snow with blood and steaming debris that was barely recognizable as human.

Its path deflected this way and that randomly. Everyone ran in every direction to avoid it, crashing into one another or accidentally flying straight into the lethal spout. It veered up the side of the height again, then spun away, vanishing down the road toward Focherd. People came out to watch the departure, young Cormac among them.

"Maybe it'll go kill Cú Chulainn and his driver," someone offered.

Cormac replied, "You idiot, that *was* Cú Chulainn." He saw Fergus mac Roich heading for the king's tent and went after him.

Ailell met them outside.

"Have you had enough?" Fergus asked.

"How many?"

"Who knows? Twenty, maybe thirty. Most are unidentifiable. And that's not counting the fourteen women who ascended Ard Aighnech with your wife but didn't come back."

"And I sent five others," Ailell confessed glumly, "to take him in his sleep."

"You'll never learn, will you? Your province may be the center of wisdom that Maeve so often espouses, but his skill supersedes your wise counsel. It's the well-handled weapon that kills."

Ailell glowered at him. "How well do you handle that weapon

of yours, Fergus?" He noted Cormac shaking his head exasperately.

"Go on," Fergus urged, "make your jokes. She's lost more warriors than you so the bull won't give her what she wants just now. But you're a long way from home. And you still have to cross Muirthemne again, *his* home."

"What can you suggest?"

"Go back to single combats. Honor his way of life that much."

Ailell seemed about to argue but finally hissed a great jet of steam into the darkness and said, "For now. But we'll send one an hour to hold him in place while the rest cross elsewhere and head to Dun Dealgun. We'll sort out a new course and strategy by then."

Fergus and Cormac walked away together. "We should go ahead of the rest," Cormac suggested. "Don't you think?"

"Probably. I just hope that, without us there to jibe him, he doesn't get trapped the way he did with mac Mofemis."

2. Class Struggle Defined

"How can they get away with this?" Senchan demanded. "How can they cheat Cú Chulainn?"

"It isn't cheating."

"What would you call it—fair play? Rotten bastards."

Laeg cocked an eyebrow. "Oh, and is it name-calling now, my brave lad? Perhaps it isn't fair—not to the modern eye. Perhaps it isn't fair to anyone, anyplace, any time. What you must understand is that you're observing two separate strata of my world in collision. Druids versus warriors. One brand of mysticism confronting the other. Here, sit down there."

Senchan got down, crossing his legs petulantly. Laeg had pulled him out of the encampment, back to the circle of stones on Muirthemne Plain. Looking at them, he realized there were only two stones unexplained. One was the strangely polished one that finished the ring. The other was the huge center stone, the one Laeg had trembled to touch years ago when this began.

The sun rode low in the afternoon sky. Senchan could hardly believe this was still the same day as he had arrived, yet that was what Laeg insisted. "Tell me what you're thinking," Laeg said.

Senchan's lips pressed together. "I," he began, but faltered and looked away.

Laeg moved around a stone and hunkered down in front of him. A wry smile played on Laeg's lips and returned the sparkle to his eye. "The Dagda bless me if you aren't worried on his account, just like Fergus."

"What if I am?"

"What? It means you've come to care how it goes for him."

"So I do. Now everything's held up because of this interruption."

Laeg sat. "No, no, not interruption—clarification. You're operating under a misguided presumption and it's vital you understand how it was, why these things that look inexplicable to you were the natural inclinations of the individuals—why Maeve scorned warrior laws and how she could support defying them. Above all else, you must come to understand this."

"Why?"

"Because without knowledge of what holds up the tale, the telling gets lost. One false turn and there's no truth thereafter. This is a good example. The order of Druids is as old as memory can recall, old as the Sidhe and the invasions that all the bards know. The Druids worship knowledge for its own sake but consider that knowledge to be of danger to the world. Since they're the only ones know just what they're guarding, I find it hard to argue with them on that point. Everything they know is kept secret: their communing with the gods—secret, both in manner and location; their skill at forming weaponry—secret; written language—secret. Just the sliver of history dividing you and me reveals their wisdom. You have your writing now, open to those who take the time to learn it, and where are the tales? Who recognizes the skill needed in the telling, save for a scattering of monks and a handful of toothless antediluvians?"

"I do."

"Yes, but Senchan, who else has shared your experience? Right now you have as much knowledge as any bard of my time who sang these adventures." He got up and strode from stone to stone as he spoke. "Druids and warriors are utterly polar. Druids nurture knowledge. Warriors slaughter it. The advantage goes to the Druids because of their secrecy: warriors fear them. Their skill with words makes them too dangerous."

"You said that before. How can words harm you?"

"Oh, come now, Senchan. Haven't I used words to provoke you, to turn you around? Hasn't your foster-father hurt you more with his curses and scorn than with his fist? Which sting lasts longest? And *his* attacks are brutishly spewed jibes. Imagine a group of mysterious people whose whole existence is bound up in the precise manipulation of language to either support or tear down individuals. Remember Levarcham, who was so skilled at her craft that all Ulster avoided her? People in my time would jump off a bridge or crawl up inside a beehive rather than confront a satirist. A good satire spreads like fire. Embarrassment hangs over it like smoke; and the wider the fire the thicker the smoke, until the shame presses so much the victim can't bear it. They die. Words kill them.

"Satirists are part of the Druidic order. They protect the order from prying warriors. Cú Chulainn has no such people at his disposal, and worse than that, Connacht is the center of Druidry. The best of them are there. His one protection is his divinity.

"Druids side with kings over warriors. Always. Cú Chulainn's specialness fends them off, yes, but the rules that govern his life as a man of Ulster do not rule Maeve and Ailell or their advisors. They exist on a level above the warriors' code, along with the Druids, and this allows them to manipulate that code."

"But Cathbad—"

"All Druids, Senchan. Cathbad's more sympathetic to the code because he once blundered along as a warrior. Nevertheless, had he not been struck down by Macha's Curse, he would have been by my side at every ford, mocking the warriors who opposed Cú Chulainn, though Cathbad was not a satirist as such."

"What is he, then? A judge?"

"That, and more. Cathbad's a rare one. He combines all aspects of Druidry, and he's renowned as are few others. He is a teacher."

Senchan's brows knitted. "But, then, wouldn't he have to side with Connacht?"

"No. His allegiance is to his province, to the king and queen on his level who govern his province, a choice elected for him by the gods. In his case, as you saw, by the Bull Dream, which the gods control. Druids did not oppose one another as warriors do. Their conflicts rage *through* the warriors."

"What about the Donn?"

"The Donn embodies the warrior in its wildness, in its willful intractability." He pushed away from Macha's stone. "But now it's time to go back, to make action of my words."

Senchan got up and walked to the last stone—the one of polished facets. He tried to pass through it and smacked his head on its cold surface.

"Not that one. We're not quite there yet. We go back through Setanta's stone." Senchan came back, rubbing the bump on his head. "The combats are far from over," Laeg explained.

3. Finnabair

Cú Chulainn's camp at Dun Dealgun lay in amongst a cluster of great stone blocks, all of which had been hauled from a quarry and deposited here, many of them already chiseled into tall standing stones, but others lay on their sides, rough and as yet undetailed as to their final appearance. Lugaid sought him and found him there, sitting cross-legged on a wide block, watching the sun rise over the hills, a wide band of purple sky under golden-edged clouds.

The King of Munster reached up from his chariot and clasped Cú Chulainn's hand. "Ailell sent me," he admitted. Laeg came up behind him and, climbing up on his rail, pulled himself up beside Cú Chulainn. "That's not such a terrible thing," he said.

"I'm beginning to wonder, myself," Lugaid replied, "but that's my lookout. Ailell's decided to stop offering his daughter to the army—"

"More like he's running out of warriors to accept the offer."

"And she's not got the sense to see how she's being used," Laeg added.

"True," admitted Lugaid. "She lacks some of what her mother has too much of."

"That's probably the cause of it just there—not enough to go around."

Lugaid mac Nois laughed. "It's refreshing to engage in such dialogue as this. I've missed it lately."

"They didn't send you out just to tell me Finnabair's been taken off the field."

"No, I'm here to pronounce the best part of the piece. Ailell wants to offer his Finnabair to you."

Cú Chulainn sat dumbfounded, his mouth hung open. Laeg scratched his hair, then said, "One can only admire his gift for subterfuge. Who could have foreseen this?"

"Surely it's a great hoax."

"I think not. He seemed fairly adamant in the particulars."

"You know me, Lugaid. I don't trust him a whit."

"I told him he's wasting his time."

"But you must tell him he isn't. That is, if he cares to assemble a celebration, lead her out and betroth us. Then I'll accept."

It was Lugaid's turn to be shocked. "How can you say that?"

"Why, it's simple. He brings her out, gives her to me as my *adaltrach*, since in no other way can I comply—and Emer must agree first—then I'll swear to leave off murdering his army for a while. Of course, my good father-in-law and his party will be expected to stay around a bit. Think of the time this gambit of his can devour."

Lugaid nodded, then broke into a grin as understanding dawned.

After he had gone off, still laughing, Laeg said, "We must be prepared for anything."

"Yes, but Ailell has more warrior in him than his wife does. Ulster *must* rise soon. The Pangs have to leave off, or else I'll drive this incursion from our province myself."

Laeg replied solicitously, "There are times, my friend, when I do not understand you—and no man or woman knows you more intimately than I."

Cú Chulainn's sparkling eyes were hooded. "I often do not know myself. Sometimes it's as if another's will seeps in and spurs me to greater deeds than I think possible, while I watch myself as from a secure place within—the mortal side standing apart and observing the godly half at its purpose."

Neither of them spoke after that. They jumped down from the stone block and went to the chariot. A short time later, two figures appeared on the hillside, the dawn now a band of fire behind them. Laeg pointed them out.

Cú Chulainn buckled on his sword, tucked his sling into his

belt. "At least no one will be disguised as a handmaiden today."
He wove his way among the assemblage of stone blocks and
pillars, pausing when he could glimpse the two coming down
the hill. At the far side of the blocks, he stepped into view and
called, "Ailell, I'm here to receive your generous gift."

The king waved and called back, "I'll betroth you two from
here if you don't mind. And she'll come back with me after—
you'll get her once all the terms are settled. But not before,
assuredly."

Cú Chulainn shaded his eyes and squinted at the man dressed
in the king's robes. It certainly was not Ailell, even though the
imitator had made a brave attempt. One more deceit had been
practiced. He could not believe for a moment that Lugaid had
been a knowing party to it; no, the King of Munster had been
tricked, too. Cú Chulainn loaded his sling from the debris
around the nearest pillar, then started up the hill.

The "king" pointed at him. "Don't you come further, treacherous wretch. I'm not willing to see eye to eye on this."

Lights flickered around Cú Chulainn's pupils.

"Um," the impostor stammered, "kings are above warriors—stay down where you belong." He glanced back up the
hill, sizing the distance to the crest. Before he could take a
step, a flying stone took him off his feet. Unintimidated by
high pronouncements, the stone passed through him and continued on.

Cú Chulainn ran up, his sword drawn. The body beneath
the robes was familiar to him. "That's the king's fool, the one
called Tamun the Stump," he muttered, more to himself than
to the girl standing rigidly beside him. The identity of the
trickster offended him more than anything Connacht had done
to him so far. They treated him as no better than a fool by this;
but they must have been certain that the deceit would work—
they had allowed the fool to come here with the real Finnabair.
She could not bring herself to look at him, but he studied her
face carefully, her figure the picture of grace even in this moment of terror. He could understand why so many warriors had
come against him for this prize; but even as he acknowledged
her beauty, his rage erased his reason.

He grabbed her piled, braided hair and dragged her off her
feet, snatched up the leg of Tamun the Corpse and pulled him
along, too. At the base of the hill, he let them loose.

Cú Chulainn selected a stone that had already been partially
worked. Mallets and chisels lay on the ground around it as if

the mason had been seized by the Pangs in the middle of a stroke. The stone would serve for the Hound's purpose. With one swift, deft cut, he sliced the stone in half vertically, so hard a blow that the groove was left smoking. Putting away the sword, he embraced one of the halves and lifted it up, over his head. Then he flung it down. The stone embedded itself in the ground. He repeated this with the second stone, and the two stuck out of the hillside like two calcified fingers as high as his head.

He picked up Tamun by the back of his tunic and one leg, and swung the body around and down onto the tip of the wider stone. The corpse cracked and split through the middle, impaled.

He turned abruptly to Finnabair. In all that time she had not dared to move. Her eyes bulged from the pressure of fear. Her repeated, flicking glances at him told her that the beautiful boy who had slain Tamun and looked her over on the hill was turning by degrees into something nightmarish. The Warp Spasm had begun to contort him, tying him in knots of fury. That by itself would have been hideous enough; but the twisting of his muscles had triggered the release of the Badb's Curse and all along the ridges of muscle that pulsed and blistered on him his skin split open like the skin of a broiling sausage, spewing blood and flesh over the stone, over the grass. Such was the Badb's intention, to destroy him by his own unnatural powers while he, in his blind rage, could not help but tear himself apart.

He roared and grabbed Finnabair by her braids again, ripping them loose from the jeweled pins that held them. Before she knew what he had done, he cut the three lengths of hair from her head. Then he gripped her around the waist with fingers swollen and as gnarled as roots, and he lifted her upside down over his misshapen head. Her skirts slid down around her torso, enclosing the both of them in a darkness redolent with the smell of her. "Hereafter," he burbled, "no one but I will satisfy you. No more carrot for your family to hang 'tween the army and me. No—more—fools!" She heard gravel scrape and sensed his turning. His hands shifted to flip her back over. He swung her down.

Driven between her legs, the tip of the stone tore her open. She shrieked in unimaginable pain. The sound, like that of a whole flock of birds, echoed and re-echoed all the way back to her father's tent. Her skirts settled over her legs and the stone that spread them. She hung there, her feet just off the ground, body twitching, head tilted to one side, her mouth slack and spilling drool. Her unblinking eyes stared through the monster that, puling, stumbled back from her. More wounds spurted open, spraying her with blood.

Now his form began to dwindle: the Badb had won; the full transformation could not take place. His eyes rolled wildly. Pink foam flecked his chin. He began to wobble back through the maze of stones, smacking into them, smearing them with red shadows of himself and coating himself with their thick gray powder. He emerged on the other side in his mortal form but nearly unrecognizable under the coat of bloody gruel.

Laeg saw him fall forward and roll the distance to the lip of the embankment and over the brink. He dropped like a stone into the swirling Nith. The dark water began to bubble and hiss. By the time Laeg reached there, dead fish covered the surface. They had broiled to perfection.

4. Turning Back the Clock

Ailell sat in a dark tent where he had ordered his daughter placed. Three Druids had cared for her since they had found her beside Tamun. She had not awakened. Her eyes would sometimes open and move, but in an ungoverned manner. A feverish sweat lay on her brow and lip, and she made tiny whimpering noises every few minutes; but she could not hear him when he called nor make any coherent sounds of her own. "Cú Chulainn has put some terrible *geis* upon her," suggested one of the Druid doctors. Ailell ignored the suggestion—the Druids had been unable to succeed with any cure. Of course they blamed the Hound. Ailell blamed himself. How did that indefatigable youth see through Tamun's disguise? Had the fool screwed up his part? Ailell had thought the likeness uncanny or he would never have allowed Finnabair to go off at all. Why had he not listened to Maeve this time and sent warriors to protect her?

His thoughts stopped at Maeve as against a wall. MacRoth

had returned from wherever she had sent him. Within an hour
he had gone off again, doggedly leading three satirists along
with him. Ailell couldn't fathom it. Later, when Finnabair was
well, he would confront his wife over this enigma. For now
he must stay at his daughter's side.

In locating Finnabair the army had found the bridge across
the Nith unguarded and no sign of Cú Chulainn. They had
pushed on from there to the ruins of the earthen fortress called
Breslach Mor. It had been an exceptional journey: no one had
died. Not one stone had come flying into their midst, not one
spear or errant chariot had appeared to hinder their march. No
river monsters, no whirligigs. Outside, mallets clopped against
tent pegs, warriors hunted up game for food, and servants blew
on sparks to get the dozens of fires going beneath the cauldrons
full of snow. Inside, Ailell tried to guess why the Hound had
let them be, why he had not killed Finnabair, and how long
they had before the demon child of Ulster set upon them again.
How long before his daughter would be well and whole?

He stretched and drew aside the fur blanket on the door,
then slowly scanned the bluish landscape of hill upon hill.
"Where do you lurk now, Warped One?" he asked. Finnabair
moaned and he dropped the fur and turned away.

The answer to his question lay not far from Breslach Mor
on a western height called Lergas. Dozens of cromlechs covered
the flat snow-covered height like monstrous petrified mushrooms. The two heroes were at the very center of the cemetery.
Laeg had made a bed of grass covered with cloaks and had put
Cú Chulainn upon it, his spear and sword at his side. Wind
slipped through crevices and made the cromlechs howl. The
stones kept the force of the wind off them, but the sound had
Laeg fidgeting and glancing fretfully into the blackness under
each capstone. He had chosen the cemetery of Lergas to ward
off the Connacht army, figuring that none would set foot in
here, while Cú Chulainn regained some strength. The idea had
not been to frighten himself to death.

He left Cú Chulainn and crept off to gather wood for a fire.
He wanted to build it up before night set in, ostensibly to keep
his friend warm; in truth he did not care for the idea of roaming
through Lergas in the dead of night for a few sticks to burn.

Upon returning, he set down his wood and lifted the blankets
to check Cú Chulainn's wounds. They still seeped like cracks
in a wine keg, and Laeg had already used the last of his herbs
to salve the worst of them. Things did not look hopeful, he

admitted grimly. He put some snow in a small pot and melted it over his fire, then added some leeks and dried marjoram he had scavenged.

Wind moaned in one of the furthest tombs; others picked up the sound like a chorus of despairing souls. Laeg edged nearer the fire. He would not be sleeping this night. The soup was thin, yellowish. The smell, at least, made him feel good.

He fed some of it to Cú Chulainn, and soon the warrior came to. His darkly ringed eyes barely flickered. His stiff mane of black hair stuck to his cheeks and neck.

"Where . . . is the army now?" he wheezed.

"Below. We're on Lergas."

"They've crossed the river, come far. Ulster?"

Laeg shook his head.

Cú Chulainn's hand brushed against his weapons. He gripped the Gai Bulga, fumbled for his sword, then used them to maneuver himself to his feet, Laeg protesting all the while. The effort of standing, even braced by the two weapons, took all the strength from him. Seized with unendurable despondency, he screamed out into sky, a warrior's scream that wound through the cromlechs, bursting out from the hill.

A thousand eyes in Breslach Mor looked up at the hill where the black gravestones stood ghostly, then at each other, then back at the food which suddenly became quite important.

A few strands of mist wove out of the tombs. Laeg did not see them at first—he was too concerned with catching Cú Chulainn as he fell, laying him down and piling the blankets on him again. After he forced the Hound to take more soup, he stoked the fire and lifted the pot to take some soup himself. That was when he saw the mist—and the form it had taken. It hung over the edge of the hill, an amorphous thing with huge eyes and teeth, the spaces between those features filling with deeper blackness every moment. The pot and wooden spoon dropped from his hands, forgotten. Never in his fiercest nightmares had he anticipated seeing the Nemain take shape. She was a huge head, shot through with stars. Her bared teeth opened and a howl emerged that shook the whole hillside.

The blackness rose up, whirling, then swept down, out of sight. Still he did not move, but listened to her howl. He knew where she had gone and he was more than glad not to be in that camp. After quickly ascertaining that Cú Chulainn would be all right, Laeg skittered through the cromlechs to the edge of the hill.

The night had split in two with the Nemain's cry. The entire camp rattled from the sound. Weapons fell over; casks blew up; teeth set to chattering so hard that the ivory cracked in some mouths. Two dozen warriors dropped dead on the spot as the blackness circled the earthen walls, unable to penetrate into the dirt, or so it seemed. The forces of Connacht huddled, shivering, their hands to their ears. They lay on top of each other and yowled like dogs or leaned up to their fires, close enough to singe their beards but close enough as well to mask the substance of night that beat at the ramparts.

Laeg, meanwhile, had been distracted by a red mist that had begun to creep down the hillside, rolling like a centipede over his feet. He rushed out of its path, then turned to watch it flow like a river of blood beneath the Nemain and into Breslach Mor. Once inside the desiccated ramparts it swelled, filling up the fortress until the fires dimmed to dusky glows. Within the mist, the warriors lost sight of one another. The Nemain spun suddenly into the sky. Her howl trailed off, died.

The mist spilled out, filling the entire valley beneath Lergas. Its color seeped into the landscape, turning everything ruddy as if beheld in the light of a blood-drenched moon. As Laeg looked on, a bright figure formed in the mist on the far side of Breslach Mor and strode into the thick wall, reappearing instantly on the near side as if it had jumped the distance. Laeg held his breath. Some instinct told him not to act out of fear and not to move just yet.

The figure became a man, dressed in clothing from another time and place. The light soaking the valley did not play upon him. The green of his cloak that floated out as if buoyed on the wind—that color could clearly be seen. Great gold and silver lines interlocked across it, and more such lines twined all along the border. A silver brooch as big as a fist rode on his breast, flanked on each side by the ram's-head tips of a huge, twisted torc. The man carried a javelin and a shiny black shield with an umbo of gold in the center and two wild, mythic horned beasts jutting from either side. His hair was short and curled, blond. The face was long, bony and somber. A helmet, resting back on his head, had a bird mounted on the tip, and Laeg could now see five prongs of a spear tip over the man's shoulder: he was dressed as if for some great battle. Laeg drew behind the nearest cromlech, then panicked and fled back to Cú Chulainn. The warrior stirred. "What's happening?" he asked. "I had a fierce dream."

"A man is coming." He was about to describe him but saw that Cú Chulainn was staring past him.

The man stood not far away, between two graves; he leaned on the butt of the javelin.

"Who are you?" Cú Chulainn asked. Laeg could barely hear him and was surprised that the man did.

"I'm your father, Lugh Lamfada, called by your cry. You've made a valiant stand, a brave defender—both of you. The Hound of Culann is great indeed." His speech was strangely accented, thought Laeg. He came forward, saying, "However, if I don't see that your wounds heal, the Morrígan and the Badb will have their fill of you."

"I cannot—the armies—"

"Enough. You've no choice. And the armies will go nowhere." Lugh put his cool hand on Cú Chulainn's brow. "Sleep. Let *me* guard Muirthemne as you once did when another hound had fallen." The warrior's eyes fluttered closed. Lugh sighed deeply and looked back at Laeg. "You've done well with your salves, defender of Ulster's defender."

Laeg acknowledged the compliment with a sheepish smile. He drew his dagger out from behind his back, returned it to its sheath.

The god cocked an eyebrow.

"How long must he sleep?"

"Three days. His wounds are infected from within by the Badb's milk. I will have to turn time back to save him. He will sleep his time in reflux and awake two days ago. So too for the army of Connacht and the cursed of Ulster."

"But Macha's Curse!"

"Will continue two nights extra—four more in all. Yet no one laboring under it will notice. They'll live it only once and they'll arrive in the same place. You and I and the army trapped by the Sidhe below, we will witness four more days of war before Ulster can stand. It is for this time that I stole away a king's sister and made this marvel."

Laeg was still trying to make sense of the tangle of time. "I don't understand the complications involved," he said.

"You're not meant to. Only those who stand outside time can see how the strands of individuals weave together and apart."

"Gods and Sidhe," Laeg muttered.

"Yes, and the dead. One day you'll unravel it, I promise." Lugh laid down his javelin. "You must rest now, too, and leave

to me your guarding. You aren't permitted to see this." The
god suddenly looked into the darkness beyond Laeg and said,
"Nor are you, young one."

Senchan flinched and went rigid. He had come to think of
himself as inviolable by the things he watched. He glanced at
Laeg but found the charioteer asleep on the blanket beside Cú
Chulainn. Then he looked back at the god and found Laeg—
the older Laeg—standing there, ghostly, beside Lugh.

Laeg said, "I've unraveled it, just as he promised, see? You
will, one day, too. If you were allowed to remain and watch
now as you'd like, you would go mad and die mad." He faded
away.

Lugh Lamfada laughed. The freed amusement encased Senchan, teasing him with gentle mockery, pushing a smile on
him, while his eyes squeezed shut and his body floated down
beside the fire. Lugh laid out a fur there before Senchan reached
the ground.

The god stood over his three charges complacently. He knew
their futures, each of them, and found each worthy of his fond
attention—even the youth from out of time.

5. An Army of Children

When he awoke, the first thing Cú Chulainn asked was, "How
long have I slept?"

"Three days," his father told him.

"Then the armies have escaped! I've failed."

Lugh sat with him. "No one has escaped you. While you
slept deeper than dreams go, the mist of the Sidhe blanketed
the army of Connacht. It lifted while you still slept, but before
the enemy could gather their wits to push on, an advancing
force was spotted, and the warriors, rather than load their wagons, took weapons down and prepared for battle."

"Ulster has risen, then."

"No, Setanta. Time has folded over on itself in order to
effect your cure, and as a result Ulster cannot come to your
aid for four days more."

"Then who came to attack?"

"It was the Boy Troop—the child trainees of Emain Macha. Too young to be ruled by Macha's Curse, they had sought this army twice through the retrogression before discovering Breslach Mor."

"They're very brave, those children. I used to play hurling with them till the sun went down. How many came?"

"One hundred and fifty, led by Conchovor's young Follamain. Ailell took charge and led a similar force out of the ruins to the plain north of here. Few of his opponents had real weapons; most carried wooden practice spears or their hurling sticks. Macha's Curse deleted many of them old enough to own their weapons."

A gloominess shrouded Cú Chulainn's voice as he asked, "And how did they fare?"

"None lived. Not Fiachu's little brother, Fiachna the Bloodspiller—a great name for one so small—nor Follamain herself, although Ailell would have preferred her for a hostage against the day of battle with Ulster. Follamain took a real sword from one of her fellows who had fallen and began slashing her way toward the king, roaring till her throat was raw that she would not desert the plain without the king's head for a trophy. She slashed warrior after warrior who tried to block her advance but finally found herself trapped between two groups at once and could not defend herself against the superior numbers and skill."

"This is more tragic . . ." Cú Chulainn broke off and turned his face away to stare up at the clouds riding the sky like soft chariots. "Think of all those who will awaken in four days to find their pride cut down . . . while they could do nothing. Was there ever a grimmer dawn?"

"Such are the consequences of the Pangs, Setanta." Lugh reached out and helped his son to stand. Cú Chulainn inhaled deeply the crisp air and wiped his watering eyes. His muscles shook off the cold. He stretched his arms, then bent down and pressed his palms flat against the earth. Scars remained from the fierce wounds but his body had re-formed, hard and tight and ready for any conflict. "Will you fight beside me to avenge that slaughter?" he asked.

Lugh shook his head. "The song sung here is yours alone. I will watch with pride in my heart. Goodbye, Setanta." He embraced his son, then strode into the sun that crested the hill between two cromlechs. The javelin spun in his hand, flashing sparks off the dawn. Soon only the sun remained.

Cú Chulainn made a fist. Strength surged down his arm. "Laeg," he called, waking his driver, "the time for single combats with these butchers is past. So many betrayals have a price." The shimmer of lights burned in his eyes. "Prepare the Sickle Chariot."

6. A Grim Vehicle

On either side of the chariot that Domnall Mildemail had given Laeg there were screens below the rails, which ran from front to back at the height of the wheels. The inner side of these screens had been hammered into trumpets and triskeles that exactly duplicated the designwork on the exterior and gave the impression that the screens were all one sheet of copper. However, the inner panels, attached to the inside of the rails, formed an enclosure and could be removed. Laeg slid them out of their grooves in the floorboards and set them aside, then turned to the implements they had concealed. Some were simple crescents, others had intricate hooks and barbs worked along their cutting edges. As Domnall had taught him to do, Laeg removed each sickle and fit it into the slot designated for it.

The first two, the largest, clipped into notches in the hubs of the wheels. Smaller ones fit into holes hidden along the bottoms of the rails and under the boards at the rear. Laeg had to slide some of the heads out of the way to attach all the sickles.

Another panel at the front opened to reveal the armor for his horses and the battle dress he would wear. He decorated the stallions first, cautious of the barbs and thorns worked onto their headgear and bridle-bits.

He drew off his tunic and cloak, rolled them up, and tucked them into one of the emptied compartments. The tunic for war was made of quilted leather like his trousers. It was sleeveless and cut open at the sides so as not to hinder his movement.

He strapped on a girdle made of pounded gold over this, decorated with rows of rings and discs. The helmet came next;

a massive structure with a squared-off base that angled out past his shoulders. Each side showed the curved horn of a ram in relief and, at the top, a stylized bird's beak projected out. The raised ridge of the beak ran all the way down the back of the helmet like a tail. For all the work and its size, the helmet weighed hardly anything at all. Laeg buckled it beneath his chin.

He unrolled a cloak of white feathers and clasped it in place on the leather tunic. Last of all, he took a small thimble-cup containing saffron stain and, with one finger, dipped in it and drew three large yellow circles on his forehead and cheeks. Now he was ready, the sun upon his face. He replaced the panels and stood back to admire the gleaming chariot.

Before climbing in, he went around to the horses and chanted to each a spell of protection that Domnall had taught him, a spell to make them appear as specters before the enemy. Finally, taking his goad, he climbed up and grasped the reins. The horses shifted, jingling their trappings. Laeg called, "It's done, Cucuc!" The hilltop of graves revealed no one.

The warrior appeared from behind a cromlech upright. He carried his full complement of weapons and armor; assorted spears, darts called *del chliss,* dozens of these; his sword hung against his leg. He had put on a black leather shirt and, over it, a tunic of twenty-seven skins that had been stitched into a thick quilt worked with beeswax to make the surface hard and glossy like horn. Laces under his arms attached the two sides of the tunic and could be undone easily, quickly. After climbing up behind Laeg, he set the spears upright in their holders. They swayed like bladed trees. He pulled his round red shield from off his back. Its edge of silver was as sharp as his spears. He placed upon his head a helmet that shielded most of his face, with wide eye-holes that offered good peripheral vision. A spike on top ended in the figure of a hound with its jaws open.

"Now, we go," he said sonorously, the helmet reverberating as from the voice of death.

The chariot shot forward, spears waving, heads swinging against each other and against scythes, the horses prancing proudly to the edge of the hill, knowing that this was what they had been trained for, this their reason for living.

Breslach Mor lay deserted, its ancient rubble augmented by fresh trash and debris. To the north they saw carrion-birds come to feast. The snow on the plain had turned muddy brown from the passing of so many. The dark track led both north and south, nearly the width of the valley itself. Cú Chulainn insisted they first go north, to inspect the scene of battle.

The birds fled at their approach. Neither of them paid the birds any heed. Their eyes were drawn ineluctably to faces of the children. Many seemed only sleeping in their downy beds, cloaks hiding their wounds, the grayness of their flesh. Faces stared up at the two men with shock and disbelief, expressions that had already outlasted their time. Cú Chulainn saw mouths everywhere calling to gods or to mothers and fathers, faint voices echoing in his head. He could not shut out the sound though he turned his attention to other things, to hands reaching for blunt weapons, willing in their posture to take up the fight again if only ... Did the distant fathers know what had happened? Would these ghosts haunt the empty playing field on Emain Macha come next spring? Yes, if only by their absence, bestowing silence. Unnatural silence was always haunted.

The floorboards creaked behind Laeg. He tilted back his head to see over his shoulder; the wide helmet blocked all but a sliver of the Hound. That proved enough. The visible arm and leg were rippling, twisting, cords of muscle rising up with ropy texture. The leg rotated with every pop of new muscled knot until it had twisted backwards below the knee. The skin turned vein purple. Finger joints swelled with lumps that cracked. Laeg goaded his horses. The chariot flew past Breslach Mor. He heard the laces of Cú Chulainn's tunic snap free. The helmet with the hound on top clattered on the floor and wedged up between Laeg's foot and one screen. The Boy Troop had done this; grief had unleashed the demon.

Filling the wide basin of a dark green valley, the army soon came into view. The thing behind Laeg heaved and growled. The mossy ground, devoid of snow, was full of ruts and gouges from those who had come before. The chariot crashed across this landscape, the sound of its approach causing those at the rear of the army to draw up. They shielded their eyes, thinking at first that a straggler in the army of children had found the resolution to attack; then they saw the enormous thing that bent the boards behind Laeg, and they began to run.

The air grew points suddenly——dozens of small darts came whizzing like wasps through their midst, each of the *del chliss* sailing until it had found four targets. People and horses sprawled across the paths of those still alive. The chaos alerted those further ahead, who slowed up to take stock of the commotion and saw the single chariot veering off to encircle them. They took up their weapons, shouted and flicked their reins, bounded off to chase the new-found foe, unaware as yet of the swollen thing hunched down in the back of it. The chariot swung around suddenly and charged into their midst. Warriors scattered in every direction, seeing the gleaming armament, but the scythes cut a swathe through them, spreading carnage like two long barrows on either side. Shredded bodies piled high.

The fiend leaped out of the vehicle. Its hair stood out in needle points, gold at the tip, red in the middle, and black at the root; a weird glow connected the points, spitting and sizzling. The forehead of the creature stuck out like a block of stone over its eyes, one of which had popped out and now dangled down the monster's cheek. The bottom half of its face was all mouth. It bellowed its rage at them and the nearest could see the lungs at the base of the gullet, glowing red as a brazier. The thing stalked forward, twisting its body with each step. Lumps ran like living things, like moles, beneath its warped and swollen skin.

The monster charged, flinging the last of its darts. It took spears from the first victims and shot them through two or sometimes three opponents at once. Some fled it and ran blindly into the path of the returning chariot. Others, bounding in from further ahead, cleared the corpses only to confront a vision that stopped them in their tracks, where the spasming monster tore them apart, flinging limbs and heads into the sky. Blood and flesh fell like hail over the whole plain. More fools rushed in every moment to add to the rain.

The monster's forehead split and black blood jetted up. The creature bellowed like a bull—many thought in their final moments how like the Donn it was. The bodies piled higher and higher around it while every weapon glanced off or bent against its rippling skin. Nothing could touch the thing, and the flow of battlers ebbed as, realizing this hard fact, they scrambled for their lives out of cold, clear reason.

The monster's corona smoked and flamed. The creature lowered its head and impaled on its spiked hair the few who remained nearby, flipping them up as a bull tosses away a hapless trespasser.

The chariot slashed through the pile of bodies and the monster bounded into it. The wheels sank deeper into the clay but rolled, spitting up rock and earth. Laeg navigated the gory obstacles littering the field. The cart shook as the Warped One shuddered down onto the floor and began to untwine. The lumps sank in, the right eyeball slid back up the cheek and into its socket; the other eye pushed back out; flesh moved like eddies of skin to reshape the creature as it shrank. The spikes of hair uncoiled like snakes and hung in a blood-clotted mane. The bright corona faded away. Pale, Cú Chulainn's head lolled onto his chest.

No one came after them.

At the scene of the incredible carnage, the king and queen counted their respective dead in disbelief—Ailell from the back of his chariot, Maeve on the ground, roaming the scarred field, shoving aside her Druids, protected by her shieldbearers.

"What happened here?" she called to her husband, her voice sharp with disgust. "I see so many of ours in the dirt but not one Ulsterman. Not one whose face I don't know."

She got an answer of sorts from the survivors, most of whom were drenched in the blood of their fellows. They described in conflicting detail the horror that had taken them.

Maeve dismissed the descriptions, but she listened to the awe in their voices, the shock of remembering. On the chariot and driver, their specifics agreed: a tall man in a helmet, with sun disks painted on his face.

"One of Domnall's students from Ablach," Ailell summed up.

"Which one, though? Fergus! Where's mac Roich? Bring him here!" she shouted.

Fergus was sought out and led forward. He grimaced at the scene of battle, an expression that the others who came with him mirrored. Fergus could not believe that Maeve needed to have the cause spelled out again. Nevertheless, he obliged her.

"Cú Chulainn?" she snarled. "You'd make him responsible for this? And the driver, his charioteer—that mac Riangabra? You make him the source of every body, every dead, your victor spoiling my plan. Then where is he? Where?"

"Gone. The Warp Spasm did this. Now he'll need to rest, to sleep deeply."

She answered derisively, "Warp Spasm. Damn your tricks and tales."

Fergus lost control of his temper at last. He grabbed three of her shieldmen and threw them out of the way, then crushed Maeve against the others so that his breath blew back her white hair. "*My* tricks? Damn your own tricks, you foul bitch! Your

lies brought the whirlwinds into our camps, cut down warriors
against the starscape, and left this ugly purlieu." He pushed
her into the open, then dragged her over to one of the piles of
bodies. Her guards looked on, unsure of what to do. Ailell
leaned against his chariot rail, his eyes those of a goshawk that
has found its prey.

"This is your reality." Fergus stuck his hand into the mass
of flesh, then smeared the warm blood over her face. "Taste
it! It's your blood—you made the hole that spilt it. My tricks,
oh mighty queen, can't compare. Go back to your dazzling
Druids and have them drag out their cauldrons for you, see if
they can dip these lifeless sausages in and give you back anything."

He turned away and stalked the gathered, taciturn Druids.
"Here, show this army your amazing skills at reviving the dead,
you quivering, secretive bone-rollers! Commune with the gods,
tell us how this fits into the great scheme. Justify it like you
always do—they're only warriors after all, aren't they? But if
I set to slaughtering you, how many do you suppose I could
get before one of you could call down doom or think up a
lampoon excruciating enough to kill me? Maybe all of you,
heh?"

"Fergus, enough!" shouted Ailell.

The Ulidian warrior cuffed a Druid out of his way, but made
no reply to Ailell, knowing who was right. He continued on,
with his own uncertain force following. He had not gone far
when he encountered MacRoth. The messenger looked tired
and worn. MacRoth read Fergus's mood instantly and stood
aside to let him pass. They eyed one another briefly with sus-
picion, but Fergus's followers prodded him on. He continued
to peer back at MacRoth. A moment later, he bumped up against
Lugaid.

"By my gods, man," said Lugaid, "we could hear you five
miles away." Behind him, Larene studied his toes. "What can
you do now that you've near strangled the queen yourself?"

"I'll tell you what I can do...I can get drunk. Care to
join?"

Lugaid clapped him on the back and they walked off to set
up a tent.

MacRoth turned away then, also. One corner of his mouth
had begun to twitch.

XV.
FERDIAD

1. MacRoth's Return

They set Maeve's tent up in a stand of leafless oaks. MacRoth followed close on her heels, but distractedly, blind to the work going on, the servants on their knees, still roping the last of the pegs. He did not come to himself until he had reached the doorway, then turned and said, "Good job, well done," gesturing at them to let them know he had noticed; they looked to him to tell them when their performance particularly pleased Maeve. A thousand insignificant gestures went unnoticed by all but MacRoth.

Inside, he could not see a thing because the shadows of the oaks lay upon the tent and no fire had yet been kindled. He listened for a sound to indicate Maeve's location. When she spoke up, he jumped.

"What are you doing there? Come and sit and have some wine."

He focused on her shadowy form in the deeper reaches and made his way to her across straw and furs. She had set out pillows for him—or for someone, he thought.

MacRoth took his cup and had just touched it to his lips when he heard a soft moan. He blinked at Maeve. The moan came again, a soft, viscerally erotic sound. "What?" he inquired.

"Finnabair," Maeve said.

"But what's she doing?" He tried to find her in the darkness, but identified only a large pile of furs behind Maeve. It shifted.

"What does that sound like to you?"

"Well, I'd rather not say." He pinched the tip of his nose.

"What she is, is in heat or something very akin to it. Ever since Cú Chulainn shoved his pillar up her, she has done nothing but lie in those moist furs like some salacious Sow Goddess. Ailell thought she was dying at first, but there is nothing particularly wrong with her any more than with rutting animals the world over, save that she is useless in future propoundments. All she wants is him, her *hound*. All she can say is his name, endearingly, while she drives herself into a state of thorough lubricity."

"How . . . unusual."

Maeve sighed heavily. "I am far more concerned with your news. Is he coming?"

"Madam, he is. The prizes you offered had no effect, as you suspected. He wouldn't come for Finnabair or half of Magh Ai or all the gold in Leinster. Once he made that clear I brought in the three satirists. The first sang a piece describing FerDiad as the recluse who hid from mankind because he had failed shamedly in his training. 'The Castoff of Emain Ablach,' was what he called him."

"How did FerDiad react?"

"You could see him wince if you looked hard enough. The second satirist went into a trance and chanted a divinely inspired poem about the 'turtle called FerDiad, who lives in a shell away from all society, cursed by his strength to love a weak man's life.'"

"And?"

"It wounded him, from the look in his eye. Wait until you see him, too. Unlike anything I've ever encountered. And you'll realize why I say that second satirist was divinely inspired."

"And what of the third?"

MacRoth swallowed some wine. "Frankly, she never got to recite. She came before FerDiad—he had ordered us out by then—as we were leaving. Her hair was all wild about her head and bardic robes, and she whispered to him that she knew a chant taught her by Levarcham, who had learned it in Ulster before they threw her out, about him and Scathach's other student, Cú Chulainn."

"Ohhh," interjected Finnabair.

"With—with that, he dropped his cup and doubled over,

crying out, 'No more, no more!' He agreed then to return here and listen to your proposal."

"So, that is the point which pricks him."

MacRoth said, "Be advised that might prove an undoing if you're not careful. His deep regard for Cú Chulainn might force him to die rather than give in. He'd likely do a lot for his dear friend."

"Then we must act to destroy his illusions on the subject. As always, MacRoth, you have brought not mere fact, but fundamental speculation. No better messenger exists."

"Madam," he replied, too overwhelmed to feign protest.

"If you have finished your wine, you may go. Know that, when this is resolved and my bull is in Cruachan, I will find some significant reward for you."

MacRoth choked on the last of his wine. He slapped his chest and got to his feet, forcing himself to wheeze, "They'll be here tonight."

"Good. I will see a meal laid out for them. FerDiad can stay in my tent until he can be accommodated otherwise. Yes, tomorrow, then. Tomorrow it will end for Cú Chulainn."

MacRoth had gone. Finnabair, in her furs, moaned, "Ah, Cucuc."

2. The New Champion: The Eighth Stone

Fergus rested his head in his wife's lap. His eyes wore the faraway look of a mind nullified by intoxicated reverie. Flidais and her husband were in their small tent, a three-sided affair with the open side facing the Black Army's central bonfire. Fergus could just see, from where he lay, the smoke rising into the gray sky past the doorway. The smell of beef and pork sizzled on the air. Besides him, Duffach and Lugaid and his crippled brother Larene (who had to make frequent journeys from the tent because his bladder no longer dealt well with more than one cup of beer) also occupied parts of the floor in semi-lucid states of abandonment. Of them all, Flidais alone remained sober—an ancient custom that still endures, as do the sober wives.

Duffach belched, tried to heave himself up into a sitting position, found that not as pleasant as he had hoped, and flopped back down.

"I'm boiled as an owl," announced Lugaid to the tent ceiling. The image struck him as particularly satisfying, and he added a long, low "who-o-o" as proof.

"How they've used us," Fergus said suddenly. "Flidais, tell me please what it is in a woman that causes us fools to follow her even though we see our folly clearly from far away."

She gazed down into his dark eyes. "Fergus, it's not what's in the woman, but what you men wish to find there—what you put in her."

Larene began laughing, an obnoxious nasal monotone that ended in a coughing fit.

"Did you allude to something basely sexual, wife?" Fergus asked.

"You see my point? Everything has a sexual side, though, to answer you. Who do *you* know that's sexless?"

Duffach decided he was cooked on this side and rolled over onto his stomach with a grunt. The sharp blue of his eyes was enisled by two pink seas. "Fergus," he said when he was comfortable, "did you marry Flidais for her wit?"

Fergus raised his head. "No, I—"

"He married me for my sex," Flidais put in. "You growling bear."

Larene fell, alternately laughing and wheezing, against Lugaid, who toppled over.

Fergus dragged himself to a sitting position. "Here we are, victims to the boy who slaughters like some spirit, unremitting and indomitable in his course. That little beardless shrimp, defender of Muirthemne, sure more Ulster's Hound than Culann's."

Duffach grunted. "I'd as soon gather up every one of us and go cut him down as hack at anything else. End it. No more treacheries, subtleties, that I don't even fathom. One open fight. Kill 'm and be done." He spat.

If he meant this to be ironic, the wryness was lost on the others. Fergus became coldly sober. "If that's your feeling, then take your black tongue from my house, you. The last thing you slew with pride were the girls in Ard Macha. Beware, Beetle, Conchovor's warriors don't peel you like a birch tree and use your hide for a tent flap in a feast hall—a warning to drunken boors to keep tight rein on their tongues."

Duffach leaned up. "And they called *you* a king once!"

Fergus struck him across the jaw with his clay cup, which shattered. Duffach fell but scrabbled up. He made it to one knee before Fergus grabbed onto his tunic and hit him again in the face. Duffach fell as far as Fergus let him before being yanked back for a third blow; but Fergus tired then and finally picked up the unconscious man and flung him out into the dirt.

Duffach's body landed at Ailell's feet. The king, with Druids and attendants who carried casks of beer, stared unfazed at the body.

"Mac Roich," Ailell called out with uncharacteristic riancy, "I'm always pleased at how my Ulstermen keep in shape." He stepped over Duffach. "Now, if you've had your workout, I'll come in and tell you about Maeve's unannounced guest."

"What do I care who she fleeces?"

"Oh, this, I think, will capture your attention—what there is left to capture, at least." He ducked inside.

It was some hours later, after the sun had set, that Fergus mac Roich, with thumping head, found himself stumbling out to the River Dee in search of Cú Chulainn's campfire. He was not too clear on why he had decided to set out. Somewhere in the midst of his beer-glazed memory, he recalled swearing to Ailell to kill the Hound. It would have been preferable to shrug that off as a dream, but Fergus knew better, even if he could not account for how he had traveled this far—a state of astonishment suffered universally by those who have drunk twice their limit. Navigation was a tight, hard thread that took every bit of brain-power left him.

He slid down an embankment, clattered onto a rocky strand, and splashed into a stream. The cold shock jarred him awake. He gathered himself up and tottered ahead, wading to his knees. It was Fergus's good fortune to tumble where he did: a hundred yards downstream would have seen him dragged under the turbid surface where this stream joined the river.

Fergus tried to get up the opposite bank. He made it halfway before slipping back down amid a spattering of pebbles and dirt.

A short figure appeared on the palisade above, a light silhouette. "You're not stealthy enough to mean anyone harm," said the figure, who by his voice Fergus identified as Cú Chulainn. "I thought the bull might have escaped from the sound of it, and maybe I was right." He reached out. "Here, now, take my hand and I'll pull you up."

"Stay back, little Hound. I might lack the underhanded skills of Maeve's favorites, but I've come for you just the same."

"Really?" Cú Chulainn lightly mocked. "It's either an incredibly skillful or expansively dim-witted warrior who comes to combat armed with a rudder rather than a sword. Or did you intend it to steer you across the Dee?"

"Don't taunt me. Ailell got my oath—"

"By applying his liquor till you're fuddlecapped?"

Fergus gathered himself up. "Nevertheless, I swore not to give you up till you yield."

"Draw your steering stick then, and have at me." He sprang off the embankment, somersaulted and landed on his feet beside Fergus. "Do your worst," he said.

Fergus fumbled the huge practice sword from his scabbard. His breath steamed and his teeth chattered. Sobriety pushed back the last of the cobwebs in his skull, bringing with it a reluctance to play this out any further. "You're too close," he said, then finally lowered the sword and said, "Faa!"

Cú Chulainn said, "Fool sot, my own charioteer will happily tell you that such rules as Ailell has invoked to bind you don't apply to unarmed men, which is what you are unless you're thinking of beating senseless a few fish. So long as the king of Connacht has your sword in his keeping, you can't *be* forced to do battle. That's established in the *fir fer*."

"But I gave my word," replied Fergus in a muddle.

"Then I will yield to you now and withdraw for the moment, provided that you'll swear to do the same before me when Ulster rises."

"Gladly would I agree to that." He stuffed the stick back into its holder and sank down wearily to a cross-legged pose.

Cú Chulainn remarked, "And here I thought that Maeve was the great intoxicator."

"She is. Let me tell you how great: there's a new combatant for you in the morning."

"I expected no less after the slaughter."

"My foster son, the vivisectionist."

Cú Chulainn grinned, then squatted down beside Fergus.

"That's more the Fergus mac Roich I've known, the hard stoic of Ulster."

"No—I'm no Ulsterman now. I'm *ecland* like any mercenary. I have no home."

"Not to me, foster father."

"Then sit a little longer and hear what this old man was to bear to you on lips cold with creeping death. The one coming at you tomorrow is your own foster-brother by Scathach, FerDiad."

All the good humor faded from Cú Chulainn's face. He squeezed his eyes shut as if a wound had opened in his belly. "Tell me that you're lying."

"I would it were so, but she has him here right now."

"What cause has he of anyone to come to *her* aid?"

"I don't know. No one gets near him. She keeps him sequestered in her tent, thinking to spring a great surprise on us all in the morning no doubt. Ailell has a spy in her household who saw him arrive under heavy robes so as to disguise his face. Her Druid satirists brought him in."

"It could be someone else, then."

"No. As I say, it's FerDiad. MacRoth had instruction to bring him."

"MacRoth." Cú Chulainn jumped up, shaking his head wildly as if to fling all this information out of his brain. "Can he have abandoned his love for me so readily? For a few cows or even Maeve's slavering lips?!" He yanked at his hair.

"I wish someone else had borne this news."

"No, Fergus. Better you than anyone. Of all the warriors on Eriu, I trust you most." For a while he stood silently beside the water, then said miserably, "Just when I think Maeve has played every possible treachery on me, she reaches into my life and finds one more path into my heart."

"It's—well, it's partly the fault of the Black Army. We related tales of you both to Maeve and Ailell early in the journey, in hope of turning them away."

Footsteps sounded overhead. Laeg appeared on the palisade. "There you are. I'd begun to wonder what you'd found and my mind conjured up impossible new treacheries."

"You should have been a seer, then," Fergus said by way of greeting. He got to his feet. "It's time I steered my way back with my 'rudder.' We'll all be on hand to witness, tomorrow. Prepare, little Hound. Believe me when I say she'll find some way to prod him against you." Outspent, he splashed across the stream.

Laeg asked, "What was that cryptic adieu all about?"

Cú Chulainn pulled himself up the bank, then told about FerDiad. "How can I prepare for something so unthinkable?"

"It's best, I think, that you spend this night with Emer. She ought to hear of this, and once battle's engaged there'll be no time. Tell her to prepare a place for you to lie afterward—we both know there are going to be great wounds to both sides. And listen to her wisdom. Ride her riddles."

"You?"

"I shall remain here to patrol the ford and guard your weapons."

"At dawn, then." He scampered off to the chariot.

Left alone above the stream, Laeg sat quietly. Soon his older, ghostly self came and passed into him, reshaping his form. "Let me tell you of FerDiad," he said abruptly. Senchan came and squatted down where Cú Chulainn had been. "FerDiad had been removed from warrior society ever since returning from Emain Ablach. His body had begun a transformation under Scathach's guidance, a transformation that continued after he had returned home, where he continued to practice, to hone his unrivaled skills."

"But didn't he love Cú Chulainn still?"

"Oh, yes. As much as I, surely."

"Then why didn't he refuse?"

"Remember what I explained to you about words, about their power? Only Cú Chulainn has exemption from the threat of satires. FerDiad may share his skills, but not his divinity. Had the Druids fashioned *full* satires rather than hinting at what they might do, then FerDiad might have killed himself out of shame.

"MacRoth had made other offers in the queen's name, including sex with herself as usual. All this was offered to him again when he arrived at the camp, and he accepted the proffered wealth but not the licentious encounter with the queen. He had altered too much in form to comply even had the desire been there—I can't say what actually lingered of his former self but I suspect that particular conatus had atrophied. That created a further threat to FerDiad, because no one ever spurned Maeve. His terse rejection of her earned him her undying resentment. She collected six mercenaries whom she passed off as warriors to guard him before the battle. In fact she intended to have them kill him once he served his purpose, for which service she'd grant them, the six, *everything* previously offered to FerDiad."

"Then he's going to win!"

"I didn't say that, did I? This is the plan, not the actuality. The two combatants have skills in different areas. No comparison is fair. Each has a, well, a gifted charioteer. Only one of the two will walk away from the combat, and Maeve has arranged to eliminate whichever one that is. And that's all I'll tell you now, except that the last dark stone in the Ring of Muirthemne is FerDiad's stone, and it's called, ironically, The Friend's Stone."

Senchan grew gloomier. "If that's the last, then he *does* win . . . except there's the one in the middle, isn't there?"

"I'm handing out no more clues, I told you."

The chill left the air. Senchan glanced around but could see no source for the sudden warmth. All was darkness. "Right now," Laeg continued, "FerDiad sleeps alone, fitfully. Cú Chulainn lies with Emer, their bodies riddling and seeking as always. It's only left for you and me to pass through that faceted stone. This will be our last pass, Senchan, our last crossing together." Laeg reached out suddenly.

Senchan took his hand. It felt empty, hard, colder than the night air. He had not anticipated this hollow sense of finality that filled him. He found that he wanted the tale to go on and on unceasingly. Eternity bound these stories; more than anything Senchan wished to become part of that, to become immortal in order to relive it all—even the fearful moments— every day, forever. To laugh with wry Cathbad and his peevish *vathi*, weep for Derdriu, and fight alongside Cú Chulainn. It seemed he had never known any other life. How could Laeg mean to end it all?

Brightness burst upon him—the late afternoon light over Muirthemne Plain. The stones threw off long indigo shadows. The one cast from Setanta's stone shaded FerDiad's as the two observers walked somberly into the hard and polished megalith, so near to the stone where they had begun their journey years earlier. Why, Senchan asked the unseen gods, could it not continue for as many more?

3. A Man Alone

Before dawn, Cú Chulainn returned to Ath Dee. Emer had sent him out dressed as if for a feast. She urged him to present himself to the armies before the combat began so that they might see his beauty to give them a comparison against the monster that had scythed their ranks the day before. As he knew that his wife's counsel always contained more meaning than appeared on the surface, he obeyed, dressed, and drove the chariot to the hill above Maeve's camp just as the sun crested the opposite horizon. His white robes burst into flame with that light, molding him into a figure of gold and purples and pinks.

The early risers below caught sight of this apparition and their cry awoke the whole army. Servants and slayers, virgins and seers, warriors of every rank, all emerged from their tents, gathered around their fires, to see the luminous observer on the hill.

They saw a short youth with his hair plaited. Two long thick strands of it hung below his shoulders—the tips blond from previous limings, the body and base of the hair black like his brows. The rest of his hair coiled in a tight knot against the nape of his neck. His pallid face could have belonged to a girl—that was what the nearest observers agreed—making him seem a gentle and fragile creature. His eyes sparkled like emeralds cut in seven facets. His jewelry was all of gold: torc, armlets, hasps, and girdle. He wore his enameled scabbard low on his hip. The shield he carried was the red circle with its gold scalloped edge and interior disks.

Maeve came out in her bulwark ring. They blocked most of her view with their helmet-top decorations. She grew waspish at having to ask for descriptions from these illiterate men and finally climbed up on backs of two of them, setting her knees on their shoulders, yoking them like a team of horses by their braids.

"That?" she scoffed when at last she saw him. "*That* is the whelp? You mean to tell me this girlish boy is the devastator of half my army? I don't believe you. I refuse to believe you. I have better warriors than that in slave's collars!"

Led by MacRoth, a tall, cloaked, and hooded figure emerged from her tent. He held his red cloak closed with a hand that was hard and shiny like a beetle's carapace. This figure's deeply recessed eyes took in the scene in sharp, swift flicks. A voice that made the bulwark members think of dry places parched by the sun issued from the red folds. "Believe it. I tell you, that is Cú Chulainn."

"But he is a child. Why, Finnabair is no older."

"That *child*, at the age of four or five, went to Emain Macha and bellowed for an enemy to kill because he thought himself disgraced by some warrior who'd refused him combat. One of Conchovor's 'wives,' called Mugain, saved the fortress and countless lives by leading all the women out against the babe. They went naked. He was so mortified, seeing their bodies displayed, that he turned red as a crayfish and hid his eyes with his cloak. The women laid hold of him somehow and threw him in a tub of water. The Warp Spasm, incipient even then—not outwardly expressed as such, but inwardly tumultuous—made the water boil and the tub burst apart. So the women dropped him in a second tub. It sizzled till the wood cracked. Mugain and the naked women finally shoved him into a tub of ice water and he cooled at last. The spasm that fueled his blood-lust retreated, leaving that beautiful, guileless child in the water, naked himself but still ashamed to witness the nakedness of the women."

"An abbreviated version has been given me before of that tale, although, naturally, when so godly a man as yourself tells me, I must accept it. Perhaps I should go naked to meet him, then kill him close up."

MacRoth eyed her skeptically. "I don't think the sight of a nude woman troubles him much nowadays."

The glowing boy on the hill retreated from sight but returned momentarily, carrying a cluster of severed heads. He held them up, called out their names. Grumblings issued from the scattered clusters; some voices began to keen, others to babble in frenzy.

And still, thought Maeve, he was too pretty for the task. Too precious a thing to live long. Like a fragile dragonfly, he must flutter and expire in a twinkling. She climbed from her warriors and ordered them back inside her tent.

Once inside, FerDiad went and sat beside his charioteer. He kept the cowl tight around his face but Maeve could feel his eyes on her every moment, like insects, and she did not care for the sensation. "Is there some question you wish to ask me?"

"Only if it's true what you told me last night—about what he said."

"That to defeat you would count as no great feat? Of course. Now I must go and be with my husband for a time. We will be on hand for your battle and I should not need to tell you that our hopes go with you and your guiding forces." She paused in the doorway. "Perhaps, after the battle, you might find time to reconsider my offer..."

The red hood shook violently its refusal.

"Ah. Well, it is a small thing." She left him, glad of the going.

"He should never have spoken that way about me. His denouncement stings like a Druid's verse."

His charioteer replied, "I don't believe for a moment that he did."

"The queen says otherwise. In any case, I've no choice so long as all the Druids in Connacht are preparing their cruel lampoons. You must go and prepare the chariot."

"This is so foolish, FerDiad. We can still escape this, just walk away."

"Where to? Where's the place the words won't find me— where I won't hear how I fell in love with him because of his feminine looks and his soft ways and made love to him on the Isle of Women, or how I came to him time and again, but was shunned in favor of Scathach's daughter and Aife. Aife. How sharply these people can tip their barbs and turn what was beautiful into an ugly, obscene union, making us monstrous."

"Why haven't they preyed on him, then? Why don't their threats work on him as well?"

"It's not the same. He isn't like others."

"Neither are you, I have to point out. Surely you remember the days with Scathach as they really were."

"Some." The rasp sounded a melancholy note. "Not all anymore. My mind's lost so much . . . as I changed."

The charioteer said, "Once, when I was your steward at Scathach's house, we went for a feast there. A huge, hairy fellow had taken the job for a while as her steward. We went across the Pupil Bridge and, at the door, Setanta deferred the honor of first position to you. You went in, but that steward, he resented you and thought you too proud, so he stuck you in the back with his cooking fork—a big, long one with three prongs like Manannán's trident."

"My armor—"

"You wore plates of horn then. Don't you remember?"

FerDiad said, "So he stabbed me from behind, the coward."

"Yes. And Setanta saw it from the doorway. He rushed in and killed that steward before he could stick that fork into your throat. Setanta carried you into another chamber, made sure your wounds were treated. That was the time you agreed to the transformation."

"I agreed. . . . Did she tell me of how my mind would . . ."

"She warned you that your thoughts would be reshaped as well, yes, that."

"What did I answer?"

The charioteer lowered his head. "You and Sentanta—all of us believed we were invincible then."

The red robe trembled. "Oh, why didn't you tell me this story when the Druids baited me? I never should have come— I loved him and we were lovers. How can I be here? Ogma, my god, how am I here?"

4. First Blood

They arrived at Ath Dee and found no one there to meet them. Here the ground was hard clay, dark but spotted with fist-sized stones. The sun had barely risen. FerDiad lay down in his depression while his charioteer kept watch. He did not have to keep it long. With Laeg at its helm, the Sickle Chariot came down the slope from the north. "Is it them?" asked FerDiad.

"It's them. Laeg, looking lean as always. Setanta behind him, doffs his cloak now, sports a purple tunic—against that his skin's like snow. Such a proud stance they're taking."

"What are you, a bard in their service? Your every word pricks."

"I had a dream last night," the charioteer tried.

"Yes, and?"

"The Hound of Culann stood upon every ford in Eriu like a giant Fomor with a leg for every stream. No one got past without paying him tribute. He stamped on those who opposed him, squashed them flat into the earth."

The red robe billowed; petrified fingers closed on the charioteer's neck. "The Morrigan has put things in your head. I need help, support, you give me paeans. Save versification for your funeral oratory—to him or me, it won't much matter. To the worms. You've been a friend. Don't desert me for feeble visions."

The Sickle Chariot came up beside theirs, wheel to wheel. Cú Chulainn said, "Who is it dwelling in that cloth cavern and claiming to be FerDiad? You've hidden your face because you know that he and I are friends."

"You were his servant, devoted yourself to his needs. He was your superior and you cleaned his weapons, brought him food."

"That's true. He was further along in training at first and I learned much from him. But still I hear nothing that merits my calling you by his name, gravel voice. Why should I trust anyone who denies such ties as he and I have for the liquid thighs of Maeve?"

"It's better to die in fair combat at the hands of a professed friend than from the slow degeneration of satirical repetition. The queen bitch would kill me either way. Choice alone remains to me."

"The third alternative's better, I think. Dead Druids don't often speak of irony."

FerDiad made a sound of exasperation—a clicking noise like the scuttling of crabs. "Oh, yes, for you that's the sweet answer. No Druids can rule you because your father's a god who rules them. But I lack your lineal good fortune."

"That's a weak argument—false in every way. No man needs listen to the false phrases poured upon him whether they raise him up or crush him down. A lie should always be squelched and the position of the liar is an irrelevancy, or else he would speak the truth."

"The more powerful the liar, the more powerful the lie."

"There we agree. And so the more powerfully do I strike him for it. Druids take one blow only, they're that lofty."

"Well, *I'm* not a liar," FerDiad proclaimed. "Your blows are all empty wind to me. I have a battle to join. We could chatter the day away and never agree. The time for that is passed. Now is the time for seeking death."

"Others have sought it before you. None has gone home unsatisfied yet."

"Perhaps, but none who know you so well have come till now, so strut some more for us, spider-mite. Thrasonical midget. You display your beauty, then boast a thousand deeds no one's ever seen."

"If you think that, go sample Connacht's army and hear otherwise. But you don't dare—you know already that none shaped by Maeve's meddling have succeeded. Count their heads on my rail. See any you recognize?"

"None."

Cú Chulainn leaned toward the cowl. "Neither do I."

One ossified hand reached up and jerked back the hood while the other unclasped the robe and let it fall. FerDiad was naked defiance.

The surfaces of his skin shone like polished horn. His whole body had grown hard in this way. At the joints the armor lay interfaced like a crab's claw, protecting the soft flesh beneath but not hindering movement. His torso had no hair on it and, like horn, striations were embedded in the surface. His genitals had been lost to a sharp tine that jutted from between his jointed thighs.

His face had also turned to horn. The cheeks had sprouted ridges, squared and planed. His cornflower-blue eyes hid in pits between the cheeks and rippled brows. Above this, his red-gold hair stuck up, a sedgy topknot. Even his ears had developed points and bumps and chiseled dimples. Horn hung in fangs around his mouth.

Cú Chulainn sought for evidence of the youth he had known in Scathach's camp. Not even the eyes revealed that person. They, too, in their way had ossified. Nevertheless, he knew this was FerDiad.

"So, you are yourself despite your dissimilar temper. I implore you now to remember our mutual love. Break off this quest for death."

"I remember nothing of it." His jumbled mind had indeed forgotten already the story his charioteer had told him that morning, that he had recounted a hundred times before. "I'm not made for love: I'm a machine of war that loves no squint-eyed demon such as you. I've never fought a girl before. I hope my honor can survive it."

"Your honor might, but you won't. Again I beg you, turn back."

"Coward. Nad Crantail proved it. I see it myself. I—" He stopped himself and turned away. "I've come too far!" His voice rattled with anguish. "Once you step off the cliff, you can't step back."

"I see that not all the hardness is on the outside, as Scathach warned. We have to begin. You were here first and you have the choice of weapons. The Druids will want to know. They've arrived while we argued. Along with an audience to entertain."

FerDiad did not look at the crowd behind him, but he called for the Druids to hear. "Darts, first!"

Laeg turned the chariot and drove back across the stream, where Cú Chulainn jumped down. He pulled off his clothing except for the wide sword girdle of gold. He reached up and Laeg handed him his round shield, then his darts.

Cú Chulainn went into the stream and, as he looked up at the rise behind FerDiad, he saw one of the Druids gesture for the combats to begin. Then he heard the Druid's voice, faintly.

FerDiad entered the stream and let his first dart fly. Cú Chulainn caught it in his shield, then flung his own, following it quickly with a second. FerDiad embedded the first in his shield as Cú Chulainn had done; the other spun off his carapace and stuck in the ground behind him.

They each drew and flung another dart, and then another and another, the darts flitting like wasps between them, wounding neither. Darts made new patterns in the enamel of their wooden shields, dotted sketches left when the used darts were drawn and thrown again, hard enough to knock a normal man off his feet. FerDiad's clawlike feet anchored him in place; Cú Chulainn's toes curled like talons around the edge of a submerged stone, rooting him.

The darts spun, whizzed, thunked all morning long. Some of the crowd drifted and returned to find the combat still enjoined. Finally, Cú Chulainn called, "Some other selection, if you would. This is fruitless."

"Hurling spears, then. My skill there will prevail."

Both men took up larger shields and long-bladed, sleek spears. FerDiad made his first throw as Cú Chulainn turned from Laeg, and the Hound barely had time to sweep his shield across himself, deflecting the spear. It struck into the streambed, the shaft vibrating. Angrily, Cú Chulainn threw his spear, but

FerDiad skimmed it easily off his shield.

Retrieving the spears took both men deeper, till the shallow ford became the distance between them. Still they drew no blood, but the effort of continuous propelling and dodging in the deeper water exhausted them quickly. They dove and swam madly for their spears so as not to give the other a free shot; this act repeatedly sent sprays of water up over the crowd, who had moved in along the river, some dangerously close.

Hours passed while the two went on, mechanically throwing, seeking an opening. Their breathing came in labored gasps, in shudders. The cold water numbed their fingers and toes. The crowd, unable to believe the duration of unblemished assault, began placing bets as to who would make the first mistake, take the first wound, and who would be the ultimate victor.

Then FerDiad scored. Cú Chulainn stepped onto a stone and it gave way beneath him. For an instant he tottered off-balance and in that instant FerDiad flung his opponent's spear. It turned on the lip of Cú Chulainn's shield, and lightly slit his arm from elbow to shoulder. Runnels of blood gathered and dripped from his hand. He stared at the wound, disbelieving. Both of the spears were in his possession now. He bellowed as he flung FerDiad's at him, then snatched up the one that had cut him, his own.

FerDiad blocked his spear and hurried to retrieve it, swimming with one arm; in his eagerness and exhaustion, he forgot the other spear's location for a stroke or two, until it flashed in the periphery of his vision. He raised his shield as best he could. The weapon skimmed it, hit the water flat and flipped up, the blade sliding between the segments of horn at his elbow and slicing into the pink tissue. He drew it out, sucking air through clenched teeth as he did. He threw it back, but the shot went wild.

After that, both of them revealed their weariness and, because of it, began to make mistakes. Neither scored anything close to a fatal wound, but by day's end both bled from dozens of gashes. Even FerDiad's plated shell had not completely withstood the violence of Cú Chulainn's throws when a fresh wound or nick had angered him. In some places, the horn had cracked or been chipped away, revealing the wet flesh beneath.

By sunset, when the Druids terminated the contest, the two were soughing with each breath. They crawled like infants after their spears. The Druids testified that the combat had been fair but would have to continue the next day in order to decide anything. For now, the army would have to remain where it was. Maeve left the scene in a fury.

The two warriors got to their feet laboriously, nodded across to each other. Each showed great respect in his weary glance; they waded into the middle of the ford, there embraced and kissed like old friends. The bond had been resurrected.

Turning away, they tossed their weapons to their respective drivers, who helped them out of the water and into their vehicles.

Awed by the day's spectacle, the crowd went off quietly; six among them wore glum faces, having to wait another day for their own glory.

5. Second Combat

The two champions spent the night on beds of rushes. Ailell sent Druids to both of them to treat their wounds. Maeve resented giving any solace to Cú Chulainn, but the king pointed out that rules of extended combat required such fair treatment when the opponent's side could not provide it and she would have to live with that. She tried giving added care to FerDiad, ordering her own healers to mix restorative drinks for him. Unfortunately for her, the plated warrior sent many of these to where Laeg sat watch over the robed figures ministering to Cú Chulainn.

By dawn the next day, both men had regained their strength and the wounds of both had glazed over from the salves applied.

They met once more at the stream, but today neither boasted nor argued with the other. FerDiad called out, "What weapon do I take up this morning?" Today Cú Chulainn chose.

"Rather than repeat yesterday's deeds," he replied, "let's take up our heavy thrusting spears and face off from our chariots." Even as he said this, he knew that neither of them would succeed at it because neither heart was truly in it.

They mounted up behind their drivers, who were on their knees. The crowd had begun to move back up the ridge to give the two teams room. Once more a Druid came forward and blessed the combat. Once more, the two friends fell to fighting.

All through that cold, lowery day they rode back and forth on the flat land beside the river. With each pass through the ford, they slammed their shields against each other and tried to perforate the other with their leaf-tipped spears. Their wounds multiplied, some so deep that the spear tips grated against bone. The planks of both chariots grew slick with blood. The drivers flung it from their hair, wiped it from their eyes. Nevertheless, the two warriors stayed upright, urging their drivers on, the horses gray with foaming sweat, eyes wild and teeth gnashing at the bits. Laeg's arms ached as they had not done since he was a novice under Domnall Mildemail. The veins stood out like tree roots all along him and his temples thundered from squinting against the strain, the sweat and blood. FerDiad's driver fared no better.

Wayward thrusts kicked sparks from the rails or cracked open one of the bobbing, swinging heads hung there. The bronze screens on both vehicles developed dents and holes. It was a wonder that neither lost a wheel rim.

Cú Chulainn spotted a Druid descending from the crowd and he called out, "Enough, FerDiad. See . . . our keeper comes . . . our horses are lathered, drivers . . . spent. Even my spear has lost its edge—look, it's curled. . . . We'll come here again, no choice." He fit the crimped spear into one of the embrasures along the edge of the floor.

The drivers brought their chariots broadside and the two bloodied warriors leaned out again, this time to hug one another, smearing each with the other's blood. They would have professed their undying love and deep esteem, but neither had enough energy left to speak the words.

The chariots parted, leaving behind a savaged, rutted ford.

6. Combat with Swords

The Druids that night were appalled by what they were expected to heal. These wounds cut too deep or stretched too wide for salves to seal: whole segments of muscle lay bared; the gloss of organs could be seen in places. Even the most arcane of prescriptions lacked any efficacy in the face of such a rending. A healing cauldron was briefly considered but rejected as too dangerous, since more often than not the warrior's personality was erased in the treatment, leaving him a healed automaton guided by some dark and wicked power, sometimes even a threat to the healer himself. No one cared to try that experiment with the likes of these two battling giants. The most the Druids could do was to lay charms and potent amulets across the worst wounds, then to chant incantations, charging the charms and sealing off the perpetual streams of blood, after which soups and potions could be ingested with some restorative effect. They dared not predict how much.

"Maeve, as you might expect, desired to move the Donn further south again," Laeg explained to Senchan, "but this time she had foiled even herself. The intense combat had captured the mind of every warrior on the plain and none was willing to aid her. The rules of *fir fer,* of honorable men, held sway. Ailell dismissed her suggestion with the simple argument that she had brought FerDiad here and now she could damn well wait for the outcome of her machination. For now, Crich Rois was her home."

"But they can't expect to really continue this another day? They can't even stand up."

"They will. They have to. If it took three or five days, the warrior fought on—that's all the creed he had—unless someone yielded. If Cú Chulainn yields here, then as he represents Conchovor on the field, he is giving Connacht safe passage with the Donn. For him not to get up is to forfeit, so long as FerDiad gets up. And neither can know if the other has come to the combat unless he gets up, so both get up."

"What if FerDiad yields?"

"Then Maeve and Ailell are enjoined from going to Cuil Sibrille for another day. In this particular instance—if you've been keeping track of your days since Lugh's intervention—such a defeat would carry us through the ninth night and Ulster would begin to recover. Of course, Maeve knows nothing of Lugh's having rolled back time. Right now, she sits in her tent, fearful that Ulster has already thrown off the Pangs, but not truly believing it. She has, in fact, surmised that the Curse may just continue so long as the danger exists—so long, in other words, as she remains in Ulster. But the fear still gnaws at her that Fergus and the Exiles receive messages from Ulster and might be conspiring to slow her army down. Ludicrous; but you see, Senchan, it's human nature to assume that all other people live up to or down to your own level. Maeve, willing as she is to defy anyone or anything because of her certainty of her own supreme privilege, is absolutely positive that every-one else she deals with would do the same as she. That's not to say there aren't some who would."

"But not Fergus mac Roich."

"Not Fergus."

Senchan folded his arms and brooded. He believed now that he had begun to understand what Laeg had been trying to teach him about the battles he had seen, but he could not yet put it into words, and that seemed important. All these bits of in-formation, of explanation and motivation, in some way were designed to clarify what Laeg wanted him to realize. The circle—and he smiled at the metaphor—the circle remained open. The ring was complete, the Friend's Stone being the last. He saw that great stone in the center as the point of total comprehension. What more did he have to realize in order to become that stone?

Laeg stood and stretched in the moonlight. His yawn became a spray of mist. "I must go back to my youth and Cú Chulainn's side. Dawn's coming soon. All the weapons have to be ac-counted for, ready for the call." Then, as though he had listened again to Senchan's thoughts, he leaned down and added, "Don't strain yourself in seeking answers in all this. What knowledge comes, comes by the story's end, and it'll fit into place on its own like a silver piece pegged into a *fidchell* board. Don't get so wrapped up in your musings that you miss the events of the day. It only goes round once. For you."

Then he was gone, a shadow.

They met again at the ford. Their wounds glistened with rawness, but the amulets and incantations had healed them enough for the potions to prove resurrectionary: they could walk, stiffly, under their own power.

Cú Chulainn crossed the river to speak with FerDiad before

the Druids signaled the beginning of combat. The chance would not likely come again. He saw the chips and gouges that he had put into FerDiad's loricate surface, wet bands of muscle beneath it, clear blood transmuting gouges into blisters in the shell, and he understood that FerDiad had fared no better than he.

"Your blue eyes have gone dark like an eclipse," he said softly, so that FerDiad alone would hear. "They've fallen into your head." He placed his hand gingerly on FerDiad's arm. "And the horn has softened like wet wood."

FerDiad tried a weak sneer. "You think to scare me from another trial by describing yourself?"

"No, dearest friend. If you'd come to me like this that first morning, I wouldn't have known you. This I'll tell you now because it's the last chance I'll have—a royal cow has enchanted all the bulls hereabout save you and me, but we're the ones dying."

FerDiad nodded. "True. That's a conundrum on the path."

"Yes, and too big to go around. Give this up. Ulster hasn't arrived yet. It would merely delay—"

"Setanta! Think what you're asking of me. Could even you bear so much shame, wear it on your face when you've not even a beard to disguise the contortion? Did you ever fight only half a fight? I fled from the barbs that tongues throw off and you want me to step into their path again, and with less claim to denial!"

Cú Chulainn lowered his head, admitting that FerDiad was right. "Of all those who might walk Eriu with me—even Emer who can run riddles like a spider weaves—there's none I love more dearly than you. My anger's been siphoned away with my blood and replaced by regret. I'd as soon stare into Balor's killing eye than take a sword against you any more."

"It's no different with me, when I can remember . . . but death is all I see now. The nearer I come, the more my mind opens to memories that might have cured me before." He reached out and wrapped his arms around Cú Chulainn.

"This rips out my soul," whispered the Hound. He freed himself from FerDiad's hold and sloshed hurriedly back through the stream, almost blind to direction. Laeg met his gaze and read all that had been said, they were that close. He turned his eyes from that penetration, lifted his chin. "Now," was all he said. Then, turning, he called, "It's your day for weapons. What's your choice?"

"Swords and shields," answered FerDiad.

Hearing this, the crowd of hundreds edged nearer, the better to witness that kind of fight. Ailell was among them, and Maeve within her ring. Fergus and Cormac stood together and fretted about the weary look of Cú Chulainn.

FerDiad had his weapons but waited for the Druid's brief blessing—the whirl of mistletoe—before wading into the water.

Cú Chulainn drew down his helmet, took up his shield, and stepped down into the cold swirl of the ford.

On foot, with swords, their movements quickened. Running and leaping played as great a part as slashing and stabbing. Both swords had been forged in Druidic ceremony; neither bent nor dulled though they hammered a hundred times. Sparks flew up from glancing blows on umbos and rims. People pressed in too closely went deaf from the screech of metal. Splinters of enamel and wood flecked the water.

Not until the afternoon did either man score against the other, but by then their previous wounds had begun to seep from the feats, the leaps and tumbles that stretched the skin, peeling it from the thin tissue that retained the precious fluids.

Cú Chulainn cut a great "V" out of FerDiad's forearm, but striking that petrified skin was like hewing rock. FerDiad responded with a feint that tricked Cú Chulainn into leaving his back open for a moment, and Ferdiad sliced away a long strip of his skin. So it went, until the two were as ashen as two birch trees and Maeve was storming back and forth through the crowd, demanding to know why, if she could overpower the whole prevaricating province, these two warriors could not knock each other down.

Finally one of the Druids came forward and said, "Hold!" The single syllable contained enormous awe and reverence; even the priests lacked the ability to cope with this. The only occurrence they could remember remotely akin to this was when two Sidhe warriors had cut a path through Cruachan, chopping each other to bits only to have their severed parts grow back together at night that they might pick up the battle again the next day. These two, though, lacked the power to heal themselves after combat.

The two fighters had dropped their shields at the cry. They slid to the ground, side by side, without a word.

Through the night both men shivered uncontrollably. Layers of skins were piled upon them, packed around them, but had no effect. Their lips turned blue as if they swam in dreams of ice. More chants and ointments and charms were applied. One Druid tried using his hazel wand over the entire ford to nurse everything. In failing, he admitted that the dolorousness of the situation would have yielded more readily to a wand of yew. The other healers did not make excuses—they could see from the beginning that this matter lay beyond their combined skill. Surely this would not go on. Surely, when the sun came up again, these two once-proud warriors would not be able to stand.

At the same time as the Druids made this prediction, in other remote parts of the province, a scattering of men tried to sit up for the first time in what seemed an eternity.

7. Death Blows

As the sky reddened and the Druids clustered to pronounce their offertory to Belenos or Aed or Neit—depending upon which province they hailed from—Cú Chulainn and FerDiad in their separate camps labored to their feet. Their charioteers helped them. Laeg leaned Cú Chulainn against the top of his head while he strapped the broad girdle around Cú Chulainn's waist, let the warrior sag across his back while he bound the sandal thongs up empurpled calves, cinching every strap fiercely. "I should be binding your flesh together instead of these thongs," he muttered, "it would go better if I did." The Hound burbled a laugh. He reached across Laeg's back, took his helmet, and fit it over his head, pressing it down over hair that was stiff with blood as if from a liming. His eyes flickered with their strange crystalline sparks—the only sign that he had the strength to fight. He scanned the weapons Laeg had laid out for him but made up his mind immediately. One weapon alone drew him; one that had not been used before against FerDiad, either here or on Emain Ablach. He had one certain skill that his opponent lacked. But his hand trembled violently when he tried to pick the deadly spear up. His fingers brushed the shaft.

In the other camp, FerDiad went suddenly cold. His eyes

opened wide, deep in their caverns. "It's today," he said hoarsely. His charioteer stepped back from him. The meaning was clear.

"Will you at least wear your iron girdle, then?"

"Yes."

"Good. Then you have a chance." He uncovered a metal device shaped like an inverted cromlech. The base looked much like a quern stone used to grind corn, a hollowed bowl that, once strapped in place, fit like a cumbrous codpiece. Leather straps harnessed it to FerDiad's shoulders. The weight pulled open some of the wounds around his collar. His carapace creaked. He let the charioteer put a leather skirt and silk tunic over him to hide the new armor.

"Now you need guard just your upper body. The lower half is safe."

"Give me more of that drink Maeve sent me. I'll need all the strength I can find. Only one of us outlives today."

These two set off and arrived at the desolate ford before Cú Chulainn. FerDiad got down and began to practice with each weapon from his arsenal, more to inure himself to the pain than to refresh his skills. He spun his shield on the tip of his spear, then flung the spear into its target before the shield dropped, and caught the shield by its straps. The early observers began to chant his name and their excitement fueled him for a while, long enough for Cú Chulainn to arrive and see him. "I can't believe his recovery," he told Laeg. "Somehow, he's got his strength back today, while mine's still in short supply. Listen, if I fall under his attack, you must curse me, belittle me the way Fergus did when the Badb tried to kill me. And listen for my call to you. Unless I see my doom in him, I can't use *it*."

Laeg stopped him by the shoulder as he tried to leave. "What that means is that you'd kill him without the Gai Bulga if possible, but that rather than die yourself, you'll kill him with it."

Cú Chulainn gathered himself up. "So?"

"Either way you have to kill him. Why let him shave you down to the bone before you do it? Why offer your throat at all?"

"Because . . . because it's all I can do." He went to the ford.

FerDiad had stopped performing by then to catch his breath. Every speck of his body burned with pain, but pain that he could control. Pain equaled life. From where he sat on the rear of his chariot, he called, "Your choice today. What do you want?"

"I want to fight in the ford. Where it's waist-deep, but without spears or any weapons at first. Let's work our feats against each other."

FerDiad's driver whispered fearfully, "The weight of that cincture will drag you down!"

"Hush." To Cú Chulainn he replied, "Nothing would give me more pleasure." In part this was true—at least Cú Chulainn had not demanded short spears in the stream. He thanked the Triple Goddess for that much hope. The crowd took up the chant again as he strode for the stream.

He and Cú Chulainn found a place where the water sloshed around their belts. They closed and began grappling with one another. The water made Cú Chulainn's flesh slick and difficult to grab hold of, while FerDiad's horn had been smooth and polished from the start. They stumbled, trying to clutch and pull, succeeding only in tearing at the new skin that covered their wounds. Rocks on the bottom cut them anew when they fell. Their battle soaked the crowd repeatedly. The air smoked with their ragged breaths, while they jumped and twisted and wriggled like eels. The grappling went on for hours.

Cú Chulainn called for his shield. FerDiad turned away and his driver threw his to him. The two men fit their arms into the straps and swung back around, colliding with a reverberating clang. They slammed into one another again and again but neither could make the other one budge. Cú Chulainn changed tactics, jumping upon FerDiad's shield and trying to swing his own down into FerDiad's head. Before he could complete this, the shield beneath him bucked and threw him off with such force that he landed on the bank. He got up immediately and somersaulted out into the middle of the ford, then onto the shield again, his toes gripping the edge hard enough to crimp it. FerDiad had expected no less and drove his knee hard into the base of the shield, a blow that ground Cú Chulainn's teeth together and flung him away like water thrown off by a dog. He landed flat on top of his own shield on the hard ground above the ford. Blood flowed down his back in webs. He did not get up.

The crowd murmured excitedly: the Hound had been dealt with at last.

Laeg recalled his instructions and ran forward, shouting, "What kind of hero is it lets himself be slapped aside like an

offending branch? Your roots can't run very deep if his like
can rip you out of the ground so easily. You callow little child,
what made you think you were capable of deeds worth remembering? Go home and learn to fight."

The crowd adopted his jeers, added catcalls of their own,
jibes of every sort, the Ulster Exiles shouting loudest of all
because they understood Laeg's purpose, while Maeve shrieked
to silence them in vain.

Cú Chulainn dug his fingers into the clay and pushed himself
up to his knees. His shield had been caved in from his elbows
and knees. He called for a change in combat—allowing all
weapons—but he did not draw the sword in his belt. Instead,
he ran down the bank and sprang, landing like a snake around
FerDiad's shoulders, battering him before FerDiad dumped him
in the water. The crowd hooted and mocked him.

Cú Chulainn shook fiercely. The water began to bubble
around him and the twisted aspect of the Warp Spasm began
to wring the beauty out of him. He rammed FerDiad. They
drove each other back and forth across the body of water,
slamming together so hard that their shields cracked and split.
The thunderclap from their collision scared the horses behind
the crowd. The horses broke free of their spancels, bolted down
the hill and into the encampment, which alarmed the cattle
enough to send them scattering ahead in all directions, pum-
meling the tents and crushing provisions. The majority of the
crowd turned reluctantly and deserted the stream in pursuit of
the animals. Just six armed warriors and three Druids remained,
grim with purpose.

The frenzied combat continued unabated. The two men drove
the water out of the stream. Fish flapped on the banks. Huge
tidal waves rushed away in both directions, spilling over as
they ran. Cú Chulainn stepped on one of the fish that lay on
the exposed bottom, and his twisted foot slipped. FerDiad,
seeing his chance to stop the monster from taking form, plunged
his sword to the hilt in Cú Chulainn's breast.

The Hound tumbled back against the bank. He stared in
amazement at the carved ivory handle protruding and the blood
spilling out around it. When he breathed, he thought he could
feel the cold metal of the blade press against his heart.

FerDiad waited, his hand raised to signal for another weapon
if Cú Chulainn did not submit now.

Cú Chulainn's face rippled as the Warp Spasm drained off.
His eyes closed under a bubbling brow. "Gai Bulga!" he cried

out in a voice full of liquid. FerDiad dropped his hand to call for his spear. His blood went cold. He sought his shield and reached for it as the water came crashing back to fill up the channel. It swirled up his body, snatching the battered shield and carrying it out of his grasp. He dove after it in desperation. Coming up, he turned to see a shining white sliver skimming along with the rushing water. Cú Chulainn was nowhere to be seen. Had the surge snatched him? FerDiad looked around for signs of the corpse.

Like a geyser, the Hound exploded out of the water. Too hurt to make his full leap, he slapped the base of his palm against the butt of the spear.

FerDiad twisted and did what he could with his chipped shield—moved it all around to try and block the shot. But the tip of the spear broke through the cracked wood and split the horny surface of FerDiad's skin. It tore out of his back, spinning him around from the part of his lung that was wrenched out with it. Then the spear glided in a wide arc and rode the stream back to Cú Chulainn.

Now the water had calmed, but the Hound had not. He was in his mettle, so practiced in this that he acted by instinct against the pain, the terrible wound, against his desire to spare his friend. He leapt high, caught the spear between his toes, and shot it across the water once more.

Weakly, FerDiad tried to hide behind his shield again, bracing his head and forearms against it, deaf entirely to his charioteer, who wanted to throw him his spear as commanded.

The Gai Bulga slid under the shield and skidded against the curve of the iron cincture, down around the projecting nub of the codpiece. One barb snapped off against the codpiece, but the force of this spun the spear up through his raised thigh. It tunneled under his skin, climbed his body, up through his abdomen. The remaining barbs snipped and snagged all his organs, dragging his insides into his chest, spleen and liver bulging out the initial wound.

FerDiad's shield smacked the water. He raised one hand, but doubled over, vomiting blood. He saw himself reflected there, a dark, alien creature with spurs and thistles for a face. The pain prodded him and he winced. When he could speak, he called, "That trick is still your best feat. It's surely caught me. Do you . . . always save the best for last?" He made a little laugh that turned into a cough. "Ah, Setanta, I'm undone!" He fell into his reflection.

Cú Chulainn rushed to him, catching him under the arms and dragging him across the stream. The effort of pulling the body from the water brought sparks to his vision. FerDiad's head slid down against the hilt of his sword that lay in Cú Chulainn's breast. The Hound gasped. "Even in death you attack." He dragged himself up over a mound and down beside the chariot. Then he and the body slid to the ground. Dizzy, half-blind, he hunched over and caressed the chiseled face that remained as hard in death as in life.

He began to weep. Distantly, he was aware of Laeg calling to him, but any meaning in the sound failed to penetrate his cloud of remorse. The voice changed, became FerDiad's voice, drawing him away. The world was turning red before his eyes and he thought that he must have died, too, and was passing now into Magh Mell. A trance of mourning settled over him and he began to chant without knowing it.

"FerDiad, I've forsaken you
 When I should have turned my back
 And made you go.
 Wouldn't disgrace have been better
 Than this state of decay we've joined?

 What for, this? Your pride? Couldn't you
 Deal with satirists—serve them up?
 Am I the only one exempt from their evil?
 Surely, you didn't do this for Finnabair—
 She's no more than a wine strainer to your blood.

 FerDiad, good friend,
 I've lost you. Now you've gone
 On your journey to your Int Ildathach,
 But I'm following, from the stroke
 You delivered upon me.

 I'll leave your torc,
 Rest in passing with you.
 We're both past caring who wins
 In contests over the Donn,
 Though I regret not aiding Ulster more.

 Glorious FerDiad, my foster brother,
 Until you arrived my time in combat was sport
 Maeve sent only lesser warriors to challenge me.

None so skilled or valiant as FerDiad
You altered everything with your arm and eye so keen."

His chant continued, drifting into tales of the training they had endured, but he made no sound to show the world that he still lived. The mellifluous chant lived with FerDiad in his mind. Laeg was presently the sole defender of Ulster.

He stopped yelling at Cú Chulainn as he saw the six assassins making their way to the river with set purpose. As one they met FerDiad's charioteer and cut him to quivering pieces.

Laeg grabbed Cú Chulainn by the hair and cursed him in the hope that anger would rouse him. Cú Chulainn's eyes remained glazed.

The six murderers carried their dripping blades into the river, past a broken shield that floated face-down.

Laeg pushed away from Cú Chulainn. He turned to the chariot and took up a spear. Hefting it, he swore to take as many of them as he could, promising Macha their hearts. He would not be cut down easily the way the other driver had been.

The six disappeared from sight behind the mound.

A sound—a scrape—came from behind the chariot. Laeg whirled around, his spear up over his head in both hands.

The tip of a sword touched him under his chin, and he froze up, staring into six blue and baleful eyes.

XVI.
ESCAPE AND PURSUIT

1. Ulster Rising

"Senoll Uathach!" exclaimed Laeg.

The long, lined, and pock-marked face broke into a canine grin. "It's me an' nobody else. And do you know the Sons of Ficce? Two good warriors, fostered to me for years now. We've been down and out, cramped and crippled up with Macha squeezing at our guts. I'll tell you, Laeg, what troubles come at you in life, there ain't none as can foul you up like Macha's Pangs of Pregnancy. That—"

He stopped speaking as he saw the first of the six assassins come into view on the mound. Senoll Uathach, an old veteran of more battles than Laeg had freckles, did not have to ask in order to see what the six had in mind. "Slings, boys," he ordered.

The six slowed up, confused by the quantity of victims awaiting them. Their hesitation was brief, however; whether they took two heads or twenty, it was all the same to them. They swung their shields off their backs and came on.

Three sling-stones flew across the ridge. One smacked a shield with a loud report like a crack of lightning. One shattered a kneecap and a third a skull. The assassins drew up again; they had gotten used to being a group of six; the idea that anyone might harm them, much less reduce their ranks, had never been considered. The four assassins let themselves be provoked to anger. They began to yell as they ran down the

slope. The Sons of Ficce took up their javelins. Laeg, aboard
the chariot, pulled Senoll up, took the reins, and snapped the
horses to a gallop. The assassins dispersed to avoid the sickles
spinning on the hubs. They saw their targets—Cú Chulainn
and FerDiad—and both looked dead. If they could just collect
those two heads, then they could escape this unbargained-for
batch of Ulstermen.

Laeg and Senoll flung two spears, grabbed two more and
drove in for a kill. Two more of the assassins fell from the
flock of spears, while the Sons of Ficce pressed the remaining
two. One assassin leaped back to avoid a blow by his attacker
and put himself in the path of a sickle that lopped him in two.
The other saw this and panicked, leaving himself open to a
straight thrust. The two of Ficce cut off the first heads of their
careers as warriors and began to dance around, shaking their
gory trophies up at the skies to show the gods they had skill.

"Mind you," Senoll observed, "them boys is daft. But they
got their heads."

"Well, whatever troubles come my way in life, I hope they're
all as incompetent as those six were. Now, go calm those idiots
down—the army's just over the hill, and they'll have ample
opportunity to expand their collection. Right now we have to
get Cú Chulainn out of here before they send along the others
to take him."

Senoll looked where Laeg pointed and he sucked in his
breath. "Never in my life have I seen wounds like that. Are
you sure there's anything worth bothering with here? Why, he
looks all but drained." His point was well taken: Cú Chulainn's
skin, where no blood coated it, had turned as gray as an overcast
sky.

"He's alive still, but he's gone to the edge of Magh Mell
with FerDiad's ghost."

"That's FerDiad?"

"What's left of him."

"I thought it was one of them crusty Fomor," Senoll said
as they reined in beside the two. Laeg got down and grabbed
hold of the corpse, but it took both men to pull him off Cú
Chulainn. Cú Chulainn's hands continued to stroke the air where
FerDiad's thorny cheek had been. Then his fingers curled and
the glaze left his eyes. He blinked wearily and groaned. Laeg
knelt in front of him. "You have to cut him open, retrieve the
Gai Bulga," Cú Chulainn whispered hoarsely. His head lolled,

nearly touching the sword hilt.

They loaded him on his chariot while Laeg went and hacked through FerDiad's back to get at the spear. It had punctured every organ in him. Cú Chulainn had to be laid on his side.

The Sons of Ficce and Senoll squeezed in around him as Laeg drove south to the house where Emer awaited them. At each stream they came to on the way, they drew up and one of the boys jumped out and returned with clean water to bathe the Hound's wounds. He went into a feverish trance after a while and pulled himself upright against a screen. Staring at nothing, he began a chant, his words nearly nonsensical to the passengers.

> *"Crimson in hair*
> *Gone down the roots*
> *Coloring the body crimson, too.*
> *Dead, ill-met at the ford.*
>
> *The tree unrooted,*
> *Birds without feathers.*
> *What's the difference*
> *From that to the unmade man?"*

"What is that he's saying?" asked one of the brothers.

"The riddles of FerDiad, I expect," Laeg called back. His attention had been drawn away to the east. Soon he called out and pointed, then waved one hand to a chariot that swept past them, seemingly out of nowhere; only Laeg had seen it. The sole inhabitant was a strikingly tall man with a gray flame of hair blowing back from his long forehead. He nodded grimly as he passed, but did not slow up. His chariot bounced and rattled as it shot ahead in the narrow brown valley.

"The plague's lifting! That was Cethern off to find the armies!" Senoll cried.

"But he had no spears with him," one of the brothers remarked.

"He wouldn't—only weapon he uses is a silver spike, long as your arm. He can put it through three men, *pfft*, like spittin' a pig."

"I hear he's a generous man," Laeg mused.

"Maybe, if you're referring to the generous crop he reaps in battle!"

* * *

The armies of Connacht were on the move away from the
ford Ath FerDiad: Maeve had named it when the Druids returned and reported the outcome—reported, that is, that FerDiad
and Cú Chulainn had slain one another. She lacked the time
to wait for proof from her six hand-picked men but rejoiced in
the assurance of double deaths while her tent was broken down.
She and her husband rode out at the head of their forces, the
Donn intractably in tow. They picked up more of their people
along the way, who had run off in pursuit of their horses.
Abandoning roads, the army cut straight up and over the rolling
terrain.

The queen sent MacRoth to look for signs of Ulster stirring
and he returned before an hour had passed. He had seen Cú
Chulainn's chariot with Laeg and three strangers in it but no
sign of the Hound. Before his queen could take her pleasure
from that information, MacRoth warned of sighting the single
chariot containing Cethern. Maeve had word of that passed
along by runners. The army watched expectantly for their new
enemy. Even with their straight retreat, they did not travel much
farther that day, only to the place called Smirromair near Mount
Oriel, because the combat at Ath FerDiad had taken up most
of the day.

Once camped, Maeve met with Ailell. He said, "I know
something of Cethern. He's called 'the Generous.' I'm sure
we'll find a way to negotiate with him. All the same, some
cautious preparation should be made.

"Rann!" he called to one of his stewards, a chubby boy, "go
find the two warriors Bun and Mecon and tell them to triple-
team the guards. Three to every post." He turned back to his
wife. "That should solve the Cethern problem." Then his brow
knitted and he began to stroke his beard. "Still, if one is up
here, there must be a hundred more up elsewhere who don't
yet know where to look. That number could be doubling every
hour. A camp may not be a wise idea now, my dear, else we'll
arise at dawn to find heads on every hillock and spears at every
horizon."

"It is a night without a moon, Ailell. And the land from
here to Cuil Sibrille is uncharted by our people."

"Fergus could lead us."

"Yes, if you can interest him in the subject at all."

"Damn him and his army. I'll melt his sword down for
snaffle-bits."

Maeve ignored his comment and mused, "The real questions now are how many hours have we before Macha's Curse is swept entirely away, and how many hours after that will lapse before Conchovor hears of our presence?"

"And what is your guess?"

"It would seem likely that the curse rode the wind, out-distancing any alarm that might have been raised. Perhaps no alarm at all was heard. My belief is that this curse will lift completely only once the danger passes—once we cross their border. The nearer we get to it, the more will find themselves able to navigate once more. But our camp should be safe. Cú Chulainn is dead. They have nothing else remotely like him, and we still have the better part of the Galeoin."

Ailell withheld his opinion on her praising of the same force she had desired to slaughter just one week before.

2. The Alarm at Emain Macha

Sualdam mac Roig came to his senses and found himself on a plateau of Slieve Cuillin. His stomach muscles ached as if he had picked up some enormous weight and in so doing had torn the fabric of his body. It did not take him long to remember what had sent him to those heights where the rain had soaked him and the snow covered him beneath his shield, his only protection against the elements. He was weak, ravenous, and aching like a man twice his age. He considered going home, but his message had to be delivered first to the king. He picked up his spear and hurried on as best he could through a sea of dead scrub grass.

Soon he came to the Midluachair Road, which stretched like a curl of smoke across the landscape. A wagon stood abandoned there. Its owner was not to be found. Perhaps the owner had fallen off when the Pangs hit and the dumb beasts yoked to it had continued blithely on. Sualdam did not care. He clambered aboard the four-wheeled vehicle and snapped the reins. The two ponies reacted sluggishly but picked up speed after Sualdam found and applied a willow whip.

Midlauchair continued past Emain Macha all the way to the tiny peninsula from which the Skerries were visible. Sualdam drove down from the road and across the plain south of the fortress, past the playing fields where his son had bested the Boy Troop in their games.

The lower rampart of the hillfort lay empty, undefended, as did the huts he had just passed. Sualdam called out. Somewhere a crow cawed as if in reply. Nothing stirred on the hill. Sualdam stopped the cart, grabbed his spear and shield, and hurried through the staggered passages between ramparts. No one challenged him; no one appeared. The three fortress buildings that Conchovor had erected stood silently, as lifeless as three skulls. He reached the top and paused to look out over the fields. It might have been an idyllic scene—plots of corn waving in the sunlight, the animals grazing carelessly—except for the lack of any human presence anywhere.

He found the entrance to Craebruad barricaded. He pounded his spear against the wall. "Is anyone about in there?"

Footsteps scuffled, then a sharp female voice answered, "I hear you. Now go away, we've trouble enough in here."

"What? Are you an idiot?"

"Hardly," came the humorless reply. "I'm a Druidess ministering to the king and all who lie here. What are you that you can move?"

"Me?" He did not know how to answer that. "I've come to warn you of what's happening."

"A little late, old fellow—it's happened already, don't you think? Now be off, leave us."

Sualdam quaked with ire. "Old? Listen you—I bring warnings of great plunder, devastations—"

"We *all* know about the crows—we *can* see the fields from up here, you know."

Sualdam shook his spear at the door. "Listen to me, you pustulating bombast—where's Cathbad? Bring me somebody who has a brain and can use it!" He jammed his spear into the barricade and tried to pry it open. "Get me Cathbad!" he shouted, then kicked the wood.

The woman shrieked, "Get away, how dare you, I'll put a *geis* on you to rot your nose."

"You'll put a *geis* on *me?*" he screamed. He flung his round shield at the door. Its razor edge stuck in the wood, knocking the spear aside. Sualdam stamped the ground, jumped up and down in a circle. He tripped over the spear shaft, cried out and fell toward the barricade. His chin hooked over the rim of the shield and the finely honed edge cut his head off.

From deeper recesses of Craebruad, a dark voice erupted, "Whatever is going on out there?"

The priestess explained in a voice still foaming with wounded pride, "Some obnoxious old messenger who wasn't dropped down by . . ." The priestess paused then, realizing that Cathbad, too, was standing up.

"Open the door," he said, exasperated.

"But—"

"Open the door, I command it. Don't annoy me, I've no patience right now. Here, get out of my way, go tend to Conchovor, he's starting to sit up."

The barricade was unbarred, drawn back. Cathbad came face to face with the bloody, scalloped shield. He stared down at the headless corpse and frowned. This was not at all the sort of unpleasant scene one wanted to deal with first thing after a curse.

Within the central chamber of Craebruad, Conchovor sat wincing, his hands pressed to his belly. He sipped at a potion the Druidess had made for him, one of indescribable foulness. His eyes pained him as if they had sunk so deep that they were squeezing against his brain. The potion made them water.

Cathbad backed in through the linen curtain. He carried a large shield like a bowl behind him.

"I know that shield," Conchovor exclaimed. To the priestess, looking on dumbly, he repeated, "I know it."

"You'll know its contents, too," said Cathbad. He set the shield on the floor between them.

Sualdam's head rested upright in the center of the wide bowl, his eyes closed in death.

"Oh, no," the king mourned. "That's my sister's husband." He looked blearily at Cathbad. "How was this done?"

The Druid shot a stiff look at the Druidess. "An unfortunate accident, a misunderstanding. That aside, Sualdam has come far to give his message and I think it only fair to hear him out." He drew the hazel wand from his belt and flourished it over the shield; he muttered something underneath his breath.

Sualdam's eyes fluttered, rolled around in their sockets, then came to rest on Conchovor. "Why, this is most uncanny," said the head. "I've just died and now I'm back again."

"Just for a while," Cathbad explained, "to tell your news."

"Cathbad? I can't see you, but I'd know that voice. At last, someone who will listen. You know, your doorkeeper's a witless louse."

"Your news, Sualdam," Cathbad urged. "My powers aren't unlimited and you wouldn't like to be one of my bodyless *vathi*, believe me. It's a diminished life. What do you have to tell?"

"Murderers!" Sualdam blurted, so abruptly that Conchovor tossed his potion. "Invasion. Plunder!"

"Who's plundering?" asked the king.

"Maeve and Ailell mac Mata—he for revenge on you, she to add the Donn of Cuailnge to her herd. Many die, hampered by Macha. Cú Chulainn went to withstand them alone, but he's fallen now. Time is short. They make their escape through Tailtiu's cemetery while a brave handful take them on. The Boy Troop's in its grave from them. Cú Chulainn—he's in his house, Emer ministering, weeping at his wounded state, knowing she can do little to save him." Sualdam screwed up his face. "Now, how did I know all that?"

Cathbad moved around in front of him. "Your news ends, Sualdam. The bridge must close now and you've got to be on the far side of it. Return to the Many-Colored World. One day we'll meet there again."

"Life ends. Cathbad. My brother, Conchovor. Remember when I set Bricriu on fire? That was a time." His voice began to fade, the color draining from his cheeks. "I wish I could have seen my son once more. . . ." The eyes shut, the lips moved a moment longer, then stopped. The wetness on his cheeks was all that remained to show that he had lived again.

Conchovor looked away from him. "Father, who else is up and moving?" Cathbad's eyes went wide at hearing himself addressed in that manner after so long. Conchovor shrugged. "The Pangs seem to have driven out the remnants of Othar. Back to his barren crag. Now, please, who?"

"Your son, Finnchad of the Silver Horns. Fergus the Messenger's child, Illan, then Coirpre, Fingin the Healer."

"Finnchad first, I'll see him. Have the Healer set out now to Muirthemne. Cú Chulainn surely needs him. We'll gather our best as they climb up, and set out after the thieves. Illan knows his father's art, so have him sound the alarm." He glanced again into the shield. "Later, we'll honor our lost ones. For now, may the Dagda guard your soul, Sualdam, and the souls of the others who fell while we were powerless. Here, help me up." He reached out.

3. A Gathering of Healers

Laeg mac Riangabra squatted at the edge of the wide plateau on which Cú Chulainn's house stood. Behind the house Mount Oriel loomed another three hundred feet, the first third of its snowy expanse dappled by orange bracken and evergreen fern. Laeg leaned against an iron-tipped javelin from his chariot stock. He wore his cloak tightly around him.

The first fires of Maeve and Ailell's encampment shone as stars on the distant landscape. The army was a dark, roiling shape—ants swarming over some decaying animal in the last glimmer of twilight. They would pass the night down there, inadvertently under Cú Chulainn's house. Had they known where they were, Laeg was certain they would have sent someone up the hill to raze the house and kill Emer. That was why he stood guard, just in case. He remained more troubled, however, by the need for a healer. Emer had some skill in the art, mostly at dressing wounds. She had coated them with what herbs she had preserved and wrapped the worst of them in muslin. More, much more, would be needed if Cú Chulainn were to arise from his bed before the battle was over. Laeg wished that the situation had been different, that the king or queen of Connacht had been so wounded, for the law in Ulster proclaimed that no person who thieved from his neighbors had the right to ask for nursing, and Laeg would have enjoyed refusing those two any aid. All of Ulster would have turned them out. He imagined them crawling from house to house, dying by inches, by hours.

The twinkling lights brought him back to himself. Perhaps he ought to sneak down into their camp and somehow snatch one of their healers, one of the ones who had come out to help when Cú Chulainn had fought FerDiad. He lowered his head into shadow out of which only steam poured. His body shifted under the cloak. The hair grew further down his back. When he raised his head again, he was older. He glanced beside himself. "Here's an unusual request for you," he said to Senchan. "I want you to take my spear and stand guard while I go down to the exiles and try to procure a healer."

"Me?" Senchan did not know what to think. Suddenly he was being asked to take an active part in the tale. His palms began to sweat. "What if someone comes? I don't know how to throw a spear."

"No matter. First of all, no one's going to come. Second, if anyone does come, what they'll see is me—for that's how you'll appear to your corporeal audience." He offered the javelin to Senchan. "Test its weight. Find the precise point of balance and learn where to hold it so that it tips neither forward nor backward. Practice with it, but don't lose it in the darkness. I won't be terribly long."

Senchan watched him, awestruck by the simplicity of it all. He studied the tip of the spear, touched it a bit too hard, and ended up sucking blood from his finger. The situation made him ambivalent—after all, what had he done to deserve such trust as this? Well, to hell with practice. He squatted down as Laeg had done, resting his weight against the spear.

From behind, a gentle voice asked, "How goes the watch, Laeg?"

Senchan jumped up. Emer stood nearby, weariness in her pose. She was such a small woman—no taller than her husband who languished within the hut. Her face, under the wrapped auburn braids, belonged to some elfin princess like the ones Senchan knew of in faery stories. She came nearer, came and put her arms around him and kissed him. Then she opened his thick blanket and tucked herself inside it for warmth. "I wish this were Samain eve, so that time could stand still for the night. He's as close now to the line of life and death as the whole world is that night. It might give him time to replenish. I keep binding him but every time I look again his tributaries are flowing. Little rivers running over their banks. Oh, Laeg, soon I fear he'll run dry. I look on his lips and think of blue."

Senchan recalled that her speech was never quite free of riddling. Not sure how best to reply, he just nodded and faced the valley nervously. His side seemed to be on fire where her hand covered his ribs. In his whole life he had never been this close to a woman. Not like this. He envisioned Derdriu flaying against the standing stone and suddenly knew that the heat from

Emer was the heat of Derdriu, and he had become the stone.

Emer said, "Soon Imbolc comes to blow away winter, and the breezes after won't chill me like this." She hugged herself to him more tightly. "I do so love you, Laeg mac Riangabra. You're a living shield without which he couldn't come back each time. He's the hard pellet and you're the sling that speeds him home. Let me bring you food, you must be starving."

"Yes, in fact . . . could you bring a double portion?"

She smiled archly, a faery face. "Of course. I shouldn't want you to starve, either, Laeg who isn't Laeg." She kissed him quickly and danced away, leaving him to wonder dazedly how and what she knew. Had she been teasing him all along, or was it when he spoke that he gave himself away?

Before Emer had returned with his food, Senchan saw Laeg climbing back from the encampment. A few others followed, no more than dusky shapes. Laeg seemed to be supporting someone. Senchan ran to help but stopped when he saw who it was: Cethern, the gray-haired warrior who had driven past so regally; only now his flowing clothes had been reduced to a bloody tatter and he kept one fist pressed tight against his middle, where his bowels were trying to squeeze through. The trailing figures, Senchan discovered, were three robed healers with oddly shaved heads.

"That's how it is," Laeg said. "I go down to get me three healers and come back with another patient."

Cethern groaned in an attempt to express mirth.

"How did you like guard duty?" Laeg whispered. "Nothing happened, of course."

Senchan hid his blush. "No. Nothing." He heard the whispered chants of the healers as they drew abreast of him, then bolted ahead to help Laeg.

In the hut they lay, Cethern beside Cú Chulainn on a bed of rushes. Emer grew dispirited to see him in such a sorry state.

Cú Chulainn stirred and opened his eyes. The lights surrounding his pupils flickered as dimly as distant stars through a cloud. He spotted Cethern, then scanned the room. His eyes rolled. He rubbed them as much as his dressings would allow. His voice was raw. "Laeg, I must be dying, for I see one of you for each of my eyes."

Laeg suppressed a grin. "There's but one of me, Cucuc."

Cú Chulainn closed his eyes for a long moment, then dared another look. His features relaxed. "So now one of you fades away—I must be getting better."

"By the minute."

He reached up to draw Laeg to him. "But tell me, was it a dream or did I slay FerDiad?"

"You did, in a great combat."

"Then, I did accompany him to Magh Mell, so red it was. . . . Who are these three characters with the amulets? Healers?"

"Fiachu mac Firaba secured them for me from Ailell's own."

"There's a proper jest."

"I thought so, too. The Ulster Exiles now know that you're alive. It seems that Maeve's bards are singing your epitaph with FerDiad's."

"I look forward to surprising her. Tell me, is this bloody stick-figure beside me Cethern the Spikewielder?"

"Is," groaned Cethern, "and if no one minds, I'd value a healer's prognosis."

Laeg moved back to let the first healer sit beside Cethern. The bearded healer moved Cethern's hand away from the wound in his belly. Cethern's intestines popped into the gap.

The healer shook his head. "This is a fatal wound. You're going to die."

"Is that a fact?" wheezed Cethern.

"It is."

"Then why don't you go before me and warn them I'm coming." He slammed his fist against the healer's forehead. The priest fell over, dead. Cethern clutched at his bowels as they tried to spring out. He tucked himself back inside the wound. With bloodshot eyes he regarded the second healer. "How do you see things?"

Reluctantly, the second man shuffled up and bent over to inspect Cethern; he was not about to sit. "I'm sorry," he said, expressing his regret at the hopelessness of the situation.

"You've good reason to be," Cethern replied. He sat up suddenly and struck the healer a blow in the face that sent him flying back into the remaining robed man. The two crashed down, the bottom man unconscious, the one on top dead.

"Cethern," Laeg said smartly, "I didn't bring these healers up here so that you might exercise your fists. I won't be able to get more, so would you mind not asking the third one for his advice until *after* he tends to you? Provided I can even get him to go near you now." He knelt and shook the last healer.

"Listen to him," Cú Chulainn argued. "How did you get such wounds?"

"Well, I—" He stopped speaking as a spear that had been standing upright where the second Laeg had disappeared suddenly floated up and settled horizontally just above the floor beside him. No one else seemed to notice it, so Cethern chose to ignore it. "I attacked the camp below. They must have had word I was coming, 'cause there were three to a post. I slew a batch—all their outer guard—but they crowded me from all sides. I could see Ailell directing them and I dragged my way toward him. Men and women took me on, replaced, as each fell, by another. It was a gauntlet I ran with the king as the goal. Just before I cleared the way to him, two of his sons—two of those boys named Maine—split open my gut and drove me back out of the camp, where I fell. They would've taken my head for sure but the two started arguing about who should have it. I lay there, listening to my fate being bickered over. That's an unnerving thing, I'll say. Then the boys came to blows and their father strode in and slapped them and sent them away, and I was forgotten. I'd've died if Laeg hadn't come along."

Laeg had awakened the remaining healer and now shoved him over to Cethern. "Now, listen to me, Spike—you let this man do his work. Don't you punch in his face or twist his neck or anything else. He has to attend to Cú Chulainn as well as you."

"All right—but only because I don't want Cú Chulainn's death on my hands."

"I thank Figol, god of knowledge, for imparting that much brain to you."

"When I'm better, I'll fix you right for such a slur."

Laeg grinned. "I shall petition for your swift recovery."

They heard a chariot approaching across the plateau. Laeg hurried out, followed by his "floating" spear.

"Your house is haunted, lady," Cethern proclaimed.

"No, I'm sure you're wrong," answered Emer. "May I give him soup?" she asked the healer. He let her spoon broth to Cethern, but after the first few spoonfuls, the broth reappeared, trickling out of the gap in Cethern's belly. Emer hesitated, then put down the bowl and wooden ladle.

"Lousy healer," Cethern muttered. "Can't even plug a leak."

Laeg returned, carrying his spear himself this time. Behind him, a short, spindly man with wavy hair came in. Laeg introduced him. "This is Fingin, Conchovor's healer. He says Sualdam brought news to Emain Macha this dawn and the king sent Fingin to tend your wounds."

The other healer bowed out of the way to the Druid of superior skill, but watched from behind as Fingin worked on Cú Chulainn. The Ulster healer unbound the bandages and studied the wounds, especially the chest wound. "A hard man gave you that. Who is your patron god?"

"Lugh Samildánach."

"All his aspects, is it? Good. I'll chant to him in all guises while I grind marrow for your wounds." To Emer, he asked, "Have you the bones you used to make your broth?" Then he went to Cethern and began to press and prod the numerous open wounds, describing them as if the healer attending him were a bard, memorizing the data. "This," said Fingin, touching his chest, "was done by two huge men, much taller than you."

"I'd been brought to my knees."

"If you say so. This was a javelin, this a sword with teeth on one edge. A woman warrior did it, unless I'm mistaken— see how she put all her force into the blow? And the angle's odd, yes, definitely a woman, much fiercer blow than by a man."

"Maeve did it—are you happy?"

Fingin went on undaunted. "And this—" he pried apart the belly wound "—was done by two who like their work. A tandem effort. Brothers, possibly?"

"Two Maines—one like his mother, the other like his father."

"Yes." He sat back on the balls of his feet, his arms crossed. He hummed tunelessly for a few moments. "And who's your family god?"

"Luchta."

"You should have asked him to make a shield for you. All you can do now is pray to him. I'll chant and make marrow balm for you, too, but the best we can hope for here is to forestall the inevitable. No, I'm afraid you've let a whole herd of bulls trample you and there's nothing for it." The second healer put some distance between himself and Fingin. "Best you should make your peace with Luchta." He stood, fatigued, and took bones and a quern stone from Emer.

Cethern's cheeks swelled and darkened. He rolled over and tried to kick Fingin, but Laeg cried, "Cethern!" and deflected the kick with his spear shaft. Cethern's foot landed on the other healer and sent him sailing out the door.

Cú Chulainn closed his eyes and groaned.

4. Senchan's Dream

The sky that night was full of stars and contained the tiniest sliver of a moon.

Laeg and Senchan did guard duty together, which consisted mostly of huddling for warmth and drinking the warm beer that Emer brought them. The fires in the valley tricked Senchan's sleepy mind into thinking it beheld a lake reflecting the stars. As he peered into the "water," one of the lights swelled like a growing bonfire and swallowed the rest.

Senchan found himself among the armies of Connacht in broad daylight. Pandemonium had seized the camp. People raced in every direction, chariots rolled, bounced, careered. Armed groups of various sizes ran every which way. The noise deafened him.

On two promontories at either end of the camp, two wide, ugly men stood. These two were hefting stones from two piles of boulders and flinging them out over the camp. The stones smacked together at the apex of their arcs and the shattered pieces rained down on the camp, striking, squashing, killing those who could not get out of their way. Senchan named the rock throwers to himself: Cu Roi mac Daire and Munremoir mac Gerrcin, two squat, troll-like creatures with arms like trees.

From the east, the fur-covered and fanged father of Cethern came bounding, leading his wild *tuath* who were likewise hirsute and snaggle-toothed. Fintan was the father's name. Among his band, Senchan saw Cethern's younger brother, Crimthan, who had no such teeth and carried weapons instead. One body of warriors, all of Munster, stood their ground to meet this onslaught.

Cethern's wife, FinBec, drove her chariot through Cruachan's camp, skewering anyone within reach as she headed for Mount Oriel and Cú Chulainn's house. She had been told that Cethern was dead.

Senchan watched how Ailell and Maeve responded to these various attacks. Warriors skirted around and came up the two

promontories from the far side, forcing the two ugly men to
leap off. Amazingly, neither died from the fall but sank into
the ground up to their thighs. Ailell had them captured before
they could wriggle free, and made them yield.

FinBec made a full sweep through the camp before continuing to Mount Oriel, unscathed. Maeve led a force around
Fintan. The only member of that family she wanted was Crimthan. The rest she had slaughtered except for the old man. Held
at bay, Fintan roared with anger and bit through the arm of one
of his captors, but he hesitated when Maeve put her dagger
against Crimthan's throat and demanded the old man pledge
his loyalty to Ailell. Fintan had no choice and complied. Maeve
released Crimthan then. She sent father and grandson away.
No one else in their *tuath* survived that attack; over a hundred
furred and fanged bodies lay, teeth bared even in death. Senchan
knew that this was the end of a race, and that these people
would be legend by his time.

Ailell and Maeve gathered their forces quickly and pushed
on for Tailtiu. On the way more groups and individuals beset
them. Senchan saw Cethern himself come swooping down from
Cú Chulainn's house. He had a wheel rim wrapped around his
middle to hold his insides in. Ailell saw the warrior cutting a
swath through the army again—straight for him as before.
Cethern foamed and raved, insanely fierce in what he knew to
be his final assault. Ailell saw this, too. He removed his king's
torc and put it around a small canted standing stone halfway
across the field. Cethern fastened his gaze on the torc, sought
and blindly hacked away at the idol, spittle dripping from his
lips, his eyes glassy, bulging. All the while that he chopped
the stone, a brace of warriors surrounded him and had an easy
time of cutting him apart. Finally one of them cut his legs out
from under him and another took off his head. The legs kicked
powerfully—one heel knocked over the chipped stone. The
arms grappled randomly, ripping up bloody grass, finally just
squeezing it. Ailell did not retrieve his torc until all the parts
of Cethern lay still.

More attacks beleaguered them as more of Ulster arose. The
royalty of Connacht tricked and defeated every enemy. Senchan
saw it all in a feverish reality where each act was too fluid,
every line too sharp and light too bright, where colors burned
his eyes and everything he saw was too close, too clear. The
names of all the challengers stacked up in his brain. The last
of them to come was Rochad.

Rochad was the young leader of a tribe, his father having died not long before the Pangs. He led his troop against Ailell with great reluctance because, at one time, the king of Connacht might have become his father-in-law. In childhood, fostered Rochad and Finnabair had been infatuated with one another and had often pretended to be married. However, Rochad's home lay in Ulster and after his fosterage he returned to his family. Now, despite many fond memories, Ailell had become the enemy and Rochad must strike him down.

Maeve described his approach to her listless daughter and was rewarded by Finnabair's stirring out of her oblivion at the mention of his name. "Rochad," she mumbled. "Rochad... I've loved him my whole life. Is he as handsome as when he lived near us?"

"More so it seems to me. Why not get up now, go out, and greet him before a conflict develops between us?"

Finnabair hurried to her mother's chariot. Two more filled with soldiers flanked it. Maeve explained to her, "I would not dare let you go out unguarded. Look at what happened the last time."

Finnabair touched her raggedly chopped hair and nodded to her mother. The warriors maintained a respectful distance as they followed her, so that she broke through the front lines seemingly unaccompanied. Rochad saw her and rushed forward. His people drew up uncertainly.

He jumped aboard her chariot. They kissed and embraced tightly, murmuring devotions. When Rochad opened his eyes, he found the chariot surrounded by a dozen armed men. He turned to the people he had abandoned, but they had already panicked and fled the field with more Connacht warriors in hot pursuit.

The soldiers escorted Maeve's chariot slowly as the queen had ordered them. Rochad and Finnabair spoke as friends—it was obvious she had not been party to his capture. She still loved him deeply as he loved her.

Maeve had ordered a small tent erected beside hers especially for Finnabair and Rochad. She declined to see him at first and simply left her daughter and the young man alone.

Rochad, whatever his skills as a warrior, lacked any defenses against Finnabair's guileless devotion. They sat beside a brazier and talked of the years that had separated them, each description erasing the passages of time, moving them closer together, until they were the children they had once been with nothing left to divide them. They made love and lay together that whole night, deaf in their vacuum of adoration to all the cries and clash of battle. They drifted warmly to sleep in each other's arms. The untended brazier burned out. In the darkness, two shapes entered the tent. They remained no more than a minute, but when they left, Rochad had disappeared.

The pain from the hands gripping him brought Rochad sharply awake. He found himself thrust naked, held upright, before the King and Queen of Connacht.

"You still love Finnabair, that is obvious," Maeve said slyly. "If you go home now, young man, she will be yours and this trifling conflict will remain someone else's concern. You no longer have a force to command in any case."

"I do love her."

"Then yield for now. How simple, and Finnabair to wife."

"I've dreamt of that since I was ten, before your Black Army killed my older brothers. I'll do as you ask."

"Excellent," said Ailell. He clapped Rochad on the back and gave him hot wine. "We'll enjoy your return to us."

This time the two guards escorted Rochad politely. They left him alone in his small tent, allowed him to dress and tell Finnabair what her parents had decided, what he had agreed to. Once the Donn had been conveyed from the province, he would come to Connacht and be wed to Finnabair. Her parents had promised. They kissed excitely and Rochad went out. The two guards took him to the perimeter of the camp, some miles back. Afterward, they wended their way back to their post, barmy with laughter, and stopped here and there to tell others how Maeve and Ailell had tricked that poor love-struck puppy Rochad into yielding without a skirmish. In this way, the tale spread swiftly through the wide camp.

The guards had not returned to their posts for five minutes when seven warrior-kings barged into the royal tent. They complained that they had caught wind of the pact struck with Rochad and had, by accident, discovered that they were *all* betrothed to Finnabair.

In the adjoining tent, the girl awoke and could not help overhearing what was being said of her. She got up and pushed her way into her mother's tent.

The loudly bickering warriors faltered in their demands at the sight of her.

Shame boiled up in Finnabair like lava at the sight of their cormorant faces. It scorched her throat; blisters erupted on her

perfect cheeks. Her nude body withered as they looked on—
even her father and mother were incapable of coming to her
aid. Her ribs protruded, the hair sprinkled from her head. She
split open where Cú Chulainn's stone had penetrated, where
hapless Rochad had penetrated. Maeve shook and began to
shriek and could not stop. Blood and gore pooled around Finnabair and she crumpled like a burning clump of grass, a skel-
eton of twigs and slough.

The spellbound onlookers were so horrified they could not
breathe. Maeve's keening had heated and thickened the air.
The shame from Finnabair spread to the seven like a disease;
none of them died from it but none escaped from that tent a
sane man. So much shame, borne all at once, had chewed a
path into their brains.

Senchan ran leadenly like a sleeper from a nightmare—to
snap bolt upright, sweating and unnaturally alert, beside Laeg.

It was night. The fires of the camp lay below . . . but closer
now. He glanced behind him and found the landscape littered
with barrow mounds and cromlechs, the latter looking like giant
fossils trying to climb out of the earth. In the midst of them
one tent had been erected.

"Where are we?"

"Where? In Tailtiu—where Ulster buries its heroes and
kings. It's a very sacred spot and no one would dare come up
here who isn't a friend."

"But when—how are we here?"

"Can't you deduce it? We're here because we're following
the armies. Cú Chulainn's in the tent, sleeping while Fingin's
marrow-mash revives him. You think you've had a dream, but
it's no dream, it's a vision. A vision like Druids have, like
Cathbad had with the bull's blood and Duffach, the night the
Nemain came. Don't ask me how you had it—I don't pretend
to comprehend these things. But it's a very good sign so far
as our benefactors are concerned."

"Then, Finnabair's dead?"

"Soon enough she will be. Regrettable by any standard."

Senchan pushed at his face. "Then, can we save her?"

"It's already happened, you see, even though it won't occur
for a few more hours, boy. You're centuries past it, really."

"*No!*" He threw off his fur and got up. "I don't care what
you say, I'm going." He ran off down the hill at breakneck
speed.

A red, dusky light surrounded Laeg. The earth shuddered

beneath him. "Oh, really?" he said as if in answer to an unheard question. "And just how shall I stop him, hmm? Let him be. He's had a powerful dream, you said so yourselves, so leave off. His time's nearly spent, after all." With a sound like a demon's belch, the red light faded. Laeg burrowed deeper into his furs.

Senchan arrived outside the tents just as Rochad was being escorted through the camp. He watched until the young warrior and his guards were lost from sight, out where a dozen large central fires stippled the night. Then he stole into the smaller tent.

Finnabair slept curled like some tiny animal, withdrawn and defenseless. Senchan cautiously drew the furs up around her neck. She had such a simple, clear beauty, one that was artless, unadorned. He sat beside her and thought of Derdriu, so much like her in many ways. Both of them victims, he thought, out of their singlehearted ingenuousness: they were born to be victimized, too honest in conduct to escape exploitation. Idly, his hand brushed through her bobbed blonde hair.

His regretful thoughts carried him into a numbness of dispirited thought, which did not release him until voices outside the tent began calling for Ailell.

Senchan stiffened, looking from the sound to the sleeping girl. Her face wrinkled as the piercing denouncements burrowed into her dreams. Senchan glanced wildly about for something to shield her with and finally, in a panic, he bent down and covered her ears with his hands. He pressed his whole weight on top of her to muffle the calls from outside. Her scent enveloped him; her hair tickled his nostrils, and he very nearly forgot his purpose, but she sighed and he pressed harder on her ears.

The yelling went on and on, with Ailell's voice, loudest of all, cutting through it, silencing the others. This had not happened in his vision and Senchan relaxed. He lifted himself off her.

Finnabair awoke. For a few moments she continued to lie there, but then pushed back the furs and got to her knees and listened to her father's strident denunciation of the seven warrior-kings. She heard Rochad's name mentioned. Immediately, she got to her feet and padded to the doorway.

Senchan pursued her, beside himself in consternation. He hadn't stopped the dreadful outcome, only delayed it. He snatched up a dented black pot from the shadows and, with both hands, struck Finnabair on the back of the head. The contents of the pot sloshed all over him. Finnabair collapsed in his arms. He flung the pot away and it clanked across the ground. The voices in the adjoining tent went silent.

Ailell stuck his head in through the tent opening. His daughter slept in a sprawl in the middle of the enclosure; she had kicked off her covers and knocked over a chamber pot, but she hadn't been awakened. Ailell thanked every god and goddess he could think of, even Macha. He crept in and replaced the furs over her. Those stupid suitors, he thought as he looked down at her, what terrible damage might their thoughtless avarice have done to her if they'd awakened her with their bickering? None of them, not one, had performed their appointed duty—to eliminate the Hound of Ulster—in order to deserve her. So far as he was concerned, none of them deserved her regardless of what they could do, a subject on which he had a few poignant ideas of his own. Satisfied that Finnabair would not awaken, Ailell crept out to rid himself of the seven fools.

Senchan tried to ignore the awful smell of himself. He tried wiping the acrid contamination off against the furs. He started to leave, then went back and, on one knee, brushed back Finnabair's hair and kissed lightly the edge of her mouth.

She sighed and said, "Cucuc."

Senchan frowned for a moment, but his discouragement evaporated. He had saved her! She was alive. Hundreds, perhaps thousands, might die before this was all over, he smelled like the ditch in back of a feast hall, but Finnabair was alive! Finally he had done something important. His life had meaning.

5. Conchovor's Force

Senchan and Laeg watched dawn come up over the hills behind them, the light outlining the graves and stones that had been so alive to Senchan the night before. His excitement had cooled somewhat since rescuing Finnabair—in part due to the sustained itching that his "bath" had caused him—but not enough to dispel his eagerness over the forthcoming battle. "What now?" he asked Laeg when he could keep quiet no longer.

"Now comes Ulster. You recall that Conchovor directed Cathbad to send a number of people to him after Fingin. Do you remember the name Finnchad of the Silver Horns?"

"One of his sons."

"Bastard sons, yes. Well, subsequently, Conchovor sent Finnchad out with orders to retrieve the heroes of Ulster. The young man, wearing the antlered crown that had earned him his name, went outside to find more people milling about, weak, tottering, but happy to be able to stand again. From on the plain he heard a pandemonium of voices, and he climbed onto the rampart to see the whole of Emain Macha teeming with warriors, a babel of heroics, some of the boasters in chariots but most on foot, and everyone blowing his own carynx as to how he would deal with the cause of the nine-day affliction, even though none of them knew what that cause might be. Finnchad jumped down from the rampart and ran back up the hill, through the crowd, to get his father.

"Conchovor returned with his son, taking Cathbad along with him. The imperious Druid silenced the horde, welcomed them, then stepped back so that Conchovor could explain to them the cause of their plight and concern. The din redoubled, threats and promises of slaughter climbing into the sky, drowned out shortly by the louder clamor of weaponry against shield face, boom and clang, carynx and bodhran. The multitude turned as one and surged away from Craebruad, a human torrent that flowed over Slieve Fuait, swept down on Fernmag, down the western edge of Crich Rois and around Lough Ramor. More men and women joined them as they pushed forward, including Eogan mac Durthact and his *tuath*.

"Below Ramor they encountered tangential Connacht forces, mostly plunderers, but with some scouts mixed in—the latter stationed on the heights of Slieve na Caille. The plunderers had no chance and were trampled. Heads went to Celtchar mac Uthidir, Amargin, Cu Roi (who had promised Ailell only to go away, but hadn't foresworn a return), and Aengus Fer Benn Uma, who like Finnchad wore horns—only his were of copper and he hung his entitlement of heads from them so that he appeared at first glance to be some many-headed monstrosity. Apparently flies did not bother him. The multitude incorporated as well the Devouring Queen of Dun Sobairche, who has no known name other than that, which may or may not refer to her skill in battle. Follamain, Laegaire, the sons of Lete and those of Fiachtna, Senoll and the Sons of Ficce, who had spent their time after delivering Cú Chulainn to his house sounding the alarm, and who joined the main body of the force with many more warriors who had assembled at their call. I could name them all night. Suffice it to say that there were so many gathered and making such noise that, as had occurred from the thunderous passage of Connacht's forces at the beginning of the raid, the Nemain was released from the tumuli atop Slieve na Caille. She swept down ahead of Ulster's advance, down onto Connacht's escaping . . ."

He stopped speaking as the dawn's light was blotted to a roiling blackness and he and Senchan were buffeted by a cold wind that seemed to come from every direction at once. The wind carried a voice on its currents—a deadly howling that whirled in a wide ring around the whole of the army. Tiny glowing creatures were flung off from the wind; evil, yellowish things with cracked, empty skin like the cast-off shells of cicadas. Their own yowls echoed the Nemain's high shriek. In the camp, people scattered, gathering their belongings, throwing implements, stores, and weapons onto wagons, tethering their terrified mounts.

"Ailell watched warriors topple from unendurable fright, others run from chittering horrors. He cursed the Morrigu, damned the Nemain to be crushed under the Dagda's foot like a slug. He shouted to the skies for all the spirits of the dead slain by Cú Chulainn to rise from their tombs and plague the Ulstermen."

Senchan glanced back worriedly at the dark graves, anticipating the emergence of armed spirits.

"No," Laeg assured him, "none are coming. Ailell's curse was devoured by the Nemain's demons, although pursuit of his words made them leave off chasing warriors. His words never reached the dead, if he ever had the power to raise them."

They watched Ailell beckon to MacRoth and yell to him in the midst of the storm. MacRoth bowed, then ran off to the west, quickly outdistancing those who had escaped at the first echo of the Nemain.

"It's time we went along, too. When the Sleep of the Marrow-Mash lifts from Cú Chulainn, we'll have arrived at the scene of the final confrontation."

XVII.
BATTLE OF THE BULLS

1. MacRoth's Views

The armies had reached Cuil Sibrille, intending to return by the same road they had followed on the way up into Ulster's heart, from the hook on the Blackwater to Cruachan. MacRoth rejoined them there. He waved the leaders to a halt as he came running up, the front ranks halted, word passed back to the king and queen, and Maeve and Ailell pushed to the front where the messenger stooped, hands on knees, catching his breath.

"I climbed the heights of Iraird Cuillen," he told them, "and from there I could see north to the tumuli sites of Slieve na Caillighe. The first thing I saw was strange lights on the plain to the north—flashing sparks as if the Sidhe had come out there. As the sun climbed higher I saw also what I thought was a layer of mist, but it wasn't mist—it was dust, a giant whirlwind full of sparks. In front of it, coming at me, all kinds of forest creatures and cattle and pigs were running, fleeing the storm, which swept along the ground, billowing and expanding out at the sides."

"Some other unnatural manifestation of the Morrigu," suggested Ailell. "I cursed the fates last night and now they plague me for it. We must turn south and try to outdistance the wind, even if we have to invade Meath as well."

"Stay and let me hear another interpretation," Maeve insisted. Fergus mac Roich had been listening to MacRoth from a discreet distance. He wore a curiously mocking smile. "What is funny, Fergus?" the queen addressed him. "Share the joke for once." The king and MacRoth turned to see him.

"What's funny is Ailell misreading the tokens of his doom with such expertise. You think that dust cloud is something arcane. It's not. That wind is the coming of Ulster. The flashes within it, all their brandished, polished weaponry glinting when the sunlight catches it. As I've said, Conchovor's come and he's ahead of you now. Once *he* discovers that, he'll turn and sweep you up." His eager eyes locked with Ailell's. "There's no way for us to go home without a fight."

Ailell brooded. "We lost a goodly number of our best—yours and mine, wife—to the late, great Hound. How are we supposed to withstand this confrontation?"

"We have enough. Our forces are surely greater in number still, but just as surely more of *them* will rise up. The best thing for us is to face them now, cut our way through them before they grow any larger, and get safely home where we can defend against all comers."

"For once your advice is persuasive," agreed Fergus. "Not based on the moment's expedience. For once you've thought ahead."

Maeve hardly acknowledged him. She addressed MacRoth: "Go back out and watch where that dust goes while we gather ourselves and prepare to meet it. We shall do as my husband suggests for now and skirt their main force by going south for a time."

"How nice to know I'm supported," Ailell cut in.

MacRoth escaped before another argument could begin and soon lost sight of his own people. Not long after that he found the outstretched whirlwind again; the head of it, he soon saw, had come to a stop at a hill called Slemain Midi on the far side of Lough Owel. From there the Ulstermen would have plenty of warning of anyone's approach through the neck of land between the three lakes of Owel, Derravaragh, and Ennell; unerringly, the Ulstermen had blocked the route that, even now, Ailell chose for his army. The Ulster Druids must be remarkably percipient, he thought, or might they even have planted the notion in Ailell's mind? Whatever the case, his job was to learn all he could. More than that could not be hoped for at this turn of events.

For many hours, his eyes as sharp as a hawk's, MacRoth memorized the faces and aspects of that gathered, tumultuous force, counting heads and weapons and vehicles. Maeve had been right; Ulster's present horde lacked superiority over hers. At least, he thought as he ran off again, that was good news to bring back.

He found his own army near Lough Sheever, a tiny body of water. Before she let him report, however, Maeve called Fergus and Cormac from their group to listen and identify the individuals described. The first few, MacRoth knew.

Conchovor: "With his hair bleached yellow, curled in waves to the middle of his back. His face is narrow in the chin and he wears his beard forked, each side twisting to a point. The elfin look of childhood still resides upon his face, in his soft gray eyes."

His son, Cuscraid: "Easily picked out by the stammer that's earned him his nickname. His hair is blond and worn identically to his father's. Also, his tunic's of the same royal green, his gold jewelry reflects the same design.

"Another leader is tall as Conchovor but older. His gray hair is thin and far back on his skull. He has yellow eyes and a face that seems chiseled from some hard wood. His nose comes to a sharp point, his cheeks go deep. A thick mustache covers his lip, as gray as his remaining hair. They call him Laegaire the Victorious. His father, Connad, is there, too, and frankly looks no older than his son—since *his* hair is curly and black.

"Others I've seen before, too. Handsome young Rochad has returned for this final battle, accompanied by his *tuath*—at least there's *one* cowardly group you needn't fear."

"How could he have defied our pact so simply?" Maeve said.

"Perhaps nearness to you two affected him," suggested Fergus. Ailell shot him a cold glare but Fergus was unintimidated.

MacRoth interjected loudly, "And Munremoir, the tree stump that walks. He's carting around a black shield now instead of stones—a shield the size of a tent. Still another is very grim and proud. Hair like a flame, swept back like a whitecap. Him I don't know." He cocked an eyebrow at Cormac.

"That might be Fedlimid the Wave."

"Another leader—his face belongs to a wolf. He has popping green eyes and bright orange hair, oiled and drawn back at the sides, loose and jagged on his forehead in front. Canine teeth, a short black beard—a face you'd never trust."

Fergus grew more excited with each depiction. "His weapon and colors, tell me!"

"The weapon . . . it's a forked javelin. Yes—the shaft cut short for close work. His color's purple, everywhere."

Fergus tilted back his head and his grin was tight. "I could ask for no more than that." He clasped his hands to his mouth and walked away, all other matters swept up and forgotten.

Ailell said to Cormac, "MacRoth just described Eogan mac Durthact, didn't he?"

Cormac nodded.

"Continue," Ailell bade.

The messenger described others whom he had not recognized. Cormac named each one: Furbaide, Conchovor's sons Fiacha (named, ironically, for Fergus's son) and Fiachna, Celtchar mac Uthidir, Amargin. It was a protracted list. Even so, when MacRoth had finished, many heroes remained unaccounted for. Conall Cernach had not arrived and his absence made Ailell feel safer; but he knew that Maeve had been right, that more were arriving every moment and that now was the time to move, while that body of fighters awaited more recruits and while Fergus chomped at the bit to get at mac Durthact.

"The time for talk is past," the king declared. He sent Cormac and MacRoth to tell everyone that war was imminent.

2. The Morrigu

Conchovor's scouts spied the forces of Connacht approaching from the northeast, a place called Ath Fene, a humid lowland full of tiny lakes, cattails, and soggy peat at present glazed with patches of ice. The king and his Druids rode out to meet this force.

Upon seeing him, Ailell and Maeve selected Druids of their own to accompany them to meet with Ulster's king. Scornful of the young man who had once made suit for his wife, Ailell would not speak with him directly.

Cathbad, in a robe of white, raised his arms above his head, holding a wand of ash between his hands. "My lord Conchovor welcomes you to the field of battle," he proclaimed.

His opposite number replied, "And the overwhelming King and Queen of Cruachan look forward to your challenge." Ailell whispered to the Druid, who then added, "The king would know what you want here."

"Will he not address me himself?" Conchovor asked, his cheeks flushing.

"He will not."

"Fine. Then you may address your questions to *my* Druid."

Cathbad glanced at him irresolutely, then cleared his throat, hemming and hawing until he concocted a reply. "We've come to request a truce till morning with you."

"Why should we want that?" Ailell asked through his Druid. "It only allows you to add to your strength."

Cathbad bent to Conchovor. "Why *should* they want it?"

"You know why. Tell them."

"Yes. Well. . . . A truce would—a truce would serve both sides. So great a battle as is no doubt about to be fought requires strength—that is, rest. Otherwise, our warriors—yours and ours—won't perform their best feats and history would speak belittlingly of our clash. If you won, that would shame you."

"If?" shouted Ailell. Then he bridled his resentment and spoke in a harsh whisper to his Druid, who said, "The king accepts, though for the need of your side, not his, as his army is *always* ready to perform to its fullest and would gladly tackle you this minute. But, rather than spend eternity listening to Ulstermen whine of how they lost the battle from lack of sleep, he grants you your nap."

"You should remind your overlord," Cathbad replied hotly, "that it's *we* have had nine night's ease while his gathering poked and prodded our territory like some halfhearted lover with a flaccid phallus. He should be thankful of the opportunity to stiffen his weapon."

Ailell's face had gone completely red and his eyes bulged from their sockets. "In the morning, then!" he barked, then snatched the reins from his driver and wheeled the chariot around. Maeve looked back at Conchovor as her husband drove them away. He *was* lovely, but Ulster would never have allowed her the power she had in Connacht, not with Macha already in power. And look at what had happened to that girl, Derdriu. Maeve pushed up beside Ailell and studied the backs of their two horses. "My, wasn't that fun?" she said.

Ailell shot her a glance to kill but Maeve continued to stare distractedly ahead all the way back.

The excitement of the camp charged Maeve as she walked through it to her red tent. Warriors huddled in clusters around small fires and when they looked up at her passing, she saw an ecstatic savagery in their faces. This was what they lived for—the coming of battle. She considered that she understood the mind of the warrior better than anyone else; after all, she had used and discarded more of them that she could count. They always displayed plenty of enthusiasm in sex but she knew that sex was merely one way of passing time between battles for them, that they loved warfare far more than sultry, coital afternoons. The few who had gone against Cú Chulainn in single combat had already won honor, if only through death. The impending fight with Ulster would change that, would give them all the chance to parade their skills, their strength. The survivors would keep alive the names of those who fell. Immortality was a curious thing.

She saw that, where there had been bickering and contention previously, there now existed only harmony and comradeship: they had become one vast being, all the parts striving for exactly the same goal, honed and oiled for this one challenge.

The distance between the two camps was that of Ath Fene. Each could see the fires of the other, the colors of the tents and tunics. Both sides sounded the alarm when three enormous ravens descended from the northern sky.

The black birds circled each camp before finally settling in the middle of the plain. A dense mist wreathed out of the ground where they landed. It whirled like a waterspout up into the clouds. A carrion wind blew through the camps and the birds twisted and grew. One became like darkness itself, a ragged spectral shape with moistly shining eyes.

The second one became the hideous sexual monster that had confronted Cú Chulainn in the guise of a Sidhe princess.

The last more than anything resembled her father, Ernmas. She was a rotted corpse, with flesh replaced by mud and detritus. Worms crawled through the holes in her.

These were the three: Nemain, the Badb, and Morrígan. They stood back to back around the whirling spout and hissed their chant. The suspired words carried to both armies, stiffening hackles.

"Welcome to the field, ripe fruits.
Put down your roots and grow here,
Wither and enrich our soil.
Spill your seeds in the delirium of battle.
Alone, here stands Ulster
Against all of golden Eriu, allied—
A division to outlast you.
It pleases us, your offer to pour out your blood
While your fundament fails,
Fertilizing your grave,
And we, ravens, pluck the savory, sightless eyes."

They paused, changed positions, and made one final chant:

"Woe betide you, Ulster! Glory to Eriu!
Tangle bodies, mangle flesh—the more we honor you!"

The whirlwind left the ground and shot into the sky, sucking the three sisters with it. The clouds slammed together thunderously and black feathers floated down over the field of battle.

3. Laeg's Telling

"They gave the armies of the other provinces all the praise and warned Ulster that it will fail!" Senchan exclaimed.

"They did that, indeed," agreed Laeg. "And you've responded just as those of Connacht, Munster, Meath, and Leinster did, as the three intended no less."

"You mean they were lying?"

"Simply a matter of interpretation. Isn't it reasonable that the Daughters of Murder itself might be more inclined to honor most those who are about to feed their obscene hunger?"

They walked up the grassy hill of Uisneach, where Cú Chulainn lay in his tent. He remained too encrusted with wounds to join the battle. Each time he had tried to rise, Fingin the Healer had forced him down again, then put him back to sleep with phrasings and lore given to all Druid healers from the god Dian Cecht, the Master of the Leech.

Around the hill a red twilight grew. The stars wheeled in the heavens; first one, then dozens, then hundreds spattered the sky and, like a sliver of the moon, arced to the horizon. The red darkness became red dawn. The entire night had passed while Laeg and Senchan ascended the hill.

Senchan turned to look out at the fires scattered across the land. He imagined how the camps had passed the night: in boasts and embraces and gestures of good luck; in calls and chants to their various gods—nearly as many in name as the quantity of *tuatha* gathered here, but some called upon by both sides, worship pitted against worship. From that Senchan saw the absurdity of calling upon deities for help when it was men who confronted you. Gods were neither for nor against you: gods were deaf. Skill was everything, action the essence.

Inside the tent, Cú Chulainn sat up with effort, throwing off layers of fur. He was bound, arms against his sides, by a cocoon of hazel twigs looped into spancel hoops. "What's happening now?" he asked.

"Early morning, gray in the sky. Time for warriors to chant in their sleep—Duffach the Dark and even Ailell. The battle's about to be engaged."

"I have to go and—"

"Nonsense." Laeg ducked into the tent and forced Cú Chulainn to lie back. Where FerDiad's sword had pierced his chest, the wound was as big as a hand. Between the bindings, it glistened icily with Fingin's salves. "Why do you think Fingin went to the trouble of tying you down? If you try and break free, I'll bring him back here and have you put to sleep again, and you'd miss the whole affair."

Cú Chulainn shot him a look of betrayal. "You wouldn't do that. We're friends."

"That's precisely why I would do it. That army below comes to clean the debris of your combats. Would you share your honor or steal theirs? Let them have their day in the sun. They won't outshine you."

"Then . . . you must stand outside and report everything that happens."

"That I'll gladly do if it keeps you here." He piled the furs over his friend again before going out.

* * *

The battle began with the morning still gray and unwarmed by the sun. Stray cattle dotted the marsh plain; during the night they had broken loose and scattered while their herdsmen slept.

"Right now the first blood of the battle is coloring the earth," Laeg called to Cú Chulainn.

Senchan looked down but saw no warriors. "What heroes are fighting?" Cú Chulainn called back.

"None. It's our herdsmen contending with Connacht's over the rightful ownership of the stray cattle. Now one of ours strikes one of theirs with a staff. Another leaps upon him, and the servant boys apprenticed to our herdsmen pry the Connachtman off and swarm over him."

"The Ants of Ulster!" Cú Chulainn cheered.

"More like hornets. Now more are running out from both sides. This battle may start over our cattle as well as our bull, with the weapons of choice being sticks."

"Where are the kings?"

"Still sleeping, though this fracas will likely awaken them, which is what the inattentive herdsmen were trying to avoid. The tops of the hills are lit by the sun but the valley will be dark for some time yet."

A shout echoed up from the plain, calling for the men of Macha to put on their arms and leather. It came in an eerie sing-song.

"That sounds like Conchovor possessed," Cú Chulainn said.

"Or else Fiachna, who sounds just like him."

Another voice took up the chant, his verse telling the Ulstermen to take back their cattle, retrieve their honor, and silence the satires before they were composed.

"That's Laegaire Buadach."

"Definitely," Laeg agreed. "Unmistakable. It's an omen, like a wind sweeping through the camp, gripping each soul as it glides through the tents. If we can hear it, so must Ailell's army this cold morning. There he is, too, out at the front edge of his army. He's gesturing fiercely. There go some of the servants from the plain. His people are gathering behind him. I can see the flash of their weapons."

"Quick, then, Laeg—drive down and warn them. Connacht intends to catch them napping!"

Before Laeg could so much as reply, a new voice rang out in the Ulster camp more loudly than its predecessors. On the hill of Uisneach they heard every word.

*"Rise up swiftly all you heroes
before the treacheries of Ailell mac Mata fall upon you
as they did upon Cú Chulainn so often.
Quick up! Defend your land and strike strongly,
knowing honor is the bracelet and ring upon your
hand!"*

"Well said," Cú Chulainn called to Laeg.

"But it wasn't you," said Senchan.

"No. It was Amargin with the Chant upon him. What's important is that the army's alerted."

The herdsmen from both sides continued to fight in the middle of soggy Ath Fene, beating one another with staffs and clubs. Suddenly they drew up, turned, and scattered, leaving the contested cattle behind. Some of the cows ran, too. A second later the sound of carynxes blaring reached the hill, a sound like many loons upon a lake.

"That's started it for real," cried Cú Chulainn.

"The warriors are coming forth naked, some of them have torn out through the backs of their tents! They were sleeping and came up running before they were awake."

"That's training for you."

"There's Conall's chariot. Footmen all around it. Across, there's Lugaid in his and a wall of men from Munster. Amargin's racing out from the other end of our camp. Now the first wave comes behind these leaders, crested by Conchovor and Cuscraid. There's no stammer in his throw—he's spit two with one shot. Ailell's had his people join in threes: three warriors, three chariots, swinging in from all sides, a pincer. They've even split up the Galeoin irregulars that way. We'll have to cut down triple-headed threats to get through them."

The hill of Uisneach shook from the thunder of those wheels, feet and hammering weapons. The two waves crashed together. Chariots tipped and overturned, horses brayed as they were pulled down. Warriors were crushed beneath the vehicles, others leaped with their spears into the thick of the fray while still others circled the perimeters and beat their shields and fouled the air with scabrous names for the enemy, bellowed threats of maiming and castration. Hot springs of blood jetted into the sky where heads flew and tumbled. Servants ducked and dove in the midst of the melee to retrieve for their masters the trophies they had won, some becoming trophies for someone else. Cattle, trapped between the fighters, were slaughtered and used for bulwarks to drop the careering chariots. Spears shot through the air like striking hawks and the sky resounded with the thump of them against shields and in breasts. Bodies crushed beneath wheels, bodies flung from the force of the blow that slew them, bodies dancing a death jig before tumbling to twitch without a head to guide them. Laeg described it all.

Senchan stared, transfixed, too overwhelmed to even blink.

"Where's eager Fergus mac Roich in all this?" called Cú Chulainn.

"I see him back in their camp. He's sitting without the slightest intention of coming to the field. The pen holding the Donn is back there, too. Three rows of warriors guarding it."

"Everything in threes—that's Druidry at work. But I can't believe Fergus sits by with Eogan mac Durthact out there."

"All the same, it's so. Others of the exiles are with him. Now Ailell runs up to him, obviously infuriated, gesturing vehemently."

"What's he saying, do you think?"

"I'm not sure." Laeg glanced at Senchan. "Shall you and I find out?" he asked quietly, with a nudge.

4. Leochain

"Neither I nor any of my people will join you!" bellowed Fergus. "How often must I swear to leave off tackling the people of Ulster before you hear me?"

"You are *useless* to me," cursed the king.

Maeve hurried over, followed by the men who had once formed her circle of defense. "What is it has our cold-blooded exile so hot now?"

"He won't go out on the field. He's turned coward on us in the end."

Maeve saw the ravening look of Fergus's eye, the urgency he held in. She could practically taste it. The very core of him opened to her, the enigma solved. He was a man of a single desire. There was room for no other. She grabbed her husband by the shoulder and said, "Give him back his sword."

"What?"

"If you want him to fight, then return the tool with which he does his work. You've had your joke long enough, husband—no longer is it a triumph of any sort."

Ailell hesitated but finally decided that he had reaped enough enjoyment from his masterly prank. "Go to my chariot," he ordered his new charioteer. "Under your pedestal you'll find a linen bundle. Bring it—and be careful of it!"

The charioteer ran off. Fergus got to his feet. Cormac, Duffach, and others gathered around. They had already dressed or undressed for battle and made no pretense of their eagerness to be out there on the plain. The driver returned and gave the bundle to Ailell. The king unwrapped it, then handed Leochain to Fergus. The warrior reached out, his fingers trembling, and gripped it. With reverence, he pressed it to his cheek. "Now I'll give you some blood," he said, "and both of us can quench our thirst. Lucky for Ailell it's not his life burns my brain. Lucky for king and queen alike." He tilted his head to one side and looked at them as if contemplating a sacrifice. Suddenly, he charged off, sweeping up his shield as he passed it, jumping into his chariot. He flung the large wooden practice weapon away, sheathed Leochain. He tore off his tunic and cloak, then snapped the reins. Behind him, the other members of the Black Army had already dispersed to enter the fight.

Fergus craned his neck in search of the swarthy features of his enemy. The soft ground was laced with ruts, acrid peat squishing underfoot, mud everywhere. More amazing still was the amount of dust kicked up from the drier points, the particles clogging throats, faces streaked by it, faces smeared darkly. Any one of them might have been Eogan's—but there! A stain of purple in the swarm. For an instant the slaughtering sea pulled apart and that sun-burned face he sought rose up and the large eyes fixed him, blinked like a lizard's, and ducked back into the fray.

Fergus bellowed at his horses and slapped his reins hard. Warriors dove away from his spitting wheels. One woman was knocked aside by his horses but came up in time to hurl an attacker into the spokes of Fergus's wheel. He leaned far out over the rail as he reached the cluster of men in purple. Leochain whipped the air, taking one head after another, making no judgment as to which of them might have cut down the sons of Uisliu, or which his own sons. He extinguished every life

as resolutely as a farmer harvesting crops. Behind he left a red
and purple road that his exiles trod.

Then there were no more warriors to protect the king of
Fernmag. The weasel's muddy face, spattered with blood, found
itself alone.

Fergus leaped the rail, his horses pounding on without him.
Eogan jabbed with his five-pronged spear and swung his razor-
edged shield to gut Fergus, but mac Roich skirted both of them
and slammed Eogan back with the shield he had brought.

Eogan's voice slithered through the sounds of battle. "Come
test me, since you've called for my death so long. How many
years has Fergus mac Roich hidden in a woman's skirts and
sworn to brave deeds undone? I don't fear your words."

"It won't be words I use to open you." He jumped forward
and struck high. The sharp shield went up and knocked Leochain aside. At the same moment the prongs of death shot out
from below. Fergus dodged quickly, but the tips scraped his
naked ribs.

Eogan sensed success and stabbed his spear in again. Fergus
held his ground till the last fraction of a second, then spun
around and with all his strength brought his sword down in a
swirl, like an executioner, and chopped the prongs away.

Eogan drew back a useless stick cut flat across the tip.
Hooked on the tips of that cruel weapon, a hundred or more
warriors had fallen; he had used it against every sword, every
feint. This left him aghast. He flung the stick away and swung
his shield with both hands in the straps, hoping to disembowel
Fergus with the cutting edge; but Fergus had watched Cú Chulainn fight FerDiad and had seen everything that a shield could
do.

Eogan tried to batter him and managed to drive him back
toward his chariot, far enough for Eogan to snatch up a spear
from one of his fallen accomplices. He tried to hem Fergus in
against the wheel of the car. Fergus knew the maneuver and
made careful retreat until his heel touched the rim. He shifted
his stance and pretended to fall back, pinned. Alert for that
moment, Eogan struck with both shield and spear. Fergus sprang
onto the wheel hub and from there made a leap against the
shield as he had seen Cú Chulainn do, using it as a springboard
to carry him over Eogan to the ground. Off-balance and out-
maneuvered, Eogan tried to swing the shield behind him, but
not before Leochain had flicked the distance like a lizard's
tongue and sent his head tumbling. The body sank as if into a

bog, doubled over the shield, then slid down the edge, performing an evisceration upon itself before it finally hit the ground.

Fergus stood among the slaughter, staring blankly at the head. The deed had been done, his son avenged, but his lust for the kill would not lift. A small, sane voice within the tumult of his mind questioned if this was how Cú Chulainn felt at the point of transformation. Fury built up like a storm inside him. He had killed mac Durthact and it meant nothing. The dead remained dead, and no one was avenged, it was just one more head rolling on a slick field of blood, one amongst a thousand. Would he have to kill the world, the universe, to be at rest?

The battle, which had allowed the two men space till then, closed in upon him again. Instinctively, Fergus began to slaughter. The blade moved ever faster in his hands. His skin turned red and blistered down his arms. Foam like a rabid dog's bubbled from his mouth. He became a death machine, silent, sweeping, insane, and inexhaustible.

Then something slammed against his sword so hard that his arms shook. A feathered spear slapped Leochain aside and Fergus came face to face with Conall Cernach. Conall, his wavy hair hanging to his waist; his bright blue eyes like sky seen from within a cave, they lay so deeply under his brow; the slight smile on his lips that never quite left no matter how much he fumed, his white tunic miraculously untarnished by the gore and mud surrounding them; Conall was a figure out of a dream, and Fergus believed it to be a dream because Conall had not been present when the battle began. Conall leaned closer and spoke in his soft rasp, "You're doing an abundance of killing here for a woman's arse. Still, I've seen men kill for less." Then Conall stepped out of the dream. Fergus glanced around but could not find him again. He thought that he must be mad, truly berserk. He turned and something slapped at his blade hard enough to throw him off-balance. He came around and found Conchovor there, glaring from within his tall, plumed helmet. Some small bit of the anger spinning inside Fergus broke off and attached itself to Conchovor, who had created the rift that put them here. Fergus howled and struck. Conchovor blocked the sword with his shield. Fergus chopped and hacked away at that shield, the famed Ochain. Conchovor could easily have wounded him on one of Ochain's projecting cones but chose to defend only in hopes of wearing down his opponent, whom he still loved.

Fergus yelled, "What are you that you stand in my way now?"

"Your better, that's who. Once your king, who was helpless to stop your boy's dying, and one who can't let you continue to slay your old friends."

At the mention of Fiacha, Fergus went deaf and blind and struck more swiftly, fiercely than ever. With one fist he knocked Ochain aside, leaving Conchovor helpless against the next blow. Leochain thirsted. Fergus brought his arms up, hands clasped together.

A body slammed into him from behind, legs wrapped around his middle, hands pulling back both his wrists so that his shield, on his back, thumped him in the head. He tried to throw the rider. The voice of Cormac blasted his ear. "Stop this, Fergus! Kill my father and you kill yourself, blotting out *any* memories you can endure. Would you banish the last of him?"

"How am I supposed to stop when the sword is still hungry?" Fergus cried in anguish.

"Go elsewhere. Go up on those hills and beat the earth till your arms are numb. But don't slay where you can't tell friend from foe!"

Fergus began to quiver, but he lowered the sword.

"Get away now, father," Cormac insisted.

"Cormac?"

"No, I won't come. His argument against you is just. If I hadn't sworn to harm no Ulstermen here I might well finish what he began." He turned smartly and led Fergus off, shielding him from attack, though not one came near him. Fergus looked on the warriors he passed with eyes unfettered of reason and no one who looked back was fool enough to get nearer.

Three hills stood to the north. Fergus climbed their heights alone. They were jagged hills, young mountains sharp with peaks. From the top, he looked down on all the fighting and could not remember the climb, the last thing in his mind being the sound of Cormac's voice instructing him to turn his anger aside. Wind whistled in his ears and he found himself wailing with it, his voice become that of another wind, rising to a bestial whine. His body shook, his teeth chattered together. The muscles worked along his arms and his fingers flexed around the hilt of his sword so tightly that the cross-hatching on it was imprinted into his palm.

His voice rose and he keened, *"Fiacha!"* The name echoed and returned, nature teasing him to greater madness. He swung

he sword, spinning from the blow. Leochain sheared through
he tip of the peak. Rock spun out and dropped onto the battle.
The peak crashed into the middle of the fray, squashing a
chariot, snapping its axle flat.

Fergus tumbled halfway down the hill. Cut and scraped, he
got up and raced to the second peak. Wind swept tears from
his eyes. *"Fiacha!"* The name scorched his throat.

5. The End of It All

"What shook the ground then?" called Cú Chulainn.

"Fergus mac Roich," answered Laeg. "He chopped the top
off a hill across the plain and now—" the hill of Uisneach
shuddered again "—he's cut into another. There's just one
properly peaked hill left and he's no doubt planning to top it,
too."

"What cause can he have?"

"Rage—he very nearly killed Conchovor from—"

"Let me free!" Cú Chulainn demanded. "Untie this hazel
loop, Laeg. I can't be held back any longer."

Laeg ducked into the tent to protest but, seeing the hard set
of Cú Chulainn's jaw, he bent down. "You should know, though,"
he said, "that Maeve entered the fray with her sword and shield.
She's cut a swath through Ulster, dropping them as if they were
stalks of corn."

The ground shook from Fergus's third blow.

The hazel bonds began to snap before Laeg touched them.
He saw Cú Chulainn's body ripple as if some live creature ran
beneath the skin of his chest. The color of him darkened,
empurpled with blood. Laeg backed away. The last of the
bindings popped and Cú Chulainn the Warped One rose up.

Laeg mentally kicked himself for relating the specifics of
Maeve's work. Now it was too late.

Maeve caught sight of some of her warriors pointing excitedly to the hill of Uisneach. There, a monstrous thing came
kidding down the hillside. At first she told herself this was

some trick of the Morrigu's, some phantom to taunt her and
terrify her army; but the twisted creature reached the edge of
battle and began slaughtering Connachtmen, and Maeve knew
then that the Hound of Ulster lived on. She withdrew from the
assault she conducted, retreating to the guarded pen that held
the Donn. Her twelve guards held that position and she replaced
them at the pen and placed them around her again. As they
were forming their wall, a sharp cramp stabbed through the
queen for a moment. She ignored it as best she could and it
soon passed. She called for two women satirists and sent them
skirting the field once they understood her plan. Next she called
MacRoth and had him make ready to move the Donn south
past Gairech.

He said, "Conall the Victorious has arrived and his addi-
tional forces are turning the tide of battle. You're needed on
the field."

"I know this, but my first concern is with the bull. See that
he escapes to Cruachan regardless of what unfolds here." With
that, she fitted on her helmet again.

The Warped One heard the singing of satires as he reached
the base of the hill. They came from behind him. He looked
about, the sunlight playing rainbows on the tips of his hair, but
could see no source of the versifying. The hidden women called
out, "Your body rots like the apples which skewer famously
in your pointy hair. All your friends have fallen—Fergus mac
Roich and the many traitors in his cause. Better you should
run onto your sword and finish yourself than live with the truth
and FerDiad's ghost." They sprang up then from behind an
outcropping of rock, nude and pink with cold, having discarded
their clothing as Maeve had directed. They expected to find
him doubled over by then or at least covering his ears. The
queen had warned that he might prove more difficult, and that
was why they had removed their garments. Intending to strut
and display themselves fully before him, the two satirists froze
at the sight of him. Their skill with words failed them utterly.

The monster with one eye dangling on his cheek addressed
them in a raw, bubbling voice. "Is this how you hounded
FerDiad? For you did, far more than I. Well, and I must answer
you now as you deserve. Regrettably, I left my sword. Something else will have to speak." He took two steps, then reached
out and smashed their heads together. The skulls cracked like
eggs.

He descended into the battle. Weaponless, he picked up abandoned chariots and hurled them at the trios of warriors Maeve and Ailell had assembled. Piles of debris, human, machine, and horse, amassed in his wake.

Across the plain he found Fergus mac Roich descending from the last of the three shorn hills.

"You, who swore friendship," Cú Chulainn burbled, "You took on my king and yours and by Macha there's no honor left. I'll strip the meat from your bones if you've done worse."

Fergus had never encountered the dark side of Cú Chulainn before, but his brain was so weary of the fight and the burden of releasing years of pent-up anger that the horror barely registered on him. He replied, "I've done nothing worse than avenge my son. Then I experienced a thing—maybe what you're feeling now—and I had to turn my hand to killing hills or else leave Ulster barren."

"Hills or no, you've a pledge with me and I'm calling it in now."

Fergus nodded, unclasping his belt. He laid Leochain at Cú Chulainn's contorted feet. "As I swore to do."

"Honorable man," the monster growled and turned away.

Fergus picked up his sword. He located his chariot and drove away from the center of battle where hundreds upon hundreds still waged a fierce effort. Seeing him go, members of the Black Army broke off from the fight and left the field. Lugaid, too, chose to side with Fergus, since he had no quarrel with Ulster. He felt that he had upheld his bargain with Connacht; they had the bull. Enough of Munster had fallen in its capture. On his way out of the thick he digressed to retrieve the trophy of Eogan mac Durthact. Fergus would probably want it when the day was done.

The loss of so many became apparent to Maeve almost immediately. She saw the packs of warriors pursuing the chariot of Fergus mac Roich. He reined in near the foot of the hill of Uisneach and Maeve, with her complement of twelve shield-bearers, skirted the field away from the last sighting of the monster in their midst and went to condemn the deserters for their behavior. As she was driven around the field, the queen felt bloated and flaccid, as if she had just eaten a huge meal rather than led an attack. More cramps flashed in her belly.

In the midst of the exiles, she had just climbed to the ground when she felt the warmth of blood trickling between her legs. This surprised her—her period was never premature. Almost never. Instead of berating Fergus, she had to order him to take command of her guards and others who had gone with him and form them into a much larger ring, to give her some privacy as well as security.

"You don't want this," Fergus warned. "Not now."

"As if I had a choice. The tides and the moon are pulling today on the descendants of Danu. Now do this—if you still serve me at all."

Fergus grumbled but marshaled the warriors into place around her, their shields up, their backs to her, giving her the sanctum she required.

While the pain clawed at her again, Maeve undressed and squatted in their midst. She pressed both hands to her belly, which had swollen up as big as if she were pregnant. The flow of blood increased, quickly doubling. The size of herself, the rush of blood, left Maeve helplessly terrified. Blood gushed like a waterfall from between her thighs, hard enough to cut channels in the ground. It drained down the hill, becoming a torrent that swept the guards off their feet and rushed on, down to the battlefield.

Maeve could do nothing other than squat there. Her belly remained enormous. The blood covered her feet. She tried to stand but the movement sent pain needling into the base of her spine. Her body seemed to her to be changing, breasts sagging a little, her hard muscles losing their perfect tone. Sweat coated her. The ends of her long white hair turned red.

A shadow fell across her. She looked up and there stood the short, beautiful, dark-haired youth she had avoided for so long. A wide pink scar divided his chest. Her blood swept around his calves with the same force that had dragged off most of her guards, but he was used to standing in torrents.

He smiled grimly at her and the lights sparkled in his eyes.

6. Cú Chulainn's Decision

Maeve could not move to save herself. No one was left standing near enough to come to her aid fast enough if she called out.

"Leave me, Cú Chulainn," she said with no hint of the fear burning inside her. "I can hardly stand against you while this inexplicable infirmity pours from me."

"Inexplicable? *I* can explain it if you'd care to hear, Intoxicator. No one body could contain so much blood, as I'm sure you know. Yet one body—your body—produced it, brought it out. See how it pours down to the plain? It's drawn back to the bodies who fell for you, the heroes, so many of whom I killed for you though my heart was in very few of them. Etarcomol. Nad Crantail. FerDiad, most of all. All perished by this hand. All from your unreasoning lust for superiority, and now their blood has mingled, damning you for your tricks and treacheries played on them. All Ulster is going to hear of this, and every time the tale of your invasion is told hereafter, the tellers will always remark on Maeve's Foul Spot: the place where blood ran in rivers."

She looked at him withstanding the blood and refused to feel shame for what had been necessary. "You'll kill me, then."

"I ought to. It would be a celebrated act that no Druid would oppugn."

She sensed a lessening in the torrent, a relaxing of her muscles. The cauldron of her belly began to recede, leaving her skin loose and scarred where it had stretched. She closed her eyes and fought back a sob.

"But I won't kill you," Cú Chulainn told her. "I like better the thought of your perpetual mortification at knowing how we speak of you, to what act you're linked. Queen of Foulness."

Triumphantly, she said, "I won your bull from you."

Cú Chulainn smiled enigmatically. "Did you? And how will you dominate *it?*"

She dropped to her knees as the last of the blood stopped

flowing. When she found the strength to look up, the dark castigator, the Hound of Ulster, was gone.

"Her blood, rushing across the plain of Fual Maetha, had ended the battle," Laeg said. "Once she had clothed herself, she mustered her remaining forces and fled for Ath Luain. Ailell remained in the dark for some time as to what had happened there at the base of Uisneach, what had created the rapids of blood. He did not learn the truth until after they had returned to Cruachan—his people were either afraid or ashamed to tell him. Most likely afraid.

"Along the road of her retreat, Maeve saw Cú Chulainn on the hillsides. Every time she caught a glimpse of him, he was ahead of her, always silently condemning her with that glitter in his eyes.

"The forces of Conchovor's army, meanwhile, led by Conall, pursued her in the belief that they were driving her out of the land. They did not know that Cú Chulainn, as Conchovor's representative champion, had given Maeve her life.

"He saw the Ulster forces closing the distance, took his sword, and climbed to the top of a triple-peaked hill just as Fergus had done. And, like Fergus, he lopped off the peaks of the hills—in such a way as to send them crashing onto the road below, sealing up the pass and segregating the two armies. The day's battle had ended. Those hills, by the way, Senchan, even in your day are called the Topless Heights of Ath Luain and Meath.

"Maeve *had* won—at least by her reckoning if by no one else's. Fergus rode up beside her with his army around him. The queen recalled that she hadn't told him off as she had meant to do before the blood had poured out of her. Now she leaned over the rail and yelled, 'You let us down today, vigorous man. You allowed us to lose our advantage when we needed it most. You made a ruin of the battle.' Everyone could hear her denunciations, which was what she had wanted. However, they also all heard Fergus's reply.

"'Indeed, I don't think so, Queen of Foulness! *Our* sole dishonor in this entire travesty lies in having followed for so long the twin hills of your hindside when we ought to have known at the start what lay between them.'

"He veered off from her then, his Black Army following. As each drew even with Maeve's chariot, he paused to catch her eye and silently vilipend her before speeding ahead. It's my belief that it was here that she truly came to despise Cú Chulainn and to become fixed upon the desire to see him dead. He had, by letting her live, forced almost constant derision upon her."

Senchan nodded, understanding. He stood, a little cramped and cold, as the late afternoon sun lighted the plain where the battle had been fought. Flocks of birds circled it, finally daring to land and feed from the strewn corpses. The ravaged peat had absorbed countless bodies' worth of blood, leaving only ensanguined puddles here and there and a bloody stench. Senchan wondered if the Morrigu were amongst the carrion flock.

"It's all over, then," Senchan said somewhat reluctantly. Then he perked up. "No, wait—what about the bulls?"

Laeg showed his pride that his pupil had reasoned the shape of the tale unaided. "Come and I'll show you." He led the way back to the low tent where Cú Chulainn had lain. He paused at the opening and let Senchan pass him, ducking, then straightening up to find them not inside a tent at all but on the plain of Magh Ai.

"Look there," Laeg pointed past him. "That's the army of Eriu returning home with their prize. And here beside us, the one who awaits this moment to the exclusion of all else."

Senchan hurled himself backward as he found the bull called Finnbennach barely an arm's length away: they had materialized inside the bull's pen! Finnbennach's eyes rolled dementedly in his blood-colored head.

7. Combat of the Bulls

Maeve and Ailell brought their bull home to a cheering throng at Cruachan. The queen praised her husband, proclaiming that it had been his cleverness that defeated Ulster. Her words pleased him, but even so he had begun to make a mental tally of possessions, hers against his, to see if she had in fact won anything at all. The matter took up so much of his concentration that he hardly heard himself tell a herdsman to go pen the Donn.

The herdsman unthinkingly obeyed, putting the dark bull of Cuailinge in with Finnbennach. The Donn saw his enemy and went straight for the red bull. He reared up on his hind legs and drove his hooves down, pinning Finnbennach's horns beneath him.

The crowd cheered Maeve's brown bull and gathered near the pen to witness a battle. However, the red bull made no attempt to wrestle free and the crowd, grumbling their disenchantment, went back to the festivities. All of them except Fergus mac Roich.

He leaned on the stone wall and studied the two creatures. "You're cut of the same cloth as Bricriu the Bitter Tongue in Ulster. I've seen a lot of your like this past *noinden,*" he told them. "You don't like anything, not even each other. Well, I can't say as I think much of you two either. Your price was too high." Some of his people called to him and he wandered away to the feast, but later returned with a slice of beef on a long flesh fork. The bulls had not changed position.

"You're neither of you living up to his reputation. I'd hate to think we clawed through this folly for two withered, weak cows." He took a section of the beef between his teeth and pulled it from the fork, at the same time strolling around behind the bulls. Close by them, he drew up suddenly and looked hard at the tines of his fork. He pulled the last of the meat off, then took the fork and stabbed the tines into Finnbennach's flank.

The bull's head jerked up hard, yanking the Donn's leg with it. The Donn's hoof caught over the other's horn and his shinbone twisted. Finnbennach pulled back to free himself and the dark bull's leg cracked at the knee. The Donn bellowed and wrenched himself free, snapping off Finnbennach's horn with a kick that sent it spinning into the sky.

Fergus laughed uproariously. "More like it!" he exclaimed. The Donn rammed Finnbennach's side and the two of them smashed into the stone wall before Fergus could move, throwing him onto his back. He sat up, bleeding where the sharp stones had gashed him, but still laughing. "Maybe you're worth something after all."

The bulls no longer required his goading. They hammered at one another, backing the full width of the pen, pawing and snorting before the burst of speed that launched them into each other, their eyes rolled up white. The ground rumbled from their collision.

The feasters of Cruachan came back out to see the battling bulls. Twilight had set in, leaving very little for them to see. They restacked the dislodged stones of the wall while the two bulls rammed each other. Maeve tried to get them to separate the beasts, but none of her herdsmen would have anything to do with it. She tried to threaten them with tortures of every sort but the herdsmen replied, "Your threat is just fulmination; theirs, now, would be a certainty." Having done with her, they strolled back to their feast, casting votes as to which bull would stand victorious come the dawn.

In the morning, the pen lay empty.

The wall, where they had replaced it, had been shattered, and the one beyond it as well. The alarm was sounded and everyone in Cruachan came out to see what wasn't there.

As the fort emptied, the cry went up and the whole populace turned to see a dark speck approaching at breakneck speed from the west. More bets were taken, but the crowd soon fell breathlessly quiet.

The speck grew larger, and they saw that it was only one of the bulls—the brown bull from Ulster. What had seemed at a distance to be the second bull turned out to be its carcass, hung on the horns of the Donn. He shook the carcass fiercely, throwing gore into the crowd, many of whom fled to the safety of Cruachan's walls.

Maeve did not hide her triumph. Ailell abided serenely; he had finished a cursory count of their losses. Later, he would let Maeve in on the totals as he had them.

The Donn ran on across Eriu, back the way he had been led. He left parts of Finnbennach strewn along his trail, where he lowered his head to drink or shook it defiantly against all the powers that had cursed him. The body on his horns grew smaller and hollower.

Back upon Muirthemne, he returned to Daire's land, seeing the places where he had grown up. Nothing about it moved him. He ran on, the tatters of Finnbennach always before him like some deflated specter. The land of his captivity fell behind, and the Donn headed into the hills of the north. There, finally, on a ridge, the heart of Finnbennach tore free: a black, shiny thing like a stone. The Donn swayed then and fell to his knees. He lowered his head, tried to will himself back onto his feet, but his broken leg would not hold. He stabbed his horns into the ground. The carcass of Finnbennach pressed like a mask against his face. Something deep inside the bull exploded. He threw back his head and gave one last plaintive bellow. Then the Donn dropped forward, his horns furrowing the ridge, and lay down on all that remained of his rival.

EPILOGUE

1. Tying Things Together

"And so it ended. Ulster honored both bulls by naming the place where they had died the Ridge of the Bull. Finding the two together supported their belief that they had in fact defeated Cruachan. The bulls symbolized it perfectly. Ulster had lost nowhere near what the rest of the isle had; Cú Chulainn had proven himself the true champion over all the provinces. The bards sang it so; the Druids read the signs.

"Sworn to respond honorably or else become the subject of derision that Maeve was becoming, Ailell made a peace with Ulster, a pact that was to hold for seven years. Peaceful, bountiful years for Ulster. Seven seething, tempestuous years for Maeve."

Laeg stood beside the Pigstone, the first and last of the circle. Where it had cracked and broken, a shiny black core was revealed, like a nut from its shell. The twilight sky streaked it with color.

Senchan asked, "What . . . what about . . ." He pursed his lips in frustration.

"I'll tell you what happened to her," Laeg answered knowingly. "She was part of Ailell's truce, the one last time he got to use her. In fact, it was the one time Finnabair used him. She begged to be made part of the prize. Her father considered how unjustly he had used her—her first love, Rochad, had perished in the battle at Ath Fene—and he complied without

375

argument. Emer accepted her into the household and she lived
with Emer and Cú Chulainn as the second wife of the house
for a time."

"Wonderful!"

"You did manage to save her, you know. You actually did.
You should be proud." He paused briefly and his silence filled
up with regret. "Now the tales are all told, Senchan, the day's
done. I'm finished with you, or very nearly."

"What about that stone?" Senchan pointed to the one in the
center.

"It belongs to another story," and there was sadness in Laeg's
voice. "Revenge's Stone."

Senchan silently repeated the name; then, beginning with
the Pigstone, he named each one by its aspect: Dominance;
Sovereignty; Honor; Leadership; the Stone of Lovers, that was
Derdriu and Naise; Macha's—the Curse Stone; then the Stone
of Combats; the Friend's Stone; and back to Dominance. A
closed ring around Revenge. "Why can't I stay and hear about
it?" he asked.

"This isn't the time of its telling. It has a different point to
make."

"But—"

"Enough! It's not my decision—I'm supervised, too, you
know."

Disgruntled, hurt, Senchan scowled at the stones. He did
not want to go home, back to the drudgery, the beatings and
beratings that awaited him as surely as the next sunup. Selden
would demand that he account for his whereabouts all day and
what was he supposed to say? No one would believe him,
however well he recounted. . . .

He forgot his self-pity in seeing the unnatural shadow he
was casting. A warm red light had effused the stones. He
whirled about.

The side of the hill below the copper screens had vanished.
An opening like a cave mouth, but glowing like an ember, had
appeared there.

Laeg trudged toward it but paused at the brink, and the
charioteer who turned around was the young one who had
accompanied Cú Chulainn. "It's necessary for me to go back
inside," he explained. "After all, I'm long since dead out here.
Only in Magh Mell do I still have substance and a future . . .
but no, that's no longer true, is it? The Sidhe would have me
put a *geis* on you, Senchan, just to be certain of your actions

henceforth. Me, I don't believe you need such an impetus, do you? You have already an inkling of what it is you're to become—those things you've seen are burning inside you like the warmth of wine. In every extremity.

"If you return here next Samain eve, I'll endeavor to meet you and show you the other story that I'm enjoined from telling right now. Remember, eve of the Samain." He glanced at the copper screens.

"You worry too much, my boy. They will believe you when you tell them. You can make them believe. They'll come to call you Torpeist, Senchan Torpeist, and through you the deeds and words will endure.

"Now I really must leave. There are some ban-Sidhe who await me with promise of a . . . well, a provocative eternity. I shouldn't care to be late for that. And neither should you, for your dinner and your first telling. The cauldron will take you back as it brought you."

He walked into the red light, which swallowed him up. Then, suddenly, he came running out from it again, down to where Senchan stood. He handed Senchan a large stoneware cup covered in Ogham slashes. "It's a good ale," he said quickly, "to settle your stomach for the journey." He winked, then sprinted back up the hill and into the light. Presently, it dimmed, withdrawing into the hill. As if from a great distance, Laeg's voice came to him: "You're a man of honor, Senchan. Never give that up!"

Then there was no light other than the band of lavender on the horizon and the stars hung in rich deep blue overhead. Senchan became aware of being cold. He hurried up the hill to the copper screens.

There sat the Dagda, awaiting him in cross-legged relief. And now he could recognize others: Goibniu the Blacksmith; Dian Cecht, Master of the Leech, of healing; the three terrible Morrigu, though their portrayals were not half so frightening as the reality; Manannán, Son of the Sea; and there, at the rear, a figure in quilted leather breeches and another figure beside him, one of hideous aspect, both of them balanced above a chariot. Senchan looked up into the stars. "Remember, eve of the Samain," he whispered.

Could they really think he would forget? Memory had become his art, his craft. To remember. He climbed into the cauldron. The water was still warm and steamy. The circle of stones glowed softly in starlight down the hill.

"I'll *be* your poet," he called to them, and toasted each with his cup of ale.

The screens swung silently shut.

GLOSSARY

Note: the final *h* is a lightly aspirated sound, lighter than a *ch* as in the Scottish "ach." In general, first syllables are stressed, and here are marked by a (') immediately *following* the stressed syllable. The long "oo" ($\overline{oo}$) is pronounced like "hoot"; the short "oo" is pronounced as in "book." Plural form is denoted by ( ).

Adaltrach (*ah'dal-trah*): a second wife, whose presence must be approved by the first wife.

An tsleg boi ac Lugh (*an slāg boy ak looh*): Lugh's spear of light.

Ben urnadna (*ban ur'nah-na*): a contracted wife, usually for a period of one year.

Brithemain (*brē'hem*): the class of judge among the Druids.

Buanbach (*bwan'bach*): a board game.

Carynx (*kair'inx*): a long-necked war trumpet, usually terminating in a stylized animal head.

Cathair (*kat'air*): a cluster of huts surrounded by a high wall.

Coibche (*kō'geh*): the right of purchase; an amount deposited with the family of an intended bride by the man wishing to marry her.

Crossan (*krō'san*): a fertility figure of wicker appearing at wedding feasts.

Cumal (*koo'mel*): a female slave.

Currach (*koor'ak*): a dugout boat.

Del chliss (*klis*): Cú Chulainn's deadly throwing darts.

Derbfine (*dair'vin-eh*): an extended family, four generations large.

Ecland (*eh'klan*): homeless, without a clan.

Epona (*eh-pō'na*): alternate name for Macha, the Horse Goddess.

Fer fognama (*fair fō'na-va*): literally, man of service.

Fer for ban thincur (*fair for ban theen'gur*): man under a woman's thumb.

Fiana (*fē-yah'na*): mercenary warriors.

Fidchell (*fē'hul*): a board game.

Fili(d) (*fil'lē*): the class of bards in Eriu.

Fír fer (*fēr fair*): true man.

Fír Ulaid (*fēr ōō'lī*): literally, true Ulstermen.

Fuil (*fwil*): blood.

Geis(a) (*gesh*/plural: *gesh'ah*): a Druidic curse capable of compelling someone to perform or to stop performing a specific act, potentially for the rest of his or her life.

Gens (*gens*): a length of time lasting nine generations.

Gentraige (*gen'trī*): pleasant or happy music; one of the three categories of music for the harp. See also *goltraige* and *suantraige*.

Glam dicin (*glom dē'kin*): a Druidic proscription, like a *geis* but in the form of a satire.

Goltraige (*gōl'trī*): sad, lamenting music.

Grianan (*grē-ya'nan*): Maeve's sunroom.

Imbas forasnai (*em'vas for'os-nī*): the gift of precognition.

Leanhuan Sídhe (*laan'oun shēē*): an enticing but evil female fairy.

Lugnasad (*loo'nas-ah*): one of the feast days in Eriu, occurring in August and celebrating the harvest.

Merrow (*mair'ō*): a sea maiden.

Nemeton (*ne'veh-tahn*): an oak grove sacred to Druids.

Noinden (*noyn'den*): a length of time lasting nine nights.

Ogham (*awch'em*): the Druidic "secret" alphabet.

Samain (*sau'win*): one of the feast days, November 1, during which the dead are capable of returning to the living world.

Sid(e) (*shēē*): mound in which the immortal Sídhe dwell.

Suantraige (*swan'trī*): a lullaby, one of the three types of song for harp.

Tarbfeis (*tar'vesh*): the bull dream, a form of induced "vision."

Tinnscra (*tin' skraw*): a woman's personal dowry at the beginning of courtship.

Torc (*tork*): a circlet around the throat, indicative of the head of a family and, by elaborateness of craft and material, of one's station in life. Kings and queens had torcs of gold.

Túatha (*Tyōō' ath*): one's tribe or people.

Vathi (*Vah' tē*): seers, in this case the living severed heads kept by Cathbad.

Wurrum (*wer' rum*): a mythical river monster.

PROPER NAMES

Aife (*ē'fe*)
Ailell mac Mata (*ī'l'ēl mak ma'ta*)
Ainle mac Uisliu (*īn'le mak ish'lōō*)
Amargin (*ahv'er-ghin*)
Ardan mac Uisliu (*ar'den mak ish'lōō*)
Badb (*bīv*)
Blai Bruga (*bl'ī brōō'ha*)
Boeve (*bōv*)
Bricriu Nemthenga (*brik'ryu nev'yen-gah*)
Buan (*bōō'an*)
Buinne (*bwin'neh*)
Cathbad (*kaf'fah*)
Celtchar mac Uthidir (*kelt'har mak ōō'he-der*)
Conall Cernach (*kō'nal kar'nah*)
Conchovor (*kōh'na-hur*)
Cormac Connlongas (*kor'mok kon'lung-yes*)
Crimthan (*krif'han*)
Crunniuc mac Agnomain (*kroon'yuk mak ah'nyō-vin*)
Cú Chulainn (*kōō hul'lin*)
Cú Roi mac Daire (*kōō roy mak dā'y-ruh*)
Cuscraid (*koos'krī*)
Dagda (*doh'da*)
Dáire mac Fiachna (*dah'ruh mak fē'an*)

382

Deichtire (*deh' ti-re*)
Derdriu (*dair' dryū*)
Dian Cecht (*dē' an haeht*)
Domnall Mildemail (*dō' nal mil' de-mal*)
Dubthach (*duf' ach*)
Emer (*ev' er*)
Eochaid Goll (*yō' hē gaul*)
Eogan mac Durthact (*ō' wen mak dōōrhaht*)
Etarcomol (*ed' ar-kō' vol*)
Fachtna Fathach (*fah' nah fach*)
Fedelm Bhanfil (*fā' delm ban' ful*)
Fedlimid mac Dail (*fal' e-mid mak dal*)
FerDiad (*fair' dē-yah*)
Fergus mac Roich (*fur' gus mak rō' eh*)
Fiachu mac Firaba (*fē' ya-hōō mak fēr' ahv*)
Finnbennach (*fin' ven-nah*)
Findchoem (*fin' gem*)
Finnabair (*fin' nū-hur*)
Flidais Foltchain (*flē' dī folt' han*)
Fraech mac Fidaig (*frāy mak fi' dāy*)
Friuch (*frē' yooch*)
Fuidell (*fwē' del*)
Galeoin (*gal' yen*)
Iollan (*yōe' len*)
Laeg mac Riangabra (*loy mak rē' yan-gahv' ra*)
Laegaire Buadach (*leer' ē bōō' yah*)
Leochain (*lō' hen*)
Levarcham (*lev' or-cham*)
Lugaid mac Nois (*loo' hē mak neesh*)
Lugh (*l ōōh*)
Macha (*ma' ha*)
Maeve (*māv*)
Maine (*mah' nē*)
Manannán (*mah' nah-daan*)
Morann (*mor' en*)
Morrígan (*mor' rē-gan*); Morrigu (*mor' rē-gōō*)
Munremoir mac Gerrcin (*mwin' re-var mak gar' cin*)
Nad Crantail (*nath kran' dal*)
Naise mac Uisliu (*nē' sha mak ish' l ōō*)
Nemain (*neh' vin*)
Ochall Ochne (*aw' kal awch' ne*)
Rochad (*rō' chah*)

Rucht (*rooht*)
Scathach (*skow' hah*)
Senchan Torpeist (*sen' kan tor' pesht*)
Senoll Uathach (*shā' nul wah' dah*)
Sétanta (*shā' dhan-da*)
Sualdam mac Roig (*swal' dhav mak roy*)
Uathach (*wah' dah*)

PLACE NAMES

Ard Aighnech (*ar ī' neh*): "ard" means "high"
Ard Macha (*ar ma'ha*)
Ath Fene (*ah fān*): "ath" refers to a ford across a river
Ath Gabla (*ah gow'la*)
Ath Luain (*ah lōō'in*)
Bernas Bo (*bair'nas bō*)
Breslach Mor (*bres'lah mōr*)
Brug na Boyne (*brōōh' na boy'nah*)
Cain Bile (*kahn bēl'eh*)
Craebderg (*krāv'dairg*)
Craebruad (*krāv'rōō-ah*)
Crich Rois (*krēē rō'ē*)
Cruachan (*krōō'a-han*)
Cuailnge (*kōō'al-nyuh*)
Cuil Sibrille (*kil siv'rel*)
Cuil Silinne (*kil sel'ēn*)
Dind Rig (*din'rēē*)
Dub (*doov*)
Dun Sobairche (*don se'ver-ka*)
Emain Ablach (*ev'in ahv'lah*)
Emain Macha (*ev'in ma'ha*)
Es Ruaid (*as rō'eh*)
Femen (Plain) (*fev'en*)
Fernmag (*farn'mah*)

Fid Duin (*f ēē d ōōn*)
Focherd (*fow' hart*)
Fual Maetha (*fwal mā' the*)
Gatlaig (River) (*gat' lī*)
Granaird (*gran' ard*)
Int Ildathach (*int il' da-thah*)
Iraird Cuillen (*ir' ard kwil' en*)
Lough (*loch*): lake
Lough Derravaragh (*loch dar' ra-var' ah*)
Lough Owel (*loch ō' wul*)
Lughlochta Logo (*lōō' law-da lō' gō*)
Maeve Sleachtadh (*māv slā' tah*)
Magh Ai (*moy ī*): "magh" means "field"
Magh Mell (*moy mel*)
Magh Trego (*moy trā' go*)
Magh Turad (*moy tir' ra*)
Midluachair (*midh' loo' a-hir*)
Moin Coltna (*moyn kolt' na*)
Muirthemne (*mur' hev-na*)
Nith (River) (*nēth*)
Rathangan (*rath' an-yan*)
Slemain Midi (*slā' wen mēth*)
Slieve Fuait (*shlēv fōō' id*)
Slieve Cuilinn (*shlēv kwil' en*)
Slieve na Caille (*shlēv' na koy' la*)
Tailtiu (*toyl' tyū*)
Temair (*tow' ir*)
Tete Brec (*tet' eh brek*)
Uisneach (*ōōsh' neh*)